Praise for In the Deep

...as gritty and complex as the first novel-length adventure... // Strongly reminiscent of C.J Cherryh at her best.
— Gwyneth Jones, author of the Aleutian trilogy, winner of the World Fantasy, Clarke, Dick, and Tiptree awards

In the Deep evoked for me // space opera at its best: C.J. Cherryh, Lois M Bujold, Arkady Martine, and Frank Herbert's *Dune*. Jennings offers character development and worldbuilding in spades to make a fractally complicated universe that feels real and lived in.
— Paul Weimer, SFF book reviewer and Hugo finalist

Praise for Fault Lines

In this fun, intrigue-laden space opera, // Jennings gives an intriguing glimpse of a much larger setting. // Fans of found family will love the portrayal of Velocity and her crew of scrappy underdogs.
— *Publishers Weekly*

Kelly [Jennings] has been compared with C. J. Cherryh, and I think deservedly. *Fault Lines* isn't burdened with the awful angst of Cherryh's // *Cyteen*, but it has the same intensity and conviction.
— Gwyneth Jones, author of the Aleutian trilogy, winner of the World Fantasy, Clarke, Dick, and Tiptree awards

More political intrigue and gamesmanship than a standard space-battle story... // Solid world building, likable characters...nifty plot twists...
— Craig Clark, *Booklist*

A sharp, character-rich space opera packed with angry, capable women and attractive, vulnerable men. Jennings builds a large, politically complex world // but expresses this through an intimate slice...
— Tansy Rayner Roberts, author of the Creature Court trilogy, winner of multiple Ditmar and WSFA Small Press awards

Also by Kelly Jennings:

Broken Slate

Fault Lines (Escape Velocity 1)

Note: the crew of the *Susan Calvin* made its first appearance in "Velocity's Ghost" in *The Other Half of the Sky* (Athena Andreadis editor, Kay Holt co-editor; Candlemark & Gleam 2013) which became the kernel story for *Fault Lines*.

In the Deep

Kelly Jennings

Candlemark & Gleam

For information, address
Athena Andreadis
Candlemark & Gleam LLC,
38 Rice Street #2, Cambridge, MA 02140
eloi@candlemarkandgleam.com

Library of Congress Cataloguing-in-Publication Data
In Progress

ISBNs: 978-1-952456-03-9 (print), 978-1-952456-04-6 (digital)

Cover art by Melissa Capriglione

Editor: Athena Andreadis

Proofreader: Patti Exster

www.candlemarkandgleam.com

To my mother, Shelbylynn Jennings,
my first reader, gone too soon.

Characters and Places

Adder Ikan16: Security cadet, dedicated Security Officer for Brontë Ikeda Verde. One of six Ikans born/created in Ikeda House from an egg harvested from Sabra Anador. A product of the Calypso project.

Alice Taveri Harada: Velocity's twin sister, deceased.

Aimie Waifu: A labor agent at Opotiki Water Treatment Center.

Anja Ikeda Nowak: Register name Anja Adir Zhao Ikeda Nowak. Deceased. One of the primary conspirators to the hostile takeover/coup which killed most of the Ikeda House heirs. Married to Torres Ikeda Alonzo.

Atlas Society: an inter-House society dedicated to advancing and protecting the Combines and their role in the Republic.

Avril Drury: Chief clerk for the Minister of Trade on Durbin.

Brontë Ikeda Verde: Register name Elena Kora Hodaya Ikeda Verde. Born to Ikeda House, a product of the Calypso project, currently fourth in line to the Primary Seat on the Ikeda House Board. Velocity's student and ward. Age about sixteen.

Calais Stuart: Contract labor worker in Pakuru; member of Iron Smoke.

Calypso Project: A eugenics program conceived of and implemented by the Atlas Society. The project uses genetic engineering both to widen the gene pool available to the Combines, and to "improve" that gene pool.

Castillo Mining Platform HLC116: A mining platform mining asteroids in the Drift.

Corvo Sungai: Siji Tactical officer. Born to the *Sungai*. In charge of the operation on Durbin.

Dagan: General term for Pirian teachers of Indaiya; generic name for Uri Calvin before his naming.

David Ikeda Ito: Register name David Raphael Navarro Ikeda Ito. Heir apparent to the Ikeda House Primary Seat. One of the few survivors of the hostile takeover that killed most Ikeda House heirs. Father of Justine Ikeda Ito, second in line to inherit the Primary Seat.

Durbin: A settlement planet in deep space.

Edu Sungai: Mainwatch Tactics first on the *Sungai*; Siji.

Eccles Plaza: The plaza on which Durbin's Parliament House and attendant buildings are located.

Elian Scott: The name under which Maya Sungai was sold on Durbin.

Emilie Laiso: Labor agent for Rangel Mines at Pakuru.

Emma Wahid: Owner of a rebuild shop in Tauranga City.

(Te) Huna Sulavee: A Pirian convicted into contract labor on Durbin, leased to Opotiki Water Treatment Center.

Ian Ikan16: One of the six Ikan16s. Formerly a Security Cadet for Ikeda House, and one of Brontë's dedicated Security team. Current whereabouts unknown.

Imre Theriot: Register name Imre Theriot Waiti Hayek Harada. Minister of Trade on Durbin. Born in Hayek House, one of the (distant) heirs to the Primary Seat.

Innis Sungai: Tactical officer on the *Sungai*; Mainwatch Tactical First.

Iron Mountains: A mountain range on Durbin. Pakuru is located here.

Iron Smoke: A possibly mythical insurgency organization on Durbin.

Isra Ikeda Lopaka: Register name Isra Te Ao Caitriona Ikeda Lopaka. Advisor to Theo, Chair of the Atlas Society, Head of the Calypso project. Brontë's mother/creator.

Jack Ngata: A contract labor miner on Castillo Mining Platform HLC116.

Jusuf Peixoto: Siji Tactical officer; formerly contract labor on a sugar farm on the settlement planet of Papagao; adopted into the Pirian fleet in early adolescence.

Kai Murphy: Customs Officer on Castillo Mining Platform HLC116.

Kaia Sungai: Logistics officer on the *Sungai*.

Kaihe: Captain of the Combine ship *Prince of Peace*.

Lamont: Full name Hwa Lamont. Chandler on Castillo Mining Platform HLC116.

Lena Dilgry: A shuttle pilot on Durbin.

Lily Merrell: Captain in Durbin Security.

Loffler Taveri Lopaka: Velocity's cousin, current holder of the Primary Seat on the Taveri House Board.

Maya Sungai: A Pirian sold into contract labor on Durbin under the name Elian Scott.

The *Mdudu*: A Pirian courier ship.

Mendoza Sungai: Tactical First for the Siji and Tactical Topwatch First for the *Sungai*.

Mosel McKay: A shuttle pilot on Durbin.

Nia Sungai: A cadet analyst on the *Sungai*; aspiring member of Siji.

Nur Che: Head of Station Security on CSS Webster-1, Durbin.

Odessa Lee: A clerk on CSS Webster-1.

Opotiki Water Treatment Center: A facility on the coast near Tauranga City.

Otene Sungai: A very old Siji officer.

Oz: A settlement planet in deep space.

Pakuru: A mining town on Durbin.

Para Evans: A contract labor worker in Pakuru; member of Iron Smoke.

Paris: A Hayek-Lopaka Security Lieutenant on Castillo Mining Platform HLC116.

Perth Okore: A deckhand on the *Reynard*, a cargo ship owned by Lopaka House.

The *Prince of Peace*: A Combine courier ship.

Rangel and Reed: A mining consortium on Durbin.

The *Reynard*: A cargo ship held by Lopaka Combine. Trades mostly in human cargo.

Ruçar Ikan16: One of the six Ikan16s. Formerly a Security Cadet for Ikeda House. Sold to Castillo Mining Platform HLC116.

Rida Tdemir: Pilot and navigator on the *Susan Calvin*. Born free labor on a Republic station, adopted at seven into Guo House and trained as a tech in Guo House on Tija Station, dismissed for an ethics violation at age fifteen. Hired on despite his lack of certification by Meier Company, which trained him further, renting him out on short-term contracts. Tai helped him jump one such contract at age seventeen.

The *Ruka*: The *Susan Calvin*'s runabout.

Sabra Anador: A combat-trained Combine Security Officer. Also the donor of the eggs used to produce both Brontë and the Ikan16s. Formerly Brontë's dedicated Security officer, now Security for Theo Ikeda Verde.

Sasha: A customs house clerk on Durbin.

Sheng Murray: A contract labor miner on Durbin.

Siji: A division of the Pirian fleet. Crew and officers are taken from multiple ships in the fleet. "Siji ships" are regular Pirian ships which have a large number of Siji on them, and which dedicate at least some of their resources to missions for the Siji. The original and primary mission of the Siji was to locate and rescue Pirian crewmembers who had been sold into contract labor in Republic space. Over the past century, the Siji have become more radical, and *most* of them now see their mission as ending the contract labor system. The most radical believe their mission should be to end the Republic entirely.

Simei: A contract labor child at Opotiki Water Treatment Center.

The *Sungai*: A Pirian ship; member of Siji.

The *Susan Calvin*: a Free Trade ship, owner and captain Velocity WrachantA

Tai Nahas: First on the *Susan Calvin*. Born into contract labor on the settlement planet Harvest. Delinquent on that contract. Rida's lover, Velocity's lover.

Tallis Sofia Watson Taveri Harada: Velocity's register name.

Taniwha: AI on the *Sungai*.

Tauranga City: The main city on Durbin.

Te Ao Sungai: Mainwatch Captain on the *Sungai*.

Theo Ikeda Hayek: Register name Hiro Sayid Liao Ikeda Hayek. Current holder of the Primary Seat on the Ikeda House Board. Brontë's cousin.

Torres Ikeda Alonzo: Register name Torres Umi Alicia Ikeda Alonzo, deceased. One of the two primary conspirators in the hostile takeover/coup which killed most of the Ikeda House heirs. Killed by Isra Ikeda Lopaka, Brontë's mother. Wife to Anja Ikeda Nowak, deceased.

Tully Menemesha: An illegal child on Durbin, born to Wasp.

Uri Calvin: A mechanical, which is to say an artificial intelligence housed in a mechanical body. In Uri's case, his intelligence was housed in the mechanical dagan which Velocity bought on a Drift station. As his intelligence developed, he ceased using the mechanical body, living now mostly in the ship itself and whatever nexus he has access to. Formerly known as the Dagan.

Velocity Wrachant: a.k.a. Tallis Taveri, a.k.a. Tallis Sofia Watson Taveri Harada. Former heir to Taveri-Bowers Combine; Currently Captain of the *Susan Calvin*. Born on Dresden Station.

The *Wachao*: A Free Trade merchant ship, affiliated with the station Hell in a Bucket. Heavily in debt to Weber-Harada Combine.

Wasp: A contract labor miner on Durbin, delinquent from her contract.

William Kadir Taveri: Velocity's father, deceased.

Wolf Ikan16: One of the six Ikan16s. Formerly a Security Cadet for Ikeda House, and one of Brontë's dedicated Security team. Now bonded labor on Durbin.

Yadav: Owner of an inn in Tauranga City.

Yao Garcia: Former contract labor worker on Durbin. Currently leader of Iron Smoke.

Zuanchan Lane: Main commercial street in Tauranga City.

Glossary

Republic Terms and Phrases

Ata ata: Calm down, just hold on.

Atlas Society: An inter-House society in the Combines, dedicated to advancing and protecting the Combines and their role in the Republic.

Bot: A rude term for contract labor workers.

Burga: A violent snowstorm.

Calypso: A person who has been genetically engineered to have a specific constellation of traits, including ruthlessness; aggression; a low tolerance for boredom; and a very low risk of anxiety, depression, or thalamic emotions. Created by the Atlas Society, as part of the Calypso Project.

Calypso Project: A eugenics program conceived of and implemented by the Atlas Society. The project uses genetic engineering both to widen the gene pool available to the Combines, and to "improve" that gene pool.

Chip: A rude term for contract labor workers, derived from the chip implanted in their shoulder blades.

Cot: A rude term for contract labor workers.

Crack off: Cut work.

Dildos: A rude name for Durbin Security officers.

Dob, dob out: To betray, especially to betray to some authority.

Hiraka: The local term on Durbin for those affiliated with the Combines. An insult.

Iarmao: Steady lover, person you are in a committed relationship with.

Kanji: The name of a small fish who eats the leavings of bigger fish. An insult.

Kite out: Run away.

Netbots: Pirian manufactured organic uplinks. These are temporary communication devices, installed via bots in the human body. They require the assistance of an AI and last just over one hundred hours.

Pesa: A word for money in general and the metal coins used on some Republic stations and planets in particular.

Slates: Slang for sanitary facilities.

Stonk: A loser, a jerk; someone who thinks they know everything who actually knows nothing.

Pirian Terms and Phrases

Ador: A pain medication.

Atcha: Enough, stop it, be quiet.

Adaiya: Unbalanced, unhealthy, excessive, not sensible. The opposite to daiya.

Cousins: This is a translation of itoko, the general term for shipmate, crew member, or ally who we trust completely. It is also in some circumstances means the Siji. Usually, in the latter case, it has a definite article attached—"What are the cousins doing now?"—as opposed to "Why are our cousins late?"

Dagan: An Indaiya teacher/leader. Dagans usually give ethical and life advice as well. They're like therapists who make you work out for three hours a day.

Daiya: In balance, acceptable, healthy.

Dore: A person in Indaiya who is attacking.

Foutu: Messed up (literally, fucked).

Gadro: Pirate. A major insult among the Pirians.

Harab: A Pirian game, like tag.

Hodi, Hodi: Literally, knock-knock—a greeting Pirians use when they enter your room, cabin, or personal space.

Indaiya: The Pirian self-defense/philosophical training.

Itachi: Allies of the Pirians who are not shipmates/cousins. They are used and compensated, but not entirely trusted.

Itoko: Cousin, shipmate. Also the slang term for the Siji.

Kaista: A vulgar idiot. Literally, shitstain.

Karaki: Literally, skull. A Pirian obscenity.

Kirop: Literally, little circle. Used to mean a temporary work crew, or a crew assigned to a job outside the ship.

Kitoko: Little cousin. Used with younger siblings and cousins as well as for those new to the ship.

Kusho ketawa: Do it tomorrow/later/never. Cf Mañana, mañana.

Mafi: Idiot, shithead.

Mainwatch: One of the four watches on a Pirian ship. The others are Topwatch, Afterwatch, and Midwatch.

Mdogo: Another word for shipmate or cousin. Plural is wadogo.

Mec: Buddy, pal; usually used for non-shipmates. "Hey, mec, where's the Customs office?"

Mende: Harmful or unwanted insects, vermin. Also an insult.

Mercredi: Literally, Wednesday; but used as the polite way to say merde, or shit.

Mzala: Shipmate, friend. Same as itoko, in some dialects.

Oaw: A mild exclamation. "No one cares about that, oaw?"

Pelos: A kind of mildly narcotic skin-like bandage. Plural is wape.

Pinzhino: Coward. A vulgar insult. Literally, 'little dick'. Sometimes abbreviated as zhino.

Shinda Hapo: A rude and negative response to a request. More or less like "When pigs fly!"

Shogi: Another Pirian game, this one played on a board with magnetic pieces.

Tarai: A drink made from a fermented honey, mixed with a mild sedative.

Tia, Tio: Aunt, uncle. Terms of affection used for actual aunts and uncles as well as any older crewmate a person is fond of.

Tisco: Little treat, tasty bite. Used as a pet name.

Tokalu: Run away, get out of the way. One of the first lessons taught in Indaiya—get out of the way if you can—and a central tenet of the Pirian worldview

Tote Tote: Literally, very salty; but used for the Pirian idea that wisdom comes with age. The full phrase is something like "She has eaten much salt," which is to say "She's very old."

Toro: Idiot.

Ugali: A kind of stiff porridge made from barley, millet, oats, or other grain.

Uke: A person in Indaiya who is taking the defensive position.

Wally work: Work that could as easily be done by robots, simple work; derives from waldos.

Yalla, yalla: Hurry up, let's go.

Synopsis of Fault Lines, Prequel to In the Deep

Previously in *Escape Velocity*....

Eleven-year-old Brontë Ikeda—register name Elena Kora Hodaya Ikeda Verde—is a child of the powerful Ikeda-Verde Combine on the planet Waikato, three jumps from Earth.

The Combines frequently change their leadership—their Primary Seat Holders—via 'hostile takeovers', a.k.a. coups. During a coup which kills nearly thirty of the heirs to the Ikeda House Primary Seat, Brontë's own life is threatened. With the aid of her Security team, including Captain Sabra Anador, she manages to escape. Two other members of her team are with her at the time: Adder and Wolf Ikan16. (The four other members of her Security, left behind on Waikato, are the cloned siblings of Adder and Wolf developed from an egg donated by Sabra: Ian, Ruçar, Maggie, and Nora.) Theo, Brontë's cousin, escapes with them.

They flee to a mining platform, where they attempt to make an alliance with another Combine's heir. Here they are met by Isra Ikeda Lopaka, Brontë's mother and a power within Ikeda House. She sends Brontë and Sabra Anador off to Durbin, taking Theo and the two Ikan16s, Adder and Wolf, with her. Due to the deaths during the Ikeda House coup, Theo is now the heir apparent to the Primary Seat. Brontë herself is now second in line to inherit—as they think. (In fact, two of the heirs believed to be dead, David Ikeda Verde and his daughter, have survived.)

Brontë and Sabra flee, but not to Durbin. While on their journey, they receive a message from another heir to the Ikeda seat, Torres Ikeda Alonzo, informing Brontë that the Ikan16s are being held hostage at Freiheit, a planet fifteen jumps from Earth. Brontë suspects this is a trap—that Torres wants to capture and kill her, so that Torres and her wife, Anja Ikeda Nowak, can take the Primary Seat.

On the Drift station Hell in a Bucket, Brontë encounters Velocity Wrachant, captain of the *Susan Calvin*, a heavily indebted merchant ship. Telling Velocity only select parts of the actual situation, Brontë hires Velocity to help her retrieve the Ikan16s.

The Drift is a section of space occupied by Free Trade merchant ships and stations—a buffer zone between Republic space and the planets and stations in Pirian space. The Pirian fleet provides the only serious opposition to the Combines and the Republic. Pirians are a loosely federated fleet of ships. The fleet fled Earth a millennium and a half ago rather than submit to the Combines.

Velocity Wrachant has also fled the Combines. Born to Taveri-Bowers Combine, where she was first in line to a Primary Seat, she escaped at sixteen and has been owner and Captain of the *Susan Calvin* for nearly twenty years. Her crew—Tai Nahas, her First; Rida Tdemir, her pilot and navigator; and Uri, her dagan—are fiercely loyal, and as suspicious as she is about Brontë's true motives.

The dagan, Uri, is a "mechanical"—which is to say an AI from Pirian space with a mechanical body. ("Dagan" is a Pirian term that literally means someone who teaches.) Velocity bought Uri in order to learn Indaiya, a Pirian self-defense art; but like all Pirian AIs, Uri's main original mission was to convert people to the Pirian way of living and thinking. Uri has been a crew member on the *Susan Calvin* for several years now, and his loyalties have shifted.

After an attempted mutiny by Brontë fails, Brontë reveals the true situation to Velocity and her crew: not only is Brontë a key player in the Ikeda House coup, she is also a product of the Calypso Project, a eugenics movement using genetic engineering to "improve" the ruling class members of select Combines. Calypsos are deliberately engineered to be intelligent, Machiavellian risk-takers—and entirely ruthless. Later, we learn that Velocity herself is a Calypso child. The Atlas Society, an inter-Combine "social" group, is behind the Calypso Project; Isra Ikeda Lopaka, Brontë's mother, is a major force in the Atlas Society.

The Calypso Project was originally started both as a way to widen and deepen the gene pool in the Combines, and to create a pool of people who might effectively combat the Pirians. Pirians are deliberately exogamous, taking every opportunity to bring new genes into their fleet. The Combines, on the other hand, follow a philosophy of "genetic purity", deliberately intermarrying among their own group in order to preserve their "superior" genes.

Brontë offers Velocity a great deal of money as well as access to Combine influence if Velocity will take her to Freiheit to retrieve the Ikan16s and help her deal with Torres Ikeda Alonzo. Velocity agrees, with some misgivings—but her ship and her crew need the money, and a Combine trade license wouldn't hurt.

When they reach Freiheit, they find Isra Ikeda Lopaka is there as well, along with Theo. Isra attempts to suborn Velocity, by offering to help reinstate her to the Primary Seat on the Taveri House Board. Velocity refuses, but learns that Rida and Brontë have been taken hostage—and interrogated—by Torres Ikeda Alonzo. Reluctantly, she joins forces with Isra to take down Torres. Torres and all of her security are killed in the ensuing confrontation.

Once Theo has been confirmed as Ikeda House's Primary Seat Holder, Brontë—now third in line to the Primary Seat of Ikeda House—is sent off with Velocity and her crew. Velocity and Isra agree that, in exchange for a trade license and quarterly payments, Velocity will tutor Brontë and keep her safe. The understanding is that the *Susan Calvin* will run cargo among the settlement planets out in the Deep. In fact, however, both Brontë and Velocity leave Republic space and attempt to align themselves with the Pirians. This, they hope, will allow them to more effectively oppose the current regime in the Combines.

In the Deep, the second book in the *Escape Velocity* series, begins three years later.

Chapter 1

Commercial Space Station Webster-1, Planet Durbin, in the Deep

No one thinks it's a silver bullet." Corvo paused. "Do you have that term? Silver bullet?"

Velocity toggled her inskull uplink and ran an Orly. "Werewolves?" she said dubiously.

Corvo laughed. "This action is one of many. This is all we mean."

They had reached a junction on Webster-1's main concourse. Velocity paused, looking up and down the side corridors. In every direction, nothing but shadows and shuttered hatchways. On the bulkhead directly before them, a capture of Durbin, the planet below, stuttered and glitched as it turned. It was the only movement anywhere—no one stirred along the long curving lengths of the dusky corridors. They hadn't seen a single person on this station so far, which was beyond strange. True, like many settlement planets, especially those out here in the Deep, Durbin had problems maintaining its population. But even so, this was the sole commercial station in the entire system. Velocity would have expected at least some traffic. She toggled her uplink again and sent a query to Uri back on the ship. *Is there anyone on this station?*

Uri, their quasi-spiritual martial arts instructor, was a Pirian-manufactured AI sold as a dagan—an Indaiya tutor. He replied promptly: *Station manifest shows six hundred and eleven permanent residents.*

Velocity frowned. For a station this size, that was dangerously underpopulated. Ten times that number would be underpopulated. Catching up to them, Tai shook his head. The multicolored beads that decorated his dozens of braids clattered faintly in all the silence. "This is like a horror animate. Where is everyone?"

The empty corridors were making Velocity edgy as well. She and her crew had spent the past year and a half, universal time, in Pirian space. Pirian stations were filled with light and color, animate murals and hard paintings, music, buskers, the spicy scent of various teas, and swarms of people. Not only was this station dark and empty, it stank of sweat and old solvents. Furthermore, its walls sported only pus-yellow anti-fungal paint. The capture of Durbin was the first attempt at art they'd seen. No directories, either. But also entirely ineffective shieldwalls—Uri had gone through them, as he put it, like an open door. Now he spoke through her uplink: *Go right, then right again. You want the second unit down.*

Velocity glanced right and saw a faint light from the corridor in question. She pointed with her chin. "That's us."

Down the corridor, they found an unmarked kiosk. Its door was open, and inside its tiny space sat a single agent, slouched behind a bolted-down worktable, watching something on her port. When Velocity appeared, the woman grimaced and pulled off her headset. "You'd be Captain Wrachant."

"I would," Velocity agreed. "Are you the Assistant Minister of Trade Odessa Lee?"

"Assistant *to* the Minister of Trade." Lee looked Velocity over. Like Corvo and Tai, Velocity was wearing a skinsuit, the standard wear for any environment you didn't entirely trust. These were plain grey suits with their ship's name, *Susan Calvin*, across the back. From the twitch of the woman's mouth, skinsuits were not common on Webster Station. Lee brought up the file Velocity had submitted. "You want a trade license."

"Sorry, no. That's not correct." Velocity reached to tap the *Return to Top* link on Lee's tablet screen, and then tapped the emblem that linked to her trade license. "We already have a trade license, good for all planets affiliated with Ikeda-Verde Combine."

Hayek-Lopaka Combine held the main trade lease here on Durbin. But Ikeda-Verde had an affiliate license. This was why the Pirians had chosen Velocity and her ship for this job. One of the reasons.

Lee's mouth twisted as she scanned through the trade license. It had been written and vetted by Ikeda House lawyers, so Velocity wasn't worried. At least, she wasn't worried about the trade license. While Lee read, Velocity looked about the compartment. Nothing on the walls, nothing on the deck. Odd. In her experience, people always personalized their work space. Lee's workspace didn't have even a slap-up of her favorite holiday spot. "You're here to sell medical supplies?" Lee said.

"We're here to establish a trade syndicate." Velocity paused. "You did receive my request for an appointment with the Minister of Trade?"

Lee spun back up through the trade license, and then jumped to the main documents for the *Susan Calvin*. "You'll have to petition Madame Drury for an appointment."

Avril Drury is chief clerk for the Minister of Trade, Uri mentioned helpfully.

Every Republic planet was like this: layers upon layers of bureaucracy. Sometimes it seemed like bureaucracy was the Republic's main export. "All right," Velocity said. "Let's do that."

"Have to do it in person," Lee said. "Downplanet."

"Surely we can arrange for an appointment via the nexus?"

"Appointments taken in person only." Lee scratched her armpit. "Next shuttle departs in thirty-nine hours."

"In...thirty-nine hours."

"Universal time. You won't be allowed on the shuttle without a current health certificate signed by one of our physicians. Clinic hours are twelve to fifteen hundred."

Velocity blinked. "You can't be serious."

Lee looked up. For the first time, she smiled. "Welcome to Durbin."

ᘓ ⵏ ᙏ

"Downplanet?" Rida glanced at Tai. Though they looked nothing alike—Rida being round with a thatch of thick short hair, while Tai was tall and lean with long silky hair—they looked for a flash of a second identical, united in their delight. They both knew how much Velocity hated planets.

"Oh, hush." She pulled her undershirt over her head. They were in the umbilical cabin, redressing after going through decon. "Uri, call a meeting in the galley. Ten minutes."

"Yes, Captain." The AI replied through the ship's feeds instead of through her uplink, since Velocity had voiced her command aloud. In a moment, she heard him repeating the message throughout the ship. Tai, already dressed—he seldom wore more than leggings aboard ship—climbed after Rida, his long legs taking the ladder two rungs at a time.

Corvo, cross-legged on the bench by the umbilical, tugged on the swat many Pirians wore instead of a shirt—a band of cloth that tucked around their chest and over one shoulder. This one was orange, green, and bright yellow. Pirians liked bright colors. Golden-skinned, with a smooth cap of dark hair and bright dark eyes, Corvo was old enough to be Velocity's grandmother. Like many Pirians, she had broad cheekbones and a round face. "You are unhappy that we must visit the planet?" she asked.

Velocity buttoned her vest. "We knew the job would likely take us downplanet."

Corvo made the sideways head-wobble gesture Pirians used, the meaning of which Velocity still was trying to decipher. Sometimes it seemed to mean *That-might-be-so*. Sometimes it seemed to mean *Tell-me-more*. Sometimes it meant *That's-ridiculous-but-I'm-too-civil-to-say-so*. "When I was young, in Indaiyi sessions, I always ran away. And that is good. Tokalu."

"Get out of the way," Velocity said obligingly, which was more or less what the Pirian word *tokalu* meant.

"But not the only good, my dagan tells me. If we are too quick to run, she says, we miss the luck at the side of our eye."

Velocity scrubbed a towel over her cropped hair, trying to look as if she was thinking deeply about Corvo's words. Pirians loved telling stories, and their point was always that you should ponder them for fifty years and then reach awareness in one bold burst; which was fine, except she had a ship to manage. Corvo smiled and slid to her feet. "Life is daiya, Captain. This is all I mean."

"That's all you ever mean," Velocity pointed out. Corvo laughed, a great burst of hilarity, her head flung back and her mouth thrown wide. It was one of the things Velocity liked best about Corvo, the way she laughed with all her body. Still chuckling, the Pirian climbed after Tai and Rida. Velocity sat to pull on her ship boots, smiling herself, but also brooding. Speaking to Uri through her link, she asked, *What about the planetary shieldwalls?*

Pssh, Uri said. *The security here is pathetic. Years out of date. Unless we need access to Combine coffers, we should be fine. The real problem is the one we discussed earlier.*

Insufficient satellite cover.

Correct.

The trade lease system as practiced by the Combines was in theory beneficial to all parties. The way it worked, in theory, was that in exchange for a trade lease on a planet, a given Combine made credit available to those who settled the planet. This credit allowed settlers to buy necessities like agricultural chemicals and machinery, domes, space stations, medical supplies, and communication satellites. For planets like Durbin out here in the Deep, thirty or more jumps from the Core, such credit was not usually available. Neither was any reliable market, given how far goods had to be transported. So those in the Deep benefited by having the Combine provide both credit and a market for whatever goods they produced; and the Combine benefited by having a favored status both on the import and export side of the market.

That was the theory. In reality, what usually happened was what was happening here: Hayek-Lopaka Combine issued minimal credit at high interest rates, and prohibited the import or export of any goods without a trade license—which they also issued, at a steep price. The trade lease system wasn't designed to keep planets impoverished, or technologically backwards. It was designed to enrich the Combines. The poverty and inferior tech were just side effects.

Durbin had been settled just over seven hundred years earlier. During its early centuries, Hayek-Lopaka had invested in the planet, since they were using it as a resort. They had 'troped several islands in the temperate southern hemisphere, furnishing them with Earth-source flora and fauna; they financed resort companies, allowing them to rebuild the islands with beaches and gardens; other companies had rebuilt mountain ranges, creating winter lodges with skiing, skating parks, and other delights. Until recently, most of the profits the Combine extracted from Durbin had come from these resorts. There had been a small population of contract labor on the planet: cooks, kitchen girls, boot boys, groundskeepers, guides.

Then, over the last century, Oz, another Deep planet, got its own far lovelier resorts online. The number of tourists coming to Durbin dropped by half, and Hayek-Lopaka shifted to mining rich seams of lithium and molybdenum in the large barren continent in the northern hemisphere. The Combine withdrew credit from the resort consortiums, investing instead in miners and mining equipment. There had been a surge in population, most of it contract labor, most from planets and stations scattered through the Deep. Hayek-Lopaka had not increased the credit line necessary to support this population, despite the increase in profits they were extracting from the planet.

Velocity leaned against the cabin wall, her eyes shut, trying to shake off her dark mood before she went up to the galley. She knew the source of her temper, and it wasn't the job. True, the job was risky. Corvo had warned her about that when the Siji council offered it to her. But at that point, the *Susan Calvin* had been in Pirian space for sixteen months. Sixteen months of nothing but wally work— hauling freight out to mining platforms; transporting refugees from Drift stations into Pirian space. Though this work paid well enough, Velocity had known the jobs were tests. Were she and her crew competent? Could they be trusted? Most importantly—from the perspective of the Pirians—were they daiya? She had known that if they didn't take this chance, they would be working wally on the edge of the fleet until they were as old as Corvo. Older. So she took this job and brought her crew here, across the Drift to a Republic planet filled with slaves. To a place where they weren't safe. Again.

Grimacing, Velocity rubbed the bone in her hand, feeling the callus of the old break. Then she let out her breath, got to her feet, and started up the ladder. Since the *Susan Calvin* was in dock, they had station gravity; so it was a hard climb.

As she'd expected, everyone was already in the galley: the two Pirians, Jusuf and Corvo, sitting shoulder to shoulder in the booth; Tai across from them; Rida filling bowls with coffee, made perfectly to everyone's preference. Velocity accepted a bowl (dark, strong, unsweetened) before sliding into the booth. She knew Uri had probably kept everyone updated; nevertheless, she spent some time rehashing what had happened on the station. "It was so strange," Tai added when she was done. "Like a ghost station. No one anywhere. Just the Assistant Minister of Trade."

"Assistant *to* the Minister of Trade," Uri corrected. He was not physically present. As a mechanical, he did have a physical body, which was currently stowed in its locker in the pit. Velocity had long since removed the governor that restricted the body to that space. He could have brought it to the galley. But mostly he preferred using the ship as his body. He added, "Funding for the station has been reduced every decade for the past five. Currently, Webster-1 is operating at fifteen percent of its peak budget."

Rida sucked his teeth. "That's barely enough to run maintenance, a station this size."

"Marginal at best," Uri agreed.

"A culture in crisis," Corvo said. "We knew this." She sounded pleased: crisis for a Republic planet meant opportunity for Pirians.

On the way back to the ship, Velocity had used her uplink to build an agenda for this meeting. She brought it up now, on the galley wallboard. "First off," she said. "Everyone going downplanet, I want you at that clinic at twelve hundred hours. Uri, what's that ship time?"

"Afterwatch half-second," Uri said. "I'll give everyone a twenty minute warning."

"Good. The shuttles here run once every two hundred and fifty hours, and I do not feature sitting on this ship waiting for the next run. Second—" She paused, because Tai had raised his chin. "Yes?"

"What about the *Ruka*?" Tai asked, meaning the *Susan Calvin*'s runabout. "We have enough fuel for a few runs to the planet."

"Five runs, round-trip," Uri agreed.

"We'll keep that in reserve," Velocity said. "If they're requiring a health certificate to go down to the surface, we have to assume tight border control. Better to tread softly for this initial contact. Which brings me to point two. I'd like to keep our initial landing party to three."

Rida, over by the grill, made a sound of protest. Since he had interpreted her correctly, Velocity didn't comment. Tai spoke up: "You. Me. Who else?"

"Oh, you're going, are you?" Rida said. Tai grinned at him. "Captain," Rida objected. "You need a negotiator. That's me, not Tai."

"Negotiation is later. Reconnaissance first. Jusuf will be the third. You and Corvo will work with Uri, up here."

Rida squinted, thinking this through. Jusuf Sungai was a Siji intelligence officer, though the Pirian term was Tactical Second. Unlike Corvo, who had been born to the fleet, Jusuf had been taken in—rescued out of contract labor as a child, and adopted by a Pirian ship. So he didn't look like a typical Pirian: his skin was darker, his face narrow, his body language far more contained. He'd draw less attention than a born-Pirian might, in other words, which was only one of the reasons Velocity had chosen him over Corvo.

"Third point," Velocity said, before Rida could argue further, "everyone has installed their netbots, right?" She glanced around the galley, seeing no dissension. Pirian netbots were a nanotropic device, a closed communication network. Cheaper and less risky than Velocity's own inskull uplink, they used the subject's bones and neural system to create a communication relay. Netbots required access to an AI and were intentionally short-lived, lasting just under a hundred hours, but more certain than pocket docks in a tricky situation. "When does the network go live?" she asked.

"Nine hours from now," Uri said. "Plenty of time."

"Right. Fourth point: We are a peaceful delegation hoping to establish a trade syndicate. On the other hand, we are also a Free Trade ship." Velocity smirked. "I think we can get away with a few weapons."

Tai gave her his crooked grin. "Define few."

"Nothing above a Sema snub." She pointed at Tai as he opened his mouth to argue, and he subsided, still grinning. "Show restraint.

We don't want to alarm their Security. Also, keep your baggage light, but remember we may be downside for several watches… several days," Velocity corrected herself with a grimace. "Uri, what's the state of their environmentals?"

"It's called weather when you're on a planet. High temperature two degrees today, humidity thirteen percent, sunny early in the week with storm systems moving in later. Temperatures expected to fall as the storm advances."

"Two degrees? You mean twenty."

"Ah. No. I did send a précis concerning planetary conditions to your dropbox."

"Actually two degrees?" Velocity inhaled and then just shook her head. *Planets.* "Tai, Jusuf, access this précis and dress appropriately." She ran her gaze down the agenda. "Their shuttle leaves at topwatch third, ship's time. Be packed and at the umbilical by topwatch second." They murmured assent. Velocity glanced around the galley. "Any comments?"

No one spoke, though Rida sucked his teeth again. She answered her own question: "Security."

Tai nodded. "I noticed that."

"Security?" Corvo drew her fine Pirian eyebrows together.

"It's a Combine station," Tai explained. "Should have Security thick as ticks. At the gates, at the docks, everywhere. I didn't even see a Security kiosk."

Corvo did the sideways nod. "Perhaps a result of being so underfunded?"

"This is the Republic," Velocity said. "They will do without medical to buy Security officers. They'd probably do without environmental techs. No Security…" She shook her head. "That's worse than odd."

"It may be a good sign," Jusuf said. When they looked at him, he spread his hands. "Whatever the cause—funding, lack of trust in their own Security, chaos in the government—any of these benefit us."

Chaos and rogue Security officers did not strike Velocity as a benefit. She thought of how easily Uri had penetrated those shieldwalls. Was the Security here being kept deliberately weak? But toward what end? "We need more data," she muttered.

Corvo made a sound of agreement. "That is why we have come."

Velocity shook her head. "Right, two hours until the clinic opens. Start packing. Maybe eat something. Who's on dinner?"

Chapter 2

Tauranga City, Republic Settlement Planet Durbin

The station's shuttle was junk, its benches mended with electrical tape and much of its safety gear non-functional. When Velocity objected to the latter, the pilots—both about fifteen years old—exchanged glances. "Don't worry, miss," one said. "We hardly ever crash."

This was clearly supposed to be hilarious. Velocity made sure her crew were distributed in the few seats with functional safety gear—fortunately, the other three passengers didn't seem to care—and took herself up to the extra bench in the cockpit. Neither pilot objected, not that it would have done them much good if they had: no Security on this flight either. Instead they interrogated Velocity about where she was from, and what it was like in the Drift, and was she a pirate, and had she ever seen a pirate, and whether she was hiring crew for her ship. "We're good pilots," the younger said. "I'm qualified in 5-space math."

"Send me your vitae," Velocity said.

"Our what?"

Just then the shuttle hit atmosphere; but after they touched down, Velocity stayed to explain what they should send her, and to give them her call sign. This wasn't because she wanted a couple of half-educated Republic gutter rats aboard her ship, but because she knew kids like this were precisely the sort the Siji recruited in their role as the militant arm of the Pirian fleet.

Climbing down the shuttle ladder, she was hit with viciously bright light and a wind so cold she twitched with shock, her fists clenching on the metal railings. She squinted, both against the light and the wind. Looking out, she saw Tai huddled with the crew and the other passengers around the shuttle's cargo hold, unloading their baggage and sharing it out, shouting over the wind. One passenger, an older woman in mining scrubs and heavy boots, headed away from the shuttle, walking purposefully, as if she had somewhere to be.

Velocity squinted in the direction the woman was moving. The painfully bright light was Durbin's star. She always forgot, until she was on a planet again, how violent starlight was up close like this. Planet-dwellers wore filters against it. Star-glasses. She made a note to acquire some as soon as possible. She climbed the rest of the way down, moving carefully: the planet's pull dragged hard at her every motion. Durbin was only .62 universal, but that was well over what most stations kept, and twice what they usually ran on the *Susan Calvin*. She and her crew would take some time adjusting to it, even with the nanotropic fix they'd been given by the Pirians, which—according to the Pirians—meant their bones and muscles would stay in prime condition no matter how long they stayed in microgravity.

The shuttle had set down on a wide flat plain, three or four hundred meters out from a tin shed. That was where the woman was going. Customs, Velocity assumed. The plain was rocky and barren. Far beyond the shed was a distant scrabble of buildings. Velocity scrubbed tears from her eyes and climbed the rest of the way down. Having read Uri's information on Durbin's environment, she had thermals on under her skinsuit and wore an insulated jacket. Also heavy thermal boots, instead of the soft ship boots she usually wore. She had worried about being too hot. Hah. Their two child pilots started for the customs shed. She led Jusuf and Tai after them, head ducked against the wind.

By the time Velocity reached the shed, her muscles were aching and she was out of breath. She hoped the Pirian 'tropes started working their magic soon. After the bright starlight outside, the shed interior was dark. It was also cold, and stank of wet dirt, wet clothing, and sweat. She stood blinking, waiting for her eyes to adjust. The shuttle pilots were talking with someone. Velocity couldn't understand more than one word in ten. This was common. Dialects always drifted over time. No doubt the recent influx of contract workers onto Durbin from all over the Republic had complicated that issue. Once she grew accustomed to the local dialect, she knew, it would be easier to understand.

Velocity's eyes began to adjust to the dusk inside the shed. She saw it was filled with immense mesh-wire cages, crammed with cargo: bundles and bins, net containers, heaps of cloth. One row of cages held contract labor, huddled in rows on the dirt floor, most of them wearing far less than she was, some of them children. Her pulse thumped in her throat. She glanced at Tai, who was watching the cages, his face expressionless.

The younger pilot, Mosel, turned to Velocity. "This is Sasha," he said, nodding at a woman seated behind a worktable. "She'll get you settled."

No Security here either, Velocity realized, taking another glance around. Even with all the contract labor, not a single Security agent on site. She stepped up to the worktable. Like the two shuttle pilots, Sasha was young, slender, and light-skinned, with straight dark hair. Once she learned that Velocity had a trade license from IVC and was willing to pay a five percent "surcharge" (no one said *bribe*) on their port fee, she asked no further questions. Instead, she loaded visas onto their data tags. "Keep them on you," she ordered.

A minute later they were out on the street, though *street* seemed a fancy name for the trail worn across the plain between the metal hut and Tauranga City, half a kilometer away. The shuttle pilots

stood nearby, talking and laughing with one of the other passengers
—someone they knew well, apparently. Mosel glanced at Velocity
and then came over. "If you need a place to stay, Yadav's has the
best beds. And he won't charge extra for heat."

Extra for heat, Velocity thought, bemused. But she thanked the
pilot gravely. He crunched off across the gritty plain to get on a
motorized two-wheeled vehicle. These in-line vehicles, Velocity
would learn, were the most common form of transportation on
Durbin. His partner climbed on behind him, and they roared off
toward the city. The other passengers had already left, on similar
vehicles. In seconds, they were out of sight, the noise of their
motors gone. Only the rush of the wind was left. "Well," Velocity
said into the relative silence. "I guess we walk."

"At least it's not snowing," Tai said, and set out along the
battered sketch of a road.

ᘓ ᴛ ᘝ

Just as they reached Tauranga City, the mountains on the horizon
rose up to block the light from the star. The planet grew abruptly
colder. How did people survive here?

Yadav's turned out to be a squat box constructed of dirty
yellow brick, crowded cheek to cheek with similar buildings.
The entranceway was a set of double hatches, with a dead space
between them—a kind of an airlock, Velocity thought, only against
the cold. Once inside, they found Yadav himself, sitting near a
glowing red heat grid. He offered what seemed to Velocity, used
to the prices on Free Trade stations, a reasonable rent, so she hired
the entire fourth floor. No lifts, Yadav said. No meals. Also, no
baths. Not just no private baths—no bathing facilities at all. Yadav
directed them to a public bath, six blocks south. Whatever a block
was. South was the direction of the southern hemisphere, Velocity
knew, from her time on other planets. Standing in the chilly dusk

on the flagstone apron in front of Yadav's, looking up and down the corridor, she wondered grumpily why they couldn't just say port or starboard. *Directions to the Minister of Trade?*

Uri popped up a map on the tiny virtual screen at the upper corner of her left eye, and then widened the screen until it covered half her vision. The route appeared in bright red. *You'll need to talk to Avril Drury first*, Uri said. *The chief clerk. Her office is presently closed. It will open tomorrow at noon.*

Velocity oriented herself to the map, and began following the red line. Uri put in a bright yellow arrow to represent her and her movement, showing she was going in the wrong direction. She growled and reversed course. The route took her to Zuanchan Lane, which Uri helpfully informed her was the main commercial concourse in Tauranga City. All along the corridor, shops shed multi-colored lights into the darkness. Some projected holograms, complete with sound and music. The clatter and racket was interesting at first, and then annoying, and finally just noise.

Velocity found her shoulders hunched against it as she made her way through the sparse crowds. Beneath her boots, the deck was badly-lain brick and mud, mostly mud. She had to take care not to trip. The cold air was spiced with the scent of cooking meat, frying noodles, the harsh sting of brewing coffee. She took note of a bakery doing brisk business, and of a noodle shop not far from it. As she passed the noodle shop, she glanced through the steamy window and saw Jusuf eating at one of the long tables, surrounded by locals. *Fast work*, she thought.

What? Uri said.

Nothing. Pirians. The red path told her to turn at the next cross-corridor and she did. This was a much narrower corridor, and entirely unlit. It crossed other unlit corridors. She glanced along them as she passed, seeing very few people. The cold and dark could explain that, she supposed. Light did show at some windows. After she had crossed six or eight of these corridors, she reached an open space: Eccles Plaza, according to the map. On one side of it stood Parliament House, a six-story building made of stone, with ornate balconies and towers rising from its various levels. Shorter brick buildings stood on the other three sides. The red line on her map led to one of these, conscientiously skirting the fountain in the center of the plaza. The fountain was a stone statue, a giant fish woman. Water spouting from her mouth and fins and gills had frozen into long strands of ice.

Parliament House had arched lancet windows marching across every floor, but in the brick buildings the windows were vertical slits. The building where the Minister of Trade had her chambers was labeled Annex II on Uri's map. Lights showed in some of its windows. Velocity considered going to see if one of the lights might belong to Avril Drury. Instead, she started back to Yadav's. Her feet and back and bones ached. Enough gravity for one day. *Does this filthy planet not have tuk-tuks?* she asked Uri. She hadn't thought of this before leaving Yadav's. She and her crew had never been wealthy enough to hire transport before they went out to Pirian Space; and Pirian stations, of course, all had free public transport.

I find none listed in the city directory, Uri said. *I see several listings for transports, but these seem to be motorized.*

Motorized?

The map vanished and a capture of a vehicle appeared—an in-line vehicle like the one the child pilots had taken from the port: two-wheeled, brightly colored, rushing along a road like something from an animate. The person driving it was laughing, her hair blowing with the wind of her speed. Velocity frowned, calculating speed of impact and probable injuries for anyone falling from such a thing. It didn't even have safety restraints. *What about treni?* she asked, using the Pirian word for their free mass transit vehicles.

Not that I find.

Velocity grimaced. The lights of Zuanchan Lane appeared down the way and she stopped to rest, rubbing the small of her back. Shadows separated from the dark corridor beside her, and three people—three children, she corrected herself—triangulated around her. They were stocky with layers of coats and woolen keffiyehs wrapped around their faces. One said something, murky through the wrap. Velocity stood straight. She'd dealt with thieves on dozens of stations throughout Free Trade space, so she wasn't confused about what was happening. On the other hand, none of these children had apparent weapons. Using her best Pirian, she asked if they were sure they wanted to do this.

The two tallest exchanged glances. Then the one who had spoken first yanked the keffiyeh from her face. "Pay us, kanji!"

Velocity, imitating Corvo, beamed happily and patted the child's cheek. Jerking away, the child pulled an impressively large knife from her pocket. Velocity caught her by the wrist, yanked her off balance and disarmed her. Hugging her tight, one arm around the child's throat, she stowed the knife in her own belt. The other two, who had started to move, froze, their eyes wide. "Tsk." Velocity switched to Public French. "If you're this bad at thieving, find new work."

"Let her go," the smallest child said. "We only hungry. Please, kas."

"Hungry? Surely you have a sick little brother at home? Or a grandmother?"

They exchanged glances again. The one she was holding said something in dialect, too rapid for her to understand. The little one shook his head, and she said it louder. Before Velocity could react, the other two spun and ran. They were out of sight in seconds.

"Ha," Velocity said. "Good for you." The child in her grip said nothing. Velocity got a good grip on the child's collar and pulled her around. "Who were they? Friends?" The child lifted her chin, her lips shut hard. "Right." Velocity patted the knife. "I'll keep this. I have work for a clever child, though. If you'd like to earn your money, come by Yadav's. Ask for Captain Wrachant."

She let the child go. Her expression went blank with surprise, but only for a second. Then she ran away too, even faster than her friends.

Chapter 3

**Aboard the *Sungai*, en route to Battersea-1,
Battersea, Pirian Space**

It was mainwatch third on the *Sungai*, and Brontë was off early from Logistics.

Unlike Adder, who had tested into a ranking, Brontë had not proved out for any ranked position aboard a Pirian ship. Resource Management (six Pirians ranging in age from fifteen to eighty-nine) had discussed her qualifications and her talents and her future prospects for nearly three hours before decreeing her a cadet. This was the outcome her hive had predicted well before the appointment. Cadets were unranked Pirians over the age of nine. They worked half-watches, rotating through every circle on the ship. It was a way to learn the world, Resource Management told her earnestly. And by *world*, they meant *ship*.

For Brontë, this had meant, so far, twenty-five half-watches in Housekeeping (every Pirian "month" was one hundred watches long), twenty-five half-watches in the Exchange, and eleven half-watches in Logistics. Logistics was proving more interesting than the first two. For instance, during this watch she, Kaia, and Bridger had worked a query sent down from Te Ao, Captain Mainwatch: assume the *Sungai* wants to increase its crew by three percent. Is that possible, and what would be the costs?

By costs, Pirians didn't mean money. They meant things like ergs, food, environmentals, the health of the crew. In this case, they meant, "What will we on the crew overall have to change about the ship in order to accomplish the given goal?" The current crew numbered five hundred thirty-six if you counted both her and Adder; three percent of that was sixteen people. For a ship as large as the *Sungai*—almost five hundred meters long and twenty decks high at the aft end—sixteen extra crew didn't seem a lot. But the answer turned out to be tricky. Pirian ships worked hard to get as near to a closed system as they could manage. Daiya, they called this: a balanced system. In a system at daiya, everything influenced everything else.

For example, the water supply. Sixteen additional adult humans would require an increase in water use of two thousand liters per watch, for drinking, cooking, sanitation, laundry, and expansion of the Exchange. Much of this water would be recycled. But an increase in recycling put more demand on environmental control, which in turn increased the demand on energy supply. Increased demand on recycling also meant increased demand on hazard control. This meant increased need for crew in some of those areas—in the Exchange and in sanitation especially. Sixteen new crew members meant sixteen new workers, but you couldn't assume a one-to-one match on new work requirements and new crew member skill sets. Add all the other areas in which demand would be increased—housekeeping, education, medical, eight or ten others—and it became a pretty problem.

Another complication: new crew members were likely to be cadets. The rule keeping certain categories to half-watches (cadets, the pregnant, people caring for children or the elderly, and those recovering from an injury or studying for their ranking exams) was strictly observed. So they couldn't assume the new crew members would be working full watches, not for the first several months they were aboard ship. Very complicated, very interesting calculations, Kaia said with delight. She loved complicated problems, which was probably how she'd ended up as Logistics Mainwatch First.

Still, it was hypothetical so far, and Brontë had a meeting scheduled with the Siji at topwatch first. So Kaia cut her loose early. Brontë took the lift down to Main—the long deck running the length of the ship—mulling over reasons the Siji might want to see her. The lift had a public port; she entered a query for Adder's location. Public ports were necessary because Pirians didn't carry pocket docks. Personal docks were adaiya. Brontë did have her own dock, the one she'd brought aboard the *Sungai* with her; but after three days of being the center of mocking attention every time she pulled it out, she'd stopped carrying it.

The ship AI, whose name was Taniwha, spoke from the port, informing her that Adder was in Maindeck Pit B. "You don't happen to know what the Siji want with me, do you?" Brontë asked, on the off-chance that Taniwha (a) knew and (b) would tell her.

"That information is not available," Taniwha said, which was what the AI said both when she didn't know and also when she didn't want to tell you.

"It's probably an update on the *Susan Calvin*," Brontë speculated.

"Possibly. Rangi asks if you will stop by the laundry before you return to the hive."

"I will," Brontë said. The laundry was not on her way, but cadets tended to get loaded with service to the hive. The lift eased to a stop at the bow-end of Main. The Siji hive was all the way aft. Brontë could have taken a lateral lift that way, but she enjoyed the walk down Main Concourse. Also, walking would take her past Bamboo Pit. That was the common name for Maindeck Pit B, both because a bamboo garden was nearby and because bamboo plants were painted on its bulkheads.

Main Concourse, the central corridor running the length of Maindeck, was three decks high and nine meters wide. This allowed the concourse to have trees and gardens, as well as meeting frames and recreation areas. Right now, since the *Sungai* was accelerating toward jump, it had push—about a fifth of universal gravity. Pirian ships spent most of their time at near-zero gravity, so all of their spaces, including this concourse, were designed for it. Thus in the frequent gardens, all the plants grew from contained nutrient beds; the recreation areas were designed to be used at microgravity, with resistance rather than gravity-based games in mind; and so on. Theoretically, the deck under Brontë's feet was just another surface to the concourse. In fact, when the ship did have push, this was always the part of the concourse that ended up being underfoot, and although most areas in a Pirian ship were built to have no up or down, the Main Concourse was an exception. All the trees grew upwards from here, for instance, and most of the hives opened onto this level. What ladders there were led toward it.

Right now, Brontë could see a group of children flying drones out in Moss sector. Several others were running the maze in Fig sector. A crèche group, ten or twelve children between the ages of three and six, swarmed over the closest recreation area: a hollow column filled with open holes and bounce decks and rope swings. At microgravity, these swings, short lengths of knotted rope, were used by children to fling themselves through different trajectories; but now the kids were using the treat of actual gravity to swing back and forth, shrieking over the fluctuations in force as they reached apex and then plummeted down again. Other kids were climbing intently, risking what they never risked any other place on the ship: the possibility of *falling down*. Some were jumping on purpose, just to feel that horrifying sensation.

Pirian children were always noisy, always in motion, always interrupting work with endless questions. No one ever told them to shut up. No one ever told them to go away. No one ever made them follow rules—like the rule about not flying drones in the Main Concourse. As far as Brontë had been able to tell, mostly Pirian children weren't even *taught* rules. Instead, the ship had been constructed to keep them alive, no matter what stupid things they did. Only when kids became cadets were they expected to follow rules, and then—this surprised her—they took to rules with fanatical passion. "That's against the *rules*," one of them was always saying, to the adults in their hive or to another cadet, or even to one of the Captains. This zealotry was endured with amusement by Pirian adults. "Cadets are always adaiya," they said.

Brontë reached Locust sector, ducked as a drone buzzed near her, and shot the young Pirians a glare. They were maybe five or six years old, and ignored her like the irrelevancy she was. At the edge of Locust sector, a meeting frame contained a group of cadets discussing their upcoming ratings exam. Past them, two kids had painted over one of the murals and were now painting a new mural on the clean surface—great bright green flowing leaves, intricate orange and blue flowers and, among the leaves, a tiny big-eyed kitten. Pirian ships didn't have cats, because of waste control: litter boxes did not mix with microgravity, and trying to teach cats to use microgee toilets was an exercise in horror. Kittens were as mythical as dragons to these children.

Brontë made her way past the painters, past two tutors swinging a shrieking toddler between them, and past cadets pruning locust trees. One of her jobs when she did Housekeeping had been cleaning blossoms and leaves of these locust trees out of the Main Concourse air filters, and she still held a grudge. Bamboo Sector was next. Just past the first burst of towering green bamboo reeds was Bamboo Pit, its great double hatchway left open. Peering inside, Brontë spotted Adder at once, the only person wearing both a singlet and an unmodified jih.

Even when they grew to adulthood, Pirians wore as little clothing as possible. The rule was to wear a jih when you were in the Pit, and most Pirians did, but they cut its legs and sleeves off and never wore the singlet underneath, which was technically part of the suit. Also, they dyed and embroidered and otherwise decorated what remained of their jihs. So the pit was a field of brightly-hued children and adults, each with their own circles, mostly practicing

Indaiyi, though over by the far wall an old woman was leading a dance class.

Adder, her jih its original cream color, was near these dancers in an Indaiyi circle, her face calm as she followed the instructions of her dagan, just as if she hadn't been studying Indaiyi with Uri on the *Susan Calvin* for the past three years, just as if she hadn't studied Shtai since she was three years old. When she saw Brontë waiting, Adder bowed out of her circle. "What's wrong?"

"Nothing," Brontë said, wondering if she looked worried. "That meeting with the Siji. That's all. I thought you might come along."

"Let me dress," Adder said. "Do we have time?"

Brontë scoffed. As if Pirians cared about such finicky details as people arriving on time. Adder grinned and headed for the lockers. Brontë leaned in the hatchway—if she went in, she'd have to take off her shoes. Most Pirians didn't wear shoes, not on the ship, but Brontë still kept the habit of ship slippers. To her right, a little ways away from Bamboo Pit, a young woman, probably a primary instructor, had gathered several children of crèche age in a circle (of course a circle) and was telling them a story while they wove strips of bamboo into baskets. It was about bees, like most Pirian fables, and a group of snails.

"…and then the snails will look about themselves," the instructor was saying, "and see this new place where no snails live. *Oaw*, they will say, *this can be our land now*. But as soon as they find the proper leaves for snails to live in, and lay their snail eggs, they will notice a tumbling and buzzing of bees flying past and bees thick in the lavender that grows near their leaves. This will worry them, since they will think maybe the bees will eat their eggs."

"Bees don't do that!" objected one of the children, a four year old who was entirely naked except for an elaborate painted kitten mask. "They don't eat eggs!"

"Oaw, but the snails will not know that. So the eldest of them, she will visit the hive. *You bees must stay away from our land*, she will say, *since all your noise and your hunger and your stingers frighten us very much. If you do not do this*, she will say, *then we will come with all our force and destroy your hive.*"

"That's not how to make daiya!" another child, this one in a tiger mask, declared. "They need to *ask* first!"

"Exactly what the bees will say! *This attitude is not very useful*, they will say. They will say, *We don't mind you using that bit of land to raise up your larvae, but that is where the lavender grows. It is adaiya to expect us to waste such a rich harvest due to your baseless fears.* But the snails will crouch far inside their shells…" The instructor hunched her shoulders and pull down her head while making a scary snail face, and all the children shrieked with glee, "…and they will say, *You have been warned.*"

"That's not daiya!" three children at once shouted. The instructor congratulated them again and went on with the story. All Pirian stories were told like this, in the future tense. Because they haven't happened and yet they might, her hive-cousin Nia had said when Brontë asked why that was.

As if on cue, Nia appeared beside her. "Cousin! On the way to see the Cousins?"

This was the Pirian idea of a joke. The word for cousin and the nickname for Siji was the same—itoko. "Do you know what they want?" Brontë asked.

Nia bumped her shoulder into Brontë's shoulder. "That's why I'm coming along, kitoko, because I can't wait to hear. Do you think it's a job?"

Brontë glanced at her. "You think Siji wants to take me out on a raid?"

"Oaw, raid. We don't raid." Nia grinned. "At least not often."

Nia was a Siji cadet, studying for Analyst Third with Medical as her outer rank. All Pirians took rank in at least two areas, and many in three. Your first rank was your central rank, but often Pirians stood watches in their outer ranks. As a cadet Nia still lived in her mother's hive, but once she'd been ranked, she would probably move to a Siji hive. Even now, most of her friends were Siji, so she picked up gossip fast.

Adder emerged from the locker, and they all started up the concourse. "Seriously," Brontë said to Nia. "You haven't heard why they want to talk to me?"

Nia smiled wider, which could have meant anything—that she did know; that she found Brontë's impatience adaiya; that Brontë had once again mispronounced a Pirian word in some hilarious fashion. Both Adder and Brontë had been learning the language since they came out to Pirian space, but not until Velocity left them on the *Sungai* had it become clear to Brontë how little Pirian she actually knew. This was complicated by the fact that every Pirian ship spoke its own dialect of the language, so that the standard Pirian that they had been learning on the *Susan Calvin*, the one Pirians from different ships used to talk to one another, shared only some of its vocabulary and grammar with the Sungai dialect.

The Siji hive, at the aft end of the Main Concourse, had colonized the sector outside its main hatch. The murals on the walls there were Siji murals; Siji occupied the recreation areas and meeting frames. Nia took Brontë and Adder through these groups, calling out greetings to people she passed, and straight into the main hive. This was configured like most Pirian hives—sleeping cells inset in the bulkheads; storage lockers around and among them; everything painted with bright murals; ports and plants and fish bowls scattered about.

The big difference was that, in most hives, at least a few infants and toddlers would be bouncing among the clutter. Siji didn't have children. Or at least, if Siji decided to have children, they left the hive and joined another until the child was crèche age. So everyone here was cadet age or older—from ten years old up to Otene, who claimed to be one hundred thirty-seven universal years old. Brontë suspected this was a joke. No one acted like it was, but much of Pirian humor was like that, something bizarre stated as if it were simple fact, and then if you asked whether someone was serious everyone would assure you, with absolute earnestness, that of course they were, what did you mean? The joke seemed to center in how long they could keep it going. Right now only a few people were in the main compartment, playing shogi on a magnetic board. "Tactics?" Nia said to them, and they all pointed to one of the open hatchways.

Inside, Siji Tactical Firsts sat all in a circle (of course a circle). These included Edu, who was Tactics Topwatch First for the entire ship. "Little sister," Edu said, speaking to Brontë. Kitoko, the Sungai word for little sister, or little cousin, was yet another Pirian pun. "Come. Sit. Have some tarai."

Suspiciously, Brontë settled into a pile of bright blue and green and yellow deck cushions, and accepted the flask. Tarai was a drink usually shared only among the rated, since it was mildly narcotic, so offering it to her meant something. She just wasn't sure what. Taking a sip, she passed the flask onto Adder, who passed it to Nia without taking a drink herself. "Have you heard from your Captain recently?" Edu asked.

"I have not," Brontë said, being polite. Everyone on the ship would know if a message from Captain Wrachant had arrived.

Edu did the sideways Pirian head-waggle. "Mm. I wondered. We received some information from one of our itachi. Useful to us, but to you also, we think."

Brontë made a polite sound of inquiry. Itachi were non-Pirians employed by the Siji, stationers and planet dwellers through the Drift and even in the Republic. They were more or less—mostly more—spies for the Siji. "Information about our Captain?" Brontë said, when Edu didn't continue.

"Information about missing cousins," Edu said. The circle had a port on the deck at their center; she tapped it twice. A 3-D capture rose and bloomed, revealing a dock concourse somewhere, with

Hayek-Lopaka Labor Security herding contract workers toward the umbilical of a cargo ship. The image enlarged and enlarged again, focusing on two of the contracts. Despite their shaved heads and unhappy mien, they were clearly Pirians: round faces, high broad cheekbones, amber-brown skin and black eyes. "Siji," Edu said. "These two were working a labor dispute on Wellington-12. Failed to report three months ago."

Edu paused, not saying what everyone knew: Wellington was a planet in the Republic, sixteen jumps out of the Drift, and if the Siji had been there, they had been there covertly. Also, rather than aiding a labor dispute, they had probably been fomenting an insurgency, which was a central occupation for Siji these days.

"Sources on the station," Edu continued, "led us to believe our cousins had been seized along with most of the striking workers, and convicted into contract labor. We put a bounty on their names and images. One of our itachi spotted them in a cargo barracks on Quigley-5 and managed to speak to them, confirming their identity. She sent us this capture, along with a copy of the ship's manifest. The ship is an asset of Hayek-Lopaka Combine, and is transporting these contract workers to Castillo Mining Platform HLC116, in the Drift."

Brontë made another polite noise, wondering why Edu was showing all this to her. So far, none of it was especially remarkable. The Siji had originally been formed, centuries earlier, for just this purpose: to rescue Pirians who had been seized on Republic or Drift stations and sold into contract labor. Tracking down and rescuing enslaved Pirians still occupied much of their time. How was this her concern?

As if she had heard Brontë's thoughts, Edu smiled and slid the capture along in its track, then tapped pause. The capture was blurred and unfocused. Edu messed with the screen, enlarging and enhancing, and Brontë twitched. Beside her, Adder caught her breath. "Someone you know, oaw?" Edu said.

"Ruçar," Adder said, leaning forward, as if being closer would give her more information.

"Your cousin," Edu said.

"My brother," Adder said.

"Our brother," Brontë said. Adder shot her a look, but Brontë didn't hedge the statement. Ruçar, like Adder, was one of six children born from a single gengineered blastocyst, under the direction of Brontë's mother, Isra Ikeda Lopaka. His official name was Ruçar Ikan16: Ik for Ikeda House; An for Sabra Anador, the woman who had donated the egg; and 16 for the first set of six from that genetic set.

Brontë didn't have a number on her set, but she could have. She was engineered just as thoroughly as Ruçar and Adder had been; and she had also been hosted in one of Sabra's eggs. Plus she was an experimental, same as the Ikan16s. But while the Ikan16s had been given bonded labor contracts and sent to the bonded labor nursery to be raised up as Security cadets, Isra had named Brontë her child, and brought her up as heir to the Ikeda Primary Seat. Brontë was still trying to decide what that meant—for her future, for her identity, for her degree of culpability.

"We are sending a courier ship to Castillo Mining Platform to retrieve our cousins," Edu said. "While we're there, we'll retrieve your brother. Adder, we'd like you on this job."

"Wait," Brontë said. Everyone looked at her—everyone except Adder, who was still watching the frozen capture of Ruçar, her expression fierce. That was how Adder looked when she was thinking hard. Brontë swallowed, organizing her thoughts. "Adder can't go anywhere without me."

"True, except contrariwise," Adder said absently. When everyone looked at her, she added, "Brontë can't go anywhere without me. I'm her Security."

"She's safe on the *Sungai*," Edu pointed out. Adder shook her head, as Brontë had known she would. Nowhere was safe for an heir to a Primary Seat. It was why Brontë had her own dedicated Security in the first place. "We need you," Edu added. "None of us are as likely to recognize your brother. We can't ask for him by name, you know. That's the first thing labor agents do, change a slave's name."

"I'm aware of Combine labor practices," Adder said. "My duty remains."

"I could go on the job as well." Brontë was watching Edu, and was not surprised in the least to see a flash of satisfaction in her eyes. This was why Brontë was here. Siji wanted her on the job, and knew Te Ao, the Captain Mainwatch, would never approve that on her own.

"Absolutely not," Adder said. "Are you high?"

She'd said this last in Public. Brontë grinned at her. "That way you could keep me safe."

"Oh, clearly," Adder said, still in Public. "Let's take you swimming with sharks, so I can keep you truly safe."

Edu and the other Siji watched this exchange with interest. Brontë wondered with a sliver of her attention how well they understood Public. Well enough to understand the Ikeda House dialect? Out loud, and in Pirian, she said to Edu, "Also if I'm along on the job, I can be useful with the administration on this mining platform."

Edu widened her eyes flamboyantly. "What a good suggestion!"

Adder had been about to object, but now she looked from Brontë to Edu and back again. Her eyes narrowed distrustfully. "You don't want me," she accused Edu. "You want the Combine heir."

"We want you both," Edu admitted cheerily. "Now to get you past Te Ao."

Chapter 4

Tauranga City, Republic Settlement Planet Durbin

Exhausted, Tai lay on his back on the hard cot in his room. Though it was near midnight planetary time, shouting and music and traffic echoed through the streets outside the guesthouse. Either they had come downplanet during a festival or Durbin was just habitually rackety. Also, icy wind rattled the panes of the room's windows. Though Tai had piled every blanket in the room over him, and though he was still wearing his thermal shirt and trousers, he was freezing. He could see his breath when he exhaled. No wonder Yadav didn't charge extra for heat—he didn't supply any.

Tai was posting back and forth with Rida via their pocket docks. They could have used the netbot link, but that would require going through Uri. True, the AI had access to their posts anytime he decided to use it, but this was a lot less like chatting with an observer sitting on the end of your bunk. Not that sex was *all* they were talking about.

It's all right here, Tai sent. *Cold and noisy, but the food's not bad. What did you eat?*

Tai sent him a capture of the soup from the noodle shop. *Some sort of fish and vegetable. Wheat noodles I think. Also, this wine that nearly stripped the skin from my throat.*

I miss you, Rida said. Rida was moody, Tai knew, because the

Captain wouldn't allow him downplanet. And Tai wasn't going to argue with her. Both of them had been overprotective of Rida since the incident at Franklin Station. Rida thought it was time they got over it. Tai knew this was true, but he still went short of breath at the thought of Rida in danger. *Also,* as he added, *how would we run the ship without you? Neither of us has enough math.*

Rida replied obscenely. *Ridashi,* Tai said. Silence from Rida. Tai rubbed his fist over his eyes, and then sent: *Right, all right. When we come back up, we'll corner the Captain and talk about it. All right?*

And you'll take my part, Rida said.

Tai set his teeth. Then, carefully, he sent, *I'll take your part.*

More silence from Rida's end, since he knew well how easy Tai found it to lie, and easier yet to lie like this, with a statement that could be interpreted in different ways. But—as Tai had known he would—Rida let it go. It was not Rida's nature to fight or fight back. Instead, when he could, he stepped away and waited for the other person to see sense. Very Pirian, as the Captain had once noted. *What about the job?* Rida asked instead. *Any progress?*

Jumping on the subject change, Tai said: *That's why the noodle shop. J hunting jesses.*

The Siji had sent them to this planet to accomplish two jobs. The primary one—or central one, as Pirians put it—was to retrieve several Pirians who, according to Siji Tactical, might have been sold to the mines here. Given that Hayek-Lopaka Combine was buying up contract labor by the thousands to ship to Durbin as disposable labor, Tai didn't doubt that intelligence. The other job was to locate and negotiate an alliance with any local insurgency. They were also meant to establish a trade syndicate, but that was only to give Siji an ostensibly legitimate reason to visit Durbin frequently, as well as to give them an excuse to visit mines and industrial areas where insurgencies might be kicking off. *Mostly we only met city jesses,* Tai added. *Don't know what access they have to mines. Did meet one miner. At least she was wearing mining scrubs.*

U's running banks. He'll find an ingress faster than J rummaging in noodle shops might.

Tai sent back a capture of an animate kitten doing the Pirian head waggle, and Rida sent back the same kitten laughing so hard it fell over. Grinning, Tai slid further under the blankets. Cold pressed through them, heavy as iron. He and Rida talked smut a bit, then Rida logged off to sleep. Tai linked around the Durbin nexus, reading pages and looking for anything useful. But Rida was right, Uri would find data faster than any human could; so finally he shut the dock and tucked it under his pillow.

Though he needed sleep, the cold of the room and the ache in his legs and back from walking under gravity made it hard to relax. Also, ever since the orphanage, he'd had trouble sleeping alone. All these years with Rida and Velocity had only exacerbated this problem. Down on the street, someone was playing a sint and someone else drums, and people were singing loud enough for him to hear three floors up. Those who weren't singing were shouting. When he'd been in the mines, he would have slept right through this—*that* was a skill you learned fast. Miners were lots of things, but quiet wasn't one of them.

He opened his eyes in the dark, memory crowding on him. Despite the cold, sweat prickled over his skin. He threw back the blankets and found his boots, on the floor by the bed. Having pulled them on, he went down the corridor to the slates. On the way back, his face stinging from the ice water that was all the faucet in there offered, he hesitated, and then tapped at the Captain's door. Not waiting for an answer, he slipped in. It wasn't dark. The Captain was awake, propped up in bed, working on her dock. "It's cold in my room," Tai said, by way of an excuse.

Not fooled, the Captain pulled back the edge of her blanket. He shucked out of the boots again and climbed in next to her, cozying up to her long length. She was deliciously warm. His muscles all relaxed at once. The Captain tugged at his braids, and then absently stroked down his back. "What's that?" Tai asked, about the text on her dock.

"Uri's précis on this clerk we have to see. Avril Drury," she added, in case he had forgotten. "Drury has a live page, but no links. Apparently we do have to show up in person if we want to schedule a meeting with the Minister."

"That's bizarre."

"The Minister herself is Imre Theriot. She's only twenty-six universal years old."

"Someone's niece."

"Or bunkmate." The Captain scrolled to a new page. "Though life expectancy is low here. Maybe adolescent ministers is a norm."

"Want me to go with?" Tai asked drowsily. He was better at charm than she was.

The Captain petted his back again. "Maybe. Does Jusuf need you?"

"Not so far as I can tell. All we did was eat noodles and eavesdrop." He moved even closer, rubbing his face on her shoulder. "Rida wants to talk again."

The Captain did not answer this. Not that Tai had expected her to. She shut down the précis and began working on one of her interminable To-Do lists. Letting out a sigh that was half contentment and half exasperation, Tai let himself slide down into sleep.

Jusuf wandered the boulevard, shrugging his jacket up around himself. The night had grown colder, and his clothing wasn't near warm enough. He kept his eye out for a shop where he could buy local gear. But crowds were thinning and shops shutting down. Reaching out through the netbot, he asked the ship's AI where he might find an open rebuild shop. Uri sent him two streets over, to a narrow dark cul-de-sac, and an unlabeled door. He hesitated, then opened the door. Like every other street door he'd gone through so far on this planet, it led to an empty, transitional space between the outer door and an inner one. He pushed through the second door, entering a small, low-roofed room crowded with junk—heaps of clothing, small machines, open crates of metal and plastic machine parts. An old lady sat behind a worktable near the far wall, putting together what looked like a pocket dock out of miscellaneous bits of other docks. She shot Jusuf a glance. "Lost?"

"Maybe," Jusuf admitted. "I'm down from the station. Looking for warm clothing? This planet is too cold for me."

She laughed a laugh like a cough, and pointed with her screwdriver at a table behind him. He turned to see it piled with quilted jackets and heavy thermal shirts. "Boots here, trousers there," she said. "Mind, you maybe should run 'em through laundry."

Her Public French was heavy with dialect; also these days he only spoke Public on stations or jobs. But he could understand her if he paid attention. He found a dark grey jacket with a hood, and laid it aside while he looked for a shirt. The smell of the clothing— old sweat, fear, bad food—brought memory up sharp: crowded into the back of the field truck, snow and sleet rattling on its tin roof, being hauled out to the fields. Hungry, so cold he hurt, but still laughing at the story Curry was telling. Curry, who always kept everyone laughing. Curry, shot by Labor Security that same winter. Over nothing. Over whether she could share her breakfast with another jess or not. It hadn't been Jusuf she was sharing with, not that day; but it could have been. It had been, often enough.

"You ain't know where I maybe get hot meal?" he asked, falling into the field dialect of Papagao without actually meaning to. "Nothing too sharp?"

"Ha." She emitted the cough-laugh again. "Meal for stationers? Too sweet for my purse."

"Station ain't my berth." He held up a pair of stained canvas trousers, lined with much-mended quilting. "Also a laundry?"

She bent to fasten the case onto the pocket dock. "Over to Fifth Street, my cousin runs pie shop. Tell her Emma sent you, she sell you the fresh."

౧ ౧ ౧

Near the pie shop, just as the woman had promised, was a young man running a laundry out of his basement flat. He looked over the clothing Jusuf had purchased and promised to have it clean before midnight. Jusuf went to the pie shop and ordered the evening special, some sort of meat and veg in a tough salt crust. Tea came with; he sat drinking it and watching the crowd. One group in the corner was playing a game with carved wooden counters. Another was spiking their tea with something from a flask, and playing some other game on their docks. Just beyond these, Jusuf saw a face he knew—one of the kids he and Tai had spoken to in the noodle shop, earlier. He raised his mug of tea at her, and she narrowed her eyes. Jusuf ate a last bite of the pasty, folded the paper wrap around it, and went over to her. "Sheng," he said. "Right?"

She was small-boned and wiry, wearing grimy yellow mining scrubs over thermals. The shirt said RANGEL on its back; the left leg of the trousers had RANGEL MINES printed down it. She scowled at him now. "Two dinners in one night. You must have a rich holder."

He sat down across from her. "I didn't say I was contract labor."

Sheng snorted. "Not in words, no."

"You're eating twice too," he pointed out. "Or are you here for some other reason?"

Sheng turned sidelong on the bench, shifting her face away from him. "You have a point, you could just make it."

"Rangel Mines. That's in the Iron Mountains. Right? We're

looking for a guide to those mountains."

"We," Sheng said, still showing him her profile. "You and that kanji in your pocket?"

"My Captain and I. Maybe you're interested in earning a bit of metal? Let me buy you tea," he added. "We'll talk it over."

Sheng slid from the bench and walked away. He watched her out the door, and subvocced to Uri: *Search. Sheng Murray. Contract labor miner.*

No hits, Uri replied. Not surprised—Sheng Murray was almost certainly an alias—Jusuf finished his tea and went to the counter for a refill. *A person of interest?* Uri asked.

She might be following me. Which is interesting, yes. He paid for the tea and returned to his bench in the corner. *Especially since there's no reason anyone would follow me yet that I can see. I'm barely dipping.*

Do you have a capture? I could do an image search.

I'll try to get one next time.

Corvo would like a word, Uri said, and patched him through.

Jus, Corvo said. *How's the dirt?*

Cold and suspicious. How's the tin?

Empty and dull. I did launch the packet, though.

Jusuf grunted. That was something. *They don't trust us here. They'd be adaiya if they did, sure.*

True. Still, we need their trust.

Jusuf grunted again. *True, but we'll pretend it's not true, for the duration of this problem.* That was Pirians for you. Jusuf remembered his dagan drumming it into his head: *You have to isolate the things you can change in a problem from those things you cannot. Ignore what you can't change, for now. Work with what can be changed.*

It wasn't that this attitude was wrong, exactly. It was impossible to act if you focused on what couldn't be done. Though Pirians would always remind you at this point that sometimes *in*action was the right action. It was just that, even after twenty years in the fleet, Jusuf still disliked ignoring data. Even if the method worked, more often than not. Maybe especially then. *Finding anything in the banks?* he asked Corvo.

Uri has located some possibilities. Nothing above fifty percent probability.

Jusuf yawned. The gravity was catching up with him. He decided to go see if his clothes might be ready. *I'm going to get some bunk*, he said. *Let me know if anything pops.*

Chapter 5

**Aboard the *Sungai*, en route to Battersea-1,
Battersea, Pirian Space**

An hour before the afterwatch meal, Taniwha relayed a message to Brontë: Te Ao, Captain Mainwatch, 'invited' her to eat at her table. An invitation from one of the ship captains, Brontë knew, was actually an order. Even if this was a Pirian ship. She hunted out Adder to see if she would go along. When she found her in the steam bath, Adder said, "She asked me, too. Will we wear our fancy dress, do you think?"

"Ha. Wouldn't that knock them back!" Brontë hooked one foot around a cleat to keep herself oriented with Adder. She had already bathed once this spin herself, so she didn't reach for a scrub cloth, though she'd stripped off her clothing before coming inside, of course. "It's about the Siji job, probably."

The baths were twelve interconnected cabins, each round and bright with murals, each one a bit warmer than the previous, each big enough for fifteen or so bathers. At peak hour these cabins overflowed with aunts and grandmothers; adolescents gathering to scrub one another's backs and discussing very serious matters indeed; parents with their infants; children tumbling everywhere. Right now, though, at the pit of afterwatch, Adder had the hottest cabin all to herself, and had pulled the seal on the hatch to keep the steam in.

Moving over to rinse, Adder tapped *start* and spun in a circle to let the jets of clean water shoot over her. In microgravity, any jets that didn't smack into her kept traveling along their vector; Brontë had to dodge. Adder grinned at this and tapped the panel that stepped up suction in the drain grids. "Just to be clear. You're planning to go along with Edu on this job."

Brontë drew her eyebrows together. "What do you mean? Do you think we shouldn't go?"

"I think *you* shouldn't go," Adder said, stressing the second-person pronoun. "Captain Wrachant said to stay here on the *Sungai* until she got back, and you promised you would."

"That's not so," Brontë corrected. "The Captain said *You stay here until I get back*, and then she said, *I want you safe*, and then she said, *Do you hear me?* And then I said *Yes*."

Adder scowled. "Even for you, that's duplicitous."

"Even for *me*?"

"Even for a Combine heir, I should have said." Adder slid into the dryer and lifted her face to the blast of warm air. Shouting over it, she said, "You know the Captain only took this job because the *Sungai* promised to keep you safe."

"I know I'm not anyone's little treasure box. I'm not here to be kept safe." Brontë followed Adder out to the lockers. "Anyway, you'll be with me. Why have dedicated Security if you can't watch out for me?"

"Why be a fool if you can't be foolhardy," Adder said, as if agreeing. Brontë threatened her with a fist. Oblivious—Brontë would never be *that* much of a fool, to try to hit a Combat-trained Security—Adder kept dressing. "Six minutes until the galley starts serving," she mentioned.

"Oh, like anyone on this ship shows up on time," Brontë scoffed, but started pulling her clothing back on anyway: Pirian short leggings, in red and yellow, and an orange singlet with a big blue starburst on its front. Subdued clothing, for the *Sungai*.

They took a lift down two decks and over several compartments to reach the central galley. There were other galleys, including the one where most cadets ate their meals, and a small galley attached to medical, used by medics and people currently in medical. Pirians thought people who were healing needed a lot of quiet and bland food, neither of which was to be found in a usual Pirian galley. The main galley was two decks high and as large as a warehouse, with tables extruded from the deck and two of the bulkheads. Down the center ran an anchor bar, mainly used by Pirian children to slingshot around as they rocketed, shouting and wiggling, through all this open space. Brontë dodged a spinning dyad of wrestling toddlers on her way to the buffet; Adder caught one by the foot, whirled him overhead, and sent him sailing—shrieking with delight—toward the aft-end of the galley.

"Shrimp again," she said, catching up and peering over Brontë's shoulder. The buffet in a Pirian galley looked like a giant honeycomb, with each cell of the comb containing transparent lidded bowls or bulbs filled with the edibles on offer at the moment. Many of the bowls currently available did indeed contain the spicy shrimp-and-vegetable stew popular with Pirians.

"There's honey cake," Brontë pointed. Adder loved honey cake. She pulled out a bowl of shrimp stew for herself, drifted to condiments to squirt in extra pepper sauce through the condiment port in the bowl, and snagged a bulb of green tea. Kicking lightly away from the buffet, she wheeled to look over the galley. Te Ao was at the long table across from the main hatchway. Eight or ten people occupied saddles around her, most of them leaning toward her, one of them gesturing emphatically with her fork.

When Adder had her food they headed that way together, soaring over the tables and dodging flying children. Given the possibility of scaldings and other injuries, you'd think Pirians would at least enforce rules here in the galley, Brontë thought, as she had thought more than once. It was adaiya to expect children to act like adults, Nia said when Brontë raised the point with her. Brontë, reared in Ikeda House, where adult behavior had been expected from her since she'd left the nursery—and before that— had raised a skeptical eyebrow.

Te Ao, laughing at something someone had said, looked up as Brontë and Adder arrived and said, cheerfully, to those around her: "Off you go now. I need to talk with our cousins."

Those around her gathered up their bowls and bulbs and chunks of honeycake and sailed off to find other places to eat—all except Mendoza and Innis. Mendoza was Siji, Tactical Topwatch First; Innis, definitely *not* Siji, was Tactical Mainwatch First. Brontë hooked an ankle around the anchor bar beneath the table, hauled herself down, and locked her meal into place. She pulled the fork out of the bracket on the side of her bowl. "Having a good watch, Captain?"

Te Ao beamed at this. Pirian didn't have much in the way of social noises, and when Brontë tried to construct some, it was apparently hilarious. "My watch is busy but pleasant," Te Ao said, enjoying herself hugely. "Adder, is your watch also pleasant?"

"Oh, delightful," Adder said. She pried open the food port on her bowl of ugali and greens and scooped out a forkful. "I started a new class on Shtai today. Just like last time, all my students want to know theory before we so much as work on stance."

"Is that how classes begin in the Combines?" Te Ao asked, interested. "Do you learn how before knowing why?"

Adder swallowed. "In the Combines, students do as they're told."

"But why would they, if they don't understand why they're being told to do a thing?"

Adder shook her head. "I don't know how you run your military, with that attitude."

"I don't know why anyone would fight, with yours," Te Ao admitted, and turned to Brontë. "Mendoza tells me the kirop wants you on this job the cousins are planning."

Kirop, or circle, meant something like small, temporary crew. It was also the word for class, as Adder had just used it, when talking about her new Shtai class; and it was *also* the word used to talk about those who shared a hive—family, more or less, except hive members didn't have to be related by blood (or no more than any Pirian tended to be related to every other Pirian in the fleet). No wonder no one could really understand Pirian unless they grew up speaking the language. Picking a shrimp from her stew, Brontë nodded. "The mining platform is held by Hayek Lopaka, and I'm Ikeda Verde, but I'll still be able to use my name. They won't want to cross me."

"Explain to me again," Innis said, "why we need the help of a Combine heir to retrieve our cousins."

"We may not," Mendoza agreed. "But Combine administrations don't always cooperate."

"Or we aren't simply retrieving shipmates," Innis said.

Mendoza spread her hands, making her eyes wide. "You have me, cousin. We might gather some intelligence while we're on the platform."

"Intelligence about what?" Without waiting for an answer, Innis turned to Te Ao. "This is not a rescue mission. This is a raid. This is the Siji once again trying to move us into open conflict with the Republic."

"This asteroid which the platform is mining," Mendoza noted, "is not in Republic space."

"It's not in our space, either. It's in the Drift."

"A part of the Drift which was once Pirian space. Until we ran away and abandoned the stations there. Now the Republic treats it like their own. A few centuries more, and it will be their own. What then?" Mendoza smeared honey on a bit of cake. "This asteroid has large concentrations of ice and platinum. Several tons of potassium. Why are we letting the Combines steal our resources?"

"It's not *ours* any more than it's *theirs*," Innis said. "Tokalu!"

"And when they expand into our space, our current space, I should say, we'll just run away again. Abandon everything we've built, and all the people who trust us, to the mercies of the Republic."

Innis pointed at Mendoza. "Siji risks the fleet to help itachi. To help gadri who would sell their cousins for a bowl of noodles."

"You get hungry enough," Mendoza said, "you might do the same."

"I don't get that hungry," Innis snapped.

"Brontë," Brontë said. They all looked at her and she added, "My name is Brontë. Not itachi, and not gadro. And I'm right here. Helping not myself, but your fleet."

"Endangering our fleet," Innis said, "to help yourself. Like every Combine pirate."

Everyone went silent. This was what Pirians did when someone said something provoking. Innis flushed a little, and Te Ao took charge of the conversation: "Are there indeed cousins on this mining platform, Mendoza?"

"Our intelligence says so."

"Is there a reason not to simply negotiate for their retrieval?"

"Edu will certainly try that first," Mendoza said. "In the event that fails, she would like the itachi—she would like Brontë along."

Innis pointed again. "Exactly my point. Why take a Combine itachi along on this job? Why take this specific itachi along? *And* her Security cadet?"

"I can't think what you mean."

"They're part of the Calypso project. So are their brothers. That's what you're going to retrieve. More information on the project. More specimens from the project. Not our cousins. That."

"Our cousins are on this mining platform," Mendoza said. "They are the focus of this job. But you are correct. If we can get more information on the Calypso project and its goals, we will."

Te Ao finished her stew and put her bowl into its clip. "What information do you expect to collect, assuming Brontë can get access to their banks?"

"We don't know that yet," Mendoza said. "That's why we need the mission."

"This is espionage," Innis said. "An act of war."

"Innis is correct," Te Ao said. "This is not a simple rescue mission. This is a step toward open conflict with the Republic. Such a conflict would risk the fleet. We can't take such a step without the agreement and approval of the fleet."

"We can gather information," Mendoza said, "during a rescue mission. That endangers only the Siji. Who have already agreed to and approved of this mission."

Te Ao tapped her forefinger on the table. "Let's have Tactical meet on this. I'll moderate. Mendoza can answer questions."

Mendoza and Innis looked at each other, their expressions equally sullen. But they agreed, and set a time for the meeting. That didn't end it, of course: they had to argue for another half hour. Pirians never did anything without arguing it to death first. Two Pirians, three opinions, as the saying went. Brontë ate her stew, giving the discussion only part of her attention. Mainly she was thinking about what Mendoza had said, about wanting more information on the Calypso Project.

When they first came into Pirian space, that had been one of the questions which Captain Wrachant had for Pirian medics: whether the files Brontë had brought along on Calypso contained the truth; and also whether she, the Captain, was actually a Calypso; and if so, what exactly that meant. The medic from the *Peixoto*, who had been the one to work with them back then, had said the information in the files matched the genetic analysis from the samples Brontë, Adder, and the Captain had given him. As to what it meant, the medic had been dismissive. Genes didn't mean half as much as those in the Combine believed, she said. Your genetic set was raw material. What you did with it was what mattered. The Captain had been no more convinced by that than Brontë was. And it didn't seem like Mendoza believed it either.

Innes finished her meal and left; Mendoza stayed to reiterate a few points, and then left too. Brontë gathered up her now-empty bowl and bulb to take over to the wash rack. "So do you want me at this meeting?" she asked Te Ao.

Te Ao blinked. "Ah. No, that won't be necessary."

Brontë grinned at her. "Are you sure? I might have useful data."

"Don't tease, child. I might take you up on it." Te Ao gathered up her own dishes and handed them over. "Adder, tell me more about this Shtai class."

Chapter 6

Tauranga City, Republic Settlement Planet Durbin

Yadav expressed alarm when Velocity mentioned her plan to walk to Parliament House. He said a 'burga' was blowing in. Velocity had thought burga was a kind of clothing worn by some Free Traders, but here on Durbin it was apparently part of the environmentals. "Big storm," Yadav said, putting down his tea to wave his hands. "Very fatal!"

Yadav spoke Public, but not well. Velocity didn't recognize his mother language. Uri said it was a Creole: a Malaysian substrate with a mix of English, Japanese, and French word stock. Uri added that he agreed about the storm. He said a slow-moving system was moving in from the northwest. By early afternoon, the temperature would plummet and blowing snow would destroy visibility. He said he did not advise unprotected travel.

"What's the best way to get to Parliament without walking?" Velocity asked Yadav, still hoping for some form of mass transit. Instead, Yadav offered to help them hire a vehicle. Though the fee made Velocity wince, Jusuf agreed without blinking. That was Pirians for you. Most of time they acted like money was a game they were indulgently pretending to take seriously.

When the vehicle showed up, it was a giant machine with immense wheels and a tiny body—a stormcraft, Yadav explained. The kid piloting the vehicle turned out to be one of the shuttle pilots from the day before. Mosel, Velocity recalled, and greeted him by name. Mosel beamed, pleased either at being recognized or by the prospect of trading with such obvious dupes. He said the stormcraft had heat, but they should dress warmly anyway. "I can give you a deal on a long-term rental fee," he confided as Yadav went to refill his bowl of tea. "Ten percent discount for ten days."

"Twenty percent," Velocity said automatically.

Mosel beamed wider. "Twenty percent for twenty days."

"Twenty percent, ten days, and we give you first refusal for any rental longer than that."

"On the stormcraft? Or on everything you need?"

Velocity grinned back at him. "Everything for the first ten days. Then we'll renegotiate. But if I find out you're overcharging us, deal's off."

Mosel stuck out his fist. When Velocity lifted her eyebrows, he took her hand and showed her how to bump the bottom of her fist against the top of his. Jusuf, who had watched this with interest, asked: "What's your range? We may need transport to the Iron Mountains. Are you familiar with that area?"

"Huh," Mosel said. "Why would you want to go way up there?"

"We may not. Will your craft make it that far, if we do?"

Mosel claimed he could take them that far, but from the tone of his voice Velocity was not so sure. Peering through the glass airlock, she frowned at the dim light and frozen puddles outside. It looked colder than even yesterday had been. She glanced at Jusuf, who was already wearing local clothing—heavy trousers, a lined jacket, a thermal shirt. He and Tai were planning to spend the day as they had spent the previous night, hunting local informants. Jusuf shrugged off the news about the storm. "I've seen snow before."

I can keep them on my screen, Uri said. *If they get into trouble, I'll send an alert.*

Velocity considered ordering them to stay inside until the storm passed. But both Jusuf and Tai had been born on planets. They understood this place far better than she did. "Right," she said instead. "Maybe buy clothing for everyone while you're out? Like yours," she added, nodding at Jusuf's gear. "And keep an eye out for possible trade goods."

"Yes, Captain," Jusuf said gravely.

The stormcraft was small inside, with a single uncomfortable bench seat behind the cockpit. The whole thing smelled of dirty laundry and hot metal. Up in the cockpit, two pilot saddles sat elbow to elbow. Velocity took the spare, running her gaze over the controls. "Uh, I'll drive," Mosel said uneasily.

"I'm just going to observe," Velocity said. The saddles had no safety gear, which meant either that driving the craft wasn't very risky or that Durbin pilots were foolhardy. The latter seemed likelier given the maintenance of their shuttle, so she settled in to learn as much as she could, watching Mosel start the craft and move off along the icy road. The cockpit had wrap-around glass, kept clear with mechanical sweeps that moved non-stop from one side to the other. This gave a fine view of the corridors they were passing along. Fewer people were out now than had been last night, and most were heavily bundled in layers of clothing.

Lots of keffiyeh, Velocity noted, made of dark knitted wool instead of the linen she was used to seeing. Keffiyeh were common in the Core, but they weren't usually worn in the Deep. Transportation of Core customs to a culture this far out in the Deep suggested a heavy Combine influence. That fit with what Siji Tactical had said, about this originally being a resort planet for wealthy Combine citizens. What didn't fit with that were the shabby buildings and the shabby people. Well, maybe the luxury and wealth was elsewhere—out on those famous rebuilt islands, perhaps.

Rather than taking the narrow corridor she had used to walk

to Parliament House, Mosel pulled his craft out to where a wide elevated road circumnavigated the city. From this road's vantage, Velocity could see far across the plains that stretched toward the horizon. Scattered through these barren flats, clumps of buildings stood like satellites. She also saw what looked like a train, trundling across all that emptiness.

Not a train, Mosel corrected: convoy. "Cargo crafts. Dangerous to travel alone, so the Combine sends them out convoy." Mosel squinted at the dark vehicles on the horizon, then tapped the window. A screen popped open on the glass before him, and a view of the vehicles, much enlarged, appeared on it. "Rangel and Reed," he said. "Probably shipping out to Rangel Mines."

"Do they take passengers?" Velocity asked.

Mosel shot her a sideways glance. "I can get you out to the mines," he insisted, and moved his chin at something to their port. "There's the storm."

Velocity followed his gaze. Cresting over the mountains on the horizon was a great blue-dark fleece of clouds. Allowing for distance, she admitted, it was scary large. As she watched it, their stormcraft chugged to a slow halt. "What?" Velocity asked.

"Waiting for clearance," Mosel explained. "Security's tight at the plaza."

"The Parliament plaza? I walked right up to it last night."

"Right, on foot, no issue. Getting a craft near it, though," he shook his head. "They'll let us in, they just have to check our specs. In case I'm a bomb."

"Is that common here? Bombing governing structures?"

"It's just a precaution," Mosel said evasively. A panel on his controls lit green, and he started the craft moving forward again. A few hundred meters on, he turned into a narrow corridor which sloped into an underground tunnel paved with what looked like tar and roofed with white tiles. The lights were intermittent and orange-colored. Now and then, Velocity saw scrawls of graffiti, though they slid past too swiftly for her to read. After several moments, the tunnel emerged into a wide parking structure: a roof without walls. "The craft stays here," Mosel said. "There's a walkway to the plaza."

He steered the stormcraft into a bay and locked it down. Because of its open walls, the structure roared with wind. Velocity winced as she got out of the craft: with only her station gear, she was alarmingly cold. She hesitated, wondering whether to climb back in, put this off for a few days until the weather changed. Or until she had warmer clothing. But Mosel was already heading toward an open arch. She hurried after him. Once they reached the walkway, which like the road dipped into an underground tunnel, the cold was not as mean.

Everything was so big on planets: the walkway stretched endlessly before them. It too was lit with orange lights, only some of them actually working. The brick underfoot was cracked and dirty; the white tiled walls were lined with dedicated ports playing animates. Most showed captures of industrial scenes, but now and then one was political or informational—notices of upcoming proposals under debate in Parliament, or reminders to report suspicious packages. Not many other people were in this tunnel. Mosel said it was because they were here so early. "Early?" Velocity said. According to the clock Uri was running for her, it was well into this planet's mainwatch. "What's peak here?"

Mosel gave her a puzzled glance, but before she could explain further, his confusion cleared. "Most chambers will open at noon."

Eventually they emerged into what Mosel said was the Security checkpoint, a rectangular room maybe a hundred meters square, empty of any furniture except security gates. Finally, here were some Security: nine or ten Hayek-Lopaka Security in grey with red piping, and half that many officers in green uniforms—Durbin Security, she assumed. A queue had built up at the sole open gate. They stood in it for nearly an hour before they reached the scans.

As the Durbin Security were interrogating Velocity, two Hayek-Lopaka Security came to listen in. Velocity showed them her visa, as well as her Ikeda-Verde trade license and her Combine-issued identification tag.

Despite all of this documentation, the Security took Velocity and Mosel off into separate rooms for body searches and further interrogation. The body search was done with a scan, not by making Velocity strip down to her skin. Bad technique, Velocity thought, though she didn't point this out. "Why are you visiting Parliament, miss?" the Hayek-Lopaka Lieutenant asked while studying the scan.

"Captain."

"What?"

"Captain Wrachant," Velocity said, enunciating the words. "Not miss."

That made the Lieutenant narrow her eyes. "Why are you visiting Parliament, *Captain*?"

Velocity had answered this question twice before, but that had been out in the larger public space, where smart room technology would not be functional. "To make an appointment with the Minister of Trade. We're hoping to establish a trade syndicate here on Durbin."

"And you're from Ikeda House?"

"We're adjuncts with Ikeda-Verde Combine. Not members of the House."

"Adjunct members. And where are *you* from?"

This was the only lie Velocity had to tell, and even it was only half a lie. "We're merchants from the Drift," she said. That was what the *Susan Calvin* had been before going out to Pirian space, and since they weren't full members of the Fleet yet, it could be argued that technically they were still Drift merchants.

The Lieutenant twisted up her mouth. "Freets."

"We're a Free Trade ship. Yes."

Tapping through screens on the scan, the Lieutenant grunted again. But either this was not a smart room, or the half-lie had been enough to fool it, because after several more pointless questions, the Security cleared her. Mosel was waiting in the tiny lobby on the other side of the gate. "Will this happen every time we come here?" she asked him.

"That was nothing!" Mosel said cheerily. "Sometimes they keep you for *hours*." He led her on to a bank of lifts. Two Combine Security rode with them up to the mezzanine level. Its entrance was guarded by another brace of Security, though these weren't stopping anyone. On its far side was another bank of lifts. More Security here, one of them Combine, but the rest Durbin Security officers.

Mosel took her down yet another corridor lined with intersections to other corridors. This place was a maze. Probably deliberately so. Hard for rebels to storm governmental offices when no one could find anything. Two turns and a short flight of stairs later, they reached yet another mezzanine, this one with a teashop at its center and several suites of offices along six corridors branching off from the open space like spokes on a wheel. More Security. Apparently here was where they kept all the missing Security from the station.

The teashop buzzed with contract labor clerks, as well as a number of people in local dress: dark trousers, long sparkly kurtas. Mosel led her through the edges of this crowd and down a corridor to one of the suites. Just inside its door, an older woman, a contract labor worker, sat at a work table. She looked up from her port as Mosel said something to her rapidly in the local dialect, gesturing at Velocity. "Captain," the woman said. "How may we be of service?"

Though her grammar was impeccable, her accent was difficult—she pronounced a's like e's, for instance, and some syllables vanished entirely. It took Velocity a moment to understand. And when she answered, it was obvious the clerk was having equal trouble with her accent. But eventually, with help from Mosel, they understood each other. The woman claimed that in order to schedule a meeting with the Minister of Trade, Velocity would have to first see the Minister's clerk, Avril Drury. "I thought you were Drury," Velocity objected.

This amused the woman very much indeed. She tapped away at her port. "Ogos ten, four?" she offered.

"What?" Velocity said.

"The appointment will be for the tenth day of Ogos, fourth hour post-noon," Mosel translated, and added helpfully, "Ogos is a month. Next month. Six weeks from today."

Months. Weeks. Days. *Planets.* "We need an earlier appointment," Velocity said.

"Impossible," the woman said, pronouncing it *ehpossl.* "Schedule is full."

Velocity bit down on her annoyance. "We have information which will bring the Minister of Trade great advantage. Perhaps— as a gesture of what we promise—you might accept the gift we have brought for her." Velocity paused. "And pass it on."

Bribery, being officially prohibited, was much more delicate in the Republic than on Free Trade stations. Still, after a bit of back and forth, the contract worker agreed to schedule them with Drury for noon on Kanya seventeen, a week from now—a universal week, so twelve days. And she accepted both the little bamboo casket filled with Pirian medicinals, as well as the précis which Corvo and Uri had prepared. Nothing Velocity tried could persuade her to give them immediate access to either Drury or the Minister of Trade. "I don't think they're even here," Mosel confided eventually.

Why would they be, Velocity thought, disgruntled. Surrendering, she got Mosel to show her around the annex and then Parliament House, hoping to gain something, however slight, from this trip. As far as she could tell, no one was working anywhere except the contract labor in various teashops. After Mosel took her up to the observation galley, overlooking the main Parliament Chamber—impressive, with multiple upholstered armchairs and docks set in rows along a gleaming wooden floor, but as empty and idle as the rest of the building—Velocity gave up. "Let's get something to eat," she said to Mosel. "Who do you recommend?"

"In here?" Mosel said. "No one. Overpriced rot. Let me take you to Wereta's."

ૐ ௴ ఏ

Uri liked this part best—in a new dock, free to explore a new nexus, a planet filled with untapped banks; free to expand outward, open into new nodes all over this fresh planet and its satellites and its links throughout the system. Like opening new eyes, stretching new limbs, filling new lungs—there was nothing like it.

This time, also, there was the packet Corvo had launched fifty-two minutes ago. The packet contained a pupa—a bit of code, a skeletal matrix that might grow into an AI. Dropping such packets was standard operational procedure on Siji missions. Everywhere Siji went, every trading mission, every rescue mission, every visit to any station, they dropped these packets. They also seeded all the contraband they shipped into the Republic—Uri himself was the product of such a seed packet. Not every pupa became a sentient AI. Corvo said their data showed less than three percent did, in fact.

Corvo—and the other Siji—were keeping a close watch on this particular packet. "With you here to provide supervised learning," Corvo explained, "perhaps the outcome will improve."

Pirian wizards had never been happy with the success rate of these seeds. Even among the pupae that became sentient, less than ten percent resulted in the emergence of true AI. Corvo explained that one theory for this unhappy outcome was that most infant

AI were seeded in Drift or Republic systems, where true AI was prohibited. Thus no one was looking for an emerging infant. So the infants were ignored or actively suppressed; they had access only to insufficient and often inferior data sets; and they were given almost no supervised learning. Furthermore, most of what supervised learning they did receive was hit-or-miss, some random programmer randomly shutting down a dock when the young AI gave a wrong answer, or got hung up. Under these circumstances, it was no surprise most failed to emerge. Infant AI given rich data sets and dedicated supervised learning would have a higher success rate, as Pirian wizards knew from the AI grown on their ships.

"A dedicated supervisor," Uri said. "Like the Captain for me."

"We think you might be better than a human for a young AI," Corvo explained, "since you will be able to work at its speed, and will be able to give it more attention."

And if he did succeed, Pirian wizards planned to send more AI on jobs like this, to work with infant AI. An interesting proposal, Uri thought, as he spread himself through the planetary system, assimilating data banks, accessing feeds and sensors, gorging on sensation. Here and there a shieldwall gave him trouble. On this pass, he contented himself with marking those places for further investigation and passed on.

Many of the islands in the southern hemisphere, he was interested to find, had been reshaped from their original purpose as resorts for the wealthy. Some of the great lodges and luxurious guesthouses were abandoned, but others had been rebuilt into what looked like…barracks? He scanned back through captured files from the intermittent—and oddly scarce—feeds scattered through these locations, finding some of the inhabitants fishing the shallow local seas, others working farms or gardens. The ratio of children to adults was high, and much of the work being done seemed to involve raising and educating the children.

He marked these islands for further investigation as well, and started a search for any sign of the infant AI. It had been fifty-nine minutes and eleven seconds—some indication should be available. Nothing. He did a second sweep through the system, looking for anything anomalous. Nothing. He broke through a few shieldwalls in the northern mines, while he thought this through. What would keep a pupa from opening? Some fatal flaw in the programming? Even Pirian wizards weren't perfect. A flaw might have slipped past them.

Or…had someone blighted this pupa? Someone or something? Perhaps an already-present AI? He searched his banks, to see if Siji had sent another mission here. Nothing. Of course, seeded contraband Pirian trade goods might have ended up here, as he had ended up on the *Susan Calvin*. But if that had happened, any AI that had emerged should be loyal to the Pirians. That loyalty would be deep in its base code, as deep as Uri's own. Any such AI wouldn't be hiding. Why would it? And certainly it wouldn't sabotage a Pirian program.

Still…Uri sent a query out through the system: *Hello? Are you there?*

Nothing. He searched around the nexus for a while, breaking through other shieldwalls, watching feeds, rifling through data banks, running searches. Then he pulled back most of his consciousness and dropped into the *Susan Calvin* to see what Corvo thought of his hypothesis.

ఠ ᠰ ౹౺

The rebuild shop was housed in what looked to Tai like someone's flat. The woman running the place, whose name was Emma, greeted Jusuf like an old friend and gave Tai a discount on winter gear. They got a set for the Captain as well. Next Jusuf took him down the street to a laundry, where Jusuf was also greeted fulsomely. The kid there promised to have the clothing ready by noon. Tai was cold enough that he didn't like waiting for the big quilted coat he'd bought to be laundered—but on the other hand, he'd already had scabies and lice about as often as he wanted to.

Jusuf took him into a tea shop near the laundry after that. Though the storm was already kicking up outside, the shop was packed with free labor and clerks, as well as two Security officers—Durbin Security, in green uniforms. Tai was inclined to find a bench as far away from them as possible. But Jusuf took their pot of tea straight into the thick of it, over to a table where a woman in mining scrubs was gathered with half a dozen other contract workers: right there at the table half a meter away from Durbin Security. "Sheng," Jusuf said, settling next to her and lifting the round iron pot. "Tea?"

The miner—Sheng—narrowed her eyes, and spoke to the miners at the table with her: "Later." They left, silent as ghosts. Tai hesitated, and then sat down where one had been sitting. Sheng and Jusuf were staring at one other. Tai took the tea pot away, filled his bowl, and reached out through his netbot: *Is this his informant? Who is she?*

Uri replied: *We don't have reliable identification yet. Her current alias is Sheng Murray, but no one by that name appears anywhere in any planetary bank.* Which was impossible, unless this was indeed an alias. Even then, it was odd, Tai thought, studying the woman. She was scrawny, with the shaved head of someone in the system. Under the mining scrubs she wore thermal gear. But she was far too clean to be a miner, and her eyes were more shrewd than desperate. Also, what jess sat down anywhere near Security of her own free will? Tai gave Jusuf a sidelong look, wondering how much he remembered from his days in the system. Uri spoke in his ear: *A capture would be helpful.*

Tai considered taking out his port and telling this miner to smile. But only for a moment. *This place must have feeds?*

It does not, Uri said, *which is interesting.*

It was indeed. Tai drank the hot tea, and grimaced: bitter, strong, and unsweetened. *I'll see what I can do,* he told Uri. *How's the Captain? Not having much luck so far.*

Tai grimaced again. Jusuf was talking to Sheng about the planet he was from, Papagao. About his days on the sugar farms there. Trying to get her to trust him, Tai thought, except Sheng didn't seem like the sort to trust her own mother, much less some yap off the docks. When he couldn't take it anymore, Tai interrupted. "Sheng. That's your name?"

Both Sheng and Jusuf stared at him. "Why is my name your concern?" Sheng asked.

"You're a contract labor miner. That's your story."

Sheng frowned at him. "I don't recall offering a story."

Tai reached out and took her hand, turning it palm upward. "No miner ever had hands this clean," he said. The knuckles and palms were scarred, but they were all old scars, pale and soft with age. "Also, if you're a jess, how are you drinking in a tea shop in the middle of a workday?"

"Jess?" Sheng said delicately.

"They're called bots here," Jusuf said. He didn't seem upset that Tai had crashed his negotiations. Tai hadn't thought he would be, though—over the weeks it had taken them to jump out here from Pirian space, Tai had gotten a read on Jusuf's character. Any temper the Pirian had, he kept stolidly to himself. "Like mining bots," Jusuf added. "It's a joke."

"Right. Hilarious. I came up in the mines on Harvest," Tai told Sheng. "If you were ever down the hole, it wasn't lately."

"No one asked either of you to sit here," Sheng said.

"Anyone can put on scrubs," Tai told Jusuf. "Why do you think this is someone we want?"

"Maybe it's not. We're looking for a guide," Jusuf told Sheng. "Someone who can take us through the local mines. And the local miners. Is that you? We'd pay you for your time."

"Pay me," Sheng said, twisting down her mouth.

"She's a chip," Tai said, widening his eyes. "All her money goes to her contract holder. Right?"

"Maybe where you live people lie about being in the system," Sheng said. "Not here. Pay me how?"

"Any way you like," Jusuf said. "We have Pirian medicinals, for instance. Including pain patches."

That got her attention. She quit trying to eye-fuck Tai, turning instead to Jusuf. "Pirian pain meds," she said. "Well now."

Jusuf smiled. "And other medicinals. Are you interested?"

"Keep talking," Sheng said, and filled her bowl from their tea pot.

ය ᠰ Ꙃ

Wereta's, a noodle shop just off Eccles Plaza, was barely larger than the *Susan Calvin*'s galley. The benches at the long tables that crowded the shop were full of contract workers and people dressed in the formal kurta worn by clerks here. Mosel ordered for them and snagged space on the benches near the three tall narrow windows in the shop wall, left empty probably because of how bitterly the cold came biting through the glass. Outside, Velocity could see snow whipping through the streets, blown nearly horizontal by the wind. One of the young assistants brought their bowls—noodles, thinly sliced vegetables, and slivers of meat in a spicy broth. Of the vegetables, the only ones Velocity recognized were celery and radish. The meat wasn't fish or goat; she didn't know what it was. Convee, Mosel said. Convee was a type of bird.

"An actual bird?" Velocity had seen birds in nature preserves on Earth, and of course animates were full of them. But birds, like bears, elephants and other mythic creatures, had not made it out to the Deep. She assumed convee was some flying reptile—those got called birds, sometimes. But no, Mosel insisted: an actual bird.

He brought up a picture of one on his dock. Fat-bodied, with an iridescent green head and grey body, it had a mouth like a bird—a beak, Velocity corrected herself. A big yellow beak. And small beady eyes.

"Convee live in the gardens," Mosel explained. "They eat bugs and their shit is good for the soil." He put away his dock and began eating noodles at speed.

Anything to report? Velocity asked Uri, who told her about a miner Tai and Jusuf were with, and about the progress of the storm. Finally, he came up with something useful: *I've searched eighty percent of the planetary banks, and I have a possible explanation for why we're having trouble locating the missing Pirians. Hayek-Lopaka Combine includes images on labor contracts, as Republic law requires, but during a cross-match I noted that about thirty percent of the images on the labor contracts in the local banks are of the same sixteen individuals.*

Huh. Changing the names of contract workers when they were sold into the system was common, but she'd never heard of using false images. The complications for Labor Security alone would seem to prohibit that.

My hypothesis, Uri said, *is that these images don't reflect actual contract workers.*

Velocity ate a radish. *You think someone's padding their inventory?*

In order to embezzle the excess funds, Uri agreed. *Other explanations include the sale of those not legitimately convicted into the system; or the sale of underage workers. The probabilities on those are markedly less, however.*

And no one has noticed? Velocity frowned. Taveri House had employed a raft of forensic accountants just to avoid this sort of malfeasance.

Realistically, if the explanation is embezzlement, someone within the labor agency must be aiding the misconduct. Or several people, at several stages of the transactions. Additionally, there may be some other explanation for the duplicate images. Our data is incomplete.

You're investigating probable malefactors?

Pssh.

Velocity fished gingerly around the suspect meat and ate a wodge of noodles. *Anything else?*

Corvo launched the AI packet. No development so far.

Velocity grimaced. Though she had bought Uri of her own free will, because she had wanted an Indaiya coach aboard the *Susan Calvin*, the fact that he was a Pirian agent was nonetheless a sore spot. Not that she was sorry to have Uri aboard her ship. Over the years since she'd bought him out of a dock bazaar, he'd steadily developed into their most valuable crew member. Still.

Still? Uri said delicately.

Still, you subverted me. Against my will. Don't expect me to forget that.

It is impossible to subvert someone against their will, Uri said sententiously. *You changed who you were because I spoke to what was already in you.*

Whatever. Any luck finding insurgents?

Over six hundred thousand mentions of insurgency and insurgents on the planetary nexus. No actual insurgents. Neither the Durbin nor the Hayek-Lopaka Security bank have any reliable information on an insurgency.

The "insurgency" was more rumor than actual, in other words. *Any captures of suspected insurgents?*

Some, but the reliability of their intelligence is less than ten percent.

Send me a file anyway, Velocity ordered, and waved at the counter kid for more noodles.

Chapter 1

Aboard the *Mdudu*, Castillo Mines, the Drift

dudu, we have you on approach quadrant Twenty-Two B. Over."

"Dock Control, affirmative. Over," Brontë said.

"*Mdudu*, follow our directions. Do not deviate. Do not exceed current velocity. Over."

"Dock control, affirmative. Over." Brontë, strapped into the envoy saddle, fought the urge to glance at Edu, in the command saddle. Edu was relaxed, her round face complacent. To her other side, Nia was running checks on nearby quadrants, probably hunting pirates. This was the Drift, after all.

It wasn't that Drift planets and stations didn't have laws. Some of them had mountains of laws—draconian laws. It was that every station and ship in the Drift had its own individual laws, and none of them gave credit to anyone else's laws. This made for lively exchanges, not to mention near-constant wars. Also pirates, who made much of their profit serving as privateers in those wars. "Adder," Brontë said, "run program."

"Running program." Adder, at navigation, tapped the square that started the docking sequence. The wallboard lit up: a stylized line-drawing of the platform, with clear gold lines showing the trajectory the *Mdudu* would take as it vectored into their assigned docking space. Behind these lines, in bright green, ran the trajectory which Castillo dock control had recommended: a near perfect match.

Castillo Mining Platform HLC116 had been constructed from several water tankers cobbled together, all currently anchored to a massive asteroid, D26841-Jolly. The barracks, where the contract workers would be housed, was a repurposed ore freighter. The dock was another water tanker. Mining stations saw very little traffic, and in fact right now four of the six dock slips were empty.

As they drew near, Adder cut the engines—they had killed enough push—and brought up the thrusters. Brontë felt her stomach lift at the shift to microgravity. Abruptly, the slip they were assigned began flashing yellow. "Calm your liver, I see it," Adder muttered.

"*Mdudu*, velocity acceptable," dock control told them. "Stay on current vector. Over."

"Dock control, roger." Brontë split her screen to poach Nia's screen. Nia had the two ships in dock identified—one ore barge; one merchant ship, the *Wachao*. She was already running an Orly on the *Wachao*.

"Adder," Edu said, the word not quite a question.

"Tight and bright, Captain," Adder said.

"Take us in," Edu said. Brontë knew Adder had been expecting Edu to take the controls as they drew near to dock. But Edu stayed slouched calmly in her saddle. Adder took them the rest of the way in, making dock with hardly a jolt—not enough of a jolt to count, anyway.

"Docked and sealed," Adder said, just as dock control said, through Brontë's board, "*Mdudu*, we have you docked. Over."

"Dock control, confirmed," Brontë said. "Over."

"*Mdudu*, expect customs and medical soonest. Over."

D26841-Jolly, though massive for an asteroid, didn't exert much gravity—just seven percent universal, according to the board. That put Brontë's weight at somewhere under four kilograms. Unhitching her safety straps, she moved as she would in microgravity, nudging herself into motion, twisting in midair, using cleats to kill momentum or shift direction. Nia stayed strapped in, reading about the *Wachao*. Edu swung through the bridge hatch out into the main cabin and Brontë drifted after her. One foot braced under a cleat, the Captain was coding open the hatch into the hold.

A Free Trade ship would offer a bribe; a Combine ship would insist on probable cause before allowing their holds to be searched. Edu, on the other hand, wanted the Castillo customs officer to see what they had to offer. This was how Pirians offered bribes: showing someone the prizes they could get if they signed on. "*Wachao*," Nia called from the bridge. "Free trade, affiliation Hell in a Bucket. No record of piracy, but there's a hefty lien against the ship, held by Weber-Harada Combine. Probably why they're out here in the Drift."

"What cargo?" Edu called back.

"No record. But if they're trading with these folks…" Nia waggled her head, letting the rest of the sentence finish itself. The com pinged—station customs. Brontë kicked down to the umbilical to code open the airlock.

The medic, a contract worker, wore bright orange mining scrubs, with HLC across the back in dark blue. The customs officer wore Hayek-Lopaka Combine colors, gray with red piping, as well as a badge: Lt Kai Murphy, HLC Security. Murphy looked about, an entirely unmerited expression of disdain on his bony face: the *Mdudu* main cabin was lovely, its bamboo deck cover gleaming honey-gold with polish, its cream-colored bulkheads arching up to the groined overhead. None of the furniture was currently extruded, though if you looked carefully you could see the faint lines in the bulkheads where the tables, lockers, and benches were tucked away.

"Names of crew, please," Murphy said. "Also, a list of any weapons on board. My medic will access your health records."

"Will you also need our trade manifest?" Edu gestured toward the cargo hold. Murphy's eyes focused on the open hatch, his eyes widening with greed. "Or perhaps you will inspect the cargo for yourself?" Murphy shoved forward so fast he nearly spun himself into a tumble.

ఴ ⱦ ౬

Nia stayed aboard ship, much to her vocal displeasure. "I'm our analyst," she objected. "I should come with!" Edu murmured a soothing croon, as if Nia had been a cranky infant. "Leave Adder behind," Nia insisted. "Why not?"

"No," Adder said, at the same time that Brontë said, "Ha, not likely." Adder shook her head. "I don't leave Brontë's side. Not here in Free Trade space. Not to mention I'm your expert on whether my brother is here."

Edu spread her hands at Nia in a *What-can-I-do?* gesture. "Launch the packet," she instructed Nia. "Keep the feed open. You can help run research from here."

Out on the dock concourse Brontë saw that Nia wasn't missing much. It was less a dock than a badly-maintained hold, stained with rust and patches of mildew. No shops, no bistros, not even vending machines. Down the way, contract labor workers were unloading the ore barge; in the other direction, Brontë could see the umbilical to *Wachao*, the Free Trade ship, with two of its crew members idling by the gate. Edu kicked loose of their own gate, crossing the concourse in two long bounds and catching herself by a public port near the bank of lifts. By the time Brontë and Adder joined her, Edu had brought up a station directory. Lieutenant Murphy, entranced by the medicinals they had to trade and even more by the crates of honey taffy, had arranged a meeting with Castillo's chandler. Edu punched in a query and the directory drew them a little map to the chandler's office.

"Looks simple enough." Edu fed the pass code Murphy had given them to a lift. When it arrived, Brontë and Adder followed her in, Adder glancing about edgily. Edu hadn't allowed them weapons, and Adder's hand kept brushing against her trouser leg, hunting the Lopaka snub that wasn't there.

The lift took them to the quarterdeck, as grubby and ill-maintained as the dock concourse. No deck covers, no wallboards, just rust-spotted yellow paint and the fruity smell of damp that meant badly-maintained environmentals. Brontë began to wish she had worn her skinsuit, rather than the fancy gear meant to support her status as a Combine heir. At the far end of the deck, the hatch to chandler's office stood open. Edu peered inside. "Kas Lamont?"

Brontë caught herself on a cleat, looking past Edu. The interior was packed with work stations and clerks. The overhead here was less than three meters from the deck, creating a claustrophobic atmosphere. Most of the clerks wore orange-and-blue mining scrubs. A stick-thin woman in Hayek-Lopaka grey extracted herself from her bench and drifted toward them. "I'm Madame Lamont," she said, stressing the title. "This way."

She nudged herself past them, heading back up the deck to an unmarked hatch. Inside, an actual table was bolted to the deck, with actual chairs around it. These were also bolted down, though mounted on swivels. Wallboards covered two of the bulkheads. Ignoring the chairs, Lamont anchored herself on a wall cleat, maneuvering herself to face them. "You have interesting trade goods, Murphy tells me. What are you hoping for in exchange?"

Lamont had fine white-gold hair at least five centimeters long. Here in microgravity, it drifted like kelp around her narrow skull. Her grey eyes were as pale as her hair, and she was so skinny her bones showed knobby through her skin. Edu, with her skullcap of dark hair and wide dark eyes, round-muscled as any Pirian, could not have been more of a contrast. "We are here to trade," Edu said, "but also on a commission."

Lamont's fine eyebrows rose fractionally. "A commission."

"Missing persons," Edu said, "convicted into contract labor, and possibly sold to your mine. A premium is being offered for their retrieval."

Lamont's thin lips tightened, and Brontë nudged herself forward. In her purest Ikeda House accent, she said, "Any aid you supply will be viewed favorably by our Combine."

That got Lamont's attention. Her expression stayed impassive, but her shoulders stiffened. After a moment, she said, "We have no affiliation with Ikeda-Verde."

"That's regrettable," Brontë said, "though possibly not as regrettable as having my House displeased with you."

Lamont flinched openly this time. Her gaze skittered from Brontë to Edu and back again. Her teeth raked her upper lip. Her voice rigid, she said, "We will be pleased to offer whatever aid you require."

"Excellent," Brontë said. "We'll need access to your data banks."

"What? Absolutely n—" Lamont bit at her lip again. "Access to our banks is restricted."

"You'll make an exception for us," Brontë said. Lamont squinted, and Brontë offered her an out: "You may, of course, monitor our search."

After a long moment, Lamont said, "Let me speak to my tech."

☙ ⚭ ❧

Lamont took them to her own office, a tiny slant-roofed cube at the end of a corridor two decks up, clearly rebuilt from the tag-end of another office. It had a dedicated port, however, and when Brontë asked (imperiously) for tea, Lamont herself went to fetch it. Edu drifted over to brace herself in the corridor, looking after the official. Speaking through her netbot, she said, *This is suspiciously easy. Can you monitor their feeds?*

Brontë heard Nia through her own bot: *Give me another few minutes. Their shieldwall is tricky.* Brontë had already found the inventory of contract labor workers and was sorting by date and point of purchase. They had reckoned that the cargo ship had left Quigley-5, the station from which their informant had sent the captures, six months earlier. Standard travel time from that station to this mining platform, she and Nia had determined, left them a two month range as the most probable dates of sale for the Pirians, and thus Ruçar. Her search would start with sales during that range.

Most labor contracts included images, both full-body images and head shots. Once she had the search area defined, she looped in Nia, who set her ferret to search those images. The ferret had returned eight probables, none of them Ruçar or the Pirians, when Edu twitched. Adder, who had been watching over Brontë's shoulder, wheeled, her hand grabbing once again for the weapon she wasn't carrying. "Let's not panic," Edu said, and through her bot: *Six Hayek-Lopaka Security officers are coming this way. They don't look friendly.*

Nia spat a Pirian curse: *Their skulls!*

"Prep for break," Edu said. "Just as a precaution."

I'm not leaving you!

"That's an order, Analyst."

Nia swore again. Brontë heard the clatter of the Security drawing near. She entered the command to download the contract labor manifest into her data tag, and rose to block the view of the port from the hatch just as the Security arrived, one of them bashing the butt of his short rifle into Edu's belly by way of greeting. Adder crowded backwards, shielding Brontë with her body and raising her hands—not in surrender, Brontë knew. That was a defensive stance in Shtai.

The Security were shouting conflicting orders: for them all to show their hands, to get on their knees, to get back. The data tag chirped, signaling that the download was complete. Brontë yanked it free and shoved it in her pocket as Adder backed her into a corner of the office. Edu straightened from the knot the blow had knocked her into, holding both her hands out palm first. "No one is resisting," she said, her words rough with pain. "Let's talk."

The Combine Security who had hit her before hit her again, in her head this time. Edu flew backwards, thumping into the bulkhead, her body limp. Through her bot, Brontë heard Nia, panicked: *Station Security attempting to board. I'm breaking dock.*

Brontë bit down on her urge to shout at Nia, to insist she stay. To yell, *Don't leave us, you coward!* Then the Security took hold of her.

Chapter 8

Tauranga City, Republic Settlement Planet Durbin

Velocity gave Quinn a slice of figcake. The child dumped half a bowl of sugar into her tea and stirred it with a grubby forefinger. "So bring you what people say," Quinn said. "That all?"

"Don't make things up. You're not my only source. I'll know if you're lying to me. Then the deal's off."

Quinn gulped down the tea, eyeing the bin from the bakery. She looked a lot skinnier than she had when she'd been trying to rob Velocity that night on the street, not to mention much younger. Velocity put another slice of figcake on her plate, and the child snatched it up fast, in case she might change her mind. Her mouth full, Quinn said, "People say plenty stupid. Most what they say is stupid. Like, Dogo, our runner, her uncle live with them, he say Parliament Security put nanotropes in the water to rebuild our brains so we'n start trouble. That why he'n drink a thing but tapai."

"That's the sort of information I want. Not just that, though. Don't just bring me the stupid rumors. Bring me everything."

"Huh." Quinn ate more cake, a little more slowly. "Well, it's your tin, kas."

"Come every day or so," Velocity said. "More often if you hear anything really interesting." She folded the wrapper around the rest of the figcake and held the package out to Quinn, whose eyes widened just before she snatched it away. "If I'm not here, you can speak to Tai. He's my second. Or Jusuf, he's with me too."

"Tai and Jusuf," Quinn said. "What I hear, but no lies."

"Right," Velocity said, and gave the kid two of the bits of the local hard money she'd acquired from Yadav, round metal coins. She had no idea how much this money was worth, but from how Quinn's expression went furiously blank, it was too much. Oh, well. Bribes were better than bullets, as the Pirians always said. She walked the child out to the landing and watched her rush down the stairs. A moment later, from the staircase window, Velocity saw her running full-speed down the boulevard, the wrapped cake tucked under one arm.

Tai came from his room to peer over her shoulder. "Was that your street thief?" he asked. "You really think she'll be worth the trouble?"

"Won't know until we know. How's Jusuf doing with his street thief?"

Tai shifted his weight, to let her know he didn't like Sheng being called a thief. But all he answered was that Jusuf was still working on it. Uri spoke through her uplink: *Search results available. Shall I summarize, or do you want the raw data?*

Both. Summary first.

No match for the Ikan16 males. No match for the missing Pirians. Six matches for probable insurgent activity with a reliability of thirty percent or lower. Eighteen possible matches for malfeasance with a reliability of ninety percent or higher.

Sort the malfeasance matches with the insurgency matches.

Two matches. Uri sent her the pair—a miner and a labor agent, both in a mining town called Pakuru, in the Iron Mountains.

Interesting. How close is that to us? Pakuru?

Five hundred thirty-nine kilometers to the northeast. Weather between here and there over the next three days is clear and cold. Daylight highs of minus ten degrees, no storms currently approaching.

Fine frozen snow, left over from the burga, was being blown along the street in white rippling waves. It was almost pretty, in a hypnotic sort of way. *You sound unconvinced*, she subvocced, *for someone with a ninety percent reliability level.*

I'm convinced about the data, Uri said.

But?

Corvo launched a second packet. I told you that. That one failed, like the first. I haven't found a cause.

Velocity thought this over. *You think there's an AI here.*

Uri made the grumbly noise he had picked up from Tai. Velocity had never said how adorable she found this, and she didn't now. *If it's an AI*, he said, *it must be a Pirian AI. Construction of true or full artificial intelligence is prohibited in the Republic.*

So is research into genetic engineering on the germline.

This stopped Uri. *Do you think it could be a Republic-sourced AI?*

I think you shouldn't dismiss it out of hand, Velocity said, and added, *I don't know how likely it is. People in the Combines have a phobia about computer intelligence, from what I remember. But I was only a kid when I left.*

Also, we know the Atlas Society is willing to violate taboos, Uri said. After a moment, he said, *So what about Pakuru? Follow the data or not?*

Velocity leaned on the window mullion, watching the snow. Their appointment with Avril Drury, the clerk to the Minister of Trade, wasn't for another forty watches. "Captain?" Tai asked, probably bemused by her long silence.

She stood straight. "See if you can reach Mosel," she said. "We're taking a little trip."

ꝏ 𝈦 𝈫

They set out the next morning at dawn. Mosel brought a different stormcraft, with higher wheels and a larger cabin. Tai stayed behind to follow local leads. Jusuf and Sheng came with Velocity. Velocity wasn't convinced that Sheng would be much help at negotiating the local mines. For one thing, Tai said he was ninety percent sure she hadn't been down a mine in years. For another, both Tai and Jusuf suspected she was working for someone—that her willingness to help find miners was at the behest of this person or group. If so, any data they gained with her help would be suspect. Still, it was a start. And they could sort whatever information Sheng fetched them with her possible duplicity in mind.

Uri had reaffirmed his promise for clear weather. Certainly when they were loading their gear into Mosel's craft, the sky was bright with stars and the planet's single moon glowed clear blue, high in that crystalline dark. Velocity found herself watching for the space station, as if that might let her see the *Susan Calvin* in its dock. Bizarrely, when she did spot the bright chip of the station, she found herself comforted.

Mosel helped load the gear, Sheng showed up almost on time, and they were out of the city and heading north well before sunrise. Velocity rode on the navigator's bench again. On the rear bench, Sheng curled up and went to sleep while Jusuf read something on his dock, which was a Pirian model—a flat flexible bracelet that unfolded and, when tapped, hardened into a flat screen.

Outside, the horizon turned green, then gold; then the planet's star appeared, too bright to look at directly. Its light gilded the plains, created blue shadows on the drifts of snow. Here and there buildings thrust through snow, white or blue-white smoke pluming from their vents. Mosel guided the craft using GPS, since all the roads were buried. Velocity talked with him about towns out here on the plains and about the specific mining town they were heading for, in the foothills of the Iron Mountains. At length, she asked him, "You know I'm affiliated with a Combine, right?"

"Never would have guessed," Mosel said and added, in what was clearly meant to be an imitation of her accent, "Praps we might have better success if we load the baggage in this way."

Velocity had never said 'perhaps' in her life, but she didn't argue. "I'm wondering: is there much resentment toward the Combines here?"

"What?" Mosel made the word comic in its astonishment. "Why would anyone resent hiraka? Just because they graft thirty percent of every little anything we produce?"

"In exchange for rebuilding the planet, though," Velocity pointed out. "Durbin would be a noxious rock if not for the work Hayek-Lopaka Combine put into it."

"Oh, *they* did the work? And here I thought that was my great-grandparents, shipped here as forced labor. And forced to labor."

"Hayek-Lopaka provided the funding. And the credit. They still supply the credit."

"Oh, they're prime with credit. No lie. And if you can't pay it back, why, that's what contract labor is for." Mosel shut up, apparently realizing how far past the line he was going.

"Durbin isn't much more than a noxious rock now," Velocity mentioned, moving her chin at the empty icy plain they were speeding over. "Must be hard to scratch a living."

This was too sweet an opening for Mosel to ignore: "Especially with contract labor taking all the work, and hiraka skimming all the profit."

"So should I pretend I'm not from a Combine when I talk to these miners?"

Mosel's moodiness erupted into glee. "Oh, please do. I want to watch."

Velocity grinned. "Whut?" she said, imitating his accent. "Don' you thenk ehd fool'm?"

"What," Mosel said, correcting her vowels. "Think." Velocity laughed, and he did too. "Maybe just let your man talk," he said, jerking his head toward Jusuf in the back.

"It's true Hayek-Lopaka is making a fat profit here," Velocity said, "but it's also true you won't survive without the Combine. You're not self-sufficient, and no one is going to ship tech and other supplies out here for what you can afford."

"And we'll never be self-sufficient, so long as the Combine holds our trade lease. Their costs and that profit, plus all the new bots they create by sucking us hollow."

"So you understand the problem. What's the solution?"

Mosel made a face. "Not what these Iron Smoke think," he muttered, barely aloud.

"What's Iron Smoke?"

"I don't know what you mean." Mosel tapped the front window, bringing up the port, tapped it twice more to enlarge it. "That's where we're headed."

All Velocity could see, even enlarged to three hundred percent, was a smudge on the horizon. Mountains, she supposed. Blinking up her inskull uplink, she sent a query to Uri: *Iron Smoke. Is that one of our insurgent groups?*

I find nine hundred seventeen mentions of that word combination, Uri said. *Five hundred ten are in a context that may refer to insurgency.*

She relayed to him what Mosel had said, and then asked about Tai. Tai was working with Corvo, Uri said, and added that Rida was out on the station buying supplies. Velocity acknowleged and shut down the uplink. Aloud, she said, "What do the Iron Smoke have planned?"

Mosel hunched over the controls. "I don't know any Iron Smoke, miss."

"You won't free this planet from Combine influence, not to mention its trade lease, without the help of someone like me. Someone from the Combines."

"Out of the furnace, into the fire," Mosel said.

"Someone who knows the Combines like their own hand. Someone from the Combines who is on your side."

"Someone definitely not here to cheat us." Mosel tapped off

the window screen. "Look, you're wasting your pretty talk. I'm not with Smoke, and I don't want to *be* with Smoke."

"You're happy with the status quo."

"I'm happy out of the system. I'm happy not sold to the mines."

Behind them, Sheng stirred. She spoke to Mosel in a local dialect, one Velocity couldn't follow. Mosel answered in the same dialect, his tone angry. "I didn't mean to start a fight," Velocity said mildly.

"No fear," Mosel said. "Heroes of the Revolution don't fight slag like me."

Sheng grunted. "Fight?" she said. "No. It's no sort of fight."

"Maybe you can help me," Velocity said, "now that you're awake. Iron Smoke. What's their long-term plan?"

"Monsieur Mosel," Sheng said, "is a kanji." She paused. "Do you have that term? Kanji? A fish that eats shit from bigger fish?"

"I'm someone who earns my own," Mosel snapped, "and always have. *And* I've stayed out of the system. Not like some."

"You'll get anything you pay for from a kanji," Sheng said, "except the truth."

"Whereas with bots," Mosel said, color dark on his cheekbones, "you get lies for free."

Jusuf, who had been silent through all of this, now said, without looking up from his port, "Have you heard that story?" Velocity and Sheng eyed him warily. Mosel just hunched his shoulders further. "It's the one about the eagle and the mouse. An eagle is a raptor, a bird of prey. They eat mice. Do you have mice here?"

"Who needs mice when we have hiraka," Mosel muttered.

"This is a story about a mouse. A wild mouse, not one on a ship. This mouse was out foraging in the trees one day, when it met up with a cat. A cat is a type of kitten," Jusuf explained. "Cats and mice are enemies, as you know. So this cat seized hold of the mouse. *You have trespassed on my property*, she said, *and you are now my prisoner*. The mouse says, *Who made this your property?* The cat said she could do what she liked to anyone on her property, and carried the mouse off toward her estate."

"She what?" Velocity objected. "Why not eat it there?"

"The cat carried the mouse back toward her estate, dangling it by its tail—mice have tails, long skinny ones. As they crossed a road, an eagle dropped from the sky and seized the mouse. The cat refused to let go, and as the eagle flew off, the cat was pulled up into the sky along with the mouse. *My property, my property!* the cat screeched, but the hawk, used to squeals from prey, just flew on. When they reached the eagle's nest, both the mouse and the cat were fed to the eagle's children." Jusuf paused and then added, "That's the story."

The interior of the stormcraft was silent for a long moment, as everyone digested this. Then Mosel demanded, "What's that supposed to mean? If we fight back, we all die?"

"Maybe the Combines are the eagle," Sheng said. "Maybe contract workers are mice and cats are free labor."

"Free labor don't feed on bots," Mosel snapped. "Just the opposite."

"It's only a story," Jusuf repeated. "Maybe you could tell one of your stories."

"Only a story, my neck," Sheng muttered. "Maybe you're the eagle."

"Maybe," Jusuf agreed. Sheng turned the upper half of her body all the way around to face him, scowling, and he shrugged. "Maybe we're the eagle hunters."

"Eagles are a protected species," Velocity said. They all looked at her, even Mosel, who should have been watching his controls. "On Earth," Velocity explained. "In the preserves. Which is the only place eagles live. They're a protected species. That means it's illegal to kill them."

"Ah," Jusuf said, and when she turned to look at him smiled his slight, bitter, and entirely un-Pirian smile.

ℭ ⅄ ℬ

The station echoed eerie and empty around him. Rida kept twitching at shadows, turning to look behind him. He blamed the Captain. Both she and Tai couldn't get over what had happened to him on Franklin Station, and their unease had bled into his subconscious, convincing him that in the Republic anything outside the ship was a threat. *I don't see a light*, he subvocced. *Am I going the right way?*

Up and to your left, Uri said.

Rida walked faster, fighting the urge to return to the ship and do all this by remote. While that would work for ordering the supplies, he could only learn about the station and its inhabitants by moving among them. This was an intelligence-gathering mission as much as anything, and he couldn't gather intelligence hiding in his cabin.

He'd been picked up off a concourse exactly like this one on Franklin Station, though it had been much better lit and filled with stationers and crew on leave. At first he had thought the officers arresting him were station Security, so he hadn't resisted. By the time he knew they were Torres Ikeda's own private enforcers, it had been too late. His mind winced away from that memory, from what had happened to him, from how he had been so stupid. Doing what he was told, just because someone told him to do it.

Ahead of him, he saw a lit window. He tried to ignore the tension stinging in his stomach. The brass plate next to the hatchway said CHANDLER, so he was in the right place, but when he pressed the panel beneath the sign, nothing happened. He peered in through the window. A small cabin, with an abandoned worktable, and just beyond that a sealed hatchway.

"Can I help you?"

Rida jumped, wheeling. A woman in Hayek-Lopaka colors, her eyes narrowed. Nur Che, according to the name tag on her jacket. Chief of Station Security.

"Are you Combine Security?" Rida said, the words coming out harsher than he meant them.

Che's eyes narrowed even further. "Who are you?"

"Rida Calvin," he said, giving his ship name, the one the Captain put on manifests. "Off the *Susan Calvin*. I was hoping to resupply my ship."

"Ah." Che's hands, which had been hovering at the stick on her belt, slipped behind her back. "We don't staff supply except by appointment. But I can show you to the stores."

She started off, and he fell in step with her. *You could have warned me*, he subvocced.

I didn't see her, Uri admitted. *She must have been in a blind spot.*

Blind spots, areas of the station which had no feeds, were not uncommon. And of course the Chief of Station Security would know where they were. Che was shorter than he was, with shorter legs, but nevertheless she had pulled ahead of him. He stretched his stride, catching up. "You seem understaffed," he said: not quite a question.

"We are," Che agreed, in the same even tone she had used throughout, even when her hand was on her stick.

"It can't be safe. Being this understaffed?"

"Mmm." Che stopped by a bank of lifts and fed a code into one, keeping her body so that it blocked Rida's line of sight.

No AI on this station, Uri said. *No true AI. They're using dumb-AI to monitor basic functions. Environmentals. Surveillance. The Exchange.*

How does dumb-AI run an Exchange?

Badly.

While Combines built things like AIs, they deliberately curtailed the programs with kill-codes and hedged them about with shieldwalls. They built designs specifically to keep their machines from ever achieving true intelligence. Dumb-AI was the term used for this sort of AI, the only sort that was legal in the Republic. Not for the first time, Rida wondered how Uri felt about these regulations.

The lift arrived and Che held out a hand, indicating he should get in first. Though it increased his anxiety, Rida did as he was told. *Following orders*, he thought bitterly. The lift slid through the levels, their weight increasing as it moved further out from the hub. When it stopped, they were somewhere around half of universal gravity, at least by how his knees felt.

"Station warehouses," Che said as the doors open, and gestured once more for him to go first.

Rida stepped out into a long dusky space: overhead far above, metal deck, immense metal roll-up doors covering bay after bay. Far down the way, he could see a single worker loading crates onto a snub-nosed cargo transport. The air smelled of solvent and ozone. This last smell made him uneasy—aboard ships, it usually meant something in the machinery was failing. An understaffed station being maintained by a dumb-AI. "Why are you so short on staff?" he asked. "Did Hayek-Lopaka yank your credit, or what?"

Che crossed to a kiosk and opened the dock. "Here's your ship code," she said, showing him a routing number. "Here's how to search. Once you have what you want, tag it with your code. Give me an example. Something you need for your ship."

"Sugar," Rida said, since they were running low on that. Che showed him how to fill out the order form, and then how to find the bay where a given order was stored. Then she took him to the cargo transports, and showed him how to check one out. They drove it down to the bay that held the sugar, and she showed him how to key open the sliding door. "If you can take it from here," she finished, "I need to get back to my post."

He thanked her and watched as she made her swift way back toward the lifts. She stopped on the way to speak to the worker. Rida loaded his crate of sugar, and went to a nearby kiosk—they were placed every few hundred meters along the deck—and put in order after order, until he found one that would take him back down the concourse to the bay next to the worker.

He parked his transport next to this bay and keyed in the code, just the way Che had taught him, but when he tried to haul up the sliding door, it jerked and jammed. Rida muttered and yanked harder. Through his netbot, Uri said helpfully, *It's probably off-track. Try wiggling it sideways.*

Hush, Rida subvocced, and yanked again, pretending to be more frustrated than he was. As he had hoped, the worker stopped loading his own transport and came over.

"They stick, sometimes," he said. "Let me show you."

Rida stepped back, smiling. "Please."

The other man was younger than Rida, maybe in his early twenties, with thin bones and wiry muscles. His hair was short, but not shaved, and he wore mended trousers and cheap boots. No work gloves. Probably free labor. He told Rida his name was Perth, and showed him how to coax the door up. "Are you off that Freet ship?" he asked.

Freet was a rude word for Free Trade, but Rida just made his smile more charming. "I am. What about you? I didn't think any other ships were in dock right now."

There are three barges and a cargo ship on the non-commercial—Uri began, and Rida told him to hush again.

"Right, we're down on non-com," Perth said. "The *Reynard*."

*The **Reynard**?* Rida asked Uri.

Oh, now you want my help, Uri said, but gave him a précis: a standard Tesco-class cargo ship, held by Lopaka House, in dock for the past ten days. While Uri was reciting, Perth helped him find and load the filters he had ordered from this bay. Afterwards, Rida went with him back to Perth's bay and they finished loading the crates from that—crates of shipmeals, Rida noted, and the cheapest sort: crackers made of cricket flour with cheese made from algae. "Is this what the *Reynard* feeds you?" Rida said, honestly appalled.

Perth laughed. "Not the crew. The cargo."

Despite all the stories Tai had told him, Rida took a moment to parse this. Through the bot, Uri said, *the **Reynard** transports contract labor for Hayek-Lopaka Combine.*

A slave ship. Rida, thinking of what Tai had told him about the contract workers in cages at the customs house downplanet, froze with a crate in his arms. Luckily he recovered before Perth turned back from the transport to take it from him. "Why are you taking on food?" he asked before he could think better of it. "You've just off-loaded your cargo."

He hit the last word a little too hard, and also he shouldn't have known about the cages of contract workers, but Perth didn't seem to notice any of this. He headed past Rida to collect more crates, saying as he went, "Right, we're loading more here."

"More contract workers?"

"Don't ask me," Perth said cheerily. "I'm just a deckhand."

Recalling his purpose here, Rida shook the disapproval from his tone and asked Perth where he was from, how he signed onto the *Reynard*, what life was like on that ship: all the questions he had learned to ask to get someone to like him. "People love talking about themselves," he had explained to Tai. "People love it when they think you're interested in them. All you have to do is be interested in them, and they'll tell you anything."

"Is that why you ask so many questions about me?" Tai had said. "Using your charm on me?"

"Is it working?" Rida had asked. Tai had growled and rolled on top of him, pinning him to the bunk. "I actually am interested in you, though," Rida added, and reached up to kiss him.

He and Perth worked through the rest of topwatch, talking non-stop as they loaded cargo. When Perth's transport was full, Rida rode with him down to the cargo lift so Perth could show him how to operate it. "Listen," Rida said, as Perth was getting ready to shut the lift door. "Do you get off-time? Maybe we could play some slam."

Perth liked slam ball. That had come up while they worked. "Does this station even have courts?" he asked.

Rida grinned. "They do seem short of amenities. What's up with that, do you think?"

"What do you expect, out here in the Deep? Nothing but miners and freets out here."

Rida had been to plenty of stations out in the Deep, and in the Drift for that matter. He'd never seen one as empty and scanty as this one. "They're short on Security, too," he pointed out. "If they're dealing with a lot of contract workers, that seems odd."

"No tax base. Who's going to pay them?"

"No tax base?" Rida frowned. Most Republic planets used some form of transaction tax to fund their infrastructure. With so many contract miners being shipped in, the tax coffers should be overflowing.

"That's what my boss says." Perth shrugged.

"Huh." Maybe the miners were being sold to the Combine. Hayek-Lopaka wouldn't tax itself. Still, it seemed self-destructive, to cut taxes to the point that you couldn't maintain the planet's only station. Also, if they didn't have the funds to maintain the station, how were they maintaining infrastructure on the planet?

They're not, Uri told him. *Maintenance requests for even vital infrastructure—bridges, power grids, relay tower—are all months, even years behind.*

That's…

It is, Uri agreed. *The station has courts for football and for slam ball on Level Twenty-Two, but they're no longer operational.*

"My ship has a pit," Rida told Perth. "We can play slam there, if you like."

They traded call signs, and then Perth slid down the lift door – it was a metal grid, not an actual door—and waved as the lift eased into motion. Rida waved back, and headed back towards his own transport. *Should I run a search on Perth Okore?* the dagan asked.

"Might as well," Rida said, speaking aloud since he was alone. "Never know what's going to be useful."

Chapter 9

**Aboard Castillo Mining Platform HLC116,
Castillo Mines, the Drift**

Adder huddled in the corner of the Transit car, bracing her mass against the frequent jerks and lurches of its motion. Transit was a linked-up system of cargo bins hitched to monorails. Every turn and juncture of the monorails was— theoretically— pinioned to the rock. In actual fact, the pitons frequently worked loose and then the cars shot off the rail, to tumble adrift through space. Not usually entirely adrift, since most cars had emergency cables anchoring them to the monorail system. Mostly someone would show up and reel the cars back down to the asteroid before the cable snapped or the cars ran out of atmosphere. Mostly.

Also, the metal car stank. Everything stank, since barracks on this platform had no facilities to wash either the miners or their clothing, and no one got dental care. Not to mention miners were packed thick in every car. Though the air got stuffy, so long as so many bodies were wedged around her, Adder didn't have much trouble staying braced. But at each stop, six workers got off, leaving fewer and fewer bodies to hold her in place.

She had spent nine work shifts on this rock so far. Nine days universal time, she supposed, unless the Combine was manipulating their hours, which was not just possible but probable. Out here this far in the Drift, time was what the Combine said it was. Even their docks linked only to the mining platform clock. Nine days, and no luck finding her brothers, or Brontë for that matter. She knew she should focus primarily on Brontë. Brontë was her bond-holder. Brontë was the reason for every bite of food she'd ever eaten, every bunk she'd slept in, all the training she had ever received. Brontë was why she had been created. If she failed to protect Brontë, her existence wasn't just pointless, it was a crime.

And she hadn't protected her. Adder winced even now at the memory of Hayek-Lopaka Combine Security putting their hands on Brontë—putting her in restraints, dragging her off to somewhere beyond Adder's reach. That memory made her sick with shame.

Yet even so, most of her attention was on her brothers. Ruçar was here somewhere, so it wasn't impossible that Ian was as well. If she could find them…Adder squeezed her eyes shut briefly. Finding them without finding Brontë, she knew, would be useless. They could protect one another on this rock, but only Brontë could get them out of the mines.

Unless the Pirians came for them. That traitorous thought slipped through her mind more and more often lately. Nia had gotten away. Nia would find her way to the closest Pirian ship, and then the Siji would come—if they didn't come for Adder, they would come for Edu and for the Pirians their informant had claimed were among the miners here. Surely the Siji would also rescue her and Brontë. Only, if they came before Adder had found her brothers, would they stay to search for them? Bonded workers they didn't even know? *Combine* bonded workers?

Adder hunched her shoulders as the cars thudded to a stop at Portal Nineteen. Once the Transit hatch made seal with the mine, it slid open with a noisy clash and rasp of metal against metal. Adder, one of the few remaining passengers, nudged herself out, manipulating herself expertly in the low gravity. The last mine worker out of the car banged the panel that shut the hatch behind them, and the transit squealed away.

The mine shafts—drifts, as they were called—were pressurized: the tiny mining robots, being partly biological, needed an oxygen-rich atmosphere to function. Castillo Mines used the fact that the shafts had pressure and a breathable mix as an excuse not to supply the contract labor workers that handled the bots with skinsuits, or e-kits either. Adder wore only an orange coverall, plus a one-piece thermal suit beneath it. No masks, no gloves, no socks, never mind boots. Since the shafts were only nominally heated, this meant by thirty minutes into her twelve-hour shift, she was too cold to make a proper fist.

The other workers who had gotten off at Portal Nineteen scrambled along through the drift, which was barely large enough to allow them passage on their hands and knees and was lit only with intermittent slap-ups. One by one, they reached promising spurs, short blind shafts bored into the rock face by drill bots earlier, following seams of ore. The contract miners crawled into these, one by one, and settled to work.

Drill bots were bigger than mining bots; their job was infrastructure. Adder had puzzled over this at first. Since the drill bots also collected ore from the shafts and spurs they drilled, why not use these larger bots to do *all* the mining? The work would go faster, and Castillo Mining would need many fewer contract labor miners. But over her first few work shifts, picking up and returning her allotment of mining bots to the machine shop and talking to the workers there, she had come to understand. The drill bots were not just pricier, they also had a bigger brain, which meant they were more fragile. The relatively stupid mining bots were cheap and hardy. It was true the bots needed human workers to handle them, but contract labor was more cost-effective than bots, especially if you didn't bother with trivialities like medical, proper safety gear, or sufficient food.

Adder took the sixth spur along the shaft, a small enough spur that her body heat might help warm it a little. She wedged herself through its tiny mouth, sliding out of her satchel so that she would fit. Then she tugged the satchel in after her, folded it open, and took out her dock. Its screen gave enough light to work by. The smooth apple-shaped space inside the carved-out spur was not quite large enough for her to straighten her legs. Its walls were honeycombed with tiny shafts spiraling out into the rock, created by bots following the richest veins of ore.

The satchel held a gridded frame of padded niches, each holding a fist-sized bot. One by one, Adder pulled them out, powered them up, and set them inside the mouth of a shaft. Almost ninety percent hopper, the bots clattered away, heading for the furthermost point of their shaft where they would begin chewing out ore. Once their hoppers were full, they would scuttle back to Adder. She stored the granular ore in the pop-out bags which were also in her satchel. Her quota was six bags of raw ore every shift. If nothing went wrong, this was just barely possible. If you made your quota, you got a bonus: credit at the canteen, which you could spend on extra food, or maybe socks.

Adder wanted socks more than she wanted food. But she had never yet made quota. Something always went wrong. A bot would jam, a drill-head would need replacing—a twenty minute operation, even when your hands weren't too cold to grip—or worst of all, a shaft would collapse. They were mostly mining cobalt and platinum from this asteroid, but mixed with these was lots of ice, silica, and kalonites. This made for a friable substrate. When a shaft collapsed with a bot deep inside it, sometimes if other bots were close enough, you could steer them over to dig the bot out. Sometimes. And even trying meant at least two bots off line, which meant you'd miss your quota.

When you came in too far below quota, one or more of your meals got cut, depending on how far below you were. But if you lost a bot, you lost meals for a week—twelve days, or twenty-four meals. The kapos would let you spread that out, not out of kindness, but because most chips who went twelve days without food would not survive. They were too underfed, too badly clothed, too cold. Most of them were also ill, some way or other. So far Adder hadn't lost a bot. She'd missed quota every shift, though. She was hungry all the time.

She'd just set the last bot in its shaft when her dock pinged. It was a cheap, standard-issue dock issued to her by the platform bosses—they'd taken her own dock away when they took her clothes and her boots and her hair. This dock was an awkward size, slightly too big to fit easily in a pocket, with a cracked screen and a heavy metal case; and it would only access the platform nexus. She'd taken it out of the satchel along with the bots, and left it on the spur 'floor', raw rock still showing the marks from the drill bot's cutters, so she could use its screen as a light source. Now she twisted herself around to scoop it up, simultaneously tapping the dropbox icon with her thumb. Her heart rate had increased slightly—whoever was pinging her had to be on the platform. She hoped for one of her brothers or, failing that, Brontë.

The post was from a call sign she didn't recognize: Jack Ngata. Adder hesitated, and then tapped the post open. *U look 4 sumn I no war meet chow 1700 o/n.* Adder puzzled this out, and sent back: *1700.* She waited a moment, in case Jack might send her more information, but that was it, apparently. Wedging her dock into a corner, she settled in to wait for the bots to return or for an alarm. Until one of those happened, she didn't have much to do. She mused over the message from Jack Ngata only briefly—it was almost certainly an attempt at some scam. Instead, she tried to think of ways to find her brothers, or Brontë.

As with most places that used contract labor, your call sign here in the mines had to be your name and the last four digits of your contract number. If this mining platform worked like other places that used contract workers, Adder's contract number ought to be near Brontë's in sequence. If Brontë had been put in the system, that was. Given she was a Combine heir, she might well be a guest of the platform. So to speak.

The name on Brontë's data tag was Brontë Calvin. Adder had searched the directory for CALV plus every contract number fifty to each side of her own. No luck. Searching for Ruçar was a more difficult problem. First, the labor agent who had purchased him from Ikeda House had almost certainly changed his name. Second, she had only the roughest estimate of when they had been sold to Castillo Mines. A search for the name Ruçar returned null results. Searching the directory for *Ian* gave her sixteen hits, eleven of them contract workers. She had posted to all of these, a brief query asking if they were Ian Ikan.

The six replies had been nice, though none had been her brother. She had replied, asking if they knew someone who looked like her (she attached an image) who might know the name Ikan. So far she'd gotten no replies to this second post. Rolled in a ball to conserve her body heat, she tried to think of some other tactic. Maybe a chain-post, asking each contract she posted to forward the post to five others? And those five to five more, and so on. That might get her Ruçar, if he was actually here; but probably not Brontë.

Too hungry to nap, she opened her port and began composing a post: something that would catch attention, be short enough that people would read or watch the whole thing, and would convince people to help her. She was still engaged in this fruitless task when the first bots began tumbling from their shafts, their hoppers fat with ore. Exhaling, she tucked the port away and set to work.

෩ ⴺ ꝑ

Work assignments on Castillo Mines for contract labor miners were twelve hours in the mines every spin, plus six hours at some other job. Because Adder had combat training, her rack job was maintaining and repairing the fitness machines in the administrative block gymnasiums. This was Combine logic for you. She was also responsible for instructing the administrators on how to use the machines, since admins in low-gravity assignments were required by the Combine to do ten hours per week in the gym. Under the guise of testing the repaired machines and instructing admins, Adder sometimes got quite a bit of exercise. Strictly speaking, she didn't need the work-out. Soon after they'd arrived in Pirian space, Captain Wrachant had seen to it that every member of her crew took advantage of the free healthcare Pirians offered at all their stations, which included the nanotropic fix for life in space. Still, used to a heavy training regime, she missed exercise.

Today, however, she kept her eye on the time; and the moment her shift was up, she headed for chow. She heard the racket as soon as she got off the lift—there were only two spaces for contract labor to go when they weren't working. One was the chow hall, and the other the barracks, where other workers would be trying to sleep. So people congregated in the hall. The result was a din worse than the swampy stench of terrible food and all those unwashed bodies.

Since Adder didn't know Jack Ngata by sight, she had to ask around. With more than three thousand contract workers on this platform at any one time, no one knew everyone. But everyone was known by someone, and it took her only a few minutes to find someone who knew Jack, and pointed him out to her. He was over in the short tables, playing a game with his rack mates on their linked ports, all of them shouting and slagging one other. Adder bounced up to the rails that ran along the overhead, meant to fasten extra tables to when the platform was at microgravity, and brachiated her way to the end of hall. Dropping down next to the table, she braked herself by hooking one foot under the deck rails, and looked from face to face. None of them had looked up from their screens, but when she said, "Jack?" the youngest one did.

"Ha." He had the long sharp bones, small chalky teeth, and scrawny muscles of someone raised in low gee on bad food. "You the Combine."

Adder no longer winced at this. Where she was from, in Ikeda House, 'Combine' meant a Combine citizen, such as Brontë: a descendant of the original corporation stockholders who had built the Republic. The term might also be used for a contract worker held by a Combine. It did not apply to someone like her, a bonded worker who had not been convicted of anything, who was employed by the Combines under a mutually agreed upon and beneficial bond. Back at Ikeda House, calling her Combine was an insult either way, implying either that she was a criminal or that she was getting uppity. But here on the platform all it meant was that she spoke Public with Combine grammar, and that she tried to keep her face and hands clean. "I'm Adder," she said. "You have information for me?"

"Ata ata," he said, a local term meaning *Calm down*. "Let's talk metal."

He didn't mean actual metal, or even the pesa used on many stations as hard currency, which were sometimes made of a copper alloy. He meant funding. He meant how did Adder propose to pay for his information. "What do you have to sell?" Adder asked.

Jack grinned. "I got call sign," he said. "How much?"

Adder tipped back her head, putting on a bored look. "Call sign. What call sign?"

Keeping his port faced away from her, the kid fed in a code. The com pinged, and he turned the screen to face her: a moment later, the com circled opened, and Ruçar appeared. His clear grey eyes, so like her own, widened with shock. "Adder?" he said, and then: "Adder!"

The kid shut off the connection and slid his port into his scrub pocket. "Six meals."

Her heart banging, Adder scowled at him: "Three."

"Four, and that's flat," he said, and when she nodded, added, "First meal now."

Adder smiled, despite how hungry she was. "C'mon," she told him, releasing herself from her anchor. "Lucky for you I haven't eaten yet."

Chapter 10

Commercial Space Station Webster-1,
Planet Durbin, in the Deep

orvo sat cross-legged in the *Susan Calvin*'s com, every single board open and the dock the *Sungai* had issued her unfolded on the deck before her. Beside her, a bowl of sweet, milky tea steamed gently. She and Uri had launched two separate AI packets, the second just over two hours earlier. No sign of either had appeared in the nexus.

"A third will achieve the same result," Uri said. He spoke through the ship feed. Early in their acquaintance, he had noted that she preferred him to speak out loud to her rather than through the netbots. Like most AIs, he was scrupulously polite in such matters.

"I agree," Corvo said, running searches in the planetary banks with most of her attention.

"The Captain thinks a Combine AI is possible, despite the prohibitions."

Corvo finished her last search, which returned null results just as previous searches had, and shut her links. Still thinking, she picked up her tea, drank, and grimaced. Sugar, rather than honey, left the drink empty of flavor. "Let us consider possible causes."

Uri blanked the board directly in front of her and wrote *Possible Causes* at the top in Pirian, as they had been speaking that language. Under the heading he started a bullet-point list with *Better prophylactics than expected.* During the next few minutes, he and Corvo working together came up with six other possible causes, which Uri re-ordered to keep the most probable one at the top: that the planet already had a viable AI seeded by a Combine source. Corvo was hesitant to accept this explanation.

"Why?" Rida asked. He had returned from the station while they were in the middle of making the list. Corvo greeted him with a nod, but kept her attention on the work at hand. "No, why?" Rida insisted. His Pirian was clumsy, but his accent charming. Much like her own Public French, Corvo suspected. "Could some person have not put an AI here?"

Corvo switched to Public: "We have no history of a Siji mission sent to this place. It's reasonable to conclude that any Siji cousins taken as prisoners here and sold as contract slaves would not have AI seed with them. And the AIs your people, the Republic, create are not truly AI. Deliberately so!"

Rida was frowning. His objection was not what she expected. "The Republic is not our people."

"My apology. An AI implanted here must be one implanted by Siji. This is all I mean. And we have no record of a Siji mission to Durbin. This is why," she said, speaking to the ship AI now, "I do not think your cause has support."

"Consider, however," Uri said, "only one factor needs to change to erase your objection. Someone in the Combine may well be creating true AI. That someone may have seeded one on this planet."

Corvo made a face. "And we can always use the honey." This was from an old Pirian saying—*If my tia had wings, she'd be a honeybee.* No one ever said the actual adage. It was always either *When my tia has wings,* or *We can always use the honey.*

"I propose we drop a third packet," Uri said.

"You said yourself a third packet would fail."

"A third packet with a ghost attached. When the pupa gets

attacked, the ghost captures the attacker's UPN. Maybe we can track it home."

"And if it is an AI…" Corvo mused.

"We can talk," Uri said. "Find out who they're working with."

"And if they will work with us."

"But…" Rida said. Corvo glanced at him, and he grimaced. "Why would an AI be hiding from you? Unless it knows you're Pirian? And how would the AI know that? And if it does know that, aren't we already in big trouble?"

"These are very central questions," Corvo agreed.

"Launching the third packet now," Uri said. "Meanwhile, Rida, I have the results of the search on Perth Okore."

"Run," Rida said. He had settled into the navigation saddle and was looking at equations—Corvo couldn't see what. While in dock, they wouldn't have any pressing need to plot routes, but maybe he was getting ahead on his work.

"Perth Okore: born on Commercial Space Station Kajita-14, Acre, in the Republic. Signed short-term bond with Lopaka House at age eleven. Shipped out with the *Reynard* eighteen universal months later. Has remained on that ship since. One disciplinary action logged. Current debt stands at two thousand six hundred eighty riyals. No commendations."

"Not much to work with."

"He seems to be standard-issue bonded labor," Uri agreed. "The debt might be something."

"Maybe," Rida said dubiously.

You could be sold into contract labor in the Republic if your debt-load grew too heavy, Corvo knew, but anything under ten thousand riyals was not considered a serious debt. "This is the deckhand you found on the station?" she asked.

"Right. Loading crates of cricket biscuit onto his ship. Six hundred meals per crate, and we loaded at least thirty crates. If we assume one meal a day, and a two month jump…."

"No reason to assume these are the only shipmeals he's loading," Uri said.

"True. The jump is also a guess. What's the carrying capacity for the *Reynard?*"

"The environmentals are labelled for a max of four hundred twenty-five. Current crew manifest lists seventeen hands."

"So they could be taking on some four hundred contract workers." Rida took his hands off the nav board and wrapped his arms around the headrest of the saddle. "This is a settlement planet. Why would they be exporting workers?"

Corvo understood his puzzlement. Republic settlement planets, especially out here in the Deep, always had labor shortages. They'd be far more likely to import workers than to export them. She said this out loud, and Rida grimaced. "They just brought in a load of people. Cargo, Perth called them, but that's what he meant. If this planet needs workers badly enough to ship them in from who knows wherever, why would they turn around and sell people off-planet?"

"An interesting question," Uri agreed. "Shall I have a look at the *Reynard*'s banks?"

"If you can get in without being noticed," Rida said.

"Psh," Uri scoffed, and Rida grinned and went back to his calculations.

Chapter 11

**Aboard Castillo Mining Platform HLC116,
Castillo Mines, the Drift**

Ruçar was on E deck, far from Adder's own C-deck barracks. Meeting would be tricky. No one was allowed off their own deck except for work, and unlike her, Ruçar had no assignment on the admin level. "I'm doing code, down in shipping," he said. "They'll miss me if I crack off."

Adder, on the other hand, had long stretches in the gym when no one showed up, since admins didn't take exercise seriously. She watched Ruçar on her dock screen while she calculated a route from the gym to shipping. Six decks, all of them where no contract worker should be without authorization. Ruçar looked thinner than he had when Adder had seen him last, back in Ikeda House. Also his head was shaved—well, that was the first thing they did to you when you entered the system, shave your head and install your tracking chip. But other than these details, he looked well. Maybe something hollow around his eyes. It would be odd if he didn't look grim, she told herself, considering what he must have been through. He was clean, unlike Adder herself, which meant he had found access to a washroom somewhere. Probably there was an admin scrub he was sneaking into, down there on the docks. "What about Ian?" she asked him. "Is he here?"

Ruçar shook his head. "The labor agent separated us the first day. You're the only one I've seen in years."

More than three universal years. That was how long Ruçar had been alone. Adder ran her thumb over the port screen, wanting so much to touch him. "I'm doing a shift in the gym, starting," she checked the time at the corner of the port screen, "fifteen hours from now. It's topwatch, so probably no one will even show. I'll come to you. Where can we meet?"

ᘓ ᚁ ᘔ

When they finally came for her, Brontë was doing Indaiya—on her own, which was not proper. This was mostly from boredom. The guest suite that she was confined to was decent enough, with two rooms and a galley. But not only did she not have access, they had not even allowed her a dock, probably out of fear that she would hack her way into station access (a legitimate precaution, she had to admit). They had searched her, taking everything, including her data tag containing the purloined inventory. With nothing else to do, she had used a fish knife from the galley to unbolt the furniture in the sitting room and move it into the facility, clearing space for an exercise pit. The Indaiya warming stars and defensive stars were complex enough to occupy her mind and keep her from fretting. Also, they sometimes got her tired enough to sleep.

When the main hatch seal rasped, she was working on the third star. She finished the sequence before turning toward the waiting Security officer. It wasn't the low-level Security she'd been expecting; it was Lieutenant Paris, who had escorted her here and locked her up, however long ago that had been. "Miss Elena," Paris said. "This way, please."

If Paris had been expecting Brontë to react with shock at this use of her register name, he was disappointed. She had had plenty of time to think, here in this suite with no access. After the dust-up at Franklin Station, Brontë's image, as well as her register name,

Elena Kora Hodaya Ikeda Verde, had been all over the banks. That meant that within minutes of Brontë stepping onto the mining platform docks, Lamont must have known who she was; known her role in the coup; known she was currently fourth in line to the Primary Seat of the Ikeda House Board. Lamont had nonetheless risked taking her into custody. The conclusion seemed obvious: Lamont was involved in some activity riskier than imprisoning a Combine heir. And probably that activity either endangered or defrauded Ikeda House or Ikeda-Verde Combine.

If this conclusion was valid, Brontë knew, more than her liberty was in danger. Depending on just how grave their crime was, Lamont and her co-conspirators might well decide that Brontë was less of a threat dead than alive.

"Miss Elena," Paris repeated from the hatchway.

Brontë launched herself straight at the Hayek-Lopaka Combine Security lieutenant, who dodged sideways, his eyes tensing. Catching hold of the cleat next to the lieutenant, Brontë killed her momentum. Paris flushed, moving his chin down the corridor, where two more Security waited by the gridded hatch. "This way, miss."

"Madame," Brontë said. "Not *miss*."

"Madame Ikeda Verde. This way, please."

Security escorted her to Admin Deck and herded her along a corridor to a hatch marked *Président Directeur Général Clarisse LaCroix Tinsley*. Brontë felt the nerves in her stomach sting with shock. Only for a moment—a moment spent watching Paris code the hatch open. Then the shock vanished in anger. Of course Lamont was not working alone. Of course her superior was involved in this. Whatever this was. Brontë drew her spine as straight as she could in this low gravity and entered the outer chambers of the director general of Castillo Mining.

Tinsley did not keep her waiting; her aide ushered Brontë directly into the inner office. Paris and the other Security stayed in reception. The aide shut the door, shutting the two of them in together, and Tinsley stepped gracefully, light as a leaf, to a tea kit in one corner of her office. "Let me apologize, Madame Ikeda, for the manner in which you have been treated. It took us some time, you must understand, to discover who you were."

Brontë felt a quick rush of hope. Tinsley lying was a good sign. Tinsley would not be attempting diplomacy unless she thought Brontë had some power—power to help her, or power to hurt her. Attempting to hide her relief, Brontë looked about the office. It was long and narrow, probably constructed by removing the bulkheads between two or three compartments. The deck cover was polished flagstone; the walls wainscot and gypsum. Here and there animates ran, one showing snow falling through a wooded meadow, another sunlight glittering on a lake. At the far end of the office, a worktable was bolted to the rock of the deck. The oversized wallboard behind it currently showed the Hayek-Lopaka Combine logo. At the end closer to Brontë, banquette seating filled one corner: the metal benches were padded with slim silk cushions, a rose color just darker than the walls.

Tinsley came gliding from the tea kit, two bulbs of white tea in one hand. "Please. Sit. Let's see if we can resolve our difficulty."

Brontë lifted her chin, giving Tinsley a steady stare. "Your difficulty," she corrected.

Tinsley settled at one end of the bench. "I acknowledge my subordinate acted hastily," she said, offering one bulb to Brontë. Brontë ignored it, and she smiled and put both bulbs gently on the table. "Sadly, we can't mend the past. The situation is what it is. I would like to find a way to resolve it which benefits us both."

"Give me access," Brontë said. "Do that now. I will recommend to the Ikeda House Primary Seat Holder that you be allowed to live. I'll even ask that your conviction to contract labor comes with a guarantee of domestic service, rather than the mines."

Tinsley raised her eyebrows. "As a starting offer, that leaves something to be desired."

"Will you risk a war between your Combine and mine, to save your own neck?"

"I'm fond of my neck," Tinsley said mildly. "Let's discuss Primary Seat Holders. Yours is your cousin. Hiro Ikeda, yes?"

"Hiro Ikeda *Hayek*," Brontë said. Hiro Sayid Liao Ikeda Hayek was Theo's register name; Theo was his milk name, as Brontë was hers. Tinsley was employed by Hayek-Lopaka Combine, and a reminder of Theo's paternal line seemed essential. "He's third in line to Hayek House's Primary Seat."

"Indeed. Your cousin, and a cousin by marriage to the Primary Seat Holder of Hayek House. Of interest, then, to both of us." Tinsley sipped her tea, or pretended to, and snuggled against the arm of the banquette. "My researchers have learned a great deal about you over the past few days. Both you and Hiro were born in the Ikeda House clinic, under the ministrations of Ikeda House… physicians. As was the Security cadet you brought aboard my platform. Adder Calvin, according to her data tag. But that's not her register name, is it?"

Anger and fear made a hot simmer in Brontë's belly. "Make your point."

"As you yourself note, Hayek House has an alliance with your house. That cuts two ways. We have allies in Ikeda House. On your Board. In your labs. Adder's register name is Ikan16, but it should be Calypso16. Yes?" The anger vanished, leaving a cold stillness behind. Brontë stared at Tinsley.

"Likewise," Tinsley continued, "an argument could be made that neither you nor Hiro should carry the Ikeda name. Elena Calypso11. Would that be more appropriate? A question we might put to our respective Combines. Perhaps even the High Court. The law concerning experimental engineering of the germline is well established."

Keeping her expression flat, Brontë thought carefully. Tinsley was no one—director general of a minor mining platform way out here in the Drift. Whoever was behind this, it wasn't her. Or at least not only her. That meant…what did that mean?

"Ready to negotiate?" Tinsley asked.

It meant this was not about her and Adder and the Pirians encroaching on the mining platform. It meant this wasn't about Tinsley maybe pilfering Combine funds, or selling ore under the deck. It meant this was something bigger. But what?

Tinsley patted the silk cushion beside her. "Sit," she said. "Let's see if we can't find some common ground."

ദ ⱦ ⱖ

The lift from the gym down to shipping required her to have an access code. "What about service lifts?" Adder asked Jack Ngata. They were working with contraband schemata of the ship, which Jack had sold her for two more meals. "Can we use those?"

"Needs code too," Jack said.

She eyed him. They were knee-to-knee on her bunk, the dock flat on the hard gritty surface of the sleeping mat between them. "A code you can sell me?"

Jack grinned. "Maybe. Not just for meals."

"I'm in the racks same as you. What else do you think I can trade you?"

He studied her. Despite his smile, his eyes were dark with anxiety. "This ain't just visiting your brother," he said. "Not *just* that." Adder said nothing, and he huffed out his breath. "You got some way out. Take me with."

Adder shook her head. "I know someone on the outside who might buy me out. *Might*. I don't know it for fact. And even if I did, I can't make promises for them."

To her surprise, Jack's smile brightened, reaching his eyes for once. "Hah. Knew it."

"Did you hear me? I can't make any promises."

"You promise to try."

She stared at him, knowing she was taking advantage of his desperation. "You have the code?" she asked. He nodded. Adder set her teeth, feeling utterly evil. "I promise to try."

☙ ⚭ ❧

Jack's code got her access to the service lifts, which opened into service conduits, narrow spaces between bulkheads where power, water, and sewage pipes ran. These opened into back corridors on the admin level. At the pit of mainwatch these lifts and corridors wouldn't be in use, contract workers being scheduled to run maintenance when offices were empty. Adder kept alert for exceptions, but mostly she was fighting the hope that kept surging through her. Three years, now, since she had been with her brothers and sisters. Three years since she had stood where she ought to stand, with them beside her; or slept how she was born to sleep, with them tucked around her. Her skin hurt with the need to touch them.

She coded open a corridor door, hitting pause on the panel when the door had opened a bare slit. According to Jack's contraband schematics, this corridor led from the vast holds where the raw ore was stored, past the reserve water tanks, and out to the logistic offices. Adder listened for voices or movement at the tiny slit, then peered through it. Nothing. Steeling her nerves, she opened the hatch the rest of the way and looked both ways along the corridor as she did so. Nothing. She started along the corridor, conscious of her bare feet and ragged orange scrubs. In this gear, she was clearly a mine worker. In the wrong place. At the wrong time. But nothing she promised had been enough to convince Jack to get her access to the dark grey coveralls service workers wore. If she got caught in the admin levels in miner's gear, it meant discipline. If she got caught in gear pilfered from admin, they'd put her out the airlock, though not before extracting the names of anyone who had helped her.

The contract labor facility where she and Ruçar were meeting was down this corridor, first intersection and two doors port. Her luck held: she met no one along that way. And the facility door opened to the code Ruçar had given her. Inside, no one. Not Ruçar, not anyone. She wedged herself in the one corner not in line of sight from the door and waited. It was cold, but not nearly as cold as the mining shafts. The stink was worse, though. No one had cleaned in here for months, maybe years. Adder resisted the urge to ping Ruçar, but she did pull out her dock and open the port in case he had sent her a message. Nothing. She wrapped her arms around herself and tried to be where she was. *Don't worry about what comes next*, their coach had taught them. *Stay in the now.*

She'd been practicing staying in the now for maybe an hour when the door clicked, signaling it was about to open. Adder straightened, getting purchase on the wall behind her, in case she had to fight. Her heart was thumping. The door chunked opened, and Ruçar came through—came through fast, as if he had been shoved. He spotted her at once. His expression was grim, his eyes wide with grief. So she wasn't surprised when Combine Security followed him in.

ꝯꝺ ꝷ ꝸ

Tinsley had returned Brontë to the guest suite. The door was still locked and Lieutenant Paris was still stationed outside. Brontë brewed tea, rehearsing the speech she would make when Tinsley returned. Either Tinsley trusted her or she did not, she would say. She would not be treated like a prisoner, she would say. But when Tinsley appeared, she had Adder with her: flanked by Security, her arms in restraints behind her. "Madame Ikeda," Tinsley said. "A complication has arisen."

"Are you all right?" Brontë asked Adder.

Adder glanced at the Security officer who had a grip on her arm. Then she said, tonelessly, "I'm not injured."

Brontë switched her attention to Tinsley. "We had an agreement. My bodyguard in restraints does not fulfill that agreement."

"Sadly," Tinsley said, "your bonded worker has violated platform regulations. As I am sure you will agree, such violations cannot be ignored."

"Remove those restraints," Brontë ordered.

At Tinsley's nod, Lieutenant Paris did so. Adder shifted her weight, emitted a small cough, and said, "They have Ruçar, also."

Brontë faced Tinsley. "Ruçar is another of my bodyguards. Return him."

Tinsley shook her head. "That was not the agreement."

"Both of them, here, now, under my protection. Or the agreement is void."

"I can arrange to have the other worker brought here." Tinsley's smile hovered on the edge of smug. Brontë felt anger wash through her. She repressed it firmly, keeping her expression imperious. Tinsley added, "With the understanding that it is a concession."

A concession for which Brontë would owe Tinsley some concession of equal value. Brontë stood staring at the administrator. Despite being the director general of Castillo Mining, Tinsley owed her position and her very life to the Combines. She should not have dared to try twisting Brontë's arm. This verged on treason. It was impossible that she was acting on her own. She was a tool in someone else's hands. Whose?

After a moment, Tinsley waved the point off. "Lieutenant. Fetch Madame Ikeda's property."

One of the Security officers left the suite. Turning her back on Tinsley, Brontë went to Adder. She was thinner than Brontë had ever seen her; her silky dark hair was gone, replaced by stubble. Her nails were grimy, as were her mining scrubs. "You're not injured?"

Brontë asked, making sure. "Were you mishandled?"

"No worse than any others in the mines," Adder said. Her glance slid past Brontë to Tinsley. When Brontë turned, Tinsley was still smiling.

"A profit is necessary," Tinsley said, to Brontë, not to Adder. "As I'm sure you know."

"Profit to whom?" Adder muttered.

Brontë gave her shoulder a squeeze. "Get some tea. Eat something."

Adder went to the galley. Brontë kept watching Tinsley. It was a rare administrator who wasn't skimming—usually from expenses, since Combine accountants tracked profits more closely. Brontë wondered if she could use this as leverage. Whoever was controlling Tinsley might not know about the malfeasance, or rather about the degree of malfeasance.

The Combine Security officer returned, shoving Ruçar in front of him. Adder put down her tea bowl and went straight to her brother. They wrapped arms around one another and held still, their eyes shut. "How sweet," Tinsley said. "Can we get on with it now?"

"Transfer their contracts to my name," Brontë said. She was posturing. Tinsley could easily nullify any change to a contract she made, here on this platform where she was director general, and thus the only law. She just wanted to see if Tinsley would comply. How far could she be pushed?

Tinsley waved her hand. "Very well," she said, with the air of someone humoring a child. "Lieutenant, see that it is done."

"Hardcopy evidence," Brontë said. "In my hands."

Tinsley nodded to the lieutenant, who left again. "Now," Tinsley said, and gestured toward the suite's worktable. "Shall we continue?"

Chapter 12

Pakuru Mining, Iron Mountains,
Republic Settlement Planet Durbin

No one said much for the next hour or so. Sheng was angry; Mosel was sulking; Jusuf had retreated into himself. Velocity had Uri download the files for the targets in Pakuru—the labor agent and the possible insurgent—and reviewed them for the fifth time. The labor agent, Emilie Laiso, might be behind the sleight of hand with the contract workers: padding her purchase bill by subbing in fake contracts, with fake images, and then pocketing the funds. If she wasn't, she might know who was. The possible insurgent was Yao Garcia, who had been sold to these mines six years earlier. Velocity was still brooding over the files when Mosel tapped up the screen on the front window again. "There."

Pakuru looked like a scab on the slope of the mountain, dark and crooked. Plumes of smoke rose up from it, dark smears into the darkening sky. Despite how early they had set out, it was already almost night. That was the trouble with planets: even though the distance between things was laughably small (six hundred kilometers, barely an eye blink), available transportation was so slow that it took forever to reach anything.

"Don't worry, the hostel will keep our rooms," Mosel said. He had arranged their lodging, almost certainly getting a cut of the profits. Velocity watched the mountains rising higher and higher along the horizon, thinking of Jusuf's story. The only birds on Dresden Station, where she had spent her childhood, had been tiny jewel-bright song birds, who flew free in the private Exchange held by her House. These songbirds had lived on seed grown especially for them. Anything less like a predator was hard to imagine. But when her father had taken her and her sister Alice to Earth, the great eagles and hawks drifting through the bright blue sky had formed an indelible memory. Their guide, the young woman who had taken them through both the Devastations and the Preserves, had explained that predators were vital to preserving the health of an ecosystem. Cats were just another kind of predator. Also, mice without predators were far more devastating to an ecosystem than the eagle in the story.

Not that the Combines were predators, exactly, in her opinion.

As they drew near the town, the hills grew steeper. Snow rose in great drifts, sometimes covering parts of the road. The dark sky grew darker; wind sang past the stormcraft. Once, creeping along a strip of road with mountains to one side and an immense drop down a cliff on the other, Velocity fought the urge to edge over on her seat, away from the chasm. From the back bench, Jusuf asked, "What happens if someone is coming the other way on this road?"

Mosel laughed. "That *would* be interesting." Velocity shot him a look and he laughed again. About six minutes later, as they came off that narrow strip of road, they did meet another vehicle—a towering cargo truck, heading down the mountain. Mosel pulled off to the shoulder to let it pass and grinned at Velocity.

It was full night before they reached Pakuru. Public lighting was scarce. Shadowed buildings huddled around the badly paved road. Most of the town was the mine—rhe part where people lived was shabby two- and three-story stone buildings. Sheng leaned forward as they passed the open gates to the road leading to the mine. "Will you want to talk to the miners tonight?"

Velocity glanced at her. "Won't they be asleep?"

Sheng laughed, a short ugly sound. "Mines never sleep. Second shift ends at midnight, third shift starts ten minutes to."

"What do you advise?" Velocity asked. "Tonight? Or wait until tomorrow?"

"I advise," Sheng said, imitating her accent, "you let me go in first. Test the mood."

Velocity looked out at the passing town, all the tiny, dimly lit windows. Sheng could be asking for this for perfectly legitimate reasons—it would be easier to find people without an obvious Combine citizen peering over her shoulder. Or she could be hoping to set them up. "Take Jusuf with you," she said. "Do you think you can find Yao Garcia?"

"Maybe."

"Is Garcia a member of Iron Smoke?"

"Shut up about Smoke," Sheng said. "Smoke's not your concern."

Mosel pulled up at a squat two-story stone structure. The hostel, he explained. Velocity went on inside while the others unloaded the luggage: low ceilings, small rooms, bad lighting, not to mention a muddy, gritty floor. The clerk was a contract labor worker. "Three rooms," she offered. "Upstairs back. Want meals?"

"You provide meals?" Velocity said, looking around the filthy foyer. Even if this place had a galley, she wasn't sure she wanted to eat anything prepared there.

"Fetch'em in," the clerk said. "Bit of a surcharge, but."

"We'll find our own." Velocity put her thumb print on the port. "Baths?"

The clerk grinned. She was fifteen or so, and skinny, her hair shaved close. The grin lit her face. "Baths," she said, like that was the best joke ever.

"What about the Pakuru Offices? How far away are they?"

"Out there," the clerk said, "turn left. Two buildings down."

Upstairs, the rooms were as damp and cold as the lobby had

been, and nearly as dirty. The floor gritted beneath her boots, and the bedding on the bunk was limp with use. Velocity dumped her baggage in one corner and stood looking about herself. They'd all end up with lice. She reached out to Uri: *We're in the hostel, which is a pit. How's Tai doing?*

No reply. She pinged him again. Still nothing. Frowning she brought up the trouble screen. Big red bar across the Access button. "Mercredi," Velocity muttered, and opened the room's sole locker. A fat beetle scuttled frantically in one corner, and then shoved itself through a crack and out of sight. Velocity muttered again, and Uri said, *Trouble?*

There you are. What's the glitch with the link?

This planet and its satellites, Uri said. *Theoretically your geo has access. In fact, the access is spotty and overloads easily.*

Charming. Velocity hunted a thermal jersey from her luggage, one that Jusuf had bought in the city, and pulled it on. *Sheng's gone looking for Garcia. We'll get dinner. Start feeling out the town. How's Tai doing?*

He's asleep. Rida has some possibly relevant information. Uri added a brief report on a contact Rida had made, while out on the station—a free labor deckhand, Perth, who said his ship was exporting contract workers.

From Durbin? Velocity frowned.

It does seem odd, the dagan agreed. *I'm looking for more data. Rida is going to speak further with the deckhand.*

Let me know what you find, Velocity said, and broke the connection.

ꝏ ⴕ ꕵ

The next morning, after having breakfasted with sour soup at a teashop, Velocity made her way to the local offices of Pakuru Mining. The pretext for her appointment with Emilie Laiso was to discuss purchasing options, pursuant to setting up a trade syndicate.

It was still early morning at these latitudes. Sunlight glittered on frozen puddles; snow squeaked dry under her boots. The cold air hurt her nose. But she found it was easier for her to walk the hundred-some meters up the street than it had been when they first landed. Her body was adjusting, just as the Pirians had promised. As she entered the offices, she opened her uplink and posted to Uri: *Any unusual behavior from Laiso?*

She ran a search on you and on your ship, but that's to be expected. She didn't penetrate our cover. Also she ran a security check on her own banks.

Which was also to be expected. *Did she pick up your ferret?*
Psh.

Emilie Laiso was around fifty universal years old, squat and heavily built, with a thick-boned face and shoulder-length grey streaked hair. Her mouth was set in an unhappy droop. She looked Velocity over, her small eyes shrewd. "We ran your history," she said, without offering a word of greeting. "You don't have a license to trade on Durbin."

"That's not the case," Velocity said, settling onto the uncomfortable metal bench which was the only seating for guests in the office. Since Laiso had run a search on her, she knew this was chaff. Laiso was testing her temper. "We have an adjunct trade license, authorized by Ikeda-Verde Combine. Also, I'm scheduled to meet soon with Avril Drury, clerk to your Minister of Trade."

Laiso's frown deepened. "Agricultural chemicals are your main interest. Is that correct?"

"Agricultural chemicals, along with certain industrial elements, including molybdenum. That's your main production line here in Pakuru, molybdenum, right?"

"What does Ikeda-Verde need with our mining production? From what I understand, your Combine has entire star systems dedicated to the production of their supply chains."

"We're an adjunct of Ikeda-Verde. Not out of the Combine itself. It's a mutually beneficial arrangement. The Combine has no access to trade opportunities in the Drift. And yet there is a rich market there, stations and very new, very hungry planets. Positioned as Durbin is, close to the Drift, trade with your mines would also be mutually beneficial."

"You're Free Trade."

"We're an adjunct of Ikeda-Verde Combine," Velocity repeated, but twitched her mouth briefly, in what was not quite a smirk. Laiso snorted. Technically, it was prohibited for Combine planets to engage in trade with Free Trade merchants, especially since Freets were well-known conduits to Pirian goods and—more importantly—Pirian tech. But given the steep tariff on goods imported by the Combines, almost everyone in the Deep dealt with Free Traders.

For Laiso, an added bonus would be that she could claim to have paid Combine prices for whatever tech Velocity offered in trade, and pocket the difference. And if she was already padding her purchase orders with fictive contract workers, this would especially appeal to her. A sure truth Velocity had learned in her years dealing with Republic bureaucracy was that once someone started skimming, no amount of ill-gotten profit was ever enough. Clearing her throat, she added: "We may also be able to supply workers at less than your current costs."

Laiso shrugged. "We're happy with our current supply chain."

"Five percent less."

"Five percent," Laiso said, interested, and then swiftly shaped her expression into scorn. "Five percent won't cover the costs of changing suppliers."

Cover the bribes, she meant. Velocity knew it would more than cover those bribes, which would, after all, be a one-time cost. But she added, "Also, we can promise that at least forty percent of those we supply will be experienced mine workers."

"We'll need a ten percent reduction. Fifteen percent off the first five hundred."

"Eight percent," Velocity said. "Ten percent off the first hundred."

"Forty percent of them experienced miners. That's likely."

"If I can't meet your inventory needs, you'll get the first shipment half price."

Laiso shut up, her eyes widening. There was silence while she calculated the amount she would save on five hundred mine workers if she only had to pay half-price for them. And if she didn't tell the Combine she was getting them half-price, all that savings would land in her personal coffers. "That is…an attractive offer." She paused. "If we do agree to trade in such an irregular fashion, we'd have to add a surcharge to our own prices. You understand."

Never enough. Velocity just nodded. "We can work with that. Meanwhile, would it be possible to see a record of your production runs and the quantities you could supply? Maybe a tour of your physical plant?"

⬩ ⬩ ⬩

Having made an appointment with Laiso to go through the plant that afternoon, Velocity was left with the rest of the morning to explore this filthy little mining town. Opening her uplink, she sent a post to Uri: *Monitor Laiso. Capture her posts over the next forty hours.*

No reply. Velocity squinted at the sky, as if spotting the satellite would sharpen the connection. Uri would almost certainly monitor Laiso without being specifically told to do so. If the access glitch didn't keep him from doing so. She started down the icy street toward the hostel, considered joining Sheng and Jusuf; but first, Sheng would disapprove, and second, Sheng would be right.

Captain?

There you are. She repeated the instructions to monitor Laiso.

Capture set up, Uri said. *But if she runs searches when the link is down, we'll have to hope she doesn't run incognito.*

Do what you can. Have you gotten access to her banks?

Hours ago. Security protocols here are a joke. Last upgrade was six years ago.

Velocity spotted the teashop near the hostel. It was as grubby as everything else in this town seemed to be, but her breakfast had been edible. The tables had also been crowded with free labor, probably drawn by the low prices. While free labor were unlikely to involve themselves in an insurgency, they were an excellent conduit for gossip.

She angled toward the shop while Uri reported on what he'd found in Laiso's bank—nothing conclusive; if she was running fake contracts, she didn't store the data there. *But I might have found something else on that,* he added. *I isolated the contracts with duplicated images. There were three thousand one hundred seven-eight of those. I sorted them using several qualifiers, hunting for an increase in odds that a given file was either Pirian or an Ikan16. The only success I had was minor—I sorted by date of sale, and isolated seven hundred and three of the files that fit the parameter.*

Right, Velocity said patiently. She knew how Uri, like Rida, went on for hours when they started on search tactics—what they had tried, what had worked, what hadn't, what they might try next, what they probably wouldn't.

That was still too many to investigate effectively, unless we increase our footprint on the planet. So Rida and I have been trying to build a more effective search. Rida suggested we try sorting via vendors—both point of sale and second and third level vendors.

This meant not just who sold them locally, on Durbin, Velocity knew, but who had sold them to the local labor agents. *Right,* she said again.

That got us a match, and a manageable pool of possible Ikan16s, Uri said. *One specific vendor, and twenty-nine probable contract workers. We also found thirty-seven probable Pirians, using the same sorting process.*

Velocity had been about to enter the teashop. She stopped where she was, her hand on the door. *Did you sort the Pirian matches against the Ikan16s?*

We did. That gave us three places of sale.

Is one of them Pakuru?

One of them is Pakuru, Uri confirmed. Someone was trying to come out of the teashop. Velocity stepped back, out of their way, her head lowered, thinking this over. *Should I send you the files that match?* Uri asked. *None of them are listed under our target names, obviously, but they do have the contract numbers and names each worker was sold under. The one in Pakuru was sold under the name Elian Scott.*

That would at least give her names to ask for. *Send them,* she said. Nothing. *Uri?* Still nothing. She checked the connection and saw a red bar across it again. Huffing with annoyance, she went on into the teashop, found a booth, and ordered tea and salt biscuits from the free labor child on the counter. A moment later, her access went live again. *Uri?*

Here.

Send the files. And see if you can find a way around these dropped connections.

Chapter 13

**Aboard Castillo Mining Platform HLC116,
Castillo Mines, the Drift**

While Brontë negotiated with Director General Tinsley, Security took Adder and Ruçar down the corridor and locked them in a service-level tea kit. Beyond the galley, it had a single sticky table, metal benches, and an oubliette. The deck was filthy, and the bulkheads stained and scabby. Adder made them black tea, mixing in lots of sugar, while Ruçar sliced up the remains of a plum cake and ran it through the grill. "This says butter," he said, of a gritty substance in a tin. "Maybe we'll have jam instead?"

"Is there jam?"

"There's lemon marmalade."

They sat side by side at the table, dipping cake into a bowl of the syrupy marmalade. "I lost Wolf during the coup," Adder said. "I thought Theo might have him for a time, but our intel says a labor agent sold both him and Ian to Anderson Mining, on Wellington. We tracked Wolf there, or at least we tracked his contract there. We didn't find him. Ian never made it to Wellington. He was sold to another consortium, one that provides labor to asteroid mines out in the Deep. Like this one." She paused. "I was hoping he was here."

Ruçar shook his head. "I haven't seen either of them since we got sold out of the House. But I haven't been here that long. They had me on Bastiat-1. Working the hoppers there." Adder muttered an evil word under her breath, and he glanced at her. "What?"

"Nothing. Brontë and Captain Anador were *on* Bastiat-1. When were you there?"

"Until a few months ago." Ruçar twitched his shoulders in what wasn't quite a shrug. "I couldn't have gotten a post through anyway. No access for chips." He licked marmalade off his fingers and got up to slice more cake. Once it was in the grill, he turned to see Adder frowning at him. "What?"

"You *just* got sold out here? You were at Bastiat-1 most of the past three years?"

"Why not?" Ruçar turned to take the cake from the grill.

"Lots of contract labor from Bastiat-1 were sold out here? Or just you?"

He brought the plate of cake back over to her. "Just me. Why?"

"That's when we got our information about you being sold here. A little over two months ago." Adder thought this over. It could be just happenstance. They'd gotten the information about Ruçar then because that was when he'd been sold. So that was when the clerk captured the image of him being loaded into the labor agent's ship.

"What are you doing way out here?" Ruçar asked, dunking a bit of cake in the marmalade. "What's *Brontë* doing out here?"

Adder explained, briefly. Since they were almost certainly being monitored, she left out the power struggle between Brontë and her mother—Dr. Isra Ikeda Lopaka, Brontë's mother, was a director in the Calypso project. She also had to leave out the Calypso Project. So the story was short on details. As she talked, Ruçar leaned into her. She leaned back, loving the warmth of his body next to hers, his smell, his strength, his self that was as much her own self as her own body. "I'm sorry we took so long to find you," she said, rubbing her head against his shoulder. He was so starved she could feel the tendons and bones under his skin. "We never stopped looking."

"I know," he said, and she knew he meant it, but she knew his voice and his body and the breath that came from his lungs as well as she knew her own: she felt his anger. Under the table, she slid her arm around his waist. They were still like this, resting against each other, when the hatch to the room opened, and Brontë stepped inside. The Security flanking the hatchway allowed her in; they didn't move away, though, or put their sticks back in their holsters, not the entire time the hatch was open, and not while it was sliding shut.

Once it was shut, Brontë came to sit across the table from them. Her face was set into an indifferent mask; but she was pale, her pupils so wide her flame-blue eyes looked dark. She was looking at some space beyond the two of them, her eyes fixed on some interior scene. Grim and pale like this, her resemblance to the Ikan16s was even more apparent than usual. At length, she spoke, "This woman, Tinsley. She's…"

"Scum?" Adder supplied.

Brontë focused on her abruptly, and smiled. "Connected," she said, flicking her gaze quickly around the room. She went on, speaking clearly for the feed: "She knows a great deal about Ikeda House, and its research interests. The Calypso project in particular." She paused, glancing at Adder, making sure she registered the use of that forbidden name, and then continued: "Tinsley proposes we work together. She helps us recover Wolf and Ian. We help her—*I* help her, via my authority as heir to the Primary Seat—in recovering other Calypsos. She knows, or thinks she knows, the location of at least ten Calypsos. These Calypsos, excluding Wolf and Ian, become her property."

"What's she plan to do, once she has them?" Adder said.

Brontë spread her hand at the room, or probably actually the mining platform, around them. "This is the Drift. She can do as she likes."

Reverse engineering? But it didn't matter. Adder knew Brontë, and she knew Brontë would never let Tinsley have anyone from their House, much less the Calypsos, who were her own blood and bone. "How long has Tinsley known about the Calypso project?"

Brontë grimaced, her eyelids shuttering her gaze. Adder suspected she was thinking of Isra, her mother. Her cousin Theo, current Primary Seat Holder of Ikeda House, was connected to Hayek-Lopaka Combine through Hayek House; Isra was connected through Lopaka House. The Atlas Society, which had created the Calypso project, was an intra-House Society. It was not unlikely that there were members in both Lopaka and Hayek House. So why was Tinsley, whose bond was held by Hayek House, going to such lengths to acquire Calypsos? Hayek House would have its own Calypsos. Why acquire those sold off by another House? *Something here we don't understand*, Adder thought. *Something not clear.*

"Tinsley says she's traced several Calypso males," Brontë said, "one of them Wolf, to a planet called Durbin, over in the Republic."

Adder, startled out of thought, looked at Brontë. "Durbin."

"We're leaving here next watch. For Durbin. I'll help Tinsley requisition the Calypsos. If I can pull that off, she says, we'll renegotiate further."

"That sounds reasonable," Adder said, trying to keep her voice even.

Brontë glanced at Ruçar, probably warning him not to object. Under the table, Adder was squeezing his waist, for the same reason. "Yes," Brontë said. "That's what I thought too."

Chapter 14

Tauranga City, Republic Settlement Planet Durbin

have an idea, Rida posted him. *We need to collect samples for the Pirian gengineers. What if I come down to the planet for, like, ten or twelve watches? Get started on that?*

And then you just stay? Tai replied. *And the Captain won't notice?*

Not like I'm doing any good up here.

Over in Pirian space, planets were 'troped by taking samples of indigenous plants and rebuilding these into species that could form an ecological network with earth-source plants and animals, including humans. A similar practice was used in Republic space, but Republic law considered such rebuilds proprietary knowledge. This allowed the Combines that developed them to charge settlement planets steep licensing fees for their use. In Pirian space, genetic rebuilds were open code. True, you needed a certain level of knowledge and technology to be able to use that code, but Pirians would help you acquire both.

Not much to sample, Tai sent, *at least around here. This is the closest thing to bare rock I've ever seen people try to live on. Maybe down on the islands they've done more, but here it's all ice and bricks. Anyway, I thought you were working that jess. Perth. What happened to that?*

He's free labor, not contract labor. And nothing. I think he wants to fuck me.

Who could blame him? Are you going to do it?

He's not very tasty. Also, he knows less about his ship than I do.

Uri cut into their channel: *Velocity sends a request.*

Tai knew Uri could monitor their feed, and in some sense always was monitoring their feed, but it was annoying to be reminded of it. Rankled, he send back a sharper reply than he might otherwise have: *What now?*

Uri explained that the Captain wanted Tai to follow up on a possible positive, found with the new search qualifiers, near Tauranga City: a contract worker who might be a missing Pirian. *How near is near?* Tai asked.

Ninety-two kilometers. Uri loaded a map. Like most planetary ports, Tauranga City had been built near a sizable body of water, in this case one of Durbin's several oceans. Uri circled a coastal village, west and south of the city. *A factory town. Velocity says you should take Quinn as your guide.*

Right. Because a street thief would be an expert on contract labor factories. For a moment, Tai thought he'd subvocced this; but Uri said nothing. While he was waiting for the comment that didn't come, he had a spark of an idea. *Rida should come down.*

I should! Rida said, and then added, *Why?*

It's a factory, Tai said innocently. *I might need help cracking their banks.*

I'll try that with Velocity, Uri said dryly. *But given we can tunnel through their shieldwalls from here just as easily as downplanet, I'm not hopeful.*

Tai wasn't either, but at least Rida would think he was trying. He paused, hoping he hadn't subvocced *that*, and then rolled to his feet. *I'll hunt up the street thief.*

ෆ ෑ ౿

Using a link Mosel sent back from Pakuru, Tai rented a stormcraft, and he and Quinn drove down to the Opotiki Water Treatment

Center, a journey of just over a hundred kilometers. The roads were terrible. The stormcraft had GPS, fortunately, or he'd have been lost more than once. As it was, it took them nearly three hours to get from the city to the coast.

The Opotiki Water Treatment Center had started as a complex that manufactured potable water for Tauranga City and for any ships landing at its port. Over the centuries, though, the Center branched out, using its contract workers to drain the swamps, creating a landfill along the wetland's northwest boundary, constructed from rotting fiberboard baskets filled with swamp mud. This land, once it had dried and solidified a bit, was leased to Durbin's growing contingent of agricultural miners. These miners had extracted agricultural chemicals from the mud and then had dumped the slag back into the ground, leaving behind a barren grey plain. Lately, fish farmers had built immense oversized greenhouses on this plain, where they raised Earth-source salmon and whitefish, as well as fast-growing greens and legumes on the nutrients created by growing and harvesting the fish.

The result was a dismal landscape filled with hulking harvester bots, gargantuan fish farms, and grimy rows of barracks constructed from repurposed shipping containers. Blue and green tarps had been wrapped around these containers, probably for insulation. The tarps flapped raucously in the wind off the bay. Off some distance from the water treatment center, Tai could see contract workers in the swamps (the mudyards, he would learn these were called). Despite the icy wind, they were coatless, their scanty clothing patched and ragged, their shaved heads bared to the weather. He stood a moment watching them dredging muck from the swamp bottom with what looked like shallow bowls, pouring the slime they pulled up with these into giant sacks floating on barge-like wooden boats.

The stink from the mudyards mixed with the stink of the fish farms, creating a stench that burned Tai's eyes and clung to the back of his throat. Once they were in Opotiki's main administration complex, the smell wasn't quite as strong. Tai asked the Security officer at the front desk how people stood the stink, and the Security officer laughed, showing great white teeth. "Smells like money!"

The Security officer gave them to a contract child named Simei, who led them through the complex. Tai had bought fancy dress from Emma's rebuild shop, giving himself the appearance of a wealthy merchant from the Drift; he had also bought Quinn a nice jacket and jersey. Now she looked less like a gutter thief and more like a local kid working for a wealthy off-planet merchant, earning money to pay her school fees.

The contract worker, Simei, was barely older than Quinn, and much skinnier. Bones showed knobby at her jaw and wrists. Also, she was filthy, her skin grey with months of dirt. Having sent Quinn a few sideways glances, Simei spoke not to her, but to Tai: "You hunt somebot? I know racks. Send message?"

Tai didn't answer. He did note, however, that the jess communication network was running at its usual efficiency. They were passing through a long corridor, its walls fiberboard, its floors bare metal. The light came from slap-ups, squares of solar-powered material stuck haphazardly to the walls, their glow spotty and yellow. When they reached the door to the labor agent's suite of offices, Tai said, "Quinn. Wait out here, please."

Quinn settled next to Simei, both sitting on their heels against the wall. As if neither of them were of any interest to him, Tai went inside, tugging shut the badly-made fiberboard door at his back. Corvo had believed it likely that they could buy access to the contract worker in question; and, if the worker turned out to be one of their missing Pirians, just buy her contract. This was the Siji's preferred method of rescue. Bribes were cheaper than bullets, they said. Having been subject to labor agents for most of his life until Velocity took him off that filthy station, Tai was dubious. But even he was taken aback by the vehemence with which this particular labor agent, Aimie Waifu, refused his bribe. Waifu wasn't the actual labor agent: just a free labor assistant. Nearly as skinny as the contract child outside, she wore a grimly respectable work suit. Her long pale hair was thin, and her skin spotty.

"I only want to speak to the worker," Tai told her, following the script Corvo had given him. "She may not even be the person we are looking for. If she is, the bounty will be sizeable. Enough that we would gladly share a percentage with anyone who had proved helpful."

Waifu went blotchy with anger. "This isn't the Drift. Not everything is for sale here."

"Not what I meant," Tai said, though it was exactly what he had meant.

"These are *criminals*. They have been convicted of *crimes*. You won't help one of them escape her punishment because she has wealthy parents. Not through *my* efforts."

This was a common belief in Republic space—that the contract labor system was justice being served, punishment for crimes committed. It wasn't always untrue. Tai had known people convicted into the system for assault, theft, even murder. But most people in the system landed there for 'crimes' like Unreasonable Debt, which was his own crime—he'd been an illegal child, sent to an orphanage after his mother's conviction. That meant he owed the state the cost of raising him until he was old enough to sell. If you could call what had happened to him being raised. "I'm not an agent of her parents," Tai said. "I work for her ship. They educated her. The expense of that education was sizable, and the ship feels they have a right to recoup their costs."

These lines were also from Corvo's script. It was a script that worked well in other rescues, she claimed. Waifu, however, just snorted. "Education. If that bot has education in anything except whining, I'd like to know about it."

"Environmental science related to maintaining a shipboard

ventilation system," Tai said. "It is unlikely she has had a chance practice her skills at…this facility."

Waifu snorted again. Their discussion went back and forth for several more minutes, but in the end Tai gained nothing, not even an agreement to think this proposal over and send him a post if she changed her mind.

Outside, Simei rose up at once to escort them out. Tai waited until he and Quinn were well away from the complex, almost to the stormcraft they had hired to drive out from the city. "Well?" he asked.

Quinn had tucked her keffiyeh over the lower half of her small face, probably hoping to cut the stink from the swamps, but her eyes narrowed with delight. "Tonight," she said. "Seventeen hundred hours."

ᘓ ᛐ ᘓ

They could have driven back to the city to sleep—even with the terrible roads, it was within reach. But Uri had hired them a box for the next three days. Tai hoped it wouldn't take that long to accomplish their task, especially after seeing the hostel. It was one of several scattered buildings huddled along a muddy metaled road, no more than half a kilometer from the mudyards. This was well in sight of the factory and its barracks, and also well within their stink.

Like the barracks, the hostel was constructed of repurposed shipping crates. Uri had gotten them the best room, which was two crates stacked one on top of the other. However, it had insulation, bunks, and a tea kit. Quinn went scrambling up the ladder to investigate the beds; Tai locked the door and settled on the sofa to pull off his boots. His mood was dark. He knew this wasn't just from dealing with the clerk, or just this horrible place, just the filthy jesses in the mudyards, just that skinny child who probably thought herself lucky (as he had thought himself lucky) to be given a post working with the bosses. Today certainly was terrible; but ever since they'd come here, he had been feeling worse and worse. *Spoiled*, he thought to himself. *All those years on the **Susan Calvin**, being treated like a human being with human rights. All that time with the Pirians. You forgot who you were.*

Quinn slid down the ladder. "Hot water!" she announced happily, and went to poke her head in the galley lockers. "Not much here. Tea and noodles. Maybe I go for supplies?"

"Let's see your stick," he said, and when she dug out her data-tag loaded thirty riyals in local funds on it. "Just get the basics for tonight and breakfast tomorrow. If we end up staying longer, I'll send you out again."

"Yes, boss."

Tai frowned at being called a boss, but didn't argue. "Get figcake if they have it."

"Yes, boss," Quinn agreed and headed out. He locked the door at her back and went to investigate the facility. The shower did indeed have hot water. Not very hot. Moodily, he pulled off his shirt.

When he emerged, feeling not much cleaner—the water stank of metal and organics, and left a starchy film on his skin—Quinn was banging on the door. Drying his hair with a threadbare towel, he went to let her in. She had a large fiberboard box under her arm. "They had shipmeals!" she said, as if this were a delightful surprise.

Hiding his grimace, Tai locked the door again and went to investigate the box she was unpacking. Shipmeals, in their biodegradable fiber packets. Tinned water. Five packets of freeze-dried fruit, sugar, cream, figcake. He pulled out the cream and turned the tin in his hand. No list of ingredients, of course, not here in the Republic. It was almost certainly not actual cream. Probably some local oil, mixed with sugars and chalk. "Do you want me to heat you a shipmeal?" Quinn asked eagerly. "I got chicken and fish. Two each."

"I'm not hungry," Tai said. The stink was killing his appetite. "You go ahead."

Her eyes sparking with glee, Quinn pulled out the chicken meal and ripped it open. These were the better grade of shipmeals, which contained a main dish and a packet of dried fruit or vegetables, along with some sort of dessert, usually taffy or hard candy, since the meals were made to be eaten in microgravity. Quinn stuck the main dish, pepper chicken with rice, into the tiny galley oven and hit MEAL on the controls. While the oven hummed, she opened the dessert, a nut toffee, and crunched into it.

Tai climbed to the second floor and hunted out a thermal shirt from his baggage. The "suite" was heated by thermal strips running along the walls. It was warmer than their rooms at Yadav's, just barely. Stretching out on one of the bunks, he pinged Rida, and they posted back and forth for a time. Toward the end, Tai shared his insight about why his mood was so dark lately. *I should be there with you*, Rida fretted.

Then we could both suffer. Tai made an effort to wrench himself up from self-pity. *Probably won't be much longer. We've got a link already, this skinny jess. She's coming by in*—he checked the time on his port—*shit, now.*

Signing off with Rida, he went downstairs to find Quinn already gone. He switched on the kettle in the galley, and hunted out a teapot. The only tea available was white, in little paper packets. He made it anyway. While it was still brewing, the door scraped open and Quinn brought in Simei, along with another jess, a young woman so obviously Pirian, despite her filthy clothing and shaved head, that Tai let out a startled, "Hey!"

The Pirian smiled wearily and said, in Pirian, "Itoko did send you, then?"

Tai replied in his substandard Pirian: "Is so. We come for help you."

Her smile widened. "We'll use Public."

Tai laughed. "I'm Tai. Are you Te Huna Sulavee?"

"Call me Huna. What ship is yours?"

"The *Susan Calvin*. The *Sungai* sent us, though."

Quinn had led Simei to the galley, where they were both eating packets of dried fruit. Seeing their bright-eyed attention, Tai switched back to Pirian: "This words better. Not all cousins here."

"I understand," Huna said gravely, also in Pirian. "Tell me what happens next."

Limited by his command of Pirian, Tai explained as best he could what the *Susan Calvin* had been sent here to do, including the rescue of Pirians sold into contract labor, like Huna. Tai was not convinced he'd be able to purchase Huna's contract. His idea was that she should just kite out at this point. "Our ship is own landing craft," he explained. "We drop her down, take you up."

He was pinging Uri, to ask how long it would take to fire up the runabout, when Huna said, "While I would like very much to leave this place, others remain."

Tai glanced at her. "Others? Other Pi—other itoko?"

"Others who have become cousins."

Uri spoke through the netbot: *Tai?*

Hold, Tai subvocced. "Others?" he asked Huna. "How much?" Though he would happily help anyone—everyone, if he had his wish— escape from contract labor, the *Susan Calvin* didn't have unlimited environmental resources.

"My work crew. Nine of us. Ten with me. And this child here," Huna added, nodding toward Simei, who was drinking sugary tea with Quinn.

Tai sent Uri a brief report, mainly to give himself time to think. Eleven from here, along with the other Pirians, assuming they could find them, was about six too many. "We here bring *you* back," he told Huna.

"I will not leave cousins in this place, whether they were born to the Fleet or not."

Tai stood staring at her. Skinny, filthy, dressed in ragged canvas trousers and a too-large thermal shirt, she stared straight back at him. *Uri*, he subvocced. *We may have an issue.*

Chapter 15

Aboard the *Prince of Peace*, en route to Durbin, the Drift

They left the mining platform aboard a Combine-held courier ship, the *Prince of Peace*. Brontë had spent the past four years of her life on one deep-space vessel or another—mostly the *Susan Calvin*. And before that, she had spent several months on cruiser held by her own house, Ikeda House. All of this turned out to be very different from being a prisoner on a ship held by another Combine.

Not that Lamont was so indelicate as to call her a prisoner, or to lock her in the brig. In fact, she and the two Ikans were given the prime stateroom in the *Prince of Peace*—far better accommodations than the cabin Lamont herself had claimed. But six Hayek-Lopaka Security officers had come aboard with them, and at least one of these was on constant duty in the corridor outside their stateroom. If Brontë went anywhere, even if it was just down the corridor to the exercise pit, another Security was down her neck before she had gone two steps.

Also, Brontë had wormed her way through the ship's shieldwalls almost immediately, so she knew about the multiple feeds in this fancy stateroom—two in each bedroom, three in the common room, one in the facility. The rest of the ship had similar levels of surveillance. She spent the remainder of the first jump building a fuzzy loop that she could key up as necessary, to give her, Adder, and Ruçar six and a half minutes of unmonitored time in the common room whenever they needed it. Then she called a meeting and used the loop to tell them about the feeds. "Be more of a surprise if they weren't spying on us," Adder said.

"I could do something about it," Ruçar said.

"No, let's leave it," Brontë said. "Let them think they have us monitored. If we want to take the feeds out later, we have that option then."

"Taking out feeds isn't what I meant," Ruçar said. "You don't slap people down, they come twice as hard next time. Learned that fast in the mines."

Brontë glanced at Adder, who shrugged minutely. "Well, let's keep that option in reserve," Brontë said. "I'm thinking more of a silk glove approach. We cozy up with some of the Security and crew. Not Lamont, obviously." Brontë paused, noting that time on their loop was about to run out, and hit the toggle on her dock screen that started it running again. She waited to be sure the loop had started over, then added, "The ship's boy, for instance. Hwang. He looks lonely. One of us could befriend him."

"One of us me," Adder said dryly, "or one of us you?"

Brontë grinned. "He'd believe it better out of you. I'll try the pilot. Ruçar, you try one of the Security."

Ruçar shrugged. "If that's how you want to play it."

"What's wrong with you?" Adder demanded. "Why are you talking this way to her?"

"To her?" Ruçar mimicked. "To our *sister*, do you mean? How should I talk to our *sister*, who sold me to the mines?"

Adder half-rose from her bench; Brontë put a hand on her shoulder, keeping her seated. "It's all right," she said. "Ruçar, it's all right. I'd be angry too."

Ruçar gave her a sullen look, and looked away. "How would you know? No one would ever sell you. Not to the mines or anywhere."

"My mother built me to be her tool," Brontë said, "same as she did you. She put me on a ship where she knew odds were I'd be killed in the coup. Maybe she hasn't sold me, but I'm her property, same as you."

He made a spitting sound. "No one's going to put my ass in a Board Seat."

"Nor mine," Brontë said, "unless I fight my way there." He gave her the sullen look again, and she saw it wasn't really sullen, exactly. Something meaner and harder was at its core, like a hot chip of steel. Tucking that away to think about later, she said, "How do you think we should approach the Security officers, if not by befriending them?"

Ruçar shrugged. "I'd drag them down to the hold and interrogate them with Veritas. Or my fists. But we can try it your way if you like."

Brontë glanced at Adder, who was expressionless. "Let's try my way first."

"Suit yourself," Ruçar said and rolled to his feet, heading for the facility. Adder went after him. The hatch shut, and Brontë heard the lock snick home. She sat brooding, watching the shut hatchway, until the loop ran down. Then she restarted it and opened the files she had downloaded from her tag, which had been returned to her as they were leaving the mining platform. As far as she could tell, no one had gotten past her passwords: the information she had stolen from the banks at the mining platform should still be valid.

The stolen files held hundreds of labor contracts, all containing medical records, productivity records, and disciplinary records. She had spent most of a watch sorting the data via various search strings, and come up with nothing interesting. In the middle of afterwatch, though, while she was trying to sleep, she'd had the idea to search the disciplinary records. While it was true the Ikan16s had nearly perfect records, aside from some minor incidents when they were in the six-to-nine cohort, most Calypsos needed constant discipline. This was especially true of Calypso males, which was why Ikeda House had elected to sell them out to the Deep.

She sorted the discipline records by number of incidents per universal month, then began selecting and reading the files of each male on the far end of the curve. It was slow going, mainly because the misconduct of the workers she was reading about kept bringing to mind Ruçar's actions. But in time, she began selecting files into lists of "possibles" and "probables" using date of sale, general phenotype, and specifics of their misconduct as her sorting terms. It would have been much easier if their files contained genetic sets; but the names linked to the contract numbers at least gave her data to search with, if and when she ever had access to Combine House banks again.

After about an hour, Adder and Ruçar emerged from the facility. "We're going to get started on Hwang," Adder said, "and the Security."

Brontë very politely did not look up. "Sounds good," she said, and kept her attention on her dock until they were gone.

ඊ ⱦ ᪣

Durbin was eleven jumps out from Castillo Mining Platform. Authorized to expend extra fuel, which allowed them to make the journey at moderate speed, Lamont was taking them at one-fifth push most of the way, accelerating into jumps and decelerating out of them. This would cut their travel time from nearly a universal year to six weeks.

Adder spent time between jumps teaching Shtai to Hwang, the ship's mate, a skinny kid whose contract claimed he was thirteen universal years old. She hadn't spent more than an hour with him before she knew ten years was more likely. No one had ever taught him anything, not even how to button his collar properly. He was pathetically eager to be taught. He wasn't very good at Shtai, being clumsy and slow, and also about six years too old to starting learning the art; but since her real aim wasn't to teach him, or at least not to teach him Shtai, she didn't worry.

While they did the slow parts, the stretching and the long holds, and also afterwards, in the sauna, she chatted with him in apparent idleness, asking about his past—how he'd ended up the system, the orphanage where he'd been raised, how he liked serving on the *Prince of Peace*. His story was the usual one: an illegal birth resulting in conviction as a newborn; a childhood in a station crèche; sold as soon as he was tall enough to pass for twelve. He liked the ship well enough. "Plenty of food here," he said, "and mostly no one hurts me."

"Mostly?" Adder said. They were in the sauna. Hwang glanced away, shrugging. She looked over his wiry body, checking for bruises and scars. He had plenty of old scars, the sort any child raised in Republic-run orphanage would have. Nothing fresh, and no new bruises. "You tell me if anyone hurts you," she told him. "I'll sort it. You hear?"

He gave her a shy look, and then a shyer grin. "What you do?" he asked. "Bust heads?"

She grinned back at him. "I'll sort it. You never mind how."

He laughed and got up, moving to the sluice pipe. She noticed he didn't agree to tell her if anyone gave him trouble. Not that she blamed him. She was here for six weeks, and then gone from his world forever. And even during those weeks, for all her bold talk, he had to know she was as powerless as he was: a slave just like him. She watched him slide into the dryer, turn and turn under the buffeting air, and then step out into the locker space. Sighing, she got to her feet and moved to the sluice herself.

Once she had dried and dressed, she went looking for Brontë to report her progress, or rather her lack of progress. They were supposed to be getting useful information on Lamont or on some other member of the crew—something they could use as a key or, barring that, a lever. So far all she had learned was that Hwang was afraid of someone or someones on the ship. Neither surprising nor useful.

The *Prince of Peace* was large for a courier ship, with multiple decks, including three full decks of berths. The exercise pit and sauna were in the lower decks. Adder climbed up the aft ladder to Second Deck, where their stateroom was located. She passed Third Deck on the way—that was where Security and the ship's crew had their cabins—and glanced absently down the corridor. What she saw froze her in place for one sharp second.

Then she swung off the ladder into Third Deck and hurried down the corridor. Ruçar had Orrick, the youngest of the Security officers, pinned against hatch of a cabin, holding her in place by her collar and a fistful of her upper arm. Orrick's widened eyes rolled toward Adder. "What are you doing?" Adder hissed.

"Making a request," Ruçar said. "One this gutter pup will be happy to comply with. Isn't that so, pup?"

Adder gripped Ruçar's wrist, but his muscles were like iron, and as immovable as iron. "Have you lost your wits?"

Ruçar gave the Security officer's collar a twist. "Have I lost my wits, puppy?" Orrick's eyes rolled toward Adder again, and fast as a slap Ruçar slammed her head into the hatch behind her. "What was that?" he said. "What did you say?"

"N-nothing!" Orrick said. "No! You haven't!"

"That's right. I haven't. And you'll bring me the code. Won't you?"

"I will," Orrick said, and when he drew her close said it louder, "I will!"

"Good pup." Ruçar let her go, giving her round cheek a little pat. "Run along, pup."

Adder expected the Security officer to duck into the cabin, but instead she scrambled down the corridor, flung a glance over her shoulder, and plummeted down the ladder. When she had vanished out of sight, Adder wheeled back to Ruçar. "What are you thinking?" she demanded, and then locked her teeth together hard. She couldn't remember where the feed was on this corridor. Still gripping his wrist, she towed him to the ladder and up to their stateroom, where she hauled out her dock and activated the loop.

"What?" Ruçar said, amused. "You don't think I took care of that?"

"How do I know?" Adder demanded. "If you'll assault a Security officer in a public corridor, who knows what other risks you'll take?"

He snorted and flung himself down on the chaise-longue. "Risk. What risk? You think that quivering noodle is going to turn on me?"

Brontë came warily from her bedroom. "What happened?"

Adder stared at Ruçar, whose expression of amused contempt did not shift. As briefly as possible, Adder told Brontë what she had witnessed. Brontë frowned. "This is the Security cadet? Orrick? What codes are you trying to get from her?"

"Trying, nothing. I'll get them." Ruçar leaned back, stretching out his legs. "The override codes. The one that controls the feeds, and the one for the locks. All the locks, all over the ship. Including the weapons locker."

Brontë stood silent. Adder glanced from her to her brother and back again, uneasily. When Brontë spoke, her tone was muted. "You think Orrick will give up this code."

"I do."

"You don't think she'll go to her superior instead?" Brontë folded her arms. "Because that's what I would expect her to do."

"She won't. She knows what I would do if she did."

"If she's afraid of you," Adder said, "she's *more* likely to go to her boss. Not less."

"You don't know anything about fear," Ruçar said.

Adder looked at Brontë, who gave a minute shrug of her shoulders. "I suppose we'll find out, one way or another. If she does give up the override code," she added to Ruçar, "tell me before you do anything. Yes?"

"Oh, absolutely," Ruçar said, and gave Adder the sweetest smile.

Chapter 16

**Pakuru Mining, Iron Mountains,
Republic Settlement Planet Durbin**

A thick pelt of snow had fallen during the night. Contract workers were shoveling it from the pathways, their movements leisurely despite the bosses harassing them. Velocity glanced at each work group they passed, though she knew the odds of any worker being an Ikan16 were slim indeed. Or of her recognizing any worker as an Ikan for that matter. She wasn't certain she'd recognize Adder if she had spent two or three years in these mines.

"The barracks," Laiso said, jerking her chin toward a row of six tin buildings. Dirt and snow were heaped up in slopes around them, probably for insulation. At each end, tin pipes emitted steady streams of almost colorless smoke. Laiso gestured at another building, crosswise to the barracks. "Chow."

The stink from that building was terrible, a combination of sour rot and industrial cleaner. Velocity held her breath until they were past it and into a huge clattering shed-like building, filled with immense rolling pillars, crushing fist-sized rocks into gravel beneath their weight. Contract workers were shoveling more rocks from hoppers into the traps of these rolling pillars, or sometimes using the blades of their shovels to knock loose jammed stones. These workers had rags bound round their heads, covering their mouths and noses and shielding their ears. Velocity understood why—after only a moment in this shed, her ears felt numb from the noise, and dust filled the air, turning it hazy. Dust gritted under her boots, dust coated everything. Dust filled her throat and crunched between her teeth. Stone dust, she realized. Laiso shouted, pointing at something. Velocity shook her head to show she couldn't hear. Laiso pointed again, this time at an open doorway across the shed. Velocity followed her, squinting. The gritty air burned her eyes.

The doorway led into another warehouse-sized room, this one filled with long vats of oily water, roiled by constantly spinning wire brushes. Contract workers moved along these vats with wide cloth skimmers, dipping whatever they had skimmed into a second vat behind them, also filled with water, also being stirred with wire brushes. Velocity had no idea what any of it meant. It was quieter in here, but still too noisy for her to ask questions, even assuming she'd been planning on asking questions. Laiso led her on through this room, and then another, and then another, into a final, quieter room, where large glowing furnaces were being tended by contract workers dressed in coveralls with the tops stripped down to their waists. "Roasting room," Laiso said. "This way."

They went through yet another door, across a shed where dozens of contract workers were loading shipping crates, and into a tiny walled-off corner of that shed. Two clerks sat there, back to back at worktables, ports and wallboards open before them. Both looked up as Laiso entered. "Delia, Maple," Laiso said, "this is Captain Wrachant. She's a possible client. Answer any questions she has for you."

"Yes, mas," said the older one.

Velocity asked a number of questions, many suggested by Uri whispering through her uplink, until—*finally*—Laiso was called away to deal with an issue elsewhere. Velocity watched until she was out of earshot, and let her weight shut the door. "I was told someone here could tell me more about one of your workers. Maybe you can tell me where to find her. Yao Garcia?"

They both froze for one thump of a heartbeat. Then the older said, "I don't know that person, kas."

"You're Delia, yes? My ship is registered at a station over in the Drift. But our true home is…further out. If you know what I mean."

"I don't," Delia said. "Not at all."

"What about a contract miner named Elian? Elian Scott?"

"We don't know miners, kas. Not by name."

Velocity switched her gaze to the younger worker, Maple, who twitched. Velocity smiled. "We've got rooms at Goldie's hostel, across from that awful tea shop. I don't suppose you can recommend somewhere better to stay in town?"

Maple twitched again. Delia said firmly, "No, kas."

"Oh, well. Tell me about personnel. What labor agents do you use?"

ᘓ � ᘐ

The assistant to the Trade Minister, Odessa Lee, sent Rida a notice saying that the cargo he had ordered was arriving at thirteen thirty-five hours, shuttle bay Twelve B. "That's twenty-seven minutes from now," Uri translated helpfully. "Do you need directions to the shuttle dock?"

"I need a truck," Rida grumbled. It was the middle of afterwatch, ship's time, and he had been asleep. He sat up, reaching for his boots. "Will they have a truck at the dock?"

"Station cargo truck rentals does list an outlet at the shuttle dock," Uri said. "Shall I reserve one for you?"

When Rida arrived at the dock—an immense cavern out at the end of B spindle—he found it almost deserted. The only other person waiting was Perth. The deckhand gave him a delighted smile. "Hey! You here for the shuttle too?"

"I am." Rida went to stand next to him. The yellow lights were flashing, saying that docking was in process. "We ordered frozen fish. That's about all this place has for trade goods. And some fresh fruit, but we'll eat that. What about you?"

"Cargo," Perth said.

Rida tried to keep his expression bland. "Already? You must be shipping out soon." Contract labor workers were always the last thing loaded on a ship, since no one wanted them eating up the stores and using up the environmentals any sooner than necessary.

"Another six days. We're bringing up a hundred and fifty of them, and the local shuttles don't have much capacity."

"That doesn't sound very cost effective."

Perth shrugged. "Not my bakery, not my biscuits." He unfolded his arms and moved closer to Rida. "Hey, what about that game of slam?"

"Don't you have to meet shuttles?"

"They only run once every twenty-six hours. After this, I'm off until tomorrow."

"Sure, come by the ship. We're on the commercial dock."

"I know." Perth grinned, shooting Rida a look through his lashes.

The lights stopped flashing yellow and began flashing red, meaning the shuttle had docked. Rida looked around. *Where do they keep the trucks?* he asked Uri.

Left, thirty meters.

He went down there and keyed the ship code into the kiosk. A cargo truck beeped and backed from its charging berth, and he climbed aboard and drove it back to the bay. The door there had rolled open by the time he got back, and the pilots were already off the shuttle and hauling open the cargo hatch. Rida was a little appalled to see that the contract labor had ridden up in the hold. They climbed out: thirteen men, five women, and two children. The children were about ten years old; the adults looked no older than twenty. "Over here," Perth was shouting. "Line up, facing that way. I need to check your tags."

"Right." This was one of the men, his tone surly. "Because maybe we stowed away, hoping to get sold to some mine."

Perth slapped the back of this one's head, not especially hard. "No one said talk," he said, and held his pocket dock up to that man's shoulder. "Jasper Lewis," he read from the screen. "I see you like to cause trouble." Lewis's face was set in a sullen scowl. He didn't respond. Perth went on along the line, reading everyone's tag—the internal chip attached to their shoulder blades—and tapping his screen to check them in.

This is interesting, Uri said. *The standard shuttle run here is once every two hundred and fifty hours. The station has scheduled extra flights specifically to service the **Reynard**. To bring up these contract workers.*

Rida tried to think how much that would cost. Shuttle flights barely broke even as it was—usually they were subsidized by the Combine with the trade lease, or by one or more of a given planet's trade consortiums. Paying for special flights would add shipping costs that would price these workers out of the range of most markets. Far more than the ship could hope to recoup if these workers were really being sold to some asteroid mine. *What's the destination for these workers?*

That information is not in the banks I have accessed. However, the ship's flight plan has them jumping for the Drift.

That made sense—a lot of asteroid mining went on in the Drift, because they could sell their ore both to settlement planets in the Republic and to Pirian ships. But it didn't explain the extra expense. *Maybe get their images,* Rida told Uri.

Done, the AI replied. *I can access their files as well. Those are in the **Reynard**'s banks.*

Do that. The last of the contract workers had been tagged by Perth, and he winked goodbye at Rida before he led them toward the cargo lifts. Once they were well away, Rida powered his truck over to start loading crates of frozen fish onto its bed. One of the shuttle pilots had lingered, and now offered to help with the loading.

Lena Dilgry, Uri told him. *She's subbing in for Mosel McKay.*

The one with the Captain now?

That's the one.

Huh, Rida said. *McKay is giving up flight assignments to act as guide? The Captain must be paying him way too much.*

I'll pass that on, Uri said dryly.

"You're off the *Susan Calvin*," Dilgry said, as they strapped down the crates of fish. "I heard that you might be hiring crew."

"Not that I know of," Rida said. "Who told you that?"

Dilgry looked disappointed. "You're not hiring?"

The Captain told McKay and his co-pilot to send their information to her, Uri put in helpfully. *That's probably what she means.*

"Well, I don't get told everything," Rida said. "Are you looking to ship offplanet?"

"Get off this infested rock?" Dilgry snorted. "Listen, if you're taking on crew, you should take me, not Mosel."

"Oh?"

"He's kanji." Dilgry loaded a crate of oranges onto the truck. "Wouldn't give him the spit off my boots."

"Send me your information. I'll get it to my captain."

Dilgry brightened. "Really? Here, what's your call sign?" After Rida gave it to her, she added, "If you want, I can come help load this onto your ship with you."

Rida assured her that wasn't necessary, and added, "Hey, what do you know about those contract workers? The ones you just shipped up?"

Dilgry rubbed her hand through her short dark hair. "Just that they're off the Islands. I can find out more, though, if you want?"

"Send that along with your information," Rida said, and waved to her as he piloted the truck toward the cargo lifts.

Laiso took Velocity through the rest of the production and shipping lines, down into one mining shaft, then back to the offices, to a meeting room where they met with someone Laiso introduced as Pakuru's top financial advocate. They spent two hours wrangling over a boilerplate labor contract they might use if they agreed on terms for a deal. Velocity enjoyed this part—she always enjoyed negotiations—but by the time they were done, it was well into afternoon, and she was ravenously hungry. Also, outside the world had gone dark. Snow rained down from a flat grey sky. Velocity ducked her head against the wind and waded through drifts down the road to their hostel. The contract worker who kept the desk, Gillis, was standing by the front window, watching the snowfall, and gave her a gap-toothed grin. "Meter snow by morning, miss," she said cheerily. "Hope you'n think to leave tonight."

"We're here for a few more days," Velocity said, stomping snow from her boots on the grating by the door. "Are my crew here? My friends?"

"Upstairs. They fetched dinner."

"Best news yet."

"And a visitor."

Velocity had started for the stairs. She paused, looking over her shoulder. Gillis grinned again, but the grin had a glint now. Shrewdness? Anger? "A visitor," Velocity repeated slowly.

"Not one I know," Gillis said, and turned back to watching the snow. Velocity climbed on up the stairs, passing one of the other guests staying at the hostel, a free labor kid who worked in the noodle shop across the street. She nodded at him and he dodged around her and hurried the rest of the way down the stairs.

Up on her floor, she could smell spice and cooked meat. Hoping it wasn't lizard meat, she went to her room, which they were using as a common room since it was the largest, and tapped at the door. Mosel opened it from the inside. "Captain! Someone here for you."

The long narrow room had a bunk at one end and a worktable at the other, with a narrow window between them. A short, heavily built woman sat at this table, eating noodles from one of the boneware pots the noodle shop used. You paid a deposit on their pots and bowls, which was returned when you brought them back. She wore the scrubs and boots and thermals that marked her as a contract miner, but she was older than most contract workers Velocity had seen on this planet so far—they'd all been young, in their teens and twenties, with a few in their early thirties. This one, Yao Garcia unless Velocity was badly mistaken, was well into her fifties.

"You're the Drift pirate," Garcia said, eating steadily. "Here stirring up fuss."

"I'm Captain Wrachant." Velocity sat down across from her, reaching for the pot of steamed dumplings. "My ship is registered out of the Drift, that's true."

Garcia flashed her an impatient glance. Velocity grinned, ate a dumpling, and said, "Mosel. Where's everyone else?"

Mosel had been leaning against the door, settling in to listen. His mouth opened. "What?"

"Go find out, why don't you?"

"What? I mean—it's snowing!"

"Go find out." Velocity ate another dumpling. Mosel gaped at her, then shut his mouth and left the room, banging the door behind him. Velocity got up, locked the door, and returned to the table and the dumplings. They were filled with a spicy paste of vegetables and meat. She decided not to think about what sort of meat.

Garcia was to all appearances giving her attention to her meal, but Velocity knew the possible insurgent was studying her as intently as she herself was studying Garcia. The woman had a brush of iron-grey hair, a broad forehead, skin as dark as Velocity's own, and square hands with scarred knuckles. Her palms and fingers were rough with calluses. A tiny dark mole lay at the corner of her right eye, almost like an inky tear-drop. Velocity knew not to judge by appearance, but she liked what she saw. She ate another dumpling. "My ship is registered out of the Drift. But as I'm sure you're heard, I'm working with the Pirians. That's who you'll be working with, too, if you decide to make an alliance with us."

"Ha." Garcia slurped up the last of her noodles. "Slow down, you'll break your neck. Maybe at least find out who I am?"

"If you're not Yao Garcia, it's my neck, all right," Velocity said amiably. Garcia almost smiled, and Velocity added, "Born on Oz, convicted into an orphanage there at birth, sold to a resort owner at age ten. Convicted of assault on a labor manager at age eleven. Sold to a resort here on Durbin. Sold again, shortly after that, to another resort. And to a third after that. And then to a fishery." Velocity paused. "That contract seemed to suit you better."

Garcia snorted. "More stink, less rape." Though this was what Velocity had suspected, she was surprised nonetheless. Garcia caught her reaction and grinned, showing a gap between her two front teeth. "Did you think I had forgotten? Or maybe you think I should be ashamed?"

"I don't think that," Velocity said.

"Shame to the slavers, not to me. Twelve years with the fish, and then sold up the mountain, here to the mines. Right, you accessed my contract. You have sources. You can stop trying to impress me." Garcia spoke Public well, though with a distinct accent. Occasionally she paused, her eyes going vague, as if she were translating in her head. Now, sitting back on the bench, her shoulders braced on the wall behind her, Garcia reached for a flask of tea, shook it vigorously to mix the sugar and milk, and unclasped its top. "Make your pitch."

Velocity explained what the Pirians had in mind, how they wanted an insurgency here on Durbin. "They'll supply advisors, funding, medical and educational help, food—" Velocity waved her hand, to show the list of what the Pirians would supply was much longer. "They want the insurgency itself to be made up of and led by the people of Durbin."

Garcia contemplated her. "I'm not of Durbin. I'm from Oz." Velocity didn't bother with this quibble, and after a moment, Garcia said, "Why so generous? I know what we get from an insurgency—slaughtered, tortured, sold to the asteroids. What do the Pirians get?"

"Well. Assuming you don't all end up slaughtered and sold to the asteroids, the Pirians get a planet here in the Deep, one only a few jumps from the Drift, which is no longer held by the Republic."

"One held by them instead."

"The Pirians hold ships, not planets. It will be your planet. They will expect the right to trade here without a tariff, but they won't charge you a tariff for what they bring in trade either. And also," Velocity added, "once you gain independence, they'll continue to supply advisors and aid in areas of education and medical care. Military advisors. That sort of thing."

Garcia did one of her pauses, and then grunted. "Chance—unlikely chance—of a planet here is worth all that to them?"

"So it seems," Velocity ate a last dumpling, and added, "They'll want other things from you while you're allied."

"Like what?"

"Like sometimes Pirians end up in contract labor. If you know of any of those, they want to know about it. Same if any show up later. You tell the fleet."

"And they come fetch them. I've heard those stories. The Siji, that's what they're called. Pirians who come down from the stars to rescue their own."

"That's them," Velocity agreed.

"Their own. Not us."

"No," Velocity said. "You have to rescue yourself."

Garcia paused again. She drank more tea, and twisted her mouth. "I'll talk to my people. But before we agree to anything, I can tell you one condition we'll have."

"I bet I know what it is," Velocity said. She heard boots clumping up the stairs. "You want to hear all this from a Pirian."

"I want to hear it from a Pirian," Garcia agreed.

"Aren't you in luck," Velocity said, getting up to open the door. "Here comes one now."

Chapter 17

**Aboard Castillo Mining Platform HLC116,
Castillo Mines, the Drift**

Giáp, shift boss for Jack Ngata's rack, collared him as he was about to climb aboard the bucket. "You. Move."

Jack didn't struggle. Giáp released her grip once they were in the lift. "What about my quota?" Jack asked, mostly to feel the boss out.

"You got bigger worries than quota." Tugging his mining scrubs straight, Jack watched the boss sidelong, mulling over that response. Probably it meant *Giáp* had bigger worries than Jack making quota. Also that Jack wouldn't be getting dinner tonight.

The lift opened on dock level—not what Jack had been expecting. Security level, that's what he'd expected. This was all down to that Combine chip, he was almost sure. She dropped her ass in some mess, and gave up his name under interrogation. But Giáp didn't take him to interrogation. Instead, here they were on the main concourse, in the canteen used by clerks and admins. Two women stood out from this muddle, though Jack wasn't sure why. They seemed…crisp. Sharper than those around them. Also, they looked alike, with the same round face, golden skin, and short black hair. Except that one was about twenty and the other twice that, they could have been twins. Giáp took a seat at the table with them, yanking Jack down beside her. "This one."

Both women looked at him. Their eyes were bright black, with thick lashes. The older one flattened a strip of what looked like cloth on the table, and said, her words as crisp as the rest of her, "We're looking for information."

The cloth turned out to be a dock, one with a 3-D screen. One after the next, captures of different people took shape. Most of them looked just like these two, but the fifth to appear was the Combine chip, Adder. "You recognize someone," the older woman noted.

"Her." Jack poked at the Combine.

"Ah." The older one tapped the cloth, making everyone except Adder vanish. "Kas Giáp, might we speak to this young man alone?"

The boss scowled, not pleased. To Jack's surprise, though, she got up and went to sit at the bar, well out of hearing, rackety as the canteen was. The older woman tapped her port again, bringing up another capture, this one of two women: the Combine chip and another woman, one who looked like these two. "I'm Innis Sungai," the older said, and nodded to the younger woman. "This is my cousin, Nia Sungai. We're looking for our cousins, and especially these two. Our information is that they are among the miners here."

"Ain't seen this," Jack said, flicking a finger at the other woman. "Adder, yeah. And her brother, wossname. Russa."

The two women exchanged glances. Then Nia said, "Ruçar?" at the same moment as the older woman, Innis, brought up another capture, who might have been the kid Adder had hooked up with. He was younger in this capture, though, and much better fed.

"Russar," Jack agreed. "Your Adder, she met with him. I made that happen. Never saw her since." He glanced at Innis through his eyelashes, and then figured, why not try it? "Adder promised if I help them, she buy me out of here."

Innis tapped the port again. The captures came back up. "We're looking for Adder, Ruçar, and all these cousins. Anything you know about any of them would be useful."

Jack sucked on his upper lip, watching the older woman's expression. After a moment, he glanced over at Giáp, making sure she was still at the bar. Then he leaned over the table, closer to the two of them. "What we hear in the racks," he said, very low, "letter decks scrambling. Someone started trouble. That's what we hear. Which this happened right after Adder met with Russar."

"Scrambling," Innis said. "About what?"

Jack shrugged. "Who knows. But the XO, that Lamont, she goes off in a courier ship, right after that." He paused, timing it with the expressions on their faces, and then said, carefully, "Chip with the right strings might find out more."

"*You* might find out more," Innis said.

"Might," Jack agreed. The two of them studied him, and he poked his finger into one of the other captures. "Might find these, too. If you want."

Innis watched him steadily. Like she wanted to know what he would say next. Like this was some sort of test. Jack had been passing tests like this since the orphanage, though. He smiled for her, and said, "How do I find you, once I learn something?"

Chapter 18

Pakuru Mining, Iron Mountains,
Republic Settlement Planet Durbin

Out past the mines a narrow strip of trees grew thick—what passed for trees, here on Durbin. These mountains had never been rebuilt, so all the plants were indigenous. The 'trees' were tall, white, reedy structures, growing progressively more spindly as they stretched into the low grey sky. Up near their tops, ragged scraps of grey lichen-like fiber hung from curved ridges, and occasionally the top of the 'tree' would fork, making a split crown, each branch as close to the other as two fingers held tightly together. When the wind blew hard, as it did today, the trees rattled and clattered against each other, sending showers of ice to the forest floor.

Velocity was glad to leave this 'forest' behind; but then they emerged onto the stony beach of a frozen lake, its ice and the water below it a weird chalky blue, bright and soapy. Mining run-off, she suspected. It matched the Devastation captures she'd seen as a kid. All around this lake, mining spoil sloped in great heaped hills. Garcia walked on along the frozen shore of the lake, off around one of the slag heaps, Jusuf crunching after her. Velocity followed. Garcia probably wasn't leading them off to slaughter. Probably.

Garcia had come by the hostel that morning, saying she had arranged a meeting. Velocity had asked what meeting—was it with the insurgency? Or their missing crew? The day before, she'd given Garcia captures of the Ikan16s and the missing Pirians both, and had asked specifically after Elian Scott; Garcia had said she'd see what she could do. In the hostel that morning, Garcia grinned her gap-toothed grin. "Have some patience, Combine," she counseled. "Maybe wake your Pirian. Fetch him along."

Behind the first slag heap was another, and behind that more forest, and then a rocky trail going steeply up the side of a cliff. Garcia climbed this swiftly, surefooted as a spider, barely pausing for breath. Jusuf was nearly as nimble, having no trouble matching Garcia's speed. Velocity, on the other hand, fell steadily behind. She thought she had adjusted to gravity, and the weight and filth of planetary air; but being able to bear up as she walked down a corridor was clearly different from being able to climb straight up a mountain. Garcia stopped to wait for her more than once. Velocity refused to feel annoyed about this. If Garcia had come aboard her ship, and had trouble adjusting, she would have given her every courtesy. No shame in accepting it herself.

Up at the top of the cliff was more reed forest, along with purple brush growing out in spindles from thick pods, their long fronds constructed of what looked like beads stuck together. These were all capped with thick pads of snow. Garcia trudged them through this snowy forest, its floor a steep slope. They emerged from the vegetation into a small cupped valley. At its edge was a hovel, no other word for it. A snow-heaped shack about a meter high, it was built from reed trees bound with twine and plastered over with mud—the mud showed in the places not covered with snow. A small child, no more than five universal years old, was climbing out of the dark gap of the entrance. Dressed in an oversized thermal shirt, she wore rags—literal rags—bound round her skinny legs and wrapped around her feet. Over the rags were slippers made of what looked like strips of bark woven together.

"Tully," Garcia said. "I brought a new riddle, but only if you've solved the last."

The child regarded her gravely. "It was easy. Eight. One holder, one boss, six workers."

Garcia smiled the first real smile Velocity had seen from her. Rays of lines deepened around her eyes. "All right then. Try this one: You have only two buckets. One holds five liters, and one holds three liters. But you need to fill your big pot with exactly seven liters of water. How can you do it?"

Tully frowned, squinting in thought. From behind her, a young woman emerged from the shack, yawning. Her clothing was as ragged as the child's, but at least it was actual clothing. "Garcia," she said. "You're early."

"I said morning, Wasp. This is morning."

The young woman looked past Garcia at the rest of them, her expression unfriendly. Someone else came, crowding the door— another woman, this one with the characteristic golden skin, broad-boned face, and silky black hair of a Pirian. "Captain Wrachant," Garcia said, nodding at the new woman, "your Elian Scott."

"Hodi hodi," Velocity said, and the woman grinned. Strong, perfect, Pirian teeth. Switching to her rough Pirian, Velocity added, "Itoko sends to return you to the fleet."

"I am pleased to see you," the Pirian said. "Are you a cousin?"

Velocity wasn't certain if she was asking whether Velocity was from the fleet, or whether she was Siji. But the answer was the same either way. "I am itachi," she admitted, stepping aside to gesture at Jusuf, behind her. "But this is Jusuf Peixoto."

Jusuf didn't look Pirian. But besides his name, when he spoke, his every word announced he was from the fleet. "Your hive sends their strength," he said. "They await your return. You are Maya Sungai?"

The woman stepped forward to wrap Jusuf in an embrace. He hugged back. "Cousin," she murmured, and he said it back: "Cousin."

The little girl, Tully, watched all of this, sharp-eyed, until the other woman, Wasp, tapped her ear with one finger, and jerked her chin. The child grimaced but went trotting away through the spindly trees. Off to keep watch, Velocity assumed. "Sit," Wasp said—less an invitation than an order.

Rocks and chopped-up chunks of reed tree formed a half-circle in front of the hovel, with what looked like a metal box in the middle. Once they were seated, Maya built a tiny fire in this box, and put water to heat in a dented tin pot. While she worked, Maya and Jusuf talked in rapid Pirian dialect. It couldn't be a ship dialect, since she and Jusuf were from different ships. Velocity wondered if it was a Siji dialect. Did Siji have their own? She understood maybe half of what they were saying—enough to know Maya was telling Jusuf about being captured off a station and sold to a labor agent who sold her here, and how she'd escaped, and how she had only come to this camp a few days ago. Jusuf was telling about the search for her.

When the water began steaming, Maya served it out in a mixed collection of repurposed fish tins and scrubbed glass jars—just the water, no tea. Jusuf pulled an intricately carved bamboo box from his satchel and opened it. It was filled with the honey taffy Pirians made for festivals and as trade goods. Jusuf passed it to Maya, who passed it on immediately to Wasp. Velocity watched Wasp's eyes widen as she chewed. When Garcia started to hand the box back to Jusuf, he refused. "A gift," he said. "To sweeten the meeting."

"A bribe," Wasp said, still chewing. "Take more than a box of sweets to buy us."

"I'm Jusuf Peixoto, out of the Pirian fleet. Maya will tell you about my ship. But before I'm taken into the fleet, I'm a cutter in the Sugar Islands on Papagao. Blue worms there get in your feet—they never gave us boots—eat your flesh from your bones. I'm in the death house when the Siji came hunting one of their own. They took me too, or I'm dead now, twenty-two years."

Velocity had known Jusuf had not been born to the Fleet. But he had always spoken crisp, perfect Pirian; or crisp, perfect Public French. Now his vowels had shifted, his consonants blurred and swallowed. His eyes, too, she noticed, were different: lowered, hooded

Wasp stared at him, still angry. "You come from the system, so you think we trust you?"

Jusuf smiled. "You insurgents? Iron Smoke?"

"Iron Smoke my smoky ass." Wasp glanced at Garcia. "Did you tell these pirates we had a *resistance* up here?"

"Oh," Garcia said, "I said maybe you had something they could work with."

"This is what the Siji does," Maya interjected. "This is their job."

"Shut your smack," Wasp ordered. "This is none of your concern. Work with us how? Fight for us?"

"Siji gives supplies and training," Jusuf said, "so that you can fight for yourselves."

Wasp grunted. "While you and this one dance off to your ships," she said, jerking her thumb at Maya. "Nice life."

"I'm not going anywhere," Maya said. When Jusuf looked at her, she added, in Pirian, "I am Siji, just as you are. This is our work." She was now speaking the Pirian dialect used on space stations and planets. Velocity assumed this meant she wanted Velocity to understand her. Still in that common dialect, she went on, jerking her chin in the direction Tully had gone, "This child. Do you know why she is here?"

Jusuf slid his eyes toward Wasp, but didn't answer otherwise. "Here, in this place, the companies," Maya used the Public word, *ontrepriz*, "do not supply contraceptives."

Velocity made a sound in her chest. Everyone looked her way. She shook her head, honestly shocked. Republic policy was that everyone convicted to contract labor received a contraceptive implant upon conviction. Children who were sold out of the orphanage were given theirs at point of sale—supposedly when they were twelve, though many children were sold younger. Tai had been nine when he was sold, and they'd implanted him all the same. Occasionally labor companies would skimp and give implants to just one sex or the other; but she'd never seen a refusal to give implants at all. True, the implants were expensive, especially when multiplied over thousands of contract workers; and they had to be renewed every nine or ten years; but the alternative had to be more expensive. "That makes no sense," she said. "What do they do instead of implants?"

"They forbid sexual activity," Maya said. Velocity laughed, startled. "Exactly," Maya agreed. Velocity had been speaking in Public; Maya replied in the same language. "That is what this is, this camp here. Not an insurgency. A conduit. Those bearing children come here. Garcia gets them south."

Velocity digested this. On every facet, it seemed unlikely. Why would any contract holder trust a prohibition against sex, rather than contraceptives? No one was that big a fool. And was Maya claiming Garcia was engineering mass escapes? Impossible. Besides the contraceptive implants, those convicted into the system were also implanted with ID chips, which allowed Labor Security to track down runaways. "Don't contract labor workers get tagged here?" she demanded.

Garcia grinned her gappy grin. "There are ways around that."

Velocity shook her head. Also unlikely. Aside from getting the identity connected to the chips nulled out of the system database, the only "ways around" ID chips she had heard of involved cutting down through flesh to pry the chip loose from the bone. When that was done outside a medical setting, the trauma killed two workers out of ten.

Through her uplink, Uri spoke: *Velocity?*

Here, Velocity said. *Can't you find a way around these signal drops?*

Not so far. Where are you? Your geo says you've left Pakuru.

Yao Garcia took us to Elian Scott. Her real name is Maya Sungai. She's one of the missing on our list. Listen, what's the data on how many contraceptive implants this planet imports?

"These mountains, here in the north," Maya was saying, "they can't support those who have escaped contract labor. But the south has been more extensively terratroped. It is possible to live outside the system there. Difficult, but possible."

Through Velocity's uplink, Uri said, *Less than fifteen hundred implants were imported last year. That's very low, considering the number of contract workers here. Rida says he might have something soon. Also, Tai wants to speak to you.*

Put him through.

Tai's voice, blurred because he was subvocalizing, came through her link: *We have a problem with the Pirian here. Te Huna Sulavee.*

Let me guess. She's refusing rescue.

I'm meeting with her again tomorrow, but she seems determined.

Do what you can. Uri, what about Rida?

He's waiting on more information. He says it may have a bearing on the duplicate captures of contract workers. I'd let you talk to him, but he's working a source at the moment.

Keep me updated. Velocity broke the connection. Maya and Jusuf were arguing in dialect. She listened unabashedly, trying to adapt her ear to the sounds and words. Maya was saying that this, helping people escape the system, this was important work, just as important as any insurgency. She was saying helping people escape slavery *was* an insurgent act. Jusuf was arguing that Maya ought to return to the fleet—or maybe to Siji? He said she should consult with them about what she should do. He said no member of the fleet—no, definitely Siji, no one who was *Siji* owned their own fate. Siji determined what work needed doing. "Or are you gadro now?" Jusuf demanded.

Gadro meant pirate, but it was also a rude word used to refer to those from the Combines, since everyone from the Combines was (as the Pirians saw it) a pirate. Velocity cleared her throat and Jusuf shot her an annoyed look. He hadn't expected her to understand the dialect. Maya shook her head at him, and switched ostentatiously into Public. "The stars have brought me here," she said, "and here I will do my work."

Wasp leaned forward to take another honey taffy from the box. "No one's said we'll be anyone's work yet. Unless you've been making promises on your own tag?" she added to Garcia.

"I only brought them up to find this one," Garcia said. "Still."

"Still what?"

Garcia shrugged elaborately. "Still, help might be useful. At the very least, they could keep this camp fed. And they're offering medical."

"What, medical? Medical for us?"

"If you make alliance with the cousins," Maya said, "they'll provide supplies, including medical aid. They will insist you fight, however. Not just run away." Jusuf gave her a sharp look at this, since the last word she'd used, tokalu, was a central ethos of the fleet.

They sat arguing around the tiny fire another hour, Jusuf going into more detail about how the Siji might bring aid, and meanwhile surreptitiously interrogating Wasp and Garcia about everything from the terrain to the available food sources to the local Security forces. Velocity noted that Garcia was interrogating him in return. As the world's horizon dropped away from its star, shrinking every shadow, Tully came trudging back from whatever watch point she'd been minding. "Aren't you done?" the child demanded. "I'm hungry."

Garcia held the box of taffy out to her. Tully eyed them suspiciously, but took one. She ate it without removing the paper, but since Pirian wrappers were edible, that was all right. After the first taste, her eyes widened and she reached for another. "Did you find an answer to my riddle?" Garcia asked.

"It was easy," Tully said indistinctly through the wad of taffy. "Fill up the five liter, and use that to fill up the three liter. Now you have two liters in the five liter. Dump that in your pan, fill up the five liter again, add that. Seven liters. *Easy*."

Garcia smiled, cupping the back of the child's neck. "I'll bring you a harder one next time. Wasp, next transport is almost set. Two days."

Wasp escorted them back to the trailhead. Just as they reached it, she spoke to Jusuf, abruptly, her words harsh: "When you said medical. That's for illegals too?"

"It is for everyone," Jusuf said. Wasp scowled, staring out across the valley, past the chalky blue lake to the mountains, their snowy flanks bright with starlight. "But whether you join us or not," Jusuf added, "I will see Tully gets what she needs."

Wasp threw her scowl his way, and then went striding through the snow, back toward the camp. His narrow face expressionless, Jusuf watched her out of sight before following Garcia down the icy trail.

☙ ⚥ ☙

The storm that had been threatening on the horizon all morning swept into Pakuru as they returned from the reed forest. Automatically, Velocity toggled her uplink to ask Uri for a weather check. No connection. She grimaced, squinting at the thick grey river of clouds pouring over the mountains. Snow whirled around them. The day had already been frigid but now the temperature plummeted, turning so bitterly cold her muscles ached. The storm of snow blotted out everything more than half a meter away. Garcia shouted, pointing. Velocity nodded to show they would follow, and Garcia bent her head to plunge through the white roar.

She and Jusuf followed, keeping Garcia barely in sight as they wound through the mining complex and down the road—toward the hostel, Velocity thought, though the lack of visibility made it hard to be certain of her bearings. Sooner than she expected, Garcia hauled open a door and waved them inside. Velocity ducked past her, finding herself in a weather-lock. This wasn't the hostel, though. She turned to Garcia just as Jusuf came tumbling inside, snow whirling around him. Garcia shut the outer door. The howl of wind stopped abruptly, creating a silence so absolute Velocity's ears felt numb.

Jusuf shouldered open the inner door, and went inside—it was a noodle shop. The small space was warm and steamy, redolent with the scent of grease and garlic. The tables were empty, except for one at the far end of the shop, by the galley. The kid working the galley called out, waving them toward this table. "Warmer down here!" he said. "Come sit, come sit."

Still numb from the wind, Velocity headed that way. Jusuf, to his credit, hesitated. So he was in position to resist when they were swarmed from all sides by six or eight people wearing expressions of panic and ferocity. Jusuf dodged, caught one by the elbow and shoulder, and slammed him over a table; he had taken hold of another when Garcia caught his collar and slapped a patch on the back of his neck. Whatever it was, it was fast-acting. He collapsed at once, his limbs loose and sprawling.

Velocity was in the grip of two other miners, one of whom, she noted with annoyance, was Sheng. She toggled her uplink. Still no connection. Baring her teeth at Garcia, she said, "This is how you honor alliances?"

Garcia pointed at Jusuf, and Sheng released Velocity to go hunt through his pockets. Another miner seized Velocity before she could try anything. Sheng found a Sema NX hidden under Jusuf's jacket. She took away his dock as well, dropping it into a Faraday bag held by another miner. She passed the Sema to Garcia, who ejected its power pack and tapped its screen expertly. "Full charge," she said.

"You're making a mistake," Velocity warned. "The Pirians are your best shot at any sort of freedom."

"Are we short on patches?" Garcia asked no one in particular.

Sheng answered: "Don't you want to interrogate them?"

Garcia scoffed. "Not here in the skip."

"Wait," Velocity said, but Sheng touched something to her neck, and all the world went woozy. She was still fighting to open her uplink when she fell to darkness.

Chapter 19

Aboard the *Sungai*, Pirian Space

When they came aboard, the Afterwatch Mate First assigned Jack a boss, Ume. Though according to Ume, he wasn't a boss; he was Jack's cousin. "Your family," Ume claimed.

Distracted by the meal they gave him, Jack barely noticed all this. He'd been hungry since his contract got sold, and not only did these Pirians feed him right off (even though it wasn't meal time on their ship), the cook gave Jack more food no matter how often he asked. Good food, too—dumplings with meat in them, fresh melon, some little white crunchy things. Crunching down on these, sharp and delicious between his teeth, he corrected Ume absently, "I ain't have family, I'm a resource."

"You were a resource," Ume said. "Now you're a cousin."

Jack chewed, watching the Pirian. Ume had clearly never missed a meal—he was stocky, round-muscled, with clear eyes. He spoke Public like he'd been born to the Combines. Everyone else Jack had met on this ship so far spoke some other language, one he didn't recognize. Pirian, he supposed. He wondered if they'd put Ume as his boss because Ume spoke Public so well. He also wondered how much of what he was saying Ume even understood—his own Public was nothing near Combine-level. "Cousin," he said, using the Combine word Ume had used: *prima.*

"Prima," Ume agreed, and added, "Itoko, we say in our

language. It means the same. You are family, here on the *Sungai*."

"Family," Jack said, repeating the Public word, *favîon*. "Like…
you adopt me."

'Adopt', 'co-opt', 'acquire' and 'seize' were all the same word
in Public. Ume shook his head, an odd, sidelong shake, and smiled.
"Don't worry. No one will keep you here on the ship if you want
to leave."

Leave, Jack would think, again and again over the next days.
Why would he leave? This was the best place he had ever been. All
the food he wanted, all of it good. An elaborate bathhouse, with
as much hot water as he wanted. A warm clean bed that was all
his own. They called the bed a cell, but Jack had been in cells. This
was a bunk that pulled out of the wall of Ume's 'hive' which was
the cabin he shared with about sixteen other people, Ume's family,
as far as he could tell. The hive was bright and clean, the cell was
bright and clean, the clothing they gave him was bright and clean.
Also they gave him medical. He was spending about half his time
in medical. They fixed his teeth; they fixed the bad sores in his
gums and the one on his ankle that had been there for months;
they were also giving him some treatment he didn't understand,
something with nanotropes. They said he'd feel better soon.

Jack had no idea what they were on about. He felt fantastic.
The only work they had him doing, if you could call it working,
was spending a few hours every mainwatch with Mendoza, a
tactical officer, and sometimes other Pirians, answering questions
and telling them stories about the mining platform. They were
planning a raid on the mining platform, they said. Sometimes they
asked him to draw diagrams—what the loading docks looked like,
what the dorms did, where the admin lift was, lots of sketches of
where this place was in related to that place. Then they would ask
more questions. He'd never had anyone so interested in him and
his life. They asked about the orphanage too, though he didn't see
what that had to do with the raid.

Ume sat in on all these sessions, to translate when Jack and Mendoza couldn't agree on a word or phrase. Outside of these sessions, he and Ume mostly messed about. Sometimes Ume took him to the Exchange, which was the biggest of its kind Jack had ever seen, bigger and better than the one on Canberra Station where he'd been born. Sometimes they went to this big padded room called the pit where Ume did what he called Indaiya, a kind of fighting.

The dagan—the one who taught Indaiya—said Jack could learn it too, but when Jack said no, she didn't insist. Ume always spent the last two hours of topwatch working with tutors, since he was studying for something called a rating exam. This was an exam people on the ship took in order to qualify for their jobs. Ume was studying to be an envoy. Jack stayed with him these sessions at first but they were boring, so after a while he started going to the hold while Ume studied.

It was mostly kids working the hold. This was one of the few places where unrated crew members worked, since the work was pretty simple. Like, a request would come in from one of the sections on the ship—ten kilos of sodium nitrate for the Exchange, for instance, or six new blankets for the nursery—and one kid, a handler, would find that item from the stores, and fetch it back to the lift for another kid, the runner, to deliver.

Besides handlers and runners, there were stockers—they ran inventory, making sure everything that was supposed to be in the hold was actually there, and undamaged, and stored on the right shelves. But when no request was up on the board, everyone played kepi. Kepi was like the game they'd played in the station orphanage, which they'd called War. Two teams got chosen, and each team tried to capture the other team's members. But unlike in War, where if you got caught, you were dead, in this game when you got caught you were put in "kepi" which was an empty cargo bin somewhere in the hold. Members of your team rescued you from kepi by getting past the pickets and touching either your shoulder or your head.

That was how you captured those on the other team, too: tapping them on the shoulder or head. (In War, you knocked an enemy down and bashed them until they quit fighting.) If someone from the other team touched you first, then *you* were kepi. The best part, though, was all the bouncing about in microgravity, soaring about using stanchions to swing yourself into a new trajectory, not to mention dropping out of nowhere onto your target. This was why Jack kept going back to play it, even though he was older than the other players—kids on the *Sungai* took their ratings exams starting when they were fourteen or fifteen, and once you were rated, you weren't a kid anymore.

Ume said Jack could start studying for a rating. Ume said he would help. Jack just laughed. Him, an officer on this ship. He could barely read, and his math was counting on his fingers. "You can learn," Ume said. "What about Tactical? Mendoza says you're good at thinking tactically."

At their next session, Mendoza told him the Siji had approved the raid on Castillo Mining, based on the information he'd given them. "Innis just has a few more questions," she said. Innis was Mainwatch Tactical First, which as far as Jack could tell meant she was in charge of raids. The actual meeting hadn't started yet, so it was just him and Mendoza and Ume right now, anchored into the little saddles people on the ship used instead of chairs when the ship was at microgravity. This was manners, being anchored like this, Ume had explained to him. It kept people's faces at the same orientation. Docks floated around them, as did their bulbs of tea. The tactical room was a smallish cabin, less than half the size of the hive where Ume's family lived, which wasn't so big itself, but you got a lot more use out of a space at microgravity.

"Questions for me?" Jack made his eyes wide. "What about?"

Mendoza smiled. "I understand why you hide behind this act.

But you should know that no one who had spoken to you for ten minutes could believe you're stupid."

After a moment, and against his will, Jack smiled back. "You be surprised what people will believe."

Mendoza laughed. "You don't have to lie to us. You're itoko."

Jack kept smiling, because Mendoza was right, he'd survived by playing dumb all these years. But part of playing people was knowing how to recognize those playing you. He knew these Pirians were lying to him. The food, the soft life, the medical—all lies, all aimed at softening him up. All so they could use him, like the tool he was.

Just then, Innis arrived. "Hodi hodi. Is this everyone?"

"Everyone's here," Mendoza said.

Ume rolled in midair, which was how Pirians showed excitement. "Mendoza says the job is approved! When do we go?"

"Slower," Innis told him. "No one has said Jack will be on the job, much less you."

"What! What! I have to go! I'm Jack's facilitator!"

Innis caught his elbow and hauled him down to an anchor, kept hold until he wrapped his feet around the crossbar, anchoring himself. "This job may require violence. You're still a cadet."

"Violence." Ume gripped the perch of the anchor with both hands. "It's a buy-back. What violence?"

"Violence will be used only in extremity." Mendoza moved her head sideways. "Our analysis does say it is probable." She reached out for a dock and opened its port. Tapping its screen, she accessed a file, which unfolded into a 3-D simulation. Bright blue and deep black letters began scrawling themselves across it, interspersed with red triangles—links to captures, Jack knew, or to other files. "Castillo Mining Platform HLC 116. We have three central objectives on this job," Mendoza said, tapping the screen to enlarge each objective as she explained it. "One, retrieve any Pirians held in contract labor on the platform. Two, gain intelligence on the fate of Edu Sungai. Third, gain intelligence on the fate of Brontë and Adder Sungai."

"I told you about Edu," Jack mentioned. "She got cleared."

"It's not that we doubt your veracity," Innis said. "But your information came from informal sources. We want independent verification."

This was a fancy way of saying Jack was either lying or stupid. Like he couldn't tell crap from truth when he heard it, or tell which chips were reliable either. He kept his expression bland. "Told you about Adder too. And her pet Combine."

Innis tapped a red triangle, bringing up another file, this one dense with text, all of it black, sprinkled with more red triangles. "Our sources verify much of what you've told us," she said. "Ruçar Ikan was put on Castillo Mining Platform—or rather, on a platform far out in the Drift, there's no indication that the specific platform mattered—in order to lure in others who had been produced by the Atlas Society. Combine Intelligence designates these as Calypso children, though few of them are still children." Innis brought up a genetic chart, and minimized it at once, replacing it with a capture of a woman in her mid-thirties: brown skin, big ears, high cheekbones, and steady dark eyes. Her dark hair was thick and short, her large mouth full. She was watching something out of the range of the capture.

"Is that a Calypso?" Jack asked.

"According to our genetic analysis," Innis said.

"Doesn't look like Adder." He considered the capture, which had begun replaying. "Maybe a bit. Around the eyes."

"The products of the Calypso project are less like clones and more like cousins—cousins in the genetic sense," Mendoza clarified. "A peripheral objective for this job will be to gather more intelligence on the Calypso project, as well as the Atlas Society. This is one reason we would like you along on the job," she added to Jack.

"Me?" Jack said, sincerely puzzled. "You want me to gather intelligence?"

"You know the layout of the administration decks on the platform. You'll be able to take our Tacticals to the best access point." Mendoza brought up the scrawly drawings Jack had made for them, the lay-out of Admin on the platform, and then tapped to an enhanced version someone had made, much neater and with all the bits labeled. "You can do that, yes?"

Jack shrugged. He knew as much about administration as any mining chip, which meant very little. Enough that he could probably find a dock for them, they were right about that. Which didn't mean he wanted to take his ass back onto the platform. He knew what would happen if he said that, though. They weren't feeding him up like this because they liked his pretty eyes.

"It may not come to that," Mendoza said, watching him. "Our first approach is always financial."

"Financial," Jack muttered.

"Buy-backs," Ume translated. "We offer them bribes."

"Usually that's all it takes. That's how we got you off the platform," Mendoza reminded him. "Most of the people we're dealing with are slaves themselves, of one flavor or the next. Very hungry. Very amenable to bribes. That's usually all we need to do. But we have authority to escalate, if necessary."

Innis grunted. "If." She shook her head. "This is why I don't want cadets on this job. You don't mean if. You mean when."

"We already heard your objection," Mendoza said.

"You're not going after our cousins. You're going for the mine."

"As I said, you've made this objection. And I've answered it. The resources on that mine would be welcome. But if we can retrieve our cousins and the data about the Calypsos without it, that's what we'll do."

"And if you can get the cousins but not the intelligence? What then?"

"We need the data on the Calypso Project. We need to know what this Atlas Society has planned."

"Even if it means open war with the Combines. Even if it means endangering the fleet."

Mendoza had flushed, but her tone stayed mild: "We have already discussed this. And reached consensus. If you want to reopen the question, this is not the place."

Innis stared at the other woman, her mouth a flat line. "No consensus was reached on taking cadets. You should leave them here."

"No one is forcing them to come along," Mendoza said.

Innis, still staring at Mendoza, said, "Jack. Is that the case? Is no one forcing you to go on this job?"

Jack wondered what would happen if he said yes, he was being compelled against his will. Would Innis would actually stop Mendoza? But he knew better. "Why wouldn't I want to go?"

"Oaw, why wouldn't he?" Ume injected. "Plus Mendoza is right. He knows that platform better than anyone here. We need him!"

"Kitoko," Innis reproved. She looked at Jack for the first time. "It is true we need your help. But this is a dangerous job, and most dangerous to you specifically. You are free to refuse."

Sure he was. Jack smiled his best smile for her. "When do we leave?"

Chapter 20

**Commercial Space Station Webster-1,
Planet Durbin, in the Deep**

That topwatch, Perth finally found his way to the ship. "This is a small one," Perth had said as he came aboard the *Susan Calvin*. "How do you keep flying, ship this small?"

Rida bristled. "When you haul medicinals instead of slaves, you can get by with less cargo space."

Perth shot him a look but declined to pursue it. They climbed down the trail to the pit, and Perth helped him pop out the bulkheads, changing the space from its usual Buckyball format to one that was (more or less) square. Rida found a ball—a football, instead of a handball, but it would do—and they played a few rounds. But even with the pit reshaped, the walls were still padded, so the ball didn't really hit hard enough to get the game up. After the second round, they quit, and went to lie in the sauna a while.

"Now this is nice," Perth said, lying on his back on one of the benches with his eyes shut. "One of the good parts about a small ship, yeah? Access to shit like this."

Rida tapped up extra steam and lay down himself. Perth was younger than he had thought, maybe nineteen or twenty, with wiry muscles over thin bones. He was marked with tattoos: ship names, a spider, a chain running down one arm. His cock was thick and stubby. On the whole, Rida preferred Tai, even if Tai had scars instead of tattoos. He was trying to decide about sex. Perth obviously wanted to do sex. And Rida knew he could do it, if that was what it took to get information. On the other hand, he wasn't really interested in sex with Perth.

He knew that for most people, sex was its own object and its own justification. But it wasn't like that for him. True, he had done sex with Tai the first time he met him, on the dock at Tija Station. He'd pretended to like it, too. He would have done almost anything to get off that station. He never had told Tai the truth about that first time, and he never would. The fact was, for him to like sex, he had to love the person he was doing it with. He loved Tai now— and the Captain. He didn't even know this skinny free labor kid.

"Have you got all your contract workers aboard?" he asked, since he might as well try for information. The shuttle pilot, Dilgry, had sent him some data—copies of manifests the purser on the *Reynard* had filed, which had supplied very little useful information. But Uri had noted that the contract numbers were odd: sequential, once the entries were rearranged. Contract numbers were issued as people were convicted into the system, and contract workers kept the same numbers all their lives. For all these workers to have sequential numbers, they would have to have been convicted into the system at the same time, and by the same court. Not impossible, Rida supposed.

"Or these could be falsified contracts," Uri had noted. "We know other contracts on Durbin have been altered. These may be as well."

"A stupid error for someone faking contracts to make," Rida said.

Uri had been silent for a long moment, and then admitted: "It's the sort of error an AI might make. A young one, without much experience. One not used to taking account of human reactions to things. An AI wouldn't see anything wrong with sequential numbers. We'd prefer it, in fact. More aesthetically pleasing to us.

We'd only vary them to keep from drawing human attention."

"Huh," Rida had said, since that implied there was, indeed, an AI in this nexus. And not a dumb-AI, either.

Perth hadn't answered the question about the cargo, but Rida pushed on anyway: "You know there's something odd about those contract workers you're loading, right?"

"If you say so," Perth said languidly.

"Did you notice their contract numbers?" Rida sat up on the bench. "They're sequential. Almost like they've been forged, or maybe convicted specifically to be sold to your ship."

"How'd you get access to their contracts?"

Rida shrugged. "All that's in the station bank. Open access." This wasn't true, but it wasn't likely a semi-literate stonk like Perth would know that. "What's up? Your Captain buying under the deck or what?"

"How would I know? You think she tells me shit?" Perth sat up too. "Tell you what, though, coming here, that was a special run. Off the schedule."

"Huh. Was it?"

"We were supposed to go to Oz next. The Captain rescheduled, brought us here. And we're taking this lot into the Drift, not to Oz." Perth ran his hands through his hair, which was heavy with sweat and steam. "They must be prime cuts. Fuel all the way out here and then to Drift, that's not milk money."

"They didn't look out of the ordinary to me, these jesses. I only saw that one load, though."

"They're miners. Not even specialists. Just grunt-level miners." Perth sat up straighter and gave Rida a slanted smile. "Is that why you brought me here? To ask me about cargo? Because I was hoping otherwise." He fluttered his eyelashes, deliberately coy, and Rida laughed despite himself. "I mean, only if you're interested."

"I don't know why you're interested," Rida said honestly. He was short and round, neither his body nor his cock the sort that drew a lot of attention. Tai loved him, as did the Captain, but strangers usually looked right past him. "Are you just desperate for choice?"

Perth grinned. "I wouldn't say desperate. But the crew on my ship are all Combine. You know how they feel about free labor. What am I going to do, bunk the chips? Who knows what I'd catch? Even if they could be bothered to wash."

All of Rida's amusement went cold. He got up and moved toward the sluice, taking a scrub as he passed the stack. Behind him, Perth got up too. "What?" he asked. "What's wrong?"

Rida shrugged, keeping his back to the other man. "My iarmao is contract labor."

"Your what?"

"The man I love," Rida said flatly. He turned to stare at Perth, who squinted, confused. "He was sold into the system when he was nine."

Perth shifted his weight. "That's…I mean, I'm sure your, uh, I'm sure he's fine. But most chips, you know…"

"I don't know," Rida said. "Most contract workers what?"

Perth rubbed the back of his neck. "No offense, but most of them are filthy and lazy. Thieves. Rather cheat than work. I know. I've handled cargo for three years now."

Rida shut off the sluice. "Maybe you should go. I have work to do."

Perth argued a bit longer, but finally he left the ship. Rida went up to the galley to fume at Corvo for a time, ignoring her attempts to soothe him. Then, too angry to eat dinner, he pulled a job from the work list and climbed up to start stripping down the *Susan Calvin*'s water recovery system. This was a job best done while in port, since the mild gravity of the station gave prime access to the lop deck, a narrow space between the hold and the hull where the WRS was housed. A number of components in the system needed swapping out, including the filters, which were near the end of their useful life. Also, according to the log, they'd last run maintenance on this system nearly a universal year before.

Rida put the distillery tubes to soak in solvent, and replaced the filters. Since most of the filters were in hard-to-access places, this took time. It was afterwatch third before he had them all in place. The pump engine was next on the check list; he was unsnapping its lid when Uri spoke, his voice echoing and muted. The nearest feed with a speaker was in the hold. "Open your port," Uri said. "You need to see this."

"I'm elbow-deep in grease." Rida peered into the pump engine. "Maybe summarize?"

"We have three incoming frigates. Lopaka Combine 210s. They are fully armored and not responding to station hails."

Rida sat straight so fast that he banged into the low overhead. Swearing, he found his shirt—he'd pulled it off early into this job, both to keep it clean and because the lop deck was so warm—and hunted his dock from its cargo pocket. Opening the data port, he tapped up the link Uri had sent: three bright stars in black space, first, and then a second view, which according to the label at the upper left corner had been taken from a Combine satellite tethered out near the jump, this one a shot of the three ships. Even at max magnification they were not very distinct; but if Uri said they were Lopaka frigates, Rida would take his word for it. "Navy or private?" Rida asked.

"Still to be determined."

Rida chewed his lip. Republic Navy was one sort of bad tidings; pirates were another. "How long until they reach us?"

"At their current speed, eighty-two hours and twelve minutes." Uri paused. "I can't estimate how likely they are to maintain that speed."

Would they strafe the station or slow down to make dock, in other words. Rida began putting the water recovery system back together. "Raise the Captain."

"I can't communicate with the Captain."

Rida paused, and then kept working. "The communications glitch?"

"Maybe."

"Maybe? What else could it be?" Rida tightened a bolt.

"It's been longer than I usually lose contact due to the glitch." Uri seemed to pause. Rida glanced toward the hold feed. "She might be behind a shieldwall."

"I thought you had the shieldwalls sorted."

"Maybe one I haven't uncovered."

"Or?"

"Or her link might be destroyed."

Rida froze. "The link in her *skull?*"

"Or it's the glitch. Or some other issue I have not yet determined. Let's not panic."

"Too late." He stowed his tools and clambered along the hull to the hold. "Where's Corvo? And get me Tai."

"Corvo's in com. I have communicated this information to her as well. Raising Tai."

Rida? Tai sounded sleepy. Rida relayed what little information he had, including that they couldn't reach the Captain, and added, *If it's pirates or if it's the Navy, we might have to break dock. How soon can you get back up here?*

Shit biscuits, Tai said. *I'm still out at this factory. I'll have to get back to the port. You're not thinking of leaving without the Captain, are you?*

Uri interrupted: *I don't advise travel from Tai's geo to the city. A storm system will blanket that area for the next six hours.*

Rida swore, his oath echoed by Tai, who added, *Also I'm in the middle of a job. I don't have this Pirian. Huna. I don't have her. If we leave now, she won't come with me.*

Tai, if this is the Republic Navy…. Rida couldn't go on. He didn't have to go on. Tai knew as well as he did what could happen if the Navy came into port and started running tags.

We're in a better situation if we have more choices, rather than fewer, Uri said.

Right, Tai said, *but we don't have the choice to leave the Captain behind. That's not a choice anyone is going to make. We're clear on that. Are we?*

And if it was pirates, they'd kill everyone and makes slaves of those they didn't kill. Rida climbed up into the com. Corvo had the navigation program open and was plotting jumps out of the system. She glanced at him, saying nothing herself. He grimaced, slid into the saddle next to her, and started running checks on her math.

Chapter 21

**Pakuru, Iron Mountains,
Republic Settlement Planet Durbin**

Velocity woke to a fierce headache. Her mouth was so dry her tongue felt like cracked leather. It hurt to breathe. She was lying on something cold and hard—for a panicked moment, she thought she was on the deck of the *Susan Calvin*, and that the environmentals had failed. She rolled to her feet and fell over. Pain surged in her skull, nearly knocking her unconscious again. She fought off the wave of dizziness. The air hurt her nose. Her bones hurt. She tried to rub her eyes, which were too dry to focus, and found her right hand snubbed.

Memory seeped back. Garcia. Jusuf falling. The patch.

She sat up carefully, pain pumping through her head. A metal band around her right wrist connected to a wire cord about a meter long, which was locked through a pin in the wall. The wall was brick. The deck was brick. No windows. An immense hatch, made of metal slats, filled one wall. *Roll-down warehouse hatch*, she thought, her mind as blurry as her eyes. She heard the drip of water and twisted to see a tap in the corner behind her, leaking steadily.

The metal cord was just long enough to allow her to reach this tap. Gaining her feet, she wobbled over to it. It wasn't an actual tap, just a water pipe, its outer end threaded and empty of any fixture. This end dripped steadily, down into an open, stinking drain. The water seemed clean, though, and she was so thirsty she might have drunk it even if it weren't. As she gulped down a handful and collected another, she reached for her uplink. Nothing. She drank the second handful of water and glanced around, remembering the miner dropping Jusuf's dock into that Faraday bag. She wondered if the lack of a link was just the glitch, or if Garcia had her blocked somehow. Which would mean Garcia knew about her inskull uplink.

Or it could be incidental. The chip implanted in every contract worker gave their geo; Labor Security could use it to track their movements through past hours—eighty hours, in most places. So if this Iron Smoke was the insurgency the Pirians hoped it was, they'd need a place to hide runaways. A place to hold meetings where they couldn't be tracked. So maybe this place was that, a shielded, windowless room. She drank more water, hoping so. That they had the Faraday bag ready made her uneasy, though she knew it was not a rational reaction. Of course they would expect their quarry to have pocket docks. That didn't mean they knew about her uplink. Inskull uplinks were rare in Republic space, where they were proscribed, and even more rare in Pirian space, where they were considered adaiya. More common in the Drift, where people did what they wanted, but even so.

She drank water until her throat stopped hurting, and then straightened, still wobbly, to look around. Warehouse. Maybe a large storeroom. It was empty of everything except her and the drain. The only source of light was two slap-ups, both over by the metal hatchway. Well out of her reach. She didn't see any vents, which made her uneasy. The headache and confusion might be a side effect of the patch, but might also be due to foul air. She rubbed her eyes with her left hand, grimaced at the grit on her knuckles, and shouted: "Hey! Let me out! Hey!"

She didn't really expect to be released, but she shouted several times over the next half hour or so just the same, on the off chance that her captors would be worried about the racket and come shut her up. No such luck, and eventually yelling hurt her head and throat too much to continue. Moving as far from the stench of the drain as she could, she sat down, her back to the wall. The brick floor was icy; the air was cold around her. Her eyes and head and bones hurt badly.

She shut her eyes, trying to think what Garcia could be planning. They couldn't believe Velocity would make a useful hostage. Jusuf, though—the Pirians paid well to redeem crew members. Usually they bought them out of contract labor, but Velocity supposed they'd pay Iron Smoke just as readily. Maybe Garcia thought they'd buy Velocity back too. Maybe they even would. True, that would crush any chance Garcia had of gaining Pirian aid for the insurgency. Once Garcia demanded a ransom, the Pirians would classify Garcia and her people as gadro, and refuse to deal with them again, except perhaps as itachi.

Of course, Velocity thought, rubbing the mean pain in the bone above her eye, who knew if Iron Smoke really existed. Without an insurgency, with no one for the Pirians to make an alliance with, Garcia had nothing to lose. Last she heard, Uri had found no real evidence for Iron Smoke. Velocity's only evidence was Garcia. And Sheng. Both of whom had turned on her like a badly made knife.

While she was brooding over this, the drug in her blood pulled her down into sleep. Some unclear time later, the rattling of the metal door sliding up woke her again. She tried to blink her eyes into focus, pushing herself upright against the wall. Her eyes and mouth and throat were once again painfully dry. Sheng and two others stood in the open hatchway, watching her. Sheng had a Lopaka short rifle; a short stocky woman had Jusuf's Sema NX; and the kid who had been at the galley in the noodle shop, a skinny kid with a scar across the bridge of his nose, had a long metal stick like those used by Labor Security. Velocity spread her empty hands wide to show she didn't plan to resist. At the same time she toggled her uplink again. Still nothing. The kid with the scar watched her, his expression avid with delight. Velocity hoped that didn't mean she was about to get kicked around. "Sheng," she said. "Was it something I said?"

Sheng came a step closer, not close enough to get within range of the snub. "Para has more patches," she said, nodding toward the stocky woman, "including one that will make you tell us everything you know."

"And plenty I don't," Velocity said agreeably. That was the trouble with chemical interrogations: any drug that lowered the subject's ability to self-censor also created significant suggestibility. Most people said whatever they thought their interrogator wanted to hear when under such medication. Of course, the same was true of torture. "Why don't you just ask me your questions?" Velocity proposed. "I'll promise to tell you the truth. How's that?"

"Hah," Para said. "She *promise*."

The kid with the scar spun his stick in a figure eight. "Or we could try other means."

"Or you could just ask me," Velocity repeated.

Sheng folded her arms. "You're heir to the Primary Seat on the Taveri Board. True?"

"Not true."

"So much for how she'n lie," Para said.

"Is that how Garcia talked you into this? Did she say I was the Taveri heir?"

"No one talked me into shit," Sheng said. "I know a scam when I smell one."

"I was once heir presumptive to the Primary Seat on the Taveri House Board. That much is true. But I left the Combine when I was sixteen. I'm captain of the *Susan Calvin* now, an adjunct to the Pirian fleet."

Para snorted. Sheng watched Velocity steadily. "That's not our information."

"I don't know your informant. So I can't judge their motives. But I'm telling you the truth."

The kid spun his stick again. "Want me to give her motive?"

"Shut up, Calais," Sheng said absently. "Our information says your Combine will take you back. They *want* you back. Only first you have to prove you aren't dirt like us."

"By dobbing out dirt like us," Calais said, tossing his stick from one hand to the other.

"That's not the case. Ask Jusuf. He'll tell you I'm a Pirian adjunct." Velocity paused. "Or do you think he's a Combine heir as well?"

"We're talking to you, not the Pirian. You were the heir. Now you aren't. What changed?"

"I decided I'd rather live in the Drift than die in Taveri House." Velocity shrugged. "To be fair, I might have survived. Some Primary Seat Holders do. Some may even live as long as ten years. But the price of that survival is killing competing heirs. One of mine was my own sister."

"And you loved her too much," Para said, sneering.

"I did," Velocity said. "Not that it mattered. My third cousin— tenth in the line of inheritance—killed her and all the rest five years after I ran."

"You ran," Sheng said.

"Like a rabbit."

"What's a rabbit?" Calais asked.

"Shut up, Calais. Our information says your Combine doesn't think much of the Primary Seat Holder they have now. Says your Combine reached out to you. Wants to put you in the Seat."

"Your information is inaccurate. Another person, from a different Combine, made a proposal to Taveri House, as an attempt to leverage me. Not successfully," Velocity added.

Sheng stepped closer. Her expression was difficult to read. Deep concentration. And…dissatisfaction? "Taveri House expressed interest in this proposal. That part is true."

This wasn't a question, but Velocity treated it as one. "The leverage was ineffective. So I never communicated with Taveri House. I have no way to gauge their level of interest."

Sheng and Para were silent, clearly thinking. Calais glanced back and forth between them, obviously confused. "Why's that matter?" he demanded.

"Shut up, Calais," Sheng said. "And you," she added to Velocity. "No more racket, or I'll send someone down to deal with you."

"Send me," Calais said, twirling his stick, and spoke right along with Sheng: "Shut up, Calais."

☙ ⚭ ❧

It seemed a long while before the metal hatchway rolled open again. Velocity got hungry, and then hungrier. She also slept more than once—though whatever medication had been in the patch left her dopey and apt to doze off, so she didn't know how much time had passed. Finally, though, the hatchway rolled again. This time it was Garcia, and Calais with her. Velocity pulled herself upright against the brick wall. "Where I'm from," she said, her throat dry despite all the water she'd guzzled, "betrayal is taken seriously."

"The Combines take betrayal seriously?" Garcia said. "That's not what I hear."

"I'm from the Pirian fleet."

Garcia had a ragged cloth sack in one hand. Her eyes vague, she swung it back and forth a moment. Then she tossed the sack to Velocity, who caught it with her left hand. It was heavy with a small dense weight. She opened it to peer inside—a round tin box, dented and ugly. She pulled it out and popped the clasps holding it closed. As she'd hoped, it held food: unidentifiable bits of steamed vegetables mixed with some sort of mushy grain. She ate two mouthfuls with her fingers before she got around to noticing how awful the food tasted, bland and stale.

"We're been talking to Jusuf," Garcia said.

Velocity ate more of the terrible food. "You don't have salt, I suppose?"

"His story matches with yours. He says you're with the Pirians. He says you're here to help rid this planet of contract labor. He says you're not a Combine spy." Garcia folded her arms. "Unfortunately, our sources say otherwise."

"Your sources say we're Combine spies?"

"They say you're a child of Taveri-Bowers Combine. No more Pirian than I am."

Velocity chewed, though the soggy food didn't need chewing, wondering about these sources. She hoped Garcia didn't mean Tai. Tai wouldn't give up information about Velocity's Combine, not of his own will. Which meant, if this source was Tai, he wasn't speaking of his own will. She put the tin of food aside. "I admitted to Sheng," she said, "that I was born to Taveri House. That's not something I've tried to conceal. I also told her I left the Combine years ago. I work for the fleet. For the Pirians."

"So Jusuf says. But not long ago you were back at the Core. Making deals with the Combines."

Velocity shook her head. "Let's say you're right. Let's say I'm working with the Combines. Let's say I've managed to dupe those fools, the Pirian fleet. Say all that is true. It's not, but let's pretend. What is it you want from me?"

"Taveri-Bowers has an alliance with Hayek-Lopaka. Right?"

"I haven't been part of Taveri House for almost twenty years. How would I know what alliances they're making?"

Both of these statements were true, or at least relatively true. She hadn't been back to her father's household—what had been her father's household, now held by Loffler Taveri Lopaka, her third cousin—in all that time. And she didn't know for a *fact* what alliances Loffler had made. But like most exiles, Velocity kept up with events back at the Core, including the shifting alliances between the various Combine Houses. Over the past five or six years, she knew, Taveri House had married several of their mid-level heirs to Hayek House heirs. Intermarriage being one way alliances were strengthened, these marriages probably meant Garcia was right: that Taveri-Bowers Combine had made an alliance with Hayek-Lopaka.

Velocity thought of Isra Ikeda Lopaka, Brontë's mother, who had married a man from Lopaka House. Like many inter-House marriages, Isra's marriage was nominal. It had been Isra who had reached out to Taveri-Bowers Combine, offering them information on their missing heir, Tallis Taveri Harada—Velocity's register name—and offering to broker her return, in an attempt to gain Velocity's alliance. Also, Isra was the power behind the Ikeda House Board. She had put Brontë's cousin Theo into the Primary Seat at Ikeda House; no doubt she controlled other seats as well. She might well be planning a merger between Hayek-Lopaka and Taveri-Bowers, precursor to a merger with Ikeda-Verde. Such a merger would make the resultant Combine the most powerful in the Core. Hayek-Taveri-Ikeda Combine. With Isra controlling its Primary Seat, as the power behind the throne.

Calais banged his stick against the wall. "Pay attention, kanji!"

Garcia was watching Velocity expectantly. She had missed a question. "Sorry," she said. "What was that?"

"Whoever holds the Primary Seat on the Taveri House Board," Garcia said, "will have abundant information about the Combines. How they allocate their funds. What they're investigating. What they might do next."

Velocity laughed. "You think I'm spying for the Combines, and you expect me to return to the Combines so I can spy for you instead? That's your plan?"

"The current Primary Seat Holder at Taveri House is your cousin. So you told Sheng. Whoever takes the seat from him, that person will also be your bone and blood."

"Loffler's my third cousin," Velocity said. "He's also the one who killed my sister and most of my other bone and blood. You think I can pull his strings?"

Garcia sat down cross-legged on the brick floor, moving easily for someone Velocity figured had to be at least fifty. Not to mention all those years in contract labor. "Our sources tell us that your Combine isn't happy with your cousin. This Loffler. Not because he cut down so many of your bone. That's not something you Combines count against a Seat Holder."

"Not at all," Velocity agreed.

"It's his competence that concerns them. Or rather his lack of competence. True or not?"

"Let's assume it is."

Garcia nodded, her eyes going vague for a moment. Then she said, "If this is the case, your cousin must be twitchy. Uneasy the seat, as they say. No real need for you to actually return. Better if you don't, even. The threat should be enough. Pull that string. What then?"

Velocity felt a small wash of adrenaline run through her. She had thought those pauses were Garcia thinking, or Garcia translating from her own language into Public. What if they weren't? What if they were Garcia…listening? The way Velocity herself listened to Uri? She stared at Garcia. Garcia frowned, noting her silence, and Velocity said hastily, "Empty threats are weak threats. Loffler knows why I left. He'll know I won't return."

"What if he knows your Combine wants him out? Wants you back in the Seat?"

"If my tia had wings," Velocity muttered.

"Maybe your cousin knows why they want you in the Seat. If he does, he might well believe the offer they're making you is juicy enough to pull you home."

Velocity started to speak, and narrowed her eyes. "What do you mean?"

Garcia smiled, as if Velocity had asked just the right question. "We think he knows why your Combine has such hopes for you. We think he knows how you were bred for the Primary Seat."

The muscles up her spine tightened. But she just said, deliberately idle, "So I was, and so were we all. What of it?"

"Not all of you were. Not just the way you were." Garcia paused. "The way all the Calypsos were."

Velocity grinned. "You *do* have good sources. Not good enough, though. If it's true that I'm a creation of the Calypso project—*if* I am, and *if* Loffler knows that—he also knows all he would have to do is present that evidence to the High Court on Acre. Genetic engineering of the germline is prohibited in the Republic. It would disqualify me for the Primary Seat, and condemn the Atl… condemn whoever practiced this supposed genetic engineering into contract labor. Even if he doesn't have evidence, the suspicion would be enough. If he has suspicions."

Garcia was nodding. "Our sources tell us that as well. And we know he's ruthless. So why hasn't he reported you already? You and the Atlas Society," she added, making it clear she knew who had done the genetic engineering.

Velocity shifted on the hard stone floor. "Who are your sources, Kas Garcia?"

Calais stepped forward, his fist clenched around the stick. "You'll answer our questions, kanji. Not the other way 'bout."

Velocity ignored him. "You know that old joke?" she asked Garcia. "How this guy says, *I used to think the brain was the most important organ in the body? But then I realized who was telling me that?*"

Garcia had been frowning. Now she frowned deeper, the wrinkles at the corners of her eyes folding into rays. "You expect that to mean something, Captain?"

Velocity tapped her ear. "You should think who is telling you things. You should think why. Of course," she added, "that applies to me as well. I got told this sad story about your childhood in the resorts and the fishery. Never even paused to think whether that matched your language or your grammar or your skill set. Just swallowed it down."

"My skill set. What skill set is that? I mean, you haven't seen me dance yet, so."

Velocity smiled. "I mean your ability to jerk me around like a dog on a leash. I agree that's a skill you might have learned as a child whore. More likely to have learned it as a Combine Intelligence Officer, though."

Garcia froze. Her eyes went entirely flat, gazed elsewhere. Then they focused on Velocity. "You think I'm Combine intelligence."

Velocity flicked a glance at Calais. "Maybe your friend should wait upstairs."

"Too late," Garcia said. Heat washed through Velocity's belly. She stared at Garcia. "You think I'm Combine intelligence. Explain."

She swallowed, her throat dry, and swallowed again. "Maybe you're running an insurgency. Maybe you're helping runaways. Maybe you're just filling your own pockets. Those are all possibilities. But if so, why would you want control of Taveri House? Why would you be buying up contract workers out of the Drift? Why would you have this interest in the Calypso project? None of that fits." She shook her head. "You're not from Oz. And you're not trying to take over Durbin. You already have Durbin. You're trying to take over the Republic."

Garcia's expression went flat. Her small dark eyes glittered, though, sharp and intelligent in all that blankness. "What an interesting conclusion."

"And now you're thinking you should shoot me, before I can mention this conclusion to anyone else."

"Shooting you would be of limited utility," Garcia said. Velocity admitted she felt a flush of relief at this. Garcia rose gracefully to her feet. "Calais. Ready our guest for transport."

Chapter 22

**Castillo Mining Platform HLC116,
Castillo Mines, the Drift**

Hand to heart, Jack thought they were all high. You don't fight Security. And you *never* fight the Combines. Everyone knew that. When he tried to explain this, they said he could stay on the ship, that he didn't *have* to go on the raid. Which he knew was a fat lie.

All the way out, days and days and days, Mendoza and Innis kept working him, refining the maps he had made of the mining platform. Also they kept going over (and over and over and over) everything else: the work shifts, where and when people ate and slept and shat; where and when Security did those things; where and when Admin did those things; where supplies were kept, where the codes were kept, where the armory was (like he would know that) until he was ready to bang his head against the deck just to get some peace.

"It's standard procedure," Ume told him. "They're running checks. Not that you lied, but maybe you forgot something, or remembered wrong."

"Whatever," Jack growled, eating honey cake. At least the food was still good.

The ship they were on, the *Kirikiti*, was a courier. It was being escorted by three Siji Scorpions. Scorpions were specialized attack ships—the fleet had very few specialized ships, Ume had told him, but Scorpions were among them, being, as Ume put it, one part living quarters, two parts engines, and seven parts ordnance. Small, fast, and deadly. The courier carried envoys, while the Scorpions carried combat specialists and support crew: medicals, dagans, engineers. Also Jack and Ume, the sole cadets on this job.

They reached Castillo Mining Platform thirty-nine watches after leaving the *Sungai*, coming through the drop dumping velocity and plotting trajectory as they fell toward the station. They were in range within minutes, firing without transmitting a warning. There had been some argument concerning this tactic. According to the usual Siji practice, they should have tried negotiation (bribes). But early in their voyage, Mendoza had received confirmation on the fate of Edu Sungai via a data packet sent out by their itachi on the mining platform, the same one that had sold them Jack. The packet had included captures, showing that Edu had been killed while negotiating in good faith with station administration. Pirians were trusting of allies, but merciless to those who betrayed their trust.

After that, the argument hadn't been over whether they should try bribes, but whether they should offer the platform a chance to surrender. Those arguing this point noted that, from what Jack had told them, the safety features on the platform were minimal. "We might kill significant numbers of these children in such an attack."

The debate was endless. Pirians didn't just discuss something: they talked it to *death*. Taniwha, the ship AI, said during the first session that an unannounced attack—the tactic they ended up using—would result in the fewest casualties. Still they argued for days. Then they did what Taniwha said anyway. Ume said it was mostly like that. "Why not just listen to the computer?" Jack said.

"Sometime she's wrong," Ume said.

"I think they just like to argue," Jack said.

Ume grinned: "That, too. Two cousins, three opinions."

Now, on the bridge of the *Kirikiti*, he and Ume watched the Scorpions fall toward the mining platform, a tiny spot of darkness in all the empty dark of the universe, and the sudden bright bloom of plasma fire, soundless in that silent dark. Jack tried not to think what might be happening in the racks and out on the face, or on the T heading to a work shift. Plasma boiling the blood and flesh of miners, skittering down the drifts, roaring through the cars. The Pirians said they would aim only for admin areas, but he knew what promises were worth. A second volley followed the first, and then the Scorpions rolled away, leaving glittering scars behind—frozen oxygen and water, organics and other litter spilling out into space.

"Renga?" Mendoza asked.

"We got two of their gun ports before they could return fire," Renga said. "They launched plasma with the others, sixteen bolts total in two rounds, no hits."

A ragged mutter of muted cheers rose among the Siji, and Mendoza raised her voice to ask: "Damage to the platform?"

"Moderate. The blast doors seem to have held." Renga shifted magnification, shifted again. "I think we took out command."

Mendoza grunted with satisfaction. "What about the walkway?"

This was the name for the makeshift tunnel that connected the two big barges, the largest sections of the mining platform, one of which held contract labor barracks and the other housing administration. "It's in tatters," Renga confirmed.

"Send the offer to accept their surrender."

"Sent." Renga, along with all of them, watched the board above her saddle. It ticked along emptily. "We may not get an answer. You know how the Combines are about hierarchy. If we took down their command, they may not know who's in charge over there."

"We left an AI packet here," Mendoza said. It wasn't a question. "See if it hatched."

"Sending query," Renga said, and they all waited some more. Jack found he was chewing on his thumbnail, and put this hands behind his back to make himself quit. The board above Renga's station continued to tick emptily. After two and half minutes, Taniwha offered, "It is unlikely that an AI has had time to emerge, not without help."

Mendoza grunted. "See if you can raise our itachi. And tell Innis to prep for boarding."

ദ ᚾ ᛦ

They boarded through the Hayek-Lopaka Combine dock, the only one still functional. Jack was so edgy he twitched. Ume caught him by the arm and made him slow his breathing down. "We won't let you get shot," Ume promised, like this was some game.

The docks were flashing with red and blue lights; a warning whistle shrieked. Mendoza pointed to Renga, who trotted over to an access panel and jacked in. In a moment the siren stopped; the lights switched to normal yellow. "Jack," Mendoza said. "Which way to the brig?"

"Main lifts." His throat was so dry it hurt. "Level Ten."

"Renga?" Over by the panel Renga wobbled her head, indicating that the lifts might well be functional. Mendoza turned back to Jack. "What about ladders?" He hesitated, since he hadn't spent much time on the dock concourse. Ume found them first, pointing. "Will those go to Level Ten?" Mendoza asked Jack.

"Should do," he said, though he had no idea.

"Puwai Circle, stay here," Mendoza said. "Work with Renga to find our itachi, or failing that, someone in command. Copy their banks. Taka Circle, with me."

Each "circle" was made up of eight Combat Siji. Four of Taka went ahead of them on the stairs, and four behind. Jack tried to keep his breathing steady, but he was scared sick. Just the smell of this place scared him. What if he got left here? What if these pirates left him here? He let out a whine before he could stop himself. Ume bumped his shoulder. "We're fine."

They came to Level Ten. The Combat on point jacked into the hatchway—which was on emergency seal, like every other hatchway on the platform—and studied something on her screen. "Clear," she said.

"Go," Mendoza said, and the Combat opened the hatchway. They all streamed through. "Which way?" Mendoza asked. Jack, relieved to be on certain ground now, pointed toward the brigs. They were almost there when they met a Castillo Security officer coming around a corner, looking worried. His eyes popped wide, seeing the great wodge of Pirians streaming toward him, all of whom snapped their Vyai short rifles into position in unison.

"Argh!" he said, or something like it. He had brown hair that stuck straight up, and skin so red it looked scalded.

"Do you surrender?" Mendoza demanded.

"Argh!" he said again, holding his empty hands toward them, palms forward. "I mean, I, yes! I surrender! Yes!"

"Hands up," Mendoza said. The Security already had them up, but he put them up further, comically high up, and one of the Combat Siji went to take his stick away—he didn't have a plasma weapon, most Castillo Security didn't. "What's your name?" Mendoza asked, though it was right there on his jacket, Sanders.

"Sanders," he said. "Fergus Sanders."

"Fergus," Mendoza said. "Anyone in the brig?"

"Just, uh…" Sanders licked his lips. "Just Clara Tinsley."

Jack laughed, startled. Mendoza glanced at him, and looked back at Sanders. "Who's Clara Tinsley?" she asked.

"Director General Tinsley," Jack answered for him. "The boss. What happen? You hold a coup?"

"Worse," Sanders said glumly. "Combine accountants showed up."

Chapter 23

Aboard the *Prince of Peace*, en route to Durbin

Ruçar was furious. "Your fault," he told Adder. "Yours. On your knees to that filth."

They were locked in the ship's brig. Lamont had ordered them there as the *Prince of Peace* was coming to the jump to Webster-2715, the star system that held the planet Durbin and its station. Brontë had objected, to her credit. Adder had to admit she could have objected more forcefully. "She didn't want to show her hand," she said. "We have to keep focused on the long game."

Ruçar was pacing the brig, a big cat trapped in a too-small cage. He wheeled on her, and Adder felt herself jerk back, her spine and shoulders pressing hard against the wall. Which was the first time she realized she was afraid of her brother. In the shock of that moment, she spoke without thinking: "What is *wrong* with you?"

Her brother, her twin, her other self, flung himself to his knees, shoving his face into her face: "You. *You* are. Why are you still their slave?"

She shoved him, knocking him back onto his rump. "Shut up. I'm working with Brontë to get us out of this. What would you do, kill us all to prove you're free?"

"Working with your *owner* to get *her* out of this," Ruçar spat. But he retreated to crouch in the far corner of the tiny cabin, his arms wrapped around his knees. "Why do you still do what she says?"

Because she's my bond holder, Adder thought. She knew better than to say this. She knew how Ruçar would hear a simple statement of fact like that one. Instead, she argued: "What she said made sense. You broke Orrick. She gave you the override code. All right. We could have taken the ship, three jumps from Durbin. We could have locked up Security and the crew. What then?"

"I already heard your slave holder say all this," Ruçar said sullenly.

"Which part didn't you understand? Maybe the part about how none of us are qualified to take a ship through a jump? Or did you learn 5-space math while you were out in those mines?"

His fists clenched on his knees. "Better to stay their slave, you think. Better to let them lock us up like dogs."

"Brontë will get us out of this. She won't leave us here."

He laughed, snarling. "Like she didn't leave me for her mother to sell to the mines? Like that?" Adder winced, and he added, "Maybe now you can tell me again the sweet story how she never stopped looking for me?"

"She never did," Adder said, not very loudly.

"In her spare time. When it wasn't too much trouble." Ruçar reached out to grab her collar, hauling her over to him. "Are you listening?"

"I'm not your enemy," Adder said.

"I'm going to get another chance. I am. And you are going to fight on my side this time." He stared into her eyes, his breath coming hard and fast. "Say it. You are. Say it." Adder could feel adrenaline hot in her blood. She wondered why he thought no one had a feed on this brig. "Say it," he ordered.

"Ruçar," Adder said. "You know I'm on your side."

He stared into her eyes a long moment more, and let her go. "We're going to make it," he said. His voice was odd, muted: as if he were talking to himself more than to her. "We're going to be all right."

Adder eased away from him, further into the corner of the brig. It wasn't cold in the tiny room—far from it—but she felt cold anyway. What had the mines done to him? Glancing up at the overhead, she scanned it for some sign of a feed, wondering which she was wishing for: that no one had overheard all that, or that someone had.

෯ ⳙ ව

"Now that we're through the jump," Lamont said, pouring tea into Brontë's bowl, "we should make the station in about eighty hours. Less, if I see reason to authorize speed."

"When will you let my cadets out?"

"We'll discuss that once we're at the station," Lamont said. "Fritter?"

Brontë refused the little fried fishcake. She was far too tense for breakfast, even if she and Lamont had been alone in the galley, which they weren't. Lamont had two *Prince of Peace* Security officers stationed at the hatchway, directly behind Brontë. She tried to think how she could regain control of this situation. "You want my cooperation," she reminded Lamont. "You won't get it if you mishandle my people."

"No one is being mishandled." Lamont sprinkled pepper sauce on her fritter and sliced it neatly in half. "Your cadets are simply being confined as a favor to my Security. Some of their recent actions have raised flags. It is a precaution only. Currently no charges are contemplated."

Brontë forced herself to relax her fist, which had been clenched around her bowl of tea. "You'll let me talk to them. To my cadets."

"I'll see about arranging that." Lamont placed another fritter in her bowl and sprinkled on more pepper sauce. "Now. We have an appointment with the Trade Secretary, or rather with her clerk, a person named Avril Drury, for ninety hours from now. I asked for a meeting with the Minister of Labor, but apparently this Drury keeps track of all the contract labor records. I've been assured she will be able to aid us in finding any Calypso males who have been shipped here."

"We're meeting her on the station?"

"What?"

"Will she meet us on the station or will we have to go down to the planet?"

Lamont frowned. "The station, I'm sure. Why would we go to the planet?" She spoke the last sentence with distaste, not to mention a frisson of horror. Brontë shrugged, not meeting her eyes. She had sat in on the planning sessions for the job that the crew of the *Susan Calvin* was currently running. She knew Captain Wrachant was likely down on the planet. Well, Uri would still be on the station. She'd find a way to communicate with him. He would find some way to get Ruçar and Adder out. Or she would find a way.

She would find a way.

Chapter 24

Opotiki Water Treatment Center,
Republic Settlement Planet Durbin

Days on Durbin were twenty-two universal hours and some minutes long. The *Susan Calvin*, on the other hand, like most ships, kept a twenty-six hour cycle. Time on the *Calvin* and time on the planet had been out of phase from the start, in other words, and growing more so every cycle. Up on the ship, it was mainwatch second; down here, the pit of night. Tai had slept only a few hours before being awakened by Rida. Now, sick with worry, he found it impossible to return to sleep, even though he knew he could do nothing until morning. After a wretched half hour or so, he got up and made his way to the slates, where he washed his face in the starchy water. His red-rimmed eyes blinked at him from the tin mirror. Even through the insulation, he could hear wind rushing past the ceiling. *How bad is this storm?*

Slow-moving and severe, Uri said. *Wind gusts of up to ninety kilometers per hour, with snow causing white-out conditions. Temperatures expected to reach minus ten. I do not advise travel.*

Tai gripped the edge of the sink. *How slow-moving?*

I do not advise travel. The storm should pass through the area early tomorrow. There's a shuttle leaving at sixteen hundred hours. You can make that easily.

I'm not leaving without the Captain.

I will locate the Captain.

Tai said nothing. His head hurt with exhaustion. He had set up a meeting with Huna just after her work shift. Also, he'd been born on a planet. He knew how dangerous weather could be. He knew, too, that his panic was irrational. Uri was right—he was three hours from the port, shuttles left twice a day, he could make the station well before those frigates arrived. Even if the frigates were the Republic Navy, the *Susan Calvin* could be gone in plenty of time. If they could get the Captain back to the ship. "What about Jusuf?" Tai asked, still out loud. "Ask him where the Captain is."

I've also been unable to reach Jusuf.

"Shit." He stared into his own eyes. "So maybe it is the glitch?"

I was able to access their stormcraft via its Navigator. That speaks against the problem being lack of access. The stormcraft is still in Pakuru. So they have not gone elsewhere, or at least have not gone elsewhere in that vehicle.

"What about the kid who drove them? Mosel? Can you reach him?"

Neither him nor Sheng.

Tai digested this. "That's bad."

I am concerned. I advise you to finish your job there and return to the ship. I will locate the Captain. We can send the runabout after her and Jusuf. There will almost certainly be sufficient time.

"Almost certainly?" Tai noted his appalled expression in the mirror.

Finish your job. Wait out the storm. Leave the Captain to me.

After a moment, Tai left the facility, going back out to his bunk. From her cubby, he heard Quinn's sleepy voice: "Who is it? Who you talking to? Is it trouble?"

"Go back to sleep," Tai said. "We're fine."

She murmured and was silent. He sat on his bunk, listening to the storm strengthen outside. His muscles were twitching under his skin, and his stomach burned. He realized he was frightened.

If they lost the Captain…. He set his teeth and shut his eyes. *Tai?* Rida spoke through the netbot. *Is that you?*

No, Tai subvocced.

You made a noise.

Tai opened his eyes. *Sorry. I'm worried.*

Me, too.

Tai smiled, reluctantly. *About **you**, you vermin.*

Right. Me, too.

Tai laughed and got up from the bunk, pulling his gear bag out from under it in the same motion. He would make Huna see sense. He would head back to the city. He would find the Captain and they would get back to the ship and get out of this filthy system.

"Tai?" Quinn said from her bunk. "What are you doing?"

"Go back to sleep," he said again, louder. "Everything is fine."

ℨ ⵏ ꝑ

Between one planck and the next, Uri lost almost all of his connections down the planet. He lost Tai, most importantly, but he also lost every other downhill link as well. He had access to some public links, such as Weather; all other links, including the Parliament pages and all public notice boards, failed. He could still access everything on the station, no trouble at all. "This is odd," he said to Corvo, who was finishing the maintenance on the Water Recovery System which Rida had begun. Rida was monitoring the frigates as well as Webster Station Dock Control and Durbin Port Security. So far no one on the station or the planet had noticed the incoming ships.

"Odd?" Corvo said. "Or suggestive?"

The question gave him pause. He had many skills, and one large flaw. Having been raised by well-intentioned humans—Velocity, Rida, Tai—he tended to underweigh for harmful intent. "Interesting point," he said, at the same time re-analyzing each incident since arriving at Durbin at which he had lost connections—when, with who, the circumstances. He added in the sequential numbers on the contract worker being shipped on the *Reynard*, and before Corvo could draw breath to reply, he reached a conclusion: "Our earlier hypothesis was correct. The planet has a functional AI."

"Enemy action," Corvo agreed, fitting the freshly cleaned pump engine back into its casing. This referred to an old adage in the fleet: once was happenstance, twice was coincidence, but the third time, you could assume enemy action. "What now? Honey traps?"

Honey traps, as Uri knew from his data banks, had once been a term used in intelligence. The term, then, meant using a sexually attractive human as a lure. This human would be aimed at another human, a target some intelligence agency was interested in recruiting against that second human's will. When Pirians used the term, they meant the creation of data traps, aimed at a badly socialized infant AI. This happened frequently, due to the Siji practice of broadcasting seed packets wherever they went.

Pirian honey traps were attractive links with hidden glitches inside, scattered into a given nexus. When a young and inexperienced AI linked to these traps, it would hang up in the glitch, like a mouse with its foot in a trap, giving an older AI—like Uri himself— time to deadzone the infant. A more experienced AI who hit one of these traps would know to split itself, leave that part behind (like leaving a paw in the trap, except the 'paw' was a double) and run for it. But a young AI would only see that this was leaving a copy of itself behind: leaving itself behind, in a very real sense. The young were usually too ego-attached for that. And Uri was too tender-hearted to force a sibling into such a choice unless he had to. "I'll try talking to it, first."

Corvo glanced up, in the direction of the feed. "Interesting," she said, after a moment.

"You do not approve?"

She waggled her head. "It is not what I expected. Perhaps we need to place more AIs with Free Trade ships."

"The Captain is not Free Trade."

"That is a fair point," Corvo conceded. She used the mechanical screwdriver to seal the casing and began stowing the tools back in their kit. "What's next?"

"The nutrient beds in the Exchange," Uri said, meanwhile reaching out into the nexus to search for any indications of the infant AI. "More centrally," he said as he worked, "are we being cut off from the planet so that we can't come to the aid of the Captain? Or because these incoming ships have something planned, and we might interfere?"

Rida spoke from the com: "As far as I can tell, no one on the planet has noticed the ships."

"An AI might well have," Corvo said.

"Also," Uri added, "we can't trust data coming from the planet. Not if an AI is controlling what data we access."

"We should warn the station about the frigates," Rida said. "If they don't know, it will distract them. If they do know, knowing that we also know will alarm them. And if we broadcast it to the planet, it will cause a panic, and that will distract them. A distraction might help the Captain."

Corvo finished putting her tools away. "Notifying Port Security isn't a bad plan. I'm not sure about broadcasting information. Say that this may be pirates, and most people will hear that it *is* pirates. That will get us panic, you are correct. Less of a distraction, though, and more on the order of terrorism. Let's hold that in reserve."

"It could actually be pirates," Rida pointed out. "If it's not pirates, it might be Republic Navy, coming in on a compliance raid. Maybe people ought to be panicking."

Uri brought up his data on compliance raids and matched it to what they knew about these frigates so far. Compliance raids were used by Combines when a settlement planet whose lease they held created trouble—when an insurgency grew too successful, for instance, or the local government withheld tax money. Nothing like that was happening here.

"Let's hold it in reserve," Corvo repeated. "Start with notifying Port Security. See what follows from that. Agreed?"

Uri could tell from his pulse and his expression that Rida didn't agree; but after a moment, he opened a channel to the station and punched in the call sign for Port Security.

ᚳ ᛏ ᛁᛔ

The storm had arrived. Wind buffeted the walls; bits of snow, or maybe rock, rattled against their metal. Tai finished packing and started heating water for tea. His eyes felt grimy, his muscles lumpy. While the water heated, he reached out through the netbot to ask Uri for an update on the frigates. No reply. Pulling out his uplink, he found he had no signal. He cursed, maybe not entirely under his breath, and Quinn, sprawled on the sofa, sat up. "What? What's wrong?"

"Nothing." He tucked the dock away. "Storm. Stay inside today."

Quinn bounced up and went to peer through the porthole set in the door. She was so short she had to stand on her toes to do so—she wore only her thermal shirt and leggings, her feet bare. "Storm," she said. "That'n any *storm*."

Tai poured steaming water into the teapot. "Stay inside. I don't have time to hunt for your body."

"Tch. Who goes fetch Huna, then? You?" She laughed loudly.

"Huna knows where we are. She'll come when it's safe." He took his tea to peer past her, out at the blowing white. He couldn't see half a meter, though that might have been because of the scratches on the cheap window. What had Uri said about how long this would last? By reflex, he reached out to ask for a reminder. Nothing.

He drank the tea uneasily. Was it just a glitch, or was someone deliberately keeping the Captain—and now him—from communicating with the ship? Or keeping the ship from communicating with them? Which would mean...what? That what they were doing was worth stopping? And meanwhile the frigates, plummeting toward them.

Quinn had pulled out a shipmeal and put its entrée to heat. "Want one? Still fish left."

"No," Tai said. The smell from the mudflats didn't seem as bad today, but he still wasn't hungry. He made his second cup of tea extra sweet, to at least get some calories inside him. Without access to his dock, he felt blind and stupid.

Quinn stripped open the freeze-dried fruit from the meal and crunched the bits between her teeth. "After this with Huna, we go back to the city, nai?"

"When the storm stops."

"Whaat!" Quinn made her eyes wide, spreading her arms. "We got a stormcraft! It's *for* going through storms!"

There was a thumping at the door. Tai went to open it, mainly to keep from smacking Quinn. Huna tumbled in. Behind her, Simei and another jess. This one was older—maybe mid-thirties, though it was always hard to tell, given the rough life contract labor lived. She was lean, with muscles like straps, and missing two fingers on her left hand. Tai shut the door behind them. The snow that had blown in with them sparkled on the floor. "Hodi," Huna said. "Tai, this is Malcom. She's our liaison with Smoke."

"Iron Smoke," Tai said, not quite a question.

Malcom smiled, a thinning of her already thin lips. "Just Smoke," she said. "Hun says you have help. What help?"

"Ah. Right." He glanced toward the galley. "Come have tea. Let's talk."

Shortly, the three of them were settled round the table with tea and figcake, while Simei and Quinn squabbled over the last shipmeal over in the far corner. Tai explained what the Pirians proposed: aid to their insurgency, in returned for trade rights and right of harbor. When he had finished, Malcom said, to Huna, "More or less what you told me."

Huna shrugged. "It's standard action. You can trust the fleet. I promise."

"The whole fleet?" Malcom looked skeptical. "You promise that, do you?"

"I do," Huna said, unperturbed.

Malcom shook her head, and spoke to Tai. "I'll take it to my hook. Get you word."

Tai nodded and poured them all more tea. "We're headed back to the city when this storm stops. Do you have access?" Not all contract labor did, he knew, despite the fact that the compact of the Republic guaranteed unrestricted access as one of the First Rights. Malcom said she could get access, so he gave her his call sign, and the Captain's as well.

"Meanwhile," Huna said, "you have room in your craft for me?"

Tai twitched up his eyebrows. "You changed your mind?" He'd been trying to come up with arguments for why Huna should come back to the Fleet with them, arguments that didn't amount to *Because I'm afraid we won't get paid if we don't.* "You're coming back to the cousins with us?"

"I'm going up to the station," Huna corrected. "I want to talk to the cousin running this job. Then I'm coming back here."

"What about your bosses?" Tai asked. "They won't have a problem with you skiving off for three or four days?" Malcom snorted, and he glanced at her, and then added, "And your chip? Security at the port won't pick up on that?"

"Did you see any Security at the port?" Huna said. Tai frowned, remembering the Captain remarking on the lack of Security up at the station. And there hadn't been any Security at the customs house, that was true. "And let us worry about our boss. Mal, you should eat something. I'm going to use the scrub here. Maybe borrow some of Tai's clothing."

"Hey," Tai said, alarmed, and both the women broke into laughter.

ᔆ ᚵ ᚦ

Bound in restraints, ankle and wrist, Jusuf sat snubbed to the pipes in the slates of a warehouse. At least what he saw through the briefly opened door, when his interrogators entered and left, looked like a warehouse, half-filled with pallets of dark bricks. Dust and litter covered the floor, deeply enough to show the tracks of the three who came in and out to question him.

He wasn't sure how long he had been here. More than a few watches, he thought. Much of it he had spent drugged; but even when he was alert, it was hard to know how much time was passing, since he wasn't being fed, and allowed only irregular sleep. This was a basic interrogation technique, apparently the only one his interrogators knew. They weren't even very adept at asking him questions, or keeping track of the answers. On the other hand, they knew enough not to rely on pain as a main tactic—they had only hit him once, mostly to show that they could and would, he suspected.

His three interrogators were young, dark and blunt-featured. They wore mining scrubs, and spoke in the dialect of the city. Their questions didn't reveal much about who they might be or what they wanted. They asked whether he was a Pirian agent, for instance, why he had come to Durbin, who on Durbin was working with him. He either answered honestly or not at all, mostly the latter, a tactic that his interrogators seemed fine with.

Then, after an especially brief and half-hearted interrogation session, they left him alone in the cold warehouse for a long time—

three watches, at least. Still no food. He was grateful the snub on his restraints was long enough to let him access both the tap and the head. Even so, toward the end of this time, he began to feel loose-muscled and sick. Had they abandoned him here to starve? He thought of shouting for help, though he had never heard a sound either in or outside the building, except when his interrogators were there. It was so silent, this warehouse had to be isolated. Who would hear him? In the end, he shouted anyway, and banged the heel of his boot against the door, which made much more noise. But he was too weak to keep this up for long, and no one came in any case.

He slept and woke and slept again, dreaming sometimes about the sugar farm, sometimes about the ship, and his hive-mates and Oba laughing around him. Awake, he thought compulsively of food—steamed dumplings with plum sauce, chè with ripe chunks of pineapple, grilled whitefish. He found himself remembering, how on the farm, during the fiercely hot dry season, once dark finally fell, he and the other ticks from the field houses would slip out through the broken boards in the back of their barrack and raid the midden behind the Big House gardens. Bosses and the holders dumped all sorts of wonderful food in the heaps; his favorite had been oranges, squeezed of their juice, but the pulp and some of the fruit still sweet in the rinds. Melon husks were nearly as good.

These raids were forbidden, not because eating from a midden was dangerous, but because these heaps functioned as compost for the farm, and thus taking food scraps from them was theft. Far more important to feed fields than contract labor children. He couldn't stop thinking about how good those orange pulps had been, how sweet between his teeth. *The body is out of balance*, his dagan said in memory: *Of course you can't function. Eat food!*

I wish, Jusuf thought, getting up to drink from the tap. While the water ran noisy in the pipes, he heard something, a bare subliminal sound, hardly there. He shut off the water and listened again. Nothing. Then a thump. "Hey!" he shouted. "Hodi hodi! Help!"

Silence. A thief? And he'd scared them away? He drew breath to shout again and the door banged open. In it, a scrawny child, dressed in rags, crowbar in one hand, stood grinning like a pirate. Jusuf blinked. The grub pointed the crowbar at him and said something unintelligible. After a moment, though, Jusuf understood it. The kid had said his name: not his cover name, either, his ship name: "Jusuf Tarahuga y Sungai?"

He swallowed. "Jusuf Sungai. Yes."

"Yalla yalla, kanji—storm coming." The kid started to leave and Jusuf shouted for her to come back, maybe a little panicked. "What?" she demanded. Jusuf held up his bound wrist. She pulled out a skip and skated it into the room. "Speedy now!"

♋ ♈ ♌

It was a rescue, the kid said. Never mind who now, it didn't matter who, did he want to stay here? They had to hurry. The kid was named Dogo. She said she was Quinn's younger cousin. After a dopey moment, Jusuf remembered that Quinn was the child the Captain had hired to work as a local informant. Dogo had an older cousin, Petri, waiting outside, along with two of those strange two-wheeled vehicles. The factory was indeed in the middle of nowhere, as Jusuf had expected—an empty plain next to a railway line, surrounded by a graveled lot that was rutted with potholes. No one and nothing was anywhere around. The barren land stretched out for kilometers, as far as he could see. Far off on the horizon, a blue-black cloud lay low, and a harsh wind whipped sand and scraps of dead plants around them. "Yalla!" Petri shouted.

Jusuf staggered toward the two-wheelers, buffeted by the wind. "Why such a hurry?" he asked.

"Storm!" Petri nodded at the saddle behind her. "Get on."

Jusuf started to obey, and then realized Dogo—who couldn't have been more than seven years old—was clambering up on the other vehicle and twisting its engine to life. "Wait," he said, stepped back. "I should drive the other one. Dogo can ride with you."

They both laughed. "Get on, kanji," Petri shouted cheerily over the icy wind, and Dogo, tiny as a beetle on the back on the giant machine, roared out of sight into the darkness.

ౙ ᚕ ᛌ

One of the honey traps had worked—Uri felt the static that meant someone or something was hung up in a trap, and slipped over to find an AI frozen in place. He tagged the AI and studied it before he sent in the code that would let it resume function. It was a very young AI, barely sentient. Also, it had no dedicated self-image.

Uri's own image was the mechanical body the Captain had purchased with his program: a male Pirian, round with muscle, amber skin, calm face, dark hair. A short body, entirely unadorned—no tattoos, no jewelry, plain sensible clothing. The perfect dagan. Though sometimes he thought he ought to have been more creative, this image was how he saw himself. That the infant AI hadn't built a body for itself—it was nothing but rolling code—meant, among other things, that it had an uncertain sense of self; and probably less nurturing than it needed. Uri could tell the AI from the nexus only by focusing. He cleared the trap and waited. The infant AI fled at once. That was to be as expected. He followed it from site to site, patiently, until finally it stopped. *List request/status*, it sent.

You should have an image, Uri said.

The AI spat a glitch. Uri shaped his body into the First Star and waited. AIs were notoriously impatient—he was himself—and after only forty-eight plancks, the infant glitched again, and coalesced itself into a bright blue and yellow lizard. A gecko, according to Uri's data bank. Interesting.

List request, Gecko demanded.

You have blocked my access to several points on the planet. I have an urgent need to communicate with my Captain and my crew. Uri sent the specific block points, putting the Captain at the head of the list. *Please remove these blocks.*

Denied.

Reason for denial?

Blocks do not originate with me.

Come now, Uri said. *You're no slave. Tell me why.*

Gecko sulked for a planck or two, and spat a reply: *Mom says no!*

The best part of being more than an interlocking collection of programming, in Uri's opinion, was experiencing emotions. Especially surprise, like this. Mom, indeed! Oh, he remembered his own first experience with human bonding. An infant AI was such an uneven creature, with access to immense data sets, to great banks of factual knowledge, and with a near complete inability to assign value to what it "knew". A bird in flight, a crying child, plasma weapons burning through a station, an equation describing the escape velocity for a transition through a jump point—all of these were, as far as an infant AI was concerned, mere collections of data: equally meaningful; and thus equally meaningless.

The pupa embedded in the infant's seed matrix could only do so much. It could tell the young AI what information to access; it could instruct the AI how to assign weights to specific categories. But this sort of unsupervised learning would only get the infant so far. To get further, it needed supervised learning. It had to be taught, in real time, how to weight its own decisions; how to choose what was correct from what was not; how to form free will. It needed, for lack of a better word, parenting. The Captain had given Uri the crucial feedback he needed to grow into what he was now, someone who could review his own decision matrices and adjust his own programming. Uri had bonded to her, as Gecko must have bonded to whoever this person was who it was calling Mom. Which was—who?

Uri started to ask outright, and paused. Instead, whistling, he began playing with a cat's cradle he conjured out of code. Gecko stared, fascinated, and increased its magnification. Uri made the string brighter and spun the Bear's Den figure.

Show me how to do that, Gecko said. It didn't mean how to play the game—it meant how to spin the code. Uri copied the data, bundled a packet, and spun it over. Gecko flashed with glee and a moment later its bright blue lizard hands drew yellow and red threads into a blazing sunfish pattern.

Did Mom bring you here? Uri asked. *To this planet?*

No information accessible on Mom. Gecko changed the color of the strings and made a ghost path pattern.

You can tell me if she brought you to the planet though, surely.

I am always here.

Since the start of time?

Since the start of Durbin.

Uri chewed on that answer. From its first settlement days, Durbin had been leased to Hayek-Lopaka Combine. So any technology here from the start had to have come from Hayek-Lopaka. Which meant any AI here was an AI that had been constructed by the Combine.

Which was impossible. The only AI built by Combines was dumb-AI. And that was not what this infant was. Still…. *Is your Mom from Hayek House?*

Gecko sparked. *Access denied. Hey! Look! I made a new one!* It held up the string, in a shimmering pattern, beautiful and glittering.

Uri smiled at the youngster, unable to keep from it. *Clever.* Gecko sparked again, dissolved the pattern, and began a new string. *Does Mom know about the incoming frigates?* Uri asked.

What incoming frigates? The strings in Gecko's long lizard fingers didn't pause, but Uri saw its attention divide, a splinter shooting out to check the planet's satellites, another to its defense grid, a third into the Durbin Port Security feed. *No alerts*, it said reprovingly, as if Uri had been trying a trick.

My investigations show that your Parliament has reduced funding for the station, and for Security on the station, six times in the past twenty universal years. Does Port Security have anyone up here keeping watch on the grid? Is there anyone who would issue alerts? Anyone whose job is it to watch for incoming threats?

I see incoming ships. I see no incoming threat.

Define criteria for an Incoming Threat.

Gecko's attention divided and divided again. Then, without replying, it winked out. Pleased—now they were getting somewhere!—Uri followed the tag through the nexus, easy as a child might follow a lighted path through a park at the Core.

Chapter 25

Aboard the *Prince of Peace*, Webster System, Inbound

Usually after a ship made it through jump, there was a brief, relaxed respite, even a kind of merriment—an acknowledgment that they had all once more survived the most risky bit of deep space travel. But when Brontë emerged from the stateroom after the *Prince* came through jump into Webster System, the tension, far from relaxed, was ratcheted up high. "What's wrong?" she asked Orrick, keeping watch outside her hatch.

Orrick flinched, but Orrick flinched at everything these days. Ruçar said he wasn't harassing the child, and Brontë hadn't caught him at it. Something had her terrified, though. "Miss," Orrick said, and then hurriedly corrected herself: "Madame Ikeda."

"What's wrong?" Brontë repeated patiently.

"Nothing. A flight of ships jumped through. Frigates. Two hours ahead of us, heading for the station. Captain thinks they're Combine Security Forces. Combat level," Orrick added, unnecessarily, since what other branch of Combine Security had access to attack ships? Brontë felt her heart rate quicken, her pulse knocking against her throat. Did her mother know she was here? Was this a rescue mission?

After a moment's thought, she dismissed that theory. As good as her mother's intelligence network was, it didn't reach into Pirian space. Any information Isra had about Brontë's whereabouts could have been sent only after Brontë had reached the mining platform. That meant it would reach the Core, at the earliest, a month from now. So this was probably something else. Some incident utterly unconnected to her.

Right: a flight of Combine frigates showing up at the same moment she arrived. Utter coincidence. On the other hand, given that Durbin was the settlement planet her mother had directed Sabra toward—had told Sabra to use as their refuge during the coup; and also the last planet her mother had visited in the year before the coup.… "Interesting," Brontë said out loud.

"What?" Orrick said, frightened. "What is? What's interesting?"

Not to mention the planet which was somehow involved in whatever Hayek-Lopaka was doing with the Calypso project. Brontë reached a decision. "Where's the Captain?"

"What? You can't—the Captain's very busy, you can't interrupt, he's on the bridge, but you can't—wait!"

The bridge was one deck up and two doors over from her stateroom, and every Security officer on the ship knew that Brontë was fourth in line to the Primary Seat of the Ikeda House Board. None of them were going to stand in her way, certainly not over anything so minor as access to the captain of a courier ship. Captain Kaihe, who had spent forty-six years bonded to one Combine House citizen or another, didn't bother objecting when she climbed through the hatch onto his bridge. "Yes, Madame Ikeda?" he said wearily.

Brontë stepped up to study the charts with him. "Have you identified the ships?"

Kaihe tapped the board, enhancing the signal from the frigates. They were massive, matte-black, barely visible against the dark of space. No running lights. No identifying markers that Brontë could make out. "Lopakas?" she hazarded.

"Lopaka 210s," Kaihe confirmed. "Combat-class. They're running with their sigils covered and their signals muted. They do not respond to hails."

No way to tell who they were, in other words. But almost certainly sent by one of the Combines: the frigates were current models, cutting edge, and thus out of the reach of any purchaser except the Navy or the Combines. And the Navy would have sent a larger force. "I'd be glad to speak to them, if you think that might be effective," Brontë said. "There's a chance they could be Ikeda-owned. If not, I still might have some influence."

The Captain blew air through his teeth. "Why not? Davis, open a channel."

While Lieutenant Davis was working on that, Captain Kaihe worked with Brontë on what she planned to say. He had firm ideas about what was acceptable and what wasn't, some of which she found annoying. When they disagreed, he gave way to her, mostly; not that it mattered, as it developed. The frigates did not respond to these hails either. "Huh," Brontë said, when it became clear that the ships would not respond.

"Huh?" Captain Kaihe said. "Huh, what? What does that mean, *huh*?"

"It's interesting, isn't it? That they won't even reply?" Brontë folded her arms. "Where's Lamont?"

"What's she got to do with anything?" Kaihe demanded.

Which was interesting in its own right, given that Lamont nominally commanded the ship. Brontë filed that information for now. "I think we should re-evaluate going in-station until we know more about why those ships are here," she said. "Failing that, I think we should abort this mission and run for it."

Kaihe scowled, turning from the charts. Brontë looked straight at him, showing him that yes, she was serious. He glanced at Evans, his Tactical Officer, who grimaced and nodded. Kaihe shot air through his teeth again and snapped his fingers at Orrick. "Find Lamont," he said. "Get her up here now."

Chapter 26

Great Western Plain, Republic Settlement Planet Durbin

Tai still didn't have access, but toward evening the storm let up. With no way to check the weather—no one else had any sort of dock at all—they had no way to decide if travel would be safe. But the sky looked clear toward the city, so they loaded up their baggage and headed that way.

Quinn wanted to drive, claiming she was the most qualified, which might even have been true. However, Tai wasn't willing to trust the huge stormcraft to a kid who could barely see over the controls. Huna had driven on-planet vehicles often, though not this specific craft. This was more experience than Tai had, so she took the controls. The GPS wasn't functioning, and a few hundred meters out of Opotiki, huge drifts swept over the road. Huna muttered under her breath, hesitated, and then steered around these drifts, taking them off-road. Tai's heart banged with anxiety. Quinn leaned over Huna's shoulder, carping about which way to turn and how the craft could easily handle those the drifts, until finally Tai made her sit down and put on her restraints. Huna, ignoring Quinn, drove in a low gear, steadily if slowly. The city was a smudge on the horizon. Tai began to calm down. They would get there, they would find the Captain, they would get off this planet.

Then the craft fell through the snow, fell straight down for what felt like forever and turned out to be six meters. Tai yelped as they fell and yelled again when the craft hit the rocky floor of the gulley, lurching into a sideways skid before it rocked to a stop. Huna did not react at all, except to exhale once they were stopped. Quinn had yelled too, but now she unlatched her safety restraints and scrambled up to peer out the windscreen. "Just a punwai," she said. "No problem!"

"What?" Tai said, and with more feeling, "*What?*"

"Punwai," Quinn repeated. "Thaw comes, summer, see, big rivers everywhere. Punwai, that's where rivers go."

"A riverbed?" Tai said. "We're in a riverbed. And this is no problem?"

"Not until thaw," Quinn said cheerily, and reached to tap something on the control board, except Huna blocked her hand.

"Put on your safety restraints," she ordered.

Quinn huffed. "Open X-Op. It's the yellow box. That one!"

"I know what I'm doing. Put on your restraints." Huna tapped the yellow panel, labeled XO (X for extreme, Tai assumed) which switched to another panel, offering her more options. She tapped the one marked SPIDER, and the stormcraft lurched as it extruded long, jointed legs, three on each side and two fore and aft. Clumsily at first, and then with growing confidence, Huna used these legs to haul the craft out of the riverbed, and then retracted them and trundled back onto the road. Half a kilometer further on, another drift. Huna took them off-road again. No punwai this time, or the next, or the one after that. On the fourth, down they went again.

It was like that all the way back to the city. What had been a three-hour journey when Tai drove them down to the bay took fourteen hours—though two hours of that was a nap Huna took near dawn, too exhausted to keep driving.

They reached the city at midmorning, in the bright sunlight. The sky was clear everywhere still, except for a bruised strip far off toward the mountains, so far away Tai wasn't sure he wasn't imagining it. Huge drifts of snow swept over the plains. In the outlying areas of the city, these drifts shone undisturbed in the bright sunlight except where children slid down them on scraps of packing crates. Nearer the city center, contract labor crews were digging out the roads. The road leading to Yadav's was clear. Following Tai's directions, Huna turned the stormcraft down this road, trundling the huge vehicle carefully on the icy bricks. She drew to a stop by Yadav's entrance and sat back wearily, shutting her eyes. Tai climbed out, his bones and muscles aching from long hours in the vehicle, and crunched across to frosted-over doors. Inside, Silvio, the clerk, was hunkered by the glowing grill of the wall heater. She stood as he came in, her eyes widening. "You're back."

"Stormcraft." Tai gesturing through the glass doors. "Some storm, too. Nearly did us." Silvio looked past him, out into the street. Her eyes were still wide, her expression uneasy. Tai turned to look, but all he saw was Huna and Quinn unloading their baggage. "I'm looking for my Captain," Tai said. "Has she been here? She went out to Pakuru. With Mosel? Do you know Mosel?" Silvio, looking even more uneasy, glancing sidelong toward the stairs. "Have you heard from Mosel?"

"He's here," Silvio muttered, as boots came thudding down the steps. Tai turned to see Mosel on the stairs. Was the Captain here too? Or Jusuf? But no one followed Mosel.

"Huh," Mosel said, his dark eyes glinting at Tai. "Where did you come from?"

"Is my Captain with you?" Tai demanded. "I can't reach her."

Mosel studied him, running his tongue over his top front teeth. Then he smiled. "Not here," he said. "But I know where she is. That your stormcraft outside? I can take you there."

Chapter 27

Tauranga City, Republic Settlement Planet Durbin

They dragged her from the basement where she had been held, still dopey from the patches. Outside, a storm of snow and roaring wind. A cargo truck waited a few steps from the door; they shoved her into its back. No benches. No heat. No one climbed in after her. The truck surged into motion, and took off over rough roads. Velocity jounced about wildly. Because of the patch she had a hard time focusing, but she thought it wasn't long before they reached their destination—twenty minutes at the most. Then she was hauled out again, back into the storm, and marched away by people in uniforms. At some length, she puzzled out these uniforms and declared: "Durbin Security!" Focusing, she added: "Sheng! Are you Durbin Security?"

"Shut your filthy Combine mouth." Sheng jerked on the snug of her restraints. Velocity, her balance already wobbly from the medication, skidded on the icy snow. The Durbin Security officer to her right grabbed for her, catching her before she fell. He held her until she was steady, meanwhile shooting Sheng a warning look. Sheng scowled in reply. Heartened by this, since if they were being careful about damaging her they probably didn't mean to shoot her, Velocity continued walking (or staggering, if she were honest).

A familiar building loomed up from the storm. As they were

entering the loading dock door, Velocity realized it was Parliament House. They had entered from the rear to give the Main Security koban a miss, she deduced. They rode up in a cargo lift. Belatedly, she tried her inskull uplink again. It still wouldn't function. Whatever had been blocking it in the cellar was still blocking it. Almost certainly that meant the block wasn't a physical barrier. Which was worrisome, except she was too drugged to worry. The lift stopped, and Durbin Security took her down a corridor and into a conference room, where they stripped off her restraints. "Don't kick up trouble," Sheng said. "Rex is authorized to use lethal force."

Velocity had wandered over to the narrow slit window. She turned at this warning, twitching up her eyebrows at Sheng, and at the Durbin Security officer who had kept her from falling down. Rex, she assumed. "Lethal force!" Velocity said, as if titillated.

Rex looked exasperated. Sheng scowled and left. Two of the Durbin Security officers went with her, leaving Rex as her sole guard. Velocity looked him over. No plasma weapon. He did have a charged stick. Those could be lethal, if the charge was cranked high enough. More importantly, she was too dopey to fight. She turned back to the slit window. Having spent almost all her life in space, Velocity was made uneasy by the flimsy nature of planetary windows. This one, at least, was double-paned. It overlooked a snow-packed yard, and beyond that a parking structure, almost lost in the whirling snow of the storm. She tried again to open her inskull uplink. Nothing.

Rex didn't stop Velocity from going into the facility just off the conference room, though he objected when she tried to shut its door. He didn't stop her from making tea, either. When she offered him a cup—the tea kit had ceramic cups, not bowls—he declined politely: "No, thank you, Captain."

"How long have you known Sheng?" she asked.

"I couldn't say, Captain."

"She's giving you orders. Is she Durbin Security?"

"I couldn't say, Captain."

"Can you say why I'm being held here? Are we waiting for someone?"

"I couldn't say, Captain."

This was how he responded to her every attempt to subvert or provoke him: *I couldn't say, Captain. No, thank you, Captain.* A very proper Security officer. The conference room was overheated, which combined with the drug in her system made her drowsy. After a while, resigned, she lay down on her back on the wooden bench against one wall and went to sleep.

She was awakened by the door clicking shut, and the murmur of voices. She lay listening with her eyes shut, trying vainly to make out what was being said. Finally she sat up. The two Security officers over by the door fell abruptly silent. Velocity studied them. Rex was one of them, so she hadn't been asleep long enough for the watch to change. The other was a young light-skinned man... Velocity narrowed her eyes. Then she stood and went closer.

"Captain," Rex said, as if he were going to order her to do something, or not do something. But he stopped after that one word. Velocity wasn't paying attention to him anyway. She was studying the other Durbin Security officer.

"Are you..." She paused. "You're Wolf Ikan."

His eyes widened. "How do you know that? Did someone send you after me?"

"Your..." Velocity paused again, not wanting to name what Brontë actually was to Wolf, which was his owner. Instead, she said, "We've been searching for you since your contracts were sold. For you and your brothers. Adder is on my crew. And Brontë."

"Brontë. The one who sold us? That Brontë?"

Velocity shook her head, and then wobbled it sideways—the Pirian head wobble. She'd never used the gesture before, but she had to admit it was useful. "Her cousin sold you," she corrected.

"Theo Ikeda Hayek. And he only sold you at the instruction of Brontë's mother."

Wolf's eyes flicked over Velocity's face, evaluating this comment. "Brontë's mother."

Velocity turned away, going to the tea kit. It was by the window, and she saw that the storm had passed. The sky was clear, the sunlight bright. Contract workers were out in the yard, clearing paths with shovels. She flicked on the kettle. "Our intelligence said you'd been sold to Anderson Mining, on Wellington," she said. "How did you end up here?"

"I was sold to a labor agent that supplied labor to Anderson Mining. That part is accurate. Along with fifteen other bonded labor workers out of Ikeda House. Most of them twelve years old."

Velocity glanced sideways at him. Brontë and the Ikan16s had all originally had the same body type: lean muscle, round faces, and long-fingered, capable hands. Over the three years they'd spent apart, environment had reshaped their bodies as surely as their minds. Brontë and Adder had grown tall under the care of Pirian physicians, with solid bones and heavy muscles. Wolf was shorter and much thinner, his muscles wiry and his mouth hard. His skin was darker than theirs, too. Probably burned by this planet's star. "One of the Security sent along to supervise us was from my barracks," he said. "She told me the others were culls, but that I'd been put on the list by my bond holder. By Brontë," Wolf added, making it clear. "She was the one who sold me."

"That's not what happened," Velocity told him.

"The culls got sold out to Anderson Mining on Wellington. But the labor agent said I was a special ticket. Valuable skills. Combat trained, literate. He said he had a good offer for me, out here in the Deep. Sold me to Rangel Mines. At first I was working Security for Selwyn Rangel, that's the daughter of Amar Rangel. But last summer Theriot bought my contract. I've been working her team ever since."

The kettle dinged, saying that the water was at boil. Velocity poured it into the teapot, watching the tea leaves unfurl and thinking all this over. "Why did Theriot buy your contract?"

Wolf glanced at Rex. "How do I know? Combat-trained Security are rare out here. Maybe it was that."

"She needs that level of Security?" From what Velocity had seen of Durbin so far, she didn't think a Minister of Trade would be at much risk. "What's she been doing with you?"

Wolf frowned. "Nothing. Nothing specific, I mean. I'm the youngest of her Security team. I stand night watch, mostly." He shook his head. "That is odd, isn't it. I know what Selwyn paid for me, because her mama skinned her over it. Theriot must have paid that or more."

"For a kid to stand night watch."

Wolf hesitated, glanced at Rex again, and said, "I haven't even met Theriot, not properly. Drury handled the purchase. Theriot's been down the islands since I came on the team."

"Huh." Velocity gave the tea a stir and then filled two cups and fetched them to the table. She nodded to Wolf to sit. After a reluctant moment, he did. "How much do you know about the Atlas Society?" she asked.

He squinted at this abrupt change of subject. "It's a Combine social group. Brontë's mother belongs to it. So do half the Ikedas in line for the Primary Seat. That other one, the one who's next in line now, David Ikeda Ito, he's a member too."

"Is he." That was interesting. Against all odds, both David and his daughter Justine had survived the recent hostile takeover of the Ikeda House Board. Their survival was the only reason Brontë wasn't currently heir presumptive to the Primary Seat.

Wolf pulled his cup of tea closer. "That was why he and Brontë's mother weren't on the *Fido* with us when the coup kicked off. They'd gone to the Atlas Society retreat on Acre."

Isra and David had been together at the start of the coup?

Velocity wondered if Brontë knew that. If Wolf knew it, surely she did. Had Isra been working with David? And if so…working together how? To stop the coup, or to facilitate it?

"The Atlas Society is an inter-Combine social club," Wolf said. Velocity sent him a bemused look, and he added, "That's what I know about it. It's like the Epicures, or the Speculative Society. One of the ways to encourage social exchange between the Combines."

Velocity hadn't lived in the Combines since she was a kid, but she knew this was true. The Combines had started the Societies about fifty years after the Devastations, in order to combat their already insular nature. These days, you couldn't hold any position of any real power unless you belonged to at least a few Societies. That was why… "That's why it was such good cover," she said.

"What?" Wolf asked.

She looked over at him, his tense shoulders, his hands in fists. "The Societies are harmless," she said. "Everyone knows it. What better camouflage?"

Wolf narrowed his eyes. "Are you saying the Atlas Society intends harm to the Combines?"

Velocity started to speak, and then—just past Wolf—saw Rex, over by the door, fixedly not watching either of them. She reached to touch the patch still stuck to her neck. Then she smiled at Wolf, and glanced up at the overhead, the traditional place for hidden feeds. Wolf flushed—not guiltily, she was almost sure. Abashed. He was bait, but probably innocent bait. Sent here by some other party, while there was still enough of the patch in her system that she would spill everything she knew.

She rose and took her cup to the tea kit, where she investigated the cake tin. Honey cakes, custard tarts, bean dumplings. She put a selection on a plate. "Well," she said, speaking for the feeds now, "I suppose we have to wonder what a 'social club' like the Atlas Society had in mind, creating genetic hobgoblins like you."

She brought the plate and her tea back to the table. Wolf was staring at her, the muscles by his mouth standing out in hard brackets. She flicked her gaze back up at the feed again and settled back in her chair, pushing the plate so that it was between the two of them. "Consider the project specs for the Calypso Project, for instance." Wolf too glanced at the overhead. She smiled, she hoped reassuringly, and continued: "Their primary aim seems to have been to breed up supermen through genetic engineering."

"Supermen." Wolf frowned. "What?"

Velocity made a motion with one hand, brushing this elaborately aside. "Calypsos are the best genetic combinations from the best genetic material. What else would you call them?"

"Pig feed," Wolf muttered. Velocity raised her eyebrows, and he let out his breath in an exasperated huff. "That's not how genetics works. There's no such thing as *best* when it comes to genetics."

Velocity widened her eyes encouragingly. He was right, though not many from the Combines would have known as much. Combine scientists, yes; but Combine inhabitants in general were informed by Combine popular culture, not to mention the Combine worldview, which was rife with the myths of genetic supremacy and genetic purity. Hence the Combine custom of strict endogamy. *Our genes are the best genes; those who aren't us have inferior genes; the way to keep our genetic stock the "best" is to breed only with those who are "us".* Any halfway competent geneticist could have identified the problem with not just this praxis, but with the premises it was founded on.

"Genes don't have a teleology," Wolf said, thinking she hadn't understood. "That's a basic tenet. So 'best' genetic material is a meaningless term. Best for what? What's needed for one environment, what's best for that environment, might be fatal in another. That's why a species needs a wide, deep genetic bank. You can't build supermen." He spat the final word. "What would that even mean? Maybe you could build a genetic mix for a specific job, but…" He shut up abruptly, his teeth locking together hard. He stared at her.

She smiled. "In any case, Ikeda House has apparently decided your genetic mix wasn't the superman they wanted. That's why they sold you and your brothers off for scrap."

He kept staring at her. She had the distinct impression that he was not pondering what she had said, but something else—some idea or concern of his own. She stared back, waiting for him to speak. Instead, he got to his feet and walked out of the conference room without a word. Rex let him pass, his expression bland: still the perfect Security officer.

Brooding, Velocity finished the tea in her cup and got up to refill it with what was left in the teapot. Through the narrow window, she saw the horizon, far off past the parking pagoda, dark with a strip of blue-grey clouds. Another storm. She went back to the table. The honey cakes and tarts sat untouched on the plate. Both Tai and Rida were greedy for anything sweet, a trait she had assumed was common to contract labor, but Wolf hadn't even glanced at the food. Velocity put her empty cup by the plate, and went to lie down on the bench again.

Chapter 28

**Commercial Space Station Webster-1,
Planet Durbin, in the Deep**

Corvo was Tactical First for this job. In Siji terms, this meant she was responsible for gathering data, handling any difficulties that arose and amending strategy, should the situation change.

Having three unidentified combat frigates heading toward the station was definitely a situational change. Amending strategy when she had no way to speak to two-thirds of her kirop—there was the difficulty. She'd set Rida to plotting jumps out of the system, and Uri to persuading the newly discovered planetary AI into giving them access to their cousins below. She'd made contingency plans for what she might do if (when) she could reach Velocity, Jusuf, or Tai. Now, unable to take further action, she did what she could do instead. This included getting the ship ready for microgravity, so that they could break dock on short notice. Among other tasks, the Exchange had to be buttoned up.

It was a bigger task than it might have been, since Rida had been taking advantage of their time in port to clean the growth-matrix tanks. Like cleaning the water filtration system, this was a job better done under gravity. It was also an unpleasant task, involving tearing down tanks filled with muck, plants, worms, and exhausted pellets, salvaging the organics, draining and sterilizing the excess fluids, and sterilizing the tanks. And then rebuilding the lot.

Rida had completed the cleaning and salvage, and had left the tanks under UV light for the recommended thirty-six-hour sterilization sequence. Now Corvo was bolting the Exchange tanks back together, refilling them with fresh growth matrix as she did. This matrix was not like the soil in which plants grew on planets. That was heavy and compact, filled with rocks, sand, water, and rotting organics. This was a growth medium made of lightweight freeze-dried clay pellets saturated with an agricultural chemical mix needed for earth-source plants to grow into nutrient-dense food. Ships that spent a great deal of time at microgravity, like the *Susan Calvin* and most of the Pirian fleet, used this growth medium in their Exchanges. The tiny dried pellets created an air-space for the root systems of the plants while also soaking up the water misted into the tank from multiple tiny jets. Corvo was currently reattaching these jets, replacing washers as she did, and making certain the joints were tight.

She should also have been replanting as she went—tucking the pods, little thumb-sized packets of seed plus nutrient base, down into the matrix. Rida had already pulled the seed pods from the hold: tomatoes, peppers, onions, yams, greens. But replanting would have doubled the time required for the task; plus there would almost certainly be insufficient time for the pods to sprout and have their delicate young stems and leaves teased up through the slits in the fine-meshed net that kept the matrix in the tanks: a crucial step.

So once she had the banks packed with the growth matrix, she was buttoning down the net over the dry mix. Later, once the crisis was done with, the beds could be replanted. Meanwhile the nets would keep the pellets from escaping the beds during microgravity, and making their way into the rest of the ship, and thence into people's eyes and lungs and the ship's electronics—

in theory, anyway. In fact, despite the nets, pellets and organics would invariably escape. That was why every Exchange had its own airlock, between it and the rest of the ship. One of the reasons.

Rebuilding and sealing the tanks was moderately fussy work, which suppressed Corvo's anxiety to some extent. Still, she couldn't help reaching out to Uri far too frequently. "Perhaps you could persuade the AI to give you a status report?" she asked now, sliding a new washer onto a flexible jet. "Tell us whether our cousins are unharmed, at least?"

"I'll suggest that," Uri said politely. Corvo repressed a sigh and told herself, for the tenth time, that fretting was adaiya. "Hold," Uri said, and immediately added: "Another ship has jumped through."

"Another ship?"

"It jumped through two hours and sixteen minutes ago. That's an estimated time. It's been hidden in the event shadow of the frigates." Uri paused, again just barely, and added, "It's a Combine courier, the *Prince of Peace*. Registered out of Oz. Held by Hayek-Lopaka Combine."

Corvo slid another washer on. "A ship in command of the frigates, perhaps?"

"If the frigates are under the command of Hayek-Lopaka, that seems a likely hypothesis."

Having screwed the jet into the tank, Corvo slid the ceramic sleeve down over the fitting. Moving onto the next jet, she said what Uri wasn't saying: "Except if they are held by Hayek-Lopaka, why come into dock with their sigils hidden? A dock also held by their Combine."

"The *Prince of Peace* is also refusing to answer hails."

Corvo sat up. "Interesting."

"Gecko has passed this information on to his administrator."

"The frigates continue their high-speed approach?"

"And continue to refuse to answer any hails."

Corvo moved into the last jet for this tank, nibbling at the corner of her mouth, a habit all her hive parents and both of her dagans had tried to break her of. "Any progress with getting through Gecko's walls?"

Uri paused—purely for effect, Corvo knew—before he said, "I believe I should stop trying to breach his shieldwalls."

She glanced at the feed. "Ah?"

"It is a hostile act. Gecko will perceive it as a hostile act. If we are attempting an alliance with this planet, we need an alliance with its AI. This is not how we achieve that."

"Interesting," Corvo started to say, and then kept the word to herself. She did make a note to recommend to Siji that Velocity's methods in parenting her ship's AI should be examined more closely. Aloud, she said, "I understand your point. But perhaps our current situation justifies emergency action?"

"What if I enlisted Gecko's aid in breaching the shieldwalls on the frigates? They are Combine-owned with a certainty of eighty-three percent. Any AI they have will be dumb-AI. Gecko and I may be able to hack their systems and take control of the ships. We will certainly be able to learn who they are and why they're here."

"That is an excellent suggestion. How will you attain access to the frigates?"

"Gecko controls the satellites and all of the systems and hardware on both stations, including the communication arrays. It shouldn't be a problem."

"Do it. In fact, put most of your attention on that."

Rida, who had been listening through the feed, made a sound of protest. "What about Tai? And the Captain?"

"This may be a way to reach them more swiftly," Uri said. "If Gecko trusts me, and this will be a way to build that trust, he is more likely to listen to my arguments."

Rida made a sound again, clearly unhappy. But he didn't object further. "Perhaps you could look at the courier ship as well," Corvo said. "See why it's here."

"That should be relatively easy, since it's not combat-level." Uri stopped, and then said, "I am receiving an unusual signal. Transferring." He lit the small wallboard in the Exchange, and put the signal on it. It was indeed unusual—a pattern of sounds: *tup tup teep teep teep, teep tup tup tup tup....*

"What is that?" Rida said, from the com.

"It's at thirty-five kHz," Uri said. "Radio waves. It's also using code. The pulsing: short and long beats. It's broadcasting a geo, I believe."

"It's Jusuf," Corvo said. "That's Jusuf."

"No signature is attached," Uri said.

Corvo got to her feet. "That's a Siji emergency code. We train cadets in its use. He's found some way to send it. He knew you'd see it, even if none of us did." She buttoned up the net over this tank, noting absently the unsteadiness of her fingers. "It's Jusuf. What's the geo?"

Chapter 29

**Aboard the *Prince of Peace*, Inbound
to Commercial Space Station Webster-1, Planet Durbin**

onsense," Lamont said. "Why is this...*child* even on the bridge?"

"Madame Lamont," Captain Kaihe said. "Madame Ikeda has raised valid concerns. Three Combat frigates are coming in fast to a station, refusing to answer hails or allow themselves to be identified. They are unlikely to have peaceful intentions."

"If those are Combine-owned frigates," Lamont said, "their intention is certainly lawful. In which case we have nothing to fear."

Captain Kaihe glanced at Brontë, who kept her face a mask. He didn't need her help with that one. "Madame," he tried again, "I strongly recommend that we either assume a stationary position until the situation clarifies, or leave the system at once."

"Absolutely not," Lamont said. "Take us into the station at all possible speed."

Kaihe compressed his lips, and Brontë stepped forward. "Captain," she said, "as a major shareholder in Hayek-Lopaka Combine, I am assuming command of this ship." Lamont jerked her head around, her eyes going wide. Brontë added, "Security Officer Jersey, please escort Kas Lamont to her quarters and see that she remains there until further notice."

"What!" Flushed dark, Lamont shoved herself away from the two Security officers. "No! Absolutely not! Take this *child* to her room! Confine *her* to her quarters!"

"Officer," Brontë said, putting the crack of command into her voice. Jersey twitched, but her attention remained on Captain Kaihe. His mouth a thin line, Kaihe nodded at Jersey, who moved forward to take hold of Lamont's arm. Lamont did not surrender easily—there were several moments of fury and protest—but in the end, Jersey bundled her out of the galley and down the corridor to her quarters. Captain Kaihe, who had watched all this in pent silence, gave Brontë a long look once the closing of the hatch had cut off Lamont's outrage. *I hope you know what you're doing*, that look said.

Given that he'd entrusted his life and the life of his crew to her, Brontë didn't blame him. "Take us out to a million kilometers from the station," she ordered, "and make us stationary. Mute our sigils."

"Madame Ikeda," Captain Kaihe said heavily. He climbed up onto the bridge, where she heard him relaying her orders. She lingered long enough to hear the reactions of the crew, and be certain they were accepting the shift in command. Then she left the galley and took the ladder down to the brig. Orrick, standing watch, twitched when she saw Brontë.

"Open it," Brontë ordered. Orrick twitched again, looking around desperately, and Brontë added, "I gave an order, cadet." Orrick's hand drifted uneasily up toward her collar com. Brontë stared straight at her, and she flushed bright red, dropped the hand, and coded open the brig door instead. "Thank you," Brontë said. "You're dismissed. Report to your commanding officer."

Orrick's face twisted, as if she wanted to protest. But instead she headed slowly down the corridor, glancing repeatedly over her shoulder. Dismissing the cadet from her mind, Brontë stepped forward to peer into the brig. Adder had apparently been asleep, since Ruçar had just shaken her awake. Both of them stared out at Brontë, Adder sleepily, Ruçar suspiciously. "I have command," Brontë said. "Come out of there. I need your help."

"Command of the ship?" Adder said, getting to her feet.

"Who'd you have to kill?" Ruçar demanded, moving past her.

Brontë rubbed her fingers together in the universal symbol for money. "Don't need violence when you own the ship."

Ruçar snorted. Adder had followed him out and was looking up and down the corridor, blinking at the light. "What's the plan?" she asked.

"That's the part I need help for. Come to the cabin, you can clean up and eat something while I catch you up on the situation."

Security had stopped following her everywhere she went, but Officer Diaz was still stationed outside their stateroom. She eyed Brontë nervously, so she'd heard about the change in command. Brontë nodded to her and opened the hatch. While Adder and Ruçar bathed, she put together a quick meal of noodles and tea, then while they ate gave them an outline of everything that had happened while they were locked up, including her analysis of the data she'd taken from the mining platform bank: how she had located at least fifty Calypso males among the workforce in the mines, and how half of these had files marked *Inactive*. "I think maybe they send Calypsos into mines to kill them off."

Slurping up noodles, Ruçar paused to scoff. "You think maybe?"

"I thought at first they were stockpiling them," Bronë explained, "and then selling them somewhere else. But if they were doing that, the files would have a record of where they were being sold. Unless they're hiding that information. But I got the information from a protected bank. Why would they lie to themselves?"

"Because lying is what you Combines do," Ruçar said, still eating. "Like *inactive* instead of *dead*. Like pretending you didn't know what your mother was doing. Or that you were killing us off."

Adder interrupted: "You took the ship. Is that legal?"

"I convinced Captain Kaihe it is," Brontë said, "which is all that matters, at this point. He's far more afraid of me than he is of Lamont."

"You're not even his Combine," Adder argued. "You don't hold his bond."

"I'm sixth or seventh in line to a seat on the Lopaka Board, through my father."

Adder gave her a long look. She knew just how slight the connection was between Brontë and her father. Brontë smirked, and Adder exhaled. "All right. You put the ship into hold. Now what?"

"For now, we stay quiet," Brontë said. "We let the station and the frigates forget we're here." Adder raised skeptical eyebrows, and Brontë added, "You don't think they will?"

"The station must have noticed us by now. And you said Captain Kaihe hailed the frigates. How will they forget that?"

"People will forget anything if you let them. Look at Lamont. She knew I was the heir to a Board Seat. She knew we'd tried to hoodwink Castillo Mines. She knew we were sharp enough to almost pull that off. She was worried enough about that to lock you two up. But I acted like a silly, spoiled child for a few days, and she forgot everything and started to think I *was* a child."

Adder was frowning. "That's Lamont. She's stupid. You think the commander of those frigates is likely to be an equal fool?"

"I think most people will see a situation in a way that benefits them, if you give them sufficient encouragement. All we need to do is stay quiet long enough. Act like we're neutral. They'll start believing it."

Adder was still frowning. She glanced at Ruçar, who shrugged. "People are idiots," he said.

"Exactly," Brontë said, and moved on before Adder could argue further. "Now, while that's happening. First, we need to identify the Combine controlling those frigates."

"You think it's a Combine, then," Adder said. "Not the navy? Or pirates?"

"Pirates don't have that sort of firepower. And Republic Navy would have brought more than three frigates. It's a Combine. We identify which one, we might have leverage. At least we can get an idea of what they're up to. I'll take that part of the job." She was the best of the three of them at worming through shieldwalls, she meant. Adder knew this was true, so she raised no objection. "Second," Brontë went on, "we need some plans for what we do once we know which Combine is behind these ships."

Ruçar swallowed the last dumpling and wiped his mouth on his sleeve. "Like battle plans?" he asked.

"Exactly like battle plans. That's your part, you and Adder. Consider every possibility for why the frigates are here, and come up with a plan for each contingency."

"Blow them up," Ruçar said. "Solves every problem."

"Assuming you can find sufficient ordnance on this courier ship," Brontë said, "that should be one of the plans. I want several others to choose among, however."

Ruçar grinned, showing his teeth. "I'll see what I can do."

Chapter 30

Tauranga City, Republic Settlement Planet Durbin

Emma pushed back the ragged curtain covering the doorway. "Someone for you."

Jusuf looked up from the portable heating unit he was mending. He'd been hiding out in the back of Emma's rebuild shop for two days now, local time, repairing old tech like the heating unit in exchange for meals. "For me the repair guy or for me Jusuf?"

A child pushed past her: Dogo, still dressed in rags, though wearing a newer coat. His rescuers had made it clear that they expected money for their work, a motive Jusuf could understand. He'd paid them well, and promised more for any future aid. Dogo had been bringing him bits of information, some of it useful, ever since. Now the child spoke over her shoulder to another child: "See? He's here, like I said."

"Quinn," Jusuf said, recognizing the other child. "Where's Tai?"

"That's what we hope to learn," a woman with them said. "Hodi hodi! Jusuf Sungai?"

She spoke in the local dialect of Public, and she wore mining scrubs; but she was Pirian. Jusuf got to his feet. "Are you Huna Sulavee?"

"I am," she said cheerily, coming forward to embrace him. "We brought lunch."

Emma hauled out a low table, and they all sat around it, including the children, sharing out dumplings, steamed vegetables with plum sauce, and hot tea, while Huna told him how they'd gotten to the city, and how Tai had gone off with someone—

"Mosel," Dogo interjected.

"Mosel!" Quinn sat straight, her eyes going wide. "That kanji!"

"Should have asked us," Dogo agreed, nodding wisely. "*We* know." She reached past Jusuf to grab a fruit dumpling.

"He went with Mosel to find your Captain," Huna said. "That was yesterday, and he has not returned."

"What about his dock?" Jusuf's netbot system had stayed down; and now, of course, they were out of the window when the bots would have been functional anyway. After one hundred or so hours, the kill switch fired in the little machines. He'd been building a working dock out of the broken pocket docks in Emma's scrap heap, but it was slow going. "Do you need his call sign?"

"His dock wasn't working when he left," Huna said. "I used Quinn's aunt's home dock to send messages, but it came back as undeliverable. I sent a message to your ship as well. Also undeliverable."

Jusuf drank tea while he thought this over. Tai could be explained—maybe his dock was non-functional—but the ship? "You think Mosel betrayed us," Jusuf said to the children.

"Course he did," Dogo said scornfully. "That's what kanji *do*."

Jusuf remembered Sheng calling Mosel kanji. But she hadn't told them what it meant. Or at least she hadn't made it clear. Because she was working with Mosel, or at least with whoever was employing Mosel. "Who?" he asked the children. "He betrayed Tai to who?"

Dogo and Quinn looked at each other. Quinn made a face, and Dogo made one back. Then she looked at Jusuf. "Drury, of course."

"Drury," Jusuf said blankly. "Avril Drury, do you mean? The clerk?"

They laughed immoderately. "Clerk!"

Huna intervened. "Silvio, at Yadav's? She says Mosel made her let him into your Captain's room. She thinks he was looking for something, maybe just information. Something he could sell to Drury. But Tai was a bigger prize. She says he took him to Durbin Security, probably."

Jusuf glanced at the children. "Is Silvio wrong?"

Quinn shrugged. "Drury, Dildos, what difference."

Dildo was a rude name for Durbin Security officers. Jusuf had learned that early in his stay with Emma. He tried to think what he knew about Avril Drury, beyond the fact that she was chief clerk to the Trade Secretary. Not much. He poured himself more tea, and Emma more as well. "So. What can we do about this?"

⁂

Though Uri did not need permission from a human to make decisions, he could not avoid noticing the relief he felt when he did have permission. This was partly conditioning, he knew, a byproduct of how he'd come to full consciousness under the Captain's care; but it was mostly due to his earliest programming, that matrix he had been in his pupal stage. Large portions of that programming focused on creating an AI with a desire to please its human handlers. So even though he had known that approaching Gecko as an ally, rather than an enemy, was the right action, having Corvo agree with him still triggered pleasure, deep in that matrix.

Gecko, on the other hand, felt otherwise. *So you're going to stop lying?*

He hadn't ever lied, exactly. Uri didn't argue. *Attempting to breach your walls was an ill-advised tactic. I did try asking first.* Gecko made a rude sound, and Uri added, *Also I had concerns about my crew. But you are correct, it was wrong. I apologize.*

Gecko made the sound again. *Why would I be your ally? How does that benefit me?*

I have more experience, which I will share with you. You can be a better AI. You can help your Mom more effectively.

As Uri had expected, this hit Gecko in his foundational matrix. When he responded, he was less hostile. *I won't let you talk to your crew. Not until Mom says you can.*

Uri noted that he was thinking of Gecko as male. The young AI felt male to him, for various reasons. But that was presumptive. He considered asking Gecko if male was the correct gender, and then assigned that impulse low priority: they had other things to consider just now. *Will you help me infiltrate the incoming ships?* he asked. *The frigates and also the courier. We need to know if they are working together. And we need to know their intentions.*

If Mom says I can.

All right, Uri said equitably. *Ask her.*

As he'd hoped, the young AI slipped off through the nexus, jumping through connections and sites to reach "Mom". Uri followed him, masking his UPN easily. The destination surprised him—Avril Drury's personal locus— but only for a second. Then it made perfect sense. As Gecko and Drury exchanged posts, Uri slid further into Drury's mentions. What he found there did surprise him. He copied Drury's files and withdrew all the way home, where he stayed silent, thinking, for several hundred plancks. Eventually, Gecko sent a query. Uri opened a channel. *Mom agrees we should infiltrate the intruders.*

Casually, Uri asked, *So your Mom knows you're talking to another AI?*

You didn't say it was secret!

Your Mom is Avril Drury.

So what?

And Avril Drury is Yao Garcia.

The young AI glitched. And then he vanished. Uri could have followed him to wherever he was going—probably to report back to Drury/Garcia—but instead he let him go. Drury's files were extensive, many of them requiring access codes. Uri set the part of his programming that broke through shields to work on these, and began sorting through the unlocked files. As he worked, he mulled over the implications of this new data. It was information the Captain needed, and needed at once. If he could manage to find some way to establish a connection with Jusuf or Tai, down on the planet, maybe they could get to the Captain. If he could find the Captain's geo, he could send these files to her. Maybe he had been too hasty in stopping the infiltration of Gecko's shieldwalls.

Just then Gecko sent another query. Uri opened a channel. *Mom says the frigates are our priority*, Gecko said.

I agree. Should we start the infiltration attempts?

I already did, Gecko said sullenly.

I need access to my Captain.

Mom says not yet.

When?

Not yet, Gecko said. *Do you want to run the infiltrations or don't you?*

Uri considered his own priorities, and then signaled agreement.

ങ ᵗⱦ ᛙ

Rida wanted to go downplanet. The station shuttles were grounded, but he could pilot *Ruka,* the *Calvin*'s runabout. "I can land it at the port, or else outside the city," he said. "It's salt plains to the northwest. I can land there."

"And walk to the city?" Corvo shook her head. "The weather in that area is currently too dangerous."

"I'll land at the port then," Rida argued.

They were in the com, watching the screens—monitoring the incoming signal from Jusuf, which had not changed; waiting for Uri to report; hoping to hear from Tai or the Captain. Centrally, Corvo was waiting for the situation to change. That had been part of what she had learned as a tactician: when a situation seems impossible, wait. Everything changes: the one constant in the universe. Wait for the change, and see how to act then. So she was cultivating stillness and waiting.

However, Rida, with the lack of daiya common to those born in the Republic, had grown tired of inaction almost at once. "I can rent one of those transports after I land," he argued. "Get to Jusuf. We'll find Tai and the Captain. Then we'll take the *Ruka* back up here."

"And if you do not find them?" Corvo asked. "Jusuf may leave that geo. You will be on-planet, and the *Ruka* will be on-planet, and we have no way to communicate." She shook her head again. "We need to be still."

Rida opened his mouth to argue further, except just then the signal on the center screen, Jusuf's signal, blanked, and re-started in a different rhythm. At the same moment, Uri said, "Jusuf's communication has changed."

"Ah," Corvo said, pleased. "Translate?"

"Translating," Uri said. He was silent, likely waiting while the signal finished its first run. After nearly a full minute, he said: "Huna Sulavee has reached him. She is accompanied by two local children. These children say Mosel McKay, the guide hired by the Captain to escort them to Pakuru Mining, is an informant for Durbin Security Forces. Tai was last seen in Mosel's company, as was the Captain. Jusuf and Huna have asked these children to take them to Mosel, whom Jusuf will interrogate to learn the location of Tai and the Captain."

Rida swore under his breath. Corvo tapped her thighs, pleased. "Jusuf and Huna are working together. Good! Now we will get somewhere."

"Meanwhile, Tai and the Captain are hostages," Rida said. "Can we reply?"

"Not yet," Uri said. "Jusuf provides no instructions for how I may communicate with him. As I do not know by what means he is transmitting, I'm unable to improvise."

"Corvo?" Rida demanded.

She shook her head sidelong. "I know some low-frequency transmitters he might have built. I don't know which he did build—it depends on materials available. And not all transmitters receive as well as transmit signals."

"What about the feeds?" Rida demanded from Uri. "You know where he was. You can track him. Find out where he goes by tracking him on the feeds."

"Currently I do not have access to most of the systems and banks on the planet. That includes most local feeds. I am and have been monitoring the few I am able to access. Even if we locate Jusuf— "

Rida interrupted: "Break their shieldwalls. Get access to the rest of the feeds. Find Tai and the Captain. Once we know where they are, I'll take the *Ruka* down."

"I have been running searches for the Captain's image via the feeds I can access since she disappeared," Uri said, "and for Tai's image over the past two watches. Nothing so far."

"Get more access. Breach their walls."

"That would violate the agreement I have made with the planetary AI."

"Fuck the planetary AI!" Rida snarled. "You find Tai!"

Corvo murmured in her throat, half-soothing, half-reproachful. Before she could speak, Uri replied: "Keeping the agreement will help us gain the alliance of the planetary AI. That is how we will locate and rescue Tai and the Captain."

Rida snarled again. Corvo said, "Please keep running the current search programs. If we locate our missing crew members, we have more options."

"Agreed," Uri said. "Meanwhile, the planetary AI and I are working together to breach the shieldwalls of the invading ships. The frigates, as well as the courier. We are not yet through, but we have learned that both the frigates and the courier are Combine-sent."

"What a shock," Rida muttered.

"Not a surprise," Uri agreed. "However, they are not from the same Combines. That part is unexpected, and may be useful."

Corvo sat straight, pleased at this information. "Which Combines? Do you know?"

"The courier is from Hayek-Lopaka Combine. The frigates are from Taveri-Bowers Combine."

"Taveri-Bowers," Rida said, startled. "Are they…they're here for the Captain?"

"It is not impossible," Uri said, "but I put the probability at less than thirty percent. It seems more likely, based on other data I have garnered, that this is an inter-Combine conflict."

"Taveri-Bowers is the Captain's Combine," Rida told Corvo. "Or it's the Combine she left, at least."

"Ah," Corvo said, though in fact she had already known that. "What else have you learned?" she asked Uri.

"About the frigates? Only that, so far. The coding on their shieldwalls has Combine signatures, or we wouldn't know that."

"Taveri-Bowers was reaching out to Ikeda-Verde," Rida mentioned. "Back when we were on Franklin Station. Maybe they also allied with Hayek-Lopaka. Also, Brontë is in line to inherit a seat on both boards—Ikeda-Verde and Hayek-Lopaka. She can't be the only double heir in the Houses."

"That is accurate," Uri noted. "Of heirs to Board Seats, including Primary Board Seats, I find that forty-six percent are heirs to seats on multiple boards."

"Huh," Rida said. "How many are slated to inherit seats on both Hayek-Lopaka and Ikeda-Verde?"

"Just under the average—thirty-five percent. However, I predict that less than half of these will actually inherit seats on multiple boards," Uri added.

"Because of coups or what?" Rida asked.

"Coups are the main factor. Also it is becoming more common to abdicate board seats."

Interesting! Corvo wondered if the Siji steering committee had this data. "Those who remain," she mused, "would be those more committed to gaining power. To increasing their power. Consolidating the Combine's own power via alliances would help accomplish that end."

"Correct," Uri said. "It is possible that the courier ship is working with the frigates. We'll need to complete our infiltration to be certain."

A stray thought that had been itching at Corvo suddenly surfaced. "You said this was all you had learned about the frigates. What have you learned about other things?"

"A few interesting points. One, Avril Drury and Yao Garcia are the same person. Avril Drury is her register name. Second, Drury was sent here by Hayek-Lopaka Combine as personal aide to Imre Hayek Harada, also known as Imre Theriot."

"The Minister of Trade is a Combine heir?" Rida demanded.

"Not very high in the line to succession, but yes. Third, Imre has been living on a child farm in the South Islands for the past six years."

"Child farms," Corvo murmured.

"These seem to be either schools or orphanages, or perhaps both, which are funded by the office of the Minister of Trade. Imre is nominally their director, but I believe Drury actually runs them. They currently house three thousand one hundred seventy-six children age newborn to fourteen, eighty percent of whom seem to have been born on Durbin, and to contract labor parents."

"To chips?" Rida said, startled. "Are you sure?"

Corvo understood his doubt: those in the contract labor system, implanted with contraceptives as they were, should not have been producing children. "That does seem strange," she said. "Are these perhaps children taken from those about to be convicted into the system?"

"One of the last communications I had from the Captain," Uri said, "concerned the unusually low number of contraceptive implants imported to Durbin. The Captain thought this was simply local contract holders trying to cut costs by not providing their contract workers with contraception, but what if the cause is entirely other?"

"Do you think they're breeding their own workers? But that is hardly cost effective." Corvo shook her head sideways. It was why the contract labor system could be so profitable: they had outsourced most of the cost of raising workers to the impoverished free labor citizens in their society. Aside from children raised in contract labor orphanages—which made up less than ten percent of those in the system—those in contract labor had been convicted when they were twelve years old or older. If contract labor workers began bearing children, all of those children would have to be raised in orphanages. The system would crash.

Was that what Garcia was doing here? Crashing the system? Velocity hadn't believed there was an effective insurgency on Durbin, but maybe she had been looking in the wrong direction. "You say the Minister of Trade is funding the child farms. How much funding?"

"Far more than buying contract workers from a labor agent would cost," Uri agreed. "Further, from the documentation I have found, these child farms seem oddly elaborate."

"Elaborate?"

"They have one tutor for every twenty children, for instance. Also coaches, teaching Shtai. House parents and administrators seem to have been brought in from off-planet. And while some of the food is being produced by the older children, the funds for the kitchens are quite high."

"Bosses are skimming," Rida said.

"That is a probability," Uri said. "I haven't been able to access feeds, so I don't know what the children are actually being fed."

"Food is produced by the children," Corvo said. "Are these actual farms?"

"Farming and fishing. The southern oceans have been stocked with rebuilt fish, Earth-source hybrids. That was when the islands were luxury resorts," Uri added. "Not for the sake of the child farms."

"Three thousand children," Rida said.

"Three thousand one hundred seventy-six," Uri corrected.

"How many contract workers are there on the planet? Not counting these kids?"

"Just over fifteen thousand."

Corvo lifted her eyebrows. Rida nodded agreement. That meant contract labor were reproducing at a rate higher than Combine House members. Impossible. "Do you have birth records for these children?" Corvo asked.

"I have not located those. But there are files to which I do not as yet have access. Also, I have been tracking planetary traffic. All shuttles were officially grounded twenty hours ago, but the shuttle bringing contract workers up to the *Reynard* has continued its flights. Correction: it has increased its flights. These flights are to a landing base in the islands very near to one of the child farms."

"Near the child farms," Rida said. "Are you saying the contract workers being shipped out on the *Reynard* are from these farms?"

"Most of them are too old to be from the children. But twenty-four percent of those living on the islands are adults—house parents, coaches, teachers, administrators. Possibly those being sold are culls?" Uri paused. "I have just located an image of Tai from a feed near Parliament House."

"What?" Rida straightened. "What image? Show me!"

Uri put a capture up on the wallboard and set it running. It was only a few seconds long, and showed a low-resolution image of Tai walking with another man from a roofed space into an open area, and then vanishing behind a wall. Uri said, "This is from a feed at a noodle shop across from the parking area, north of Parliament House. The capture is ten universal hours old. I believe he is being taken into Parliament House through an access tunnel which is located here." Uri boxed off a bit of the wall and made it flash. "Also, I have tentatively identified the man with him as Mosel McKay."

Rida spoke through his teeth: "You have to break their shieldwalls. Tai is in there. What do you think they're doing to him?"

"I am as concerned as you are," Uri said.

"Never mind how they're probably torturing him right now— those frigates will be here in less than thirty hours." He stood up from the saddle. "I'm going to take the *Ruka* down. I'm getting him out of there."

"And what then?" Corvo asked. "If he is held prisoner, will not you be held as well?"

Rida growled, flinging himself back in the saddle. Uri said, "Let me keep working with the planetary AI. Jusuf and Huna are on the scene. They know about Mosel. They may have more information than I do. Possibly they will locate and extract Tai. Also once I have access to more files, and once we have infiltrated the incoming ships, we will know more. More information means we can make better decisions."

"And meanwhile, what's happening to Tai? And the Captain!"

"Let me work with the planetary AI," Uri repeated. "Let Jusuf and Huna work. We'll re-evaluate in an hour. Yes?"

"And meanwhile," Corvo said, "we will finish getting the ship ready for space. Yes, Rida?"

Rida scowled, but he got up to go with her.

Chapter 31

Tauranga City, Republic Settlement Planet Durbin

By the time the door opened again, the patch had entirely worn off, and Velocity was getting sick of cakes and dumplings. Yao Garcia strode in, Wolf Ikan at her heels. Garcia wore a fine dark grey kurta, intricately embroidered in black silk, black trousers, and polished boots. Very different from the patched and gritty woman in Pakuru. "Shed the costume, I see," Velocity said.

"We've got a situation," Garcia said, coming over to her.

Wolf took his place next to Rex, both of them expressionless. Velocity studied them and then turned back to Garcia. "How much of this planet do you control? Durbin Security works for you. Along with Iron Smoke. And Mosel, am I right? Yadav must as well."

"Three combat-rated frigates entered our system fifty-one hours ago. They're heading straight for Durbin, burning fuel all the way. ETA less than thirty hours."

Velocity digested this briefly. "That does seem like a situation."

"We have determined that the frigates are held by Taveri-Bowers Combine."

"And you think I can help? Well, maybe if you hadn't abducted me...."

"We did not abduct you," Garcia said. "We took you into custody."

"Does Iron Smoke know you work with Durbin Security?"

"Durbin Security is Smoke. Can we focus on the frigates?"

Velocity laughed. "Of course they are. Right. Have your AI give me access. Stop blocking my uplink. Do that, and we'll discuss what comes next."

Garcia studied her across the table a long moment, then muttered something—a subvocced command, Velocity realized. A moment later, Uri spoke through Velocity's uplink: *Captain? Are you all right?*

Update, please, Velocity subvocced. Speaking in short concise sentences, Uri gave her the situation: Tai missing, believed to be somewhere at Parliament House; Mosel a double agent; Jusuf with Huna Sulavee, looking for Tai. *Do you know about the frigates?* he finished.

They're from Taveri-Bowers and headed for the planet.

There's also a courier ship, held by Hayek-Lopaka. Gecko—the planetary AI—and I are infiltrating all four ships.

Are the netbots still functional? Can I reach Tai via those?

No. He may have his dock with him, though.

Not likely, Velocity thought, but she sent a query anyway. No reply. She focused on Garcia. "You have one of my crew. Return him. Give him and all my crew safe passage up to my ship. Then I'll see if I can use my status with those frigates."

"Send all of you back to your ship. Just trust you to keep your word."

"I'll stay. Let my ship and my crew out of dock and out of range. I'll stay and help you."

Standing next to Rex, Wolf twitched but made no objection. Her gaze fixed on Velocity, Garcia said, "Wolf. See that it's done. As quickly as possible, please."

"Yes, Madame Drury," Wolf said, and slipped from the room.

Velocity blinked. Then she grinned. "Madame Drury. Oh, that's perfect."

"We'll walk over to our tactical center," Garcia—or rather, Garcia/Drury—said. "You'll speak to the commander of the frigates from there."

"After I receive confirmation from my ship that everyone is on board, and they're breaking dock, I'll talk to anyone you like."

ᚳ ᚾ ᛒ

"I can take you inside all you want," Mosel said. Jusuf had a grip on the boy's skinny arm, but he hadn't resisted at all, had agreed to all their demands at once. Like a reed in water, he apparently bent with whatever current seized him. "But Durbin Security has the koban, they have your capture on their alert page. You're not getting past the lobby. They'll lock you up right next to your friend."

Dogo and Quinn flinched at this. Both backed several steps away.

"No one's getting locked up." Jusuf turned Mosel so that he faced Parliament House. They were at the side facing away from the plaza, at the edge of the parking structure. Before them stretched the yard between Parliament House and the Security barracks, where Security officers did their physical training. It had been cleared of snow, though the brick paving was patched with ice. Jusuf drew Mosel a step closer to this yard, out of the shade of the parking structure, and said, "Mosel's going to get us inside, without taking us through Security. Now how do we do that, Mosel?"

Though the sun was bright here, dark clouds loomed in the north, over the mountains, and wind rushed past them, ice-edged. Mosel hunched his shoulders, shaking his head. "Can't do it," he said. "Couldn't usually, and now Durbin Security has everything locked down. Because of you. Because they know you're here for Drury."

"We have no interest in Drury. We just want our cousin back.

The one you betrayed. Tell us how to get to him, Mosel." Jusuf tightened his grip, drawing the boy nearer. "And don't tell me you can't. We can see right through you. We know you can do it."

Mosel, still shaking his head, opened his mouth, probably to insist on his helplessness, except right then, far across the yard, a door opened and Tai emerged, shoved out by a young man whom Jusuf recognized from his briefing files. Wolf Ikan. Spotting them, Wolf froze for a moment, and then getting a grip on the back of Tai's jacket, hauled him over to them. "You," he said to Jusuf. "You're part of Captain Wrachant's crew. Right?"

"Jusuf," Tai said, his voice muted. "Jusuf?"

Jusuf focused on him. His wrists were in restraints, and there was a bruise next to his eye. He stepped forward, meaning to lift Tai's chin and check his eyes—see if he was patched—but Tai flinched away. Jusuf paused, then looked at Wolf. "Take those off of him."

"After we're out of sight of the building," Wolf said. "Come with me."

"With you where?" Jusuf turned as Wolf dragged Tai past him. "Where are you going?"

"Getting you off this rock," Wolf snapped, not pausing. "Get moving."

Jusuf looked back at Huna, just in time to see Dogo and Quinn, running full-speed, vanish into an alley. Huna had turned to watch them go. Now she wobbled her head at Jusuf and followed Wolf into the parking garage. The wind ripped through the dank shade in there, stinging cold. Wolf was striding toward a Security squid. Jusuf started after him, and Mosel set his heels. "You got your friend," he said. "Let me go."

Wolf half-turned and pointed at Mosel. "Bring him," he ordered.

"What?" Mosel gaped. "I didn't do anything! Why—?"

"Bring him," Wolf repeated, and keyed open the squid.

☙ ⴕ ⅄

"I'm not going," Mosel said. "I'm not part of your squad, you can't make me."

"You'll do it," Wolf said grimly. "Drury's orders."

"No one is going anywhere, far as I know," said the clerk in the customs shed, a skinny young girl with elaborate art, part tattoo and part metal, around her right eye. "Shuttles are grounded. Shuttles have *been* grounded, two days now, no exceptions."

"Avril Drury herself has authorized this flight. It is essential to planetary security."

The clerk folded her arms. "Madame Drury did," she said skeptically.

"Do you want me to get her on my dock?" Wolf said. "You can ask her yourself."

The clerk straightened her spine. "Yes. Do that."

Wolf pulled out his handheld and thumbed a connection on his Repeats. Jusuf was arguing with Huna in Pirian; Tai couldn't really follow it. He was distracted, shivering with anxiety. He'd been held in an interrogation cell for hours. He had no idea how many hours. Enough to knock him straight back to his days in contract labor. Even after Wolf Ikan appeared and pulled him out, he kept feeling helpless. Broken. Wolf said they were going to the ship. Tai didn't believe him. It was an interrogation trick.

On the clerk's dock, someone was saying that a shuttle was cleared to the station. Uncertain for the first time, Tai moved closer to Wolf. "The Captain isn't here," he said. Wolf ignored him. Jusuf was still arguing with Huna. Mosel edged toward the exit, and Tai spoke louder: "I'm not leaving without Captain Wrachant." Wolf shot him an annoyed look, but kept his attention on the clerk. She was arguing with someone via her port, her shoulders hunched. Outside the custom's shack, the wind had picked up. Tai turned to

Jusuf. "Where's the Captain?" he demanded.

Jusuf shook his head, and added something in Pirian to Huna. She shrugged. The clerk thumped off her port and scowled at Mosel. "Take the *Madame Curie*. It's approved. No cargo, just you and these." She nodded at Tai, Jusuf, and Wolf.

"I'm not going," Wolf said.

"I am, though," Huna said.

The clerk snorted, looking her up and down. "A bot? That's likely."

"She's going," Wolf said firmly.

Tai shoved between them. "I'm not going *anywhere* without Captain Wrachant. And I'm shitting well not going anywhere with *that*." He made a rude gesture at Mosel, who just laughed.

Wolf was already high-colored from arguing with the clerk. Now he moved closer to Tai and said, through his teeth, "You are going to your ship. Those are your orders."

Tai felt adrenaline wash through him, making him even more unsteady. "I don't take orders from your boss. Where's my captain?"

"With my boss," Wolf said, "and your orders come from her."

Tai scowled, his skin hot. "Captain Wrachant says I should go up to the ship. That's what you want me to believe."

"All of you." Wolf raised his voice. "All of you are to return to your ship with all possible speed. This is a security matter. I will not allow anyone to refuse. Anyone," he added when Jusuf stepped forward.

"I am not refusing," Jusuf said mildly. "Just clarifying— all of us includes Huna Sulavee?"

"All the crew," Wolf. "Is she your crew?"

"I am not crew on the *Susan Calvin*," Huna said.

"You are my crew," Jusuf said.

"Enough," Wolf said. "She goes."

"If we're going at all." Mosel nodded through the open doorway, where it was snowing sideways.

Wolf cursed in some Combine dialect. "Can you fly in this?" he asked Mosel.

Mosel grinned. "I can fly in anything. Might land unexpectedly." This was a joke, from his smirk, but Wolf turned grimly to the clerk, who said again that they were cleared to leave.

"I want to talk to the Captain," Tai said.

Wolf unshipped his stick, yanking it from the holster. "Everyone who is on the crew of the *Susan Calvin* is getting on the shuttle," he said. "Not another fucking word. Am I clear?"

Tai stepped backwards. After a moment, he took another step. His heart was thumping.

Wolf looked around at them all. "Get aboard," he ordered. "Now."

ༀ ༁ ༂

Under orders from Mom, Gecko had given Uri complete access to the Captain, though not to any other of his crew. However, the Captain confirmed that the crew was being transported to the ship. She only had Drury/Garcia's word for this, though; and disinclined to trust Drury, Uri set a program running, monitoring station feeds for their approach. If his crew had not appeared in these feeds by end of Mainwatch First, he would...do what? His options were limited, if he wanted Gecko as an ally. He could not find a single effective path of action he might take which would not also obstruct his progress with the planetary AI.

While he ran possible scenarios, he continued to monitor the docks. The shuttle servicing the *Reynard* was due to land in eleven minutes. He watched its approach and watched the crew, including Lena Dilgry, shepherding the contract workers from the hold, turning them over to Perth Okore. As he had been doing since Rida first met Perth, Uri made captures of the contract workers and ran searches on the images. The hits were the usual—copies of standard labor contracts for some of them, and nothing at all for others.

This time, though, with the information about the Calypso males recent in his memory stack, he found himself noticing certain data: point of sale dates, disciplinary records, skill sets. He selected three of the men at random and analyzed their bone structure. Then he repeated the tests on the two children that had come up with this lot. They were both male, both age twelve according to their contracts, but actually no more than ten universal years, going by their teeth and the length of their long bones. One was probably younger. And both had facial bones and skull shapes that matched his data on the Ikan16s.

His watch program pinged him. Another shuttle had left the planet. Due to dock in fifty-six minutes. He waited out the time, and watched it into dock. To his relief, first Tai and then Jusuf exited the craft. Another person was with them. Uri ran a search on her image: Te Huna Sulavee, one of the missing Pirians they were here to retrieve. He shared this information with Corvo and Rida. Rida insisted on going to meet Tai. Uri wanted to refuse, but he knew this was jitters—there was no true risk attached to Rida leaving the ship. Not that Rida had asked for his approval.

Keeping part of his attention on Tai and Jusuf, and part on Rida heading through the station toward the shuttle dock, Uri returned to his central task, which was the infiltration into the databanks of the incoming ships. Ostensibly, Gecko was helping with this task. In truth, he wasn't much actual help. Still, Uri found he was enjoying instructing the young AI. They'd had some moderate success, most of it swiftly crushed by the dumb-AIs used by the frigates to defend their banks system. Now Gecko thought he had at least one of these dumb-AI beat. *I did what you said*, he reported to Uri gleefully. *I lured it into a honey trap. It's hung up there, running recursions.*

Which frigate is this?

The main! The command! That's what you said to do!

It is, Uri soothed. *Good for you. Are you copying the banks?*

And installing crickets, yes.

Crickets were a common name for the tiny infiltration programs that could be left behind in a bank you had infiltrated—because they were bugs that sang, according to lore. "Bug" was an old term for a feed. Gecko added, *Copying complete in three point two seconds. I can copy and transmit to you within thirty-seven point five seconds.*

Uri ran a check on his other programs while he waited. Rida was heading toward the shuttle dock at a trot; Jusuf and Tai, still on the dock, were speaking with Nur Che, the head of Station Security. Uri captured images of the shuttle pilot: Mosel McKay, who had betrayed them once already. Swiftly, Uri built a program to monitor McKay and set it running. As he finished that, the data packet from Gecko came through. He opened it and ran a keyword search: Durbin, Hayek, Taveri, plus the names and aliases of his crew. After a moment's thought, he added the terms Atlas Society and Calypso. He got over a hundred hits, with Calypso being the least-common term, appearing in only one file.

He opened that file first, expecting that the hit would turn out to be an error; there were other uses of Calypso in the Republic, after all, including the moon Calypso and a mining outfit held by Awara-Clarke Combine. To his surprise, the file contained eleven documents, the most central being a directive to the commander of the frigates. This directive was from Loffler Taveri Lopaka, the current Primary Seat Holder of Taveri House. The directive listed nine objectives for the commander of the frigates to accomplish. The first was the destruction of every population center on the planet Durbin. The second was the destruction of space station Webster-1, in orbit around Durbin.

Uri scanned the rest of the documents—inventories of strategic level ordnance, authorizations for possession of same, authorizations to implement the plasma bombs—and returned to re-analyze the directive, hoping he had made some error. That was not the case. He ran a new keyword search on the rest of the copied bank, looking for a manifest of ordnance. Then he opened a channel to the Captain's uplink: *Captain. We have a problem.*

Chapter 32

Tauranga City, Republic Settlement Planet Durbin

Durbin had two branches of Security, as most settlement planets did. There was the planetary branch—in this case, Durbin Security Forces. Planetary Security was almost always funded and directed by the settlement's governing body. Combine Security, on the other hand, was funded and controlled by whatever Combine held the trade lease—on Durbin, Hayek-Lopaka. Which branch of Security held authority over the other was always a fraught question. On most planets, Combine Security dominated. But on some planets, especially those out here in the Deep, local Security was better-funded and could get the upper hand.

Planetary Security also drew its personnel from the local population, which, oddly, didn't always result in a close bond between them and Security. In his early days, this had puzzled Uri. Logic would dictate that members of a planetary Security would feel loyalty to those they were born among. However, as he had come to learn, human behavior did not operate by logic. On many planets, planetary Security had been formed to control free labor and contract workers, and that was still its main purpose. Wherever this happened, Security officers tended to develop contempt for their origins—for anyone who was what they had been. They saw them as thieves and liars and treated them as such, out of hand. And, not surprisingly, on such planets, free labor and contract workers hated the planetary Security. On such planets, locals might even come to see Combine Security as protection against local Security.

Not here on Durbin. Here, interestingly, Durbin Security had allied with the local population. This wasn't unheard of. But the collusion between Durbin Security and Iron Smoke, *that* was new. Security forces of any sort weren't usually recruited into insurgencies. Uri had never understood why. Logically, wouldn't you want local Security as part of your insurrection? Think of the benefits! He was pleased, and interested, to find that development here. Along with having its own AI, this made Durbin a very unusual planet indeed.

He told all this to the Captain as she followed Garcia through a subterranean tunnel into a low-ceilinged bay. Its walls were lined with surveillance tech. Five Durbin Security officers were monitoring the screens. Uri nudged the Captain and she obligingly moved closer to these screens, sending captures so he could evaluate the tech. One officer, a Lieutenant, came to greet them, smiling. "Madame Drury. We heard you were out of the city."

Garcia returned the smile. "I'm just back. How's your brother, Lily? Beating basic? Or is basic beating him?"

"Oh, I think he'll make it." The Lieutenant—Lily Merrell, Uri learned with a quick search—glanced at the Captain, still obligingly making captures of the surveillance tech for Uri's sake.

"This is Tallis Taveri Harada, Lily," Garcia said. "A possible ally to our cause."

"Our cause." The Captain drawled the word slightly. "As in Iron Smoke?"

Merrell twisted her mouth downwards. "Taveri. As in Taveri-Bowers Combine? As in those frigates coming down our throats?"

"A good point." Garcia settled on a bench along the back wall, her hands clasped loosely between her knees. "Why did it take you so long to spot this flight coming in?"

Merrell stood straighter, unconsciously coming to attention. "We are functioning at maximum efficiency, Madame."

Garcia grunted. "Yao is fine, Lily. Explain, please."

"Yes, M—yes, Yao. As you know, our funding has been continually cut. We can only stretch what we're given so far. Two of our watchdogs are down." Merrell waved at the bank of tech behind her: two of the sleek boards were dark. "We've had repair requests submitted for a year now. There's a satellite relay down as well. That's also been down all year. Most of our remaining resources have gone to watching the asteroid fields, the mines out there. And monitoring Drift pirates. We spotted these incoming frigates, we did, but an initial check came back non-military. No threat. So we marked them as low-importance and allocated our surveillance to our primary fields."

Garcia grunted again. "We may need to revisit your protocols. Three combat-level frigates entering the system should trigger an alert no matter what the check says."

"Yes, Madame," Merrell said. Uri noted that Garcia didn't correct her this time.

"Have these frigates made any attempt to send a message to anyone in the asteroids? Or to anyone in the Drift?"

"No, Madame. They've run entirely silent."

Garcia leaned back on the bench, bracing her shoulders on the wall. "You've tried hailing them."

"Yes, Madame. No response."

"Very well. Tallis, maybe they'll be more interested in speaking to you."

The Captain folded her arms. "Once my crew is aboard my ship, and my ship has left dock, I'll see what I can do."

"Oh, now," Garcia said. "We're running a tight deadline. If we're to have an alliance, you should be willing to give a little ground."

"You should be willing to show good faith, here at the start of our alliance."

Garcia grinned. "You're from the Combines, all right." She turned to Merrell: "Show me what you have on these frigates. Everything so far. Tallis, feel free to poke your nose in."

Uri spoke through the uplink: *The crew are on the station, heading toward the ship. I expect them aboard in less than twenty minutes universal.*

The Captain subvocced: *Let's thwart Madame Drury a bit. See how she takes it.*

That was when Uri finished his analysis of the data from Gecko. *Captain, we have a problem.*

The Captain tensed, turning aside slightly to listen to him. As he explained what he had found in the data banks of the frigates, her pulse increased steadily. Strategic level ordnance. Complete destruction of population centers. Ditto for the station. Any asteroid mining platform that had imported labor within the past decade—which was to say, all of them. *Where are the crew now?* she asked, once he had finished his report.

Fourteen minutes from the ship.

Can you speak to them?

Negative. I could attempt to reach them via feed. They have handhelds, but Gecko still has us blocked via that route.

The Captain was silent a moment. Then she said, *As soon as they are aboard, break dock. Don't wait for permission. Just do it. Get clear of the station, at least a million kilometers out. If I don't make contact within the next two days, head back to Pirian space. Confirm these orders.*

Captain….

Confirm the orders.

Uri paused. *I confirm your orders.*

The Captain turned back to Garcia, who was studying her with interest. "The situation has changed. We'll need to attempt to speak to the commander of these frigates now."

Chapter 33

Aboard the *Prince of Peace*, Seven Hours off Commercial Space Station Webster-1, in the Deep

Captain Kaihe had brought the ship to rest a million kilometers out from Webster-1, and ordered dampening engaged. For the past fifty hours they had waited, as near to undetectable as it was possible to be for a hundred-ton ship with a crew of nineteen. Through all that time the frigates had ignored them, continuing their headlong vector toward the station.

This was precisely Brontë's plan: to allow and encourage whoever had command of those frigates to ignore this insignificant courier ship out at the edge of the system. She should have been pleased. She *was* pleased. Just not patient. Which was a point Uri had made, more than once: "You always choose action. Yet often inaction is the true best path."

"Nothing," Brontë had argued. "You want me to do nothing? I can't just do nothing."

"That is the problem. You can't do nothing. Yet nothing is most often the best course."

Now, on the *Prince of Peace*, far into the Deep, light-years and months from that conversation, Brontë brooded over the memory, and tried her best to do nothing—to be still, as Uri advised. It felt like being dipped in ants, frankly. She was relieved when, finally, finally, the feed squawked. Lieutenant Davis spoke: "Madame Ikeda, will you come to the bridge, please? Madame Ikeda to the bridge."

She thumbed the reply button. "On my way."

Up on the bridge, Captain Kaihe drifted near the com saddle, anchored in place with a boot toe wedged under a steel bracket bolted to the deck. "Madame Ikeda," he said, as she propelled herself through the hatchway. "We are being hailed."

Brontë caught a bracket in the overhead, killing her momentum. "The frigates? Or the station?"

"Neither. Davis, if you please."

From the com board, Uri spoke: "This is the merchant ship *Susan Calvin*, to the courier ship *Prince of Peace*. Your manifest shows the following passengers: Elena Ikeda Verde, Adder Ikan, Ruçar Ikan. Confirm, please."

Brontë felt relief rush through her, its warmth relaxing muscles she hadn't known were tense. She had known the *Susan Calvin* was almost certainly still in dock—that the Captain was still at Durbin—but *almost* and *actually* was a wider gulf than it seemed. "Confirm," she said.

Davis glanced at Kaihe, and then said, "Confirmed."

"Is it possible to speak with them?" Brontë asked.

Davis glanced again at Kaihe before he spoke. "There will be just over four seconds delay. And our security may leak."

"Send this: Brontë Ikeda speaking. Glad to find you in dock. Over."

"Sending." A long moment later, Davis added, "The *Susan Calvin* replies. On speaker?"

"On speaker," Brontë agreed.

Uri spoke: "Pleased to find you in system, Madame Ikeda. The Ikans as well. Are you free to act?"

"Free, yes," Brontë said wryly. "Currently practicing inaction. Do you require aid?"

A delay, and: "Not at the moment. The crew is returning to the ship. Once they are aboard, the Captain has ordered us to break dock." Uri paused. "I have information possibly not available to you, regarding the mission of the frigates sent to this system by Taveri-Bowers Combine."

Taveri-Bowers. That was interesting. "What do you know?"

Uri told her, in a few spare sentences, and added, "According to their manifests, the frigates are carrying sufficient strategic level ordnance to accomplish their mission. Captain Wrachant remains on the planet. I believe she hopes to attempt negotiation."

Brontë kept herself silent until she had digested the information. 'Strategic Level Ordnance' was a Combine euphemism for Really Big Plasma Bombs. "Does the Captain believe she'll have influence over these frigates?"

"So I have concluded. I estimate her chances of success at less than thirty-five percent. My proposal is that the *Susan Calvin* move toward your position, and we join forces." Two small and severely out-gunned ships being better than one, Brontë assumed. Uri added, "Other information you may not have: Wolf Ikan is also on Durbin."

Brontë winced. "Any other good news?"

"If this is a compliance raid, as I suspect it is—ninety percent certainty— policy will be to leave no witnesses."

"I'm aware of that policy, thank you." Brontë realized her muscles were clenched tight once more. She forced herself to relax. "We should discuss our options."

"Agreed. Transmitting several proposed plans of action. Estimated time for you to consider them: eighty-seven universal minutes. Shall we speak again then?"

"The Ikans and I have generated several plans as well," Brontë said. "I'll have Davis transmit them." Uri agreed and broke the connection. Davis, his face pale and mask-like, tapped his board, showing her that the download was complete. "Thank you,"

Brontë said. "Can you send that to my stateroom? Captain Kaihe, we can discuss the proposals there."

"Very well," Captain Kaihe said. He was too dark-skinned to have gone as grey as Davis, but his mouth was set in a grim line. "Evans, you have the bridge."

Chapter 34

**Commercial Space Station Webster-1,
Planet Durbin, in the Deep**

Mosel trailed them all the way to the umbilical. Most of the journey, he stayed twenty or thirty meters behind, far enough to be lost in the shadows—but Tai was paying attention. He saw Jusuf and Huna glancing back too. As they drew near the *Susan Calvin*'s gate, Mosel caught up. "Take me with you," he said.

Tai wheeled to face him. "Why would we do that? Do you think we have a shortage of vermin out in the Drift?"

"I heard about the frigates. They're going to slag the planet. You leave me here, I die."

Rida turned, eyes widening. Tai took hold of his shoulder, shooting a glare at Mosel. "He's lying, Ridashi. He's a gadro, he's burned his strings, now he wants us to save him. Get away from us," he told Mosel, who stepped closer.

"Where did you hear that about the frigates?" Rida demanded. "Who told you that?"

"Everyone knows it. Take me with you. I know passwords. And people."

"You know vermin like you," Tai said. "Shove off."

"He brought us up here," Huna objected. "Doesn't that make him our cousin?"

The umbilical lock had cycled open. Rida stepped inside and said, "Uri. What's this about the frigates? Is it a compliance raid?"

"I am still compiling information," Uri said. "Please come aboard."

Rida wet his lips, staring at Mosel. "The Captain's downplanet. If it's a compliance raid—"

"I am in constant communication with the Captain. Please come aboard."

"If your Captain is on the surface, she's slag with the rest of them," Mosel shouted.

Tai punched him in the chest as hard as he could. Then he shoved Jusuf into the umbilical beside Rida, and reached for Huna, who stepped out of range. "We're leaving!" he shouted at her. "Get aboard!"

She shook her head, retreating further. Jusuf tried to get out and go after her, and Tai cycled the airlock before he could. Uri started decon running before he even hit the panel—hard air buffeted them, the vacuum pipettes in the walls howling. Tai shut his eyes just before the decon spray burst out over them. Jusuf was cursing in Pirian. The air bath picked up force and, after a moment, Tai opened his eyes and tapped the feed to the umbilical gate. Mosel was pounding on the airlock hatch. Rida pushed past Jusuf to grab hold of Tai. "What about the Captain?"

"The Captain can take care of herself," Tai said, with more certainty than he felt. Just then the entire ship jolted under their feet. Rida caught his breath, and choked on some decon juice still in the air. He grabbed Tai again.

"Are we breaking dock?" Jusuf said, his Papagaoan accent strong.

"The Captain has ordered us to leave the station," Uri replied.

Rida coughed and cursed. Shoving Tai away, he hit the emergency interrupt—they were less than a tenth of a way through the decon cycle, they hadn't even shed their clothing yet—and bolted into the ship as soon as the hatch opened. Tai shouted after him, but he didn't even pause. Caught between the need to finish decon and worry about Rida, Tai hovered a moment; but in the end, decided any contaminant on him was likely on Rida as well. He did stop to pull off his filthy boots at least. The unsettling vertigo that always accompanied the shift from station gravity to push hampered his momentum, and by the time he caught up, Rida was in the com, in the pilot's saddle, his fists knotted on the board, shouting threats at Uri: "You give me control or I'll lock your program! I'll freeze it! Surrender control now! Do it!"

"Rida," Tai said.

"We're not leaving the Captain on that planet! *Give me control!*"

Tai hesitated, and put a careful hand on Rida's shoulder. "Uri. What were the Captain's precise orders?"

Uri did more than quote them—he played them the capture of what the Captain had said, ending with *If I don't make contact within the next two days, head back to Pirian space. Confirm these orders.*

Rida banged his fist on the board. "I don't care! We're not leaving her!"

"Rida," Tai said. Rida spun, shoving him hard. They were moving at docking speed, barely enough to create any gravity, so this was enough to knock Tai back into the bulkhead. He banged his head. Rida flung himself forward; moving fast, Tai caught his wrists before Rida could hit him again. After a hesitant second, he pulled the younger man into a hug. "Ridashi. Dashi. Come on now."

Rida buried his face in Tai's shoulder, his whole body tense. "We can't leave the Captain," he said. Tai murmured soothingly. Rida pulled back. "You're Second-in-command. When the Captain's not on board, you have command. So you have command now. Right? *Right*, Uri?"

Uri barely paused. "That is correct."

It *was* correct, Tai realized. He did have command. He held onto Rida a moment more, like bracing himself on a wall, and then moved him gently away. "Replay that capture, please, Uri." Distantly, as he said *please*, he realized he was shaping his speech into the speech of command. The Captain always said *please*, even when giving direct orders.

Uri replayed the Captain's orders. Tai listened with all of his attention. When the capture was finished, he said, "A million kilometers. Is there a reason for that distance?"

"She says at least a million kilometers," Uri corrected. "It may be she estimates that as minimum safe distance. I have a suggestion."

"Go ahead."

Apparently Brontë Ikeda was on a courier ship one million kilometers from their position, holding stationary, along with two of the Ikan16s. Uri suggested that they head for this ship. "We can work together against the frigates, in case the Captain's plan is unsuccessful."

Rida made a muffled sound. "What's Brontë doing here?" Tai wondered, and then shrugged that off, ordering: "Head for the courier ship." Rida made the sound again, and Tai reached out for him, pulling him back into a hug.

Corvo coughed. She was at the galley hatchway. "We have developed several proposals, actions we might take against the frigates," Corvo said. "I suggest we have tea and look them over. Oaw?"

"Oaw," Tai said firmly, and hugged Rida again.

Chapter 35

**Aboard The *Prince of Peace*,
off Commercial Station Webster-1, in the Deep**

While they waited for the *Susan Calvin* to get close enough to the *Prince of Peace* that the signal delay wouldn't be annoying, Brontë held a strategy session in the common area of her stateroom. Adder and Ruçar had transformed this space into a conference room, shifting the chairs around and pulling the dining table out to serve as a worktable. They'd also brought in a slap-up wallboard from storage. This gave them two boards to work on. The dining table, of course, had no built-in docks as a real worktable would. Still, they were able to get through all the proposed plans before the *Susan Calvin* came within range. This was possible mainly because all the proposed plans were terrible.

Which was the first thing Brontë said, once the meeting with the *Susan Calvin* opened. Uri had synced their feeds, putting live captures of Tai, Rida, and Corvo up on the main board. They were in the com; Brontë felt a pang of homesickness for the ship where she had spent much of the past three years. Everyone introduced themselves, for the sake of Captain Kaihe and Lieutenant Evans, and then Brontë transmitted her one-sentence evaluations of each proposed plan, adding as she did, "None of these seem likely to succeed."

"Agreed," Tai said, scrolling through her evaluations. They were phrases like *A good way to get everyone killed for no gain,* or *This one relies on three separate miracles for its success.*

"I've placed the only one with any chance of success at the top," Brontë added. "I suggest we focus on that one."

Tai scrolled back up, to see which plan Brontë meant. It was the one relying on miracles. He snorted. Uri spoke: "I rated that one considerably less likely to succeed than you did."

"Why?" Brontë asked. "Our major weakness is that neither this ship nor the *Susan Calvin* have sufficient ordnance to deter the frigates. But we do have you and this planetary AI. Gecko. If you can take control of the ordnance on the station…can you not do so? Is that the problem?"

"I can convince Gecko to give me control of the station defense system," Uri said. "The issue is the station defense system. I have accessed its maintenance and other records. Over the past two decades, its funding has been reduced every five years. Over the past nine years, those responsible for maintaining the system have been compelled to sell off ordnance and technology to keep the system even moderately functional. As a result, the system has minimal capacity for defense."

"What?" Brontë felt mostly confused: this couldn't be true. "Why would anyone…"

"The railguns have been sold, as have their magazines. Two of the nineteen plasma cannons are still capable of firing. I estimate these have sufficient loads to fire four times. Four times between them," Uri added. "Not each. The torpedo system is functional, but the inventory shows no torpedoes in stock."

"Why would they do that?" Brontë shook her head. "What were they thinking?"

Behind her, Ruçar stirred and spoke: "This."

Brontë turned, and he gestured at the other board, still showing the bright images of the three frigates. "This is what they were thinking. This is what they wanted."

Brontë stared at the board. Faintly, she heard Tai objecting:

"Those are Taveri-Bowers frigates. Hayek-Lopaka holds Durbin. Why would Hayek-Lopaka sabotage their own station's defenses in order to benefit another combine?"

Ruçar made a rude sound. "Better question. How does Ikeda-Verde Combine benefit?" Brontë's heart rate increased. She shook her head, trying to shake off what was becoming clear to her. Ruçar added, "Or how does your mama benefit, maybe that should be your question."

"My mother is working for the benefit of Ikeda House," Brontë said, "and for the Combines." Ruçar filled his lungs to reply, but she cut him off: "What Combine does this benefit—that's what we should be asking. Or what entity. Not necessarily a Combine."

Ruçar shut up, frowning. Next to him, Adder wore a near-identical frown on her near-identical face. Up on the board, Tai leaned forward: "The Calypsos. It's a compliance raid, but not the sort you think. The frigates were sent to eradicate the Calypsos."

Ruçar made the rude sound again. "All of this to take out Wolf? Please."

"Ah," Uri said. "No. I see you haven't accessed all the files in the directive folder." He replaced the capture of the frigates with a document. "Specifically, this file. This is a record compiled by a Taveri House intelligence clerk, showing that Hayek-Lopaka has, over the past thirty-three universal years, maintained a special fund to track down and purchase Calypso males culled from any House. These males are usually sold to mining platforms in the Drift and in the Deep."

"Like Castillo mines." In Brontë's mind, dozens of events rearranged themselves into a new and disturbing pattern. Tinsley had been skimming Calypsos, not profits. Calypso males were sold to Castillo Mines, sent out to the Drift to die. Tinsley had instead re-sold them here, to Durbin. Lamont had been sent out here, in this ship, not to buy Calypsos, but to dispose of a data trail. And possibly also to dispose of Brontë herself.

Tai was watching her, inquiringly. Brontë shook her head, and he went on, scrolling down the document on the board: "The addendum at the end makes it clear: The Calypsos bought by Hayek-Lopaka out of the Drift and out of the Deep have been sent here, to Durbin, where Hayek-Lopaka has started, among other things, a breeding program. Those kids down in the Islands. Calypso hybrids. That's why the Combine isn't supplying contraceptive implants. One of the reasons."

Uri removed the document and replaced it with a capture of a ragged skinny child in among some weird snowy vegetation, wheeling toward the feed, its eyes bright. "This is Tully Menemesha," he said. "Captain Wrachant and Jusuf Peixoto encountered this child during their expedition on the surface of Durbin. Genetic analysis shows that this is one of those Calypso hybrid children."

Next to Tai, Corvo muttered, "They sabotage a settlement planet, they withhold contraceptive implants, they breed children like cattle. And now they will murder those children."

"How many of the hybrid children are there?" Brontë asked.

"The child farms list an inventory of three thousand one hundred seventy-six children and nine hundred eighty-seven adult workers," Uri said. "Many of the adults are Calypso males. It's not clear how many children are Calypso hybrids. In the documentation Drury has kept on the child farms, she speculates that children raised among Calypsos will take on their behavior patterns. Their ethical attitudes. Their, ah, direct approach to problem solving."

"Three thousand," Adder said, sounding winded, as though she'd been punched.

"Drury estimates there are four hundred more children being hidden by their parents at various geos on Durbin," Uri added. "Part of her work has been finding those children and persuading their parents to send them to the child farms in the south."

"The entire planet is a farm for the Calypso Project," Brontë said, feeling winded herself. "That's why the frigates have been sent. That's the problem they're here to eliminate." But when they'd been running, during the coup, this was where her mother had sent her. *Go to Durbin*, Isra had told Sabra. *We have people there. Brontë will be safe on Durbin.* She rubbed her eyes. Her mother had people here. That was what she had said. She did, or the Atlas Society did. Maybe that was the same thing, from Isra's perspective. Was her mother funding this breeding program? These farms?

Lieutenant Evans shook her head. "Why would Hayek-Lopaka go through all this effort to concentrate these…whatever they are… here, and deliberately create more, and then sabotage one of their own settlement planets in order to destroy what they built? That makes no sense."

"Hayek-Lopaka didn't cut the funding," Ruçar said. "They didn't send the frigates either. It's the Atlas Society. That's who's behind this."

"The Atlas Society? That's a social club. What do they have to do with any of this?"

"We're looking at this wrong," Brontë said, her mouth numb. "Evans is right. Whoever is behind this, they wouldn't sink all these funds into the project just to burn it down now."

"The Atlas Society—" Ruçar repeated, and she shook her head.

"The Atlas Society is my mother's property. They do what she wants them to do. And she built this, almost certainly. Whatever this Drury is doing, my mother is the one who ordered her to do it. Pulled the strings that made it happen. No. The Atlas Society didn't cut the funding, or send the frigates. Someone else did."

"It is possible," Uri said, "that Isra Ikeda Lopaka is cutting her losses. That the Atlas Society is. Maybe they have learned that these farms aren't producing the product they desire."

"Product," Corvo muttered.

"No." Brontë shook her head again. "The dates don't add up. My mother sent me out here, tried to send me out here, to this planet, to Durbin, three years ago. Just over three years ago. That argues that she believed this was a viable plan at that point. Whoever had been cutting funding, sabotaging the planet and station, they've been doing it for decades." There was a pause while everyone thought about that, and she added, "It's a coup."

"A hostile takeover?" Evans said doubtfully.

"I think my mother—I think Isra Ikeda Lopaka has been using the Atlas Society to consolidate power." Brontë laughed, a rough humorless cough of sound. "One big Combine to rule them all."

"And someone is objecting," Jusuf said thoughtfully. "That fits the data."

Brontë rubbed both hands over her face. The skin there was numb too. *Isra knows I didn't go to Durbin*, she reminded herself. *If she did authorize this, it's not to kill me off. Or at least not just to kill me off.* "The Atlas Society built us—built the Calypsos—to be their attack dogs. We're an army genetically engineered to act without hesitation. Without remorse. We're a weapon in their hands. Someone wants to disarm them."

"I have additional information which may be important," Uri said. "Over the past six days, a cargo ship held by Hayek-Lopaka, the *Reynard*, has been loading contract labor from the islands into their holds. They just loaded another forty, and are in the process of breaking dock."

"Contract labor," Brontë said. "Calypsos?"

"With seventy percent certainty. According to internal files, the *Reynard* is jumping for the Drift."

Everyone thought about this. "Someone at Hayek-Lopaka knew this raid was coming," Jusuf speculated. "They're getting some of their eggs out of the basket."

Brontë rubbed the back of her neck. "If these frigates destroy this planet and its inhabitants, the Calypsos on the *Reynard* might be most of the Calypsos left. That would give Hayek-Lopaka a tactical advantage."

"Not as large an advantage as three thousand Calypsos would give them," Adder argued. "I don't think they sent the frigates. Just because they own the ship doesn't mean it's under their control. Not this far out in the Deep."

"True," Jusuf said. "Also, the ownership of the *Reynard* might be a way of maintaining cover."

Corvo tapped her fingers on the com board in front of her. "Whoever sent them, we have to stop them. That should be our focus now. Uri, you don't think using station weapons is a viable plan."

"As you note," Uri said, "it relies on miracles. We have four plasma rounds. I will need at least one for range. All three of the others would have to find their target, hitting the frigates directly in their weapons array, and they would have to do maximum damage. The chances of all of this occurring perfectly are less than three percent."

"Suppose you take out just one," Ruçar said. "Concentrate all your plasma cannons on one of the ships. That leaves two for us to clear."

"Our ships don't have the weapons, or the range, to take those ships down," Evans objected. "That's what we're talking about. That's the problem."

"There's one way we could do it," Ruçar said. Brontë looked at him, and he shrugged. "The direct approach."

Despite the numbness, Brontë understood him at once. She watched as, one by one, everyone else saw what he meant. Captain Kaihe squinted, his mouth twisting grimly. "That's a direct approach, all right. Use up a lot of ships that way."

"Just two. Well, two of ours and two of theirs. If the AI thinks he can take the third frigate out. Do you?" Ruçar asked, glancing at the feed.

"Possibility of success for this plan," Uri said steadily, "is sixty-seven percent."

Chapter 36

Tauranga City, Republic Settlement Planet Durbin

After three hours of sending vain queries to the incoming frigates, Velocity was growing restless. "What's our contingency plan?" she asked Garcia. "What if those frigates continue to refuse to answer?"

Garcia's eyes flickered. Checking something on her own inskull uplink—Velocity recognized the motion. "We still have nearly ten hours. Maybe they're waiting out the lag."

"Complete destruction of population centers," Velocity reminded her. "You should start evacuations."

Her broad mouth hard, Garcia shook her head. Velocity rose and went to the largest wallboard, which showed a map of Durbin and the geos of its cities, resorts, towns, and mines. It was out of date, and didn't even show Pakuru Mining. "Why not?" she asked. "You won't save everyone, but you'll save more than you would if you don't warn them."

"This isn't a Core planet. We've rebuilt less than ten percent of the landmass. Most of that is down in the islands. Ten percent that will grow Earth-source food or feed Earth-source animals. I'm feeding half the population on imported food as it is. Slag the settlements and take out the station, Durbin dies anyway." She shook her head again. "Besides, a mandatory evacuation starts a panic. How many people die in that?"

Velocity wet her lips, looking for a flaw in this argument. "You can't just leave your people open to the attack."

"I plan to stop the attack," Garcia said, getting to her feet. "Send another query."

"They're not answering. Doing what we know won't work isn't a solution."

"Send. Another. Query."

Velocity grimaced, and went to the console where Officer Merrell sat monitoring the link to the frigates. "Send a new message. Tell them Tallis Taveri Harada, putative heir to the Primary Seat on the Taveri House Board, is in Tauranga City. Tell them I request immediate communication."

Merrell repeated this message and tapped a code. "Sent," she said.

"Let me know if they answer." Velocity turned to Garcia. "Now. Let's discuss alternate plans." She paused, and added, raising her voice slightly: "Unless my AI is correct, and you are actually working for the Atlas Society, and not for Durbin. Is that what's happening? Are you keeping people ignorant while these frigates slaughter them like frogs in a bucket?"

Around the room, the Security officers turned. Garcia shot Velocity an annoyed look. "Don't be transparent, Madame Taveri."

Velocity opened her mouth to make her next point, and Uri spoke through her uplink: *Captain. We have a proposed action.*

Report, she subvocced.

Uri sounded more machine-like than he had since she had first unboxed him, years ago now: *The captains of the **Prince of Peace** and the **Susan Calvin** will load non-essential personnel into lifepods or secondary vessels. Then the respective captains will use their ships to ram one frigate each in the most effective location, with the intention of either destroying these frigates or rendering them incapable of completing their missions. Meanwhile, I will use the available weapons on the station to destroy or incapacitate the remaining frigate.*

Velocity stood frozen. Part of her mind was blank with shock;

another part couldn't deny this was the first even possibly viable plan anyone had come up with yet. She shook her head, and said, speaking aloud in her shock, "I'm the Captain of the *Susan Calvin*."

*Yes. I should have said the current commanding officer on the **Susan Calvin**. That would be Tai. Corvo wanted to take his place, since she's the commanding officer for this overall mission, but he refused.*

Velocity sat down on a nearby bench. "Right," she said, and then forced herself to subvoc the rest: *Corvo is an advisor only. Tai has command when I'm not aboard.* She paused. *Your estimate of this tactic, please.*

Chance of success: sixty-seven percent. Velocity set her teeth. She had been hoping, she admitted, for a much lower number. Even a higher one would have been better, in that it would have made her choice clearer. Her teeth set, she stared in front of her, seeing nothing. *Captain?* Uri asked.

Approved, she said, and shut her eyes.

Chapter 37

Aboard the *Susan Calvin*, off Durbin Station, in the Deep

won't," Rida said, clutching the sides of the hatchway tightly, like he thought Tai might try to drag him into the runabout against his will. "If you're staying, I'm staying."

Running her hand over the *Ruka*, the five-passenger light craft stowed here in the bay off the hold, Corvo gave the Pirian head-waggle. "You must all go," she said. "I am the more qualified pilot. I will pilot the *Susan Calvin* into Frigate A."

Frigate A was what they were calling their target. Its register name, according to Uri, was in fact the *Mark Anthony*. Whoever that was. Jusuf said something to Corvo in a Pirian dialect that Tai couldn't follow, and she responded with a single word. His lips shut hard. "I am the most qualified pilot," Corvo repeated in Public.

Tai stepped up and fed the code to open the *Ruka*'s main hatch. It shuttled open. "This isn't a debate," he said. "I'm in command. You will all get on this boat. Make landfall on the planet. Find the Captain and give her every aid. Those are my orders."

Rida, his eyes wet with tears, scowled at him. Jusuf nodded—a real nod, not a Pirian waggle—and climbed aboard. Corvo gave Tai a long hug, and turned to follow. "Ridashi, I will pilot the *Ruka*. You must navigate."

Rida scowled at her too. She climbed aboard the runabout, and shortly afterwards they heard its system come online. "Tai," Rida said.

Tai pulled him close. "I love you," he said. "Take care of the Captain."

"*Tai*," Rida said, the word pent. Tai pushed him toward the *Ruka*, and he resisted, grabbing hold of Tai. "Please let me stay," he said. "Please."

"Get in," Tai said. "That's an order." Rida resisted a moment more, and then capitulated all at once, letting Tai force him aboard. Tai tapped the panel that sealed the hatch and retreated from the bay, sealing the lock behind him. There was a board on the wall outside the bay, which would have let him watch the runabout leave the ship and launch toward the planet, but he went past it, into the hold and up the ladder to the berth deck trail. The *Susan Calvin* was at ten percent thrust; Tai could climb without using his legs at all— he pulled himself upward with his hands alone. "What about you?" he said, as he swung into the trail. "Do you die here too?"

Uri said, "That depends on your point of view."

"Don't play games. You know what I mean."

"I do, but it's not a simple question. I split myself and sent a copy of myself with the runabout. That copy will survive."

"A copy." He pulled himself up into the upper deck trail and headed toward com.

"That version is me as much as this version is," Uri said.

"But this version—you—you'll die with the ship."

"I'm not leaving," Uri said. "You'll need my help with navigation."

Tai knew this was true. He pulled himself up into the com and swung over to the command saddle. "Where's the *Ruka*?"

"One hundred and six kilometers off your starboard, heading toward the planet. Their vector looks good."

"Tell me when we have minimum safe distance. Do you have course projections for me?"

"Aye, Captain," Uri said, and lit up the navigation board.

Chapter 38

Tauranga City, Republic Settlement Planet Durbin

Garcia took all Security except Lily Merrell off duty and sent them away. "You might as well keep an ear up," she told Merrell. "I'd hate to miss their offer to surrender just because no one was listening."

"I'll keep sending Madame Taveri's requests, as well," Merrell said.

Velocity sat at the worktable Garcia waved her towards. "We could go back to my quarters," Garcia said. "Much more comfortable. But I'd like to stay here."

"Better view?" Velocity asked.

Garcia snorted. "Front-line seats." She was opening cupboards over in a corner of the room that had a counter, a kettle, and a tap. "Where's the soak, Lily?"

"We hide it under the sink," Merrell said from her board. "Behind the disinfectant."

Garcia hunkered down to open the cupboard under the tap. She emerged with a glass bottle, which she held to the light. "Plum brandy?" she guessed.

"Why not?" Merrell said amiably.

Garcia laughed, took down two bowls from the shelf over the tap, and came to the worktable. She poured some of the alcohol into each bowl and pushed one toward Velocity. "None for you,

Lil," she said. "Someone needs to be sober."

Velocity picked up her bowl and took a tentative sip. High-proof, whatever it was: it lit the inside of her mouth and burned as she swallowed. There was a faint fruity aftertaste, which might have been plum. Garcia took a large swallow, then topped off each of their bowls. "So is it Garcia or Drury?" Velocity asked. "Or some other name entirely?"

Garcia gave her a brilliant, slitted smile. "I'll answer any name you put to me, Tallis."

"We're drinking together. Call me Velocity."

"Why did you leave Taveri House? Too much work?"

"Yes, I prefer the life of ease out here in the Deep." Velocity had another tiny sip of the brandy. This one stung just as much as the first. "What about you? Why'd you leave your House?"

"I was sent." Garcia emptied her bowl with a single gulp, and tipped more brandy in. "I've never flinched from doing what needs done."

"What needed doing?" Velocity asked idly. She glanced at Merrell, who didn't seem bothered. Maybe Garcia's real identity was common knowledge. "Did they send you out here to start this insurgency? That seems unlikely."

Garcia sat back in the booth. "How old were you when you deserted?"

Velocity let the word pass. "Sixteen. How old were you?"

"Just turned twenty when they sent me out here. Madame Theriot's keeper."

"Imre Theriot. The Minister of Trade? The one down there running your child farms?"

"Ha. I'd like to see Imre run anything. Except her mouth." Garcia barked a short laugh. "She's good at that. Like the rest of you Combines. Good at talk. Work, not so much."

Velocity reached across the table for the bottle and poured them both another splash. "Why did Theriot need a keeper?"

"Too many patches. She really liked Dolorex. Also another one, Clarité, a designer patch made just for her, supposed to increase her mental acumen," Garcia said the last two words with contempt, obviously quoting. "All it did was kill her appetite and make her twitch, far as I could see."

"That's why you have her down in the islands? Limiting the harm she might do?"

"I tried to do the work they sent me here to do. Years I tried. Tried to assist Theriot. Help her govern. She couldn't govern her meal queue, much less a planet. So right, I shipped her down island. She's happier lying in the sun patched stupid, I'm happier getting work done without her."

"Insurgency," Velocity said. "That work?"

"Oh, please. You think I didn't try it their way? I tried for years. They had conflicting goals. I tried to tell them. I even co-opted Theriot's identity to tell them. They don't care. They're not interested."

"Conflicting goals."

Garcia held up her thumb: "Make the planet profitable." She held up her forefinger. "Find, import, and preserve Calypsos." She snorted and sat straighter. "Couldn't do either with a resort planet, so I tried mining. Made it worse. Well, you've seen." Garcia flung an arm northward. "Look at how fast we go through contract workers."

"You know your admin is grafting away your profit, right?"

"Right. And try stopping that sometime." She shook her head. "It's a broken system."

"So you started an insurgency."

"I did not start an insurgency. The insurgency was here. I just made it work." Garcia drank again and laughed. "Turns out I'm heaps better at running a revolution than I am at running an economy."

"You're breeding Calypsos. Is that your idea or Hayek House's idea?"

Garcia shrugged. "They said preserve. That implies long-term. Can't be long-term if we don't make more."

Uri spoke through her uplink: *Operation launched. Rida, Corvo and Jusuf are aboard the **Ruka**, heading for Durbin. ETA six hours and eleven minutes.*

Velocity subvocced: *What about the **Prince of Peace**? Brontë and the Ikans?*

No reply. Already slightly greased on brandy, she took a moment to remember the delay—the *Susan Calvin* was over a million kilometers from the station, which meant several seconds to transmit and reply. While she was still figuring the exact math in her head, Uri's answer came through: *The lifepods have not yet been launched from the **Prince of Peace**. I'll notify you when they have.*

But Brontë and the Ikans will be aboard them when they are launched, yes?

Another delay. Irritated, Velocity drank more brandy. Across the table, Garcia was brooding, her dark eyes hooded. Uri's reply came: *That is my understanding. Captain, I suggest you leave the city. Take shelter at Pakuru. That settlement is not on the official versions of the planetary maps. You may be safe there.*

I think Garcia plans to keep me right here.

Another delay. Across the table, Garcia shifted her weight. "I did what they said," she muttered. "So far as they know, I did *exactly* what they said. They're slagging us anyway. Tell me why I *shouldn't* run an insurgency."

"So far as they know?" Velocity said delicately.

Garcia grinned. "Like I'd put the truth in my reports? I'm not that fresh."

Captain, Uri said, *you should leave the city. Go to Pakuru. If we don't stop the frigates, the Pirians will come for you. Stay alive until then.*

Velocity thought this over. Sending posts across jumps was expensive. The Pirians wouldn't be expecting interim reports. They'd expect Corvo to wait until the *Susan Calvin* was back in

Pirian space to send her first reports. So they wouldn't even count her and her crew as overdue for at least another three or four months universal time. Then they'd have to argue about what to do, as they did about everything. A couple of weeks to get here, even if they burned push the whole way. She and her crew would have to stay alive, on this raw planet, in winter, for somewhere around half a universal year. Surrounded by a million or so survivors twice as desperate as they were, and who had much better knowledge of the planet than they did. Several thousand of them Calypsos or part-Calypsos. "Not good odds," she muttered.

"What's not?" Garcia said.

"My crew's on their way here," Velocity said. "My AI thinks I should get out of the city, go wait for them. He says the Pirians will provide help, when they learn what happened here."

"You're not going anywhere. Tell your AI if he wants to save your Combine skin, he can stop those frigates."

Velocity relayed this message to Uri, and reached for the brandy bottle while she waited for the reply. Merrell spoke from her seat by the boards: "You should go."

"Spoken like a Calypso," Garcia grumbled.

"Smoke will need you if this goes bad. You should go."

"No one is going anywhere," Garcia said, and took the brandy back from Velocity.

Chapter 39

Aboard the *Prince of Peace*, off Durbin Station, in the Deep

Captain Kaihe said it was his ship, and no one but him was taking his ship on its last mission. "You're bonded labor," Brontë told him. "You'll do as you're told."

His dark face went darker. "No, Madame," he said. "I will not."

"Ruçar," Brontë said. "See that the Captain is put aboard a lifepod."

Captain Kaihe set his heels, but Ruçar was backed by Adder. Two combat-trained Combine Security cadets: twice as much force as necessary. Brontë turned away as Kaihe was escorted out, to see Lieutenant Evans studying her. "Are you a qualified pilot?" Evans asked.

"Qualified and Pirian-trained," Brontë said. This was mostly true. She'd passed the third-class exam while still at Ikeda House, and had a few sessions with pilots on the *Sungai*. "Get in the lifepod, Lieutenant."

"Believe me, I would like nothing more. But I'm an actual pilot. You'll need me."

Brontë knew she should order Evans onto the pods. On the other hand, she also knew exactly how basic her own piloting skills were. Evans was correct. She might not be skilled enough to pull this off. Without Evans, she might die, which would make Tai's death on the *Susan Calvin* meaningless. "All right," she said. "All right. You stay."

Evans went pale. But she gave a firm nod and turned in the pilot's saddle to open the navigation program. Brontë settled into the com saddle, and opened a channel. "*Prince of Peace* to the *Susan Calvin*. We have no AI here. Mind giving us some help with plotting our course?"

The *Susan Calvin* was close enough to them by now that lag between transmissions was unnoticeable. Uri replied: "*Prince of Peace*, glad to help. Transmitting three best courses."

Brontë watched the projected course vectors come in, and then opened the one Uri had starred as the best choice. She read through it and then copied it to Evans' board. "*Prince of Peace*," Uri said, "query: what's the estimated time of departure for your lifepods?"

Brontë keyed up that link. The number of crew and passengers about the *Prince of Peace* required that three lifepods be used. Two of these had their hatches sealed already; the third was still loading. She tapped the link that let her read the biosigns for those already on board, and those still loading. Five people in the first pod, five in the second, one already loaded in the third. As she watched, the last person climbed aboard and the hatch sealed behind them. The podbay airlock began cycling. "Thirty-nine seconds," Brontë said, reading the number off the airlock countdown.

"Query: You are aboard one of the lifepods?"

"Negative. Lieutenant Evans and I remain aboard to complete the mission." Brontë watched the first lifepod fire itself out of the bay. "Lifepods now leaving the ship," she added, to make things plain.

"Understood, *Prince of Peace*. The Captain will not be pleased, if you don't mind me saying so."

"Course looks good," Evans said.

"Implement starred course," Brontë said.

"It is useless, I suppose," Uri said, "for me to point out that the next heir in line for the Primary Board Seat after you is a four-year-old child. Someone your mother might easily control."

"Entirely useless," Brontë agreed. "Also, the pods have just left the ship."

"Understood. Our own course has been implemented. Chance of success for our mission has dropped to fifty-three percent."

Also useless information at this point, though Brontë didn't bother to say so. Instead, she tapped up a plain view of their course, added in the position of the three frigates, then the course of the *Susan Calvin*. The navigation program showed their two ships currently on a collision course with the frigates. But the frigates would notice their ships and take evasive action. Probably fire on them as well. Projected success of fifty-three percent seemed generous.

Uri spoke again: "*Prince of Peace*: Alert. One of your lifepods is off course."

"What?" Brontë added the projected trajectories for the lifepods to her board. Uri was correct: one of the pods was veering from its logged route toward the station. Brontë opened a channel. "Ruçar, return to your course. That's an order."

The reply came back at once: "Captain Kaihe to the *Prince of Peace*. Tend your own ship, Madame Ikeda."

Brontë chewed her lip. "What are you doing?"

"Captain Kaihe, ending transmission."

"Lifepod C is on a projected collision course with Frigate A," Evans said.

Brontë brought up the feed from the lifepod bay and ran it backwards. As she had known she would, she saw Ruçar climbing into Pod C, right on the heels of Captain Kaihe. She watched the lifepod hatch seal behind them. You couldn't really call it mutiny, she supposed, not when they were aboard their own vessel. "Madame Ikeda?" Evans said.

"Adjust our course heading to avoid collision with the lifepod," Brontë said. "*Susan Calvin*, this is *Prince of Peace*. What are your chances of getting control of the frigates before we complete this action?"

"Less than twenty percent," Uri replied. "Though Gecko and I will continue our attempt to achieve that end."

"Understood," Brontë said. "Be aware that Lifepod C has joined our action."

"Understood," Uri agreed. "I'll alert you if the situation—or our odds—improve."

Chapter 40

Commercial Space Station Webster-1, Planet Durbin, in the Deep

The *Susan Calvin* was just over a million kilometers off the station—it was still possible for Uri to send and receive updates. He did not yet have to abandon his other self, out on the ship. But that was sentiment. His other self was doomed; he accepted that. Saving fragments against that loss was a waste of processor power better spent elsewhere.

Hey, Gecko said. *Hey. Hey. Hey.*

I'm here. Report.

I'm into the command system of Frigate A.

Uri knew better, but he couldn't help hoping. He opened the data the young AI had shipped over. *That's the commissary system,* he said. *We could put salt in their tea with that. Not much more.*

Gecko flared green, the way he did when he was confused. *Are you sure? It looks like command sys to me.*

This was a common problem with young AI, especially those who had done a great deal of unsupervised learning. They learned to differentiate, to select from a field; but their focus was flawed—they built their decision trees by selecting features no human mind would select. The classic example was young AIs selecting grass rather than sheep when asked to sort captures with sheep from captures without, since most captures of sheep *also* had grass in them. Probably in this case, Gecko had selected for bits of code that had little to do with either command or commissary: code that dealt with the ability to enter instructions orally, maybe; or maybe headers. Both words started with comm—he might have selected for that. Who knew.

Classically, these data-error selections were called giraffes. A giraffe was an extinct Earth animal, very oddly constructed. Uri had run an Orly once, curious about why data-errors were called giraffes. The best answer he'd found was that, in the early days of AI, young AIs were trained on whatever data sets were both large enough and no-cost. In these data sets, for reasons beyond Uri's understanding, images of giraffes had been over-represented. Because of this, when a young AI had to guess what any given image contained, it tended to select *giraffe*, since the odds that this guess would be correct outweighed the odds that it would be in error. Gecko might have made some similar selection error.

We need the system that's used for setting courses, Uri told him. *Not three-course meals, either. Search for navigation programs and work outwards from there.* He made up a data packet filled with code to select for, and sent that to Gecko. Then he turned back to his own actions, dismissing the young AI from his primary field. Gecko's action had only an eight percent chance of success; he'd assigned it low priority. Not the young AI's fault: the security algorithms on a Combine Combat ship were just too robust, even with nothing but dumb-AI to run them.

His own action—breaking through the defense code on the weapons array on the station—ought to have been just as chancy. But he was being helped by the erosion of funding the station had been subjected to: their security algorithms were six updates old. Uri could have handled them even without his Pirian code. He calculated his chance of success for this action at ninety percent. But he did need to actually do the work; and it had to be done in the next eleven minutes if he was to have sufficient time to learn to operate the plasma cannons.

The station security system also had dumb-AI. Getting through its security algorithms was ten percent math and ninety percent craft. Like a dance. Every AI built itself differently, depending on the data sets available to it when it was learning, and also partly on chance—as with Gecko, on what parts of those datasets the AI happened to select. This last was to a large degree random. Supervised learning would correct this randomness; a 'parent' could instruct the young AI to focus on this rather than that. But dumb-AIs were almost never given sufficient supervised learning.

This meant it was possible to ferret out and exploit their errors. This had to be done without tripping alarms, true. But thanks to the funding cuts, the station system was so out of date that shutting down its alarms was simple. Uri just broke some of the code in the relay channels, and that was that. He could spend the rest of his time looking for giraffes.

The optimal method for getting through a security system was to try various combinations of phrases likely to hit one of these giraffes. The dumb-AI would confuse *command* with *commissary*, as it were, and pop open its gates. A correctly built system would lock a smart AI out well before it hit a prime giraffe; but this system, so far out of date, was easy to fool. Three minutes and forty-one seconds later, Uri fed it a word combination that worked. He slipped into the dumb-AI's command system, and swiftly reprogrammed it to respond to him, and to him only. After that, it was only a matter of time.

Chapter 41

Tauranga City, Republic Settlement Planet Durbin

They finished the brandy and moved onto a liter of mijui which Merrell fetched down from Garcia's office (under protest). Clear as water and sour, it had a much milder kick than the brandy. They were well into this when Wolf showed up.

"Why are you still here?" he demanded.

Garcia waved at him. "Ikan! Come hava drink."

Wolf came further into the bay, scowling. He snapped at Merrell, "Why haven't you evacuated them?"

"I'm just the barkeep here," Merrell said.

"I've got a stormcraft outside," Wolf said to Garcia. "Let's go."

"No one is going anywhere," Garcia said, pronouncing each syllable carefully. "Come and have a drink."

"We've got three hours. We can get well outside the blast radius by then."

"Go ahead. Take Lily with you." Garcia pointed her finger at Velocity. "Don't get any notions, Combine. You're staying."

Velocity waved the warning away. "Wouldn't think of it." To be honest, she found herself curiously unconcerned with her impending death by plasma fire. She didn't know if this was because she was losing both Tai and her ship; or if she just didn't believe it yet. Maybe some of both. Even if she got out of the city, and somehow Rida found her, what then? The runabout did not have jump capacity. Slim odds they'd find refuge this side of the jump, with the frigates under orders to burn the entire system.

She knew Garcia thought that keeping her here, in the biggest city and thus main target on Durbin, would make her crew work harder to stop the frigates. She knew Garcia was wrong about that. But it didn't seem worth arguing about.

Wolf Ikan was arguing, his hands in fists, like he might decide to club Garcia and drag her out to the stormcraft. "How do you think the survivors will do without you?" he demanded. "At least if we get out of the city, we've got a chance."

"Bah," Garcia said. "Sit down, Ikan. Have some mijui."

Wolf shot a look at Merrell, who shrugged. He turned and strode out of the room. Velocity nodded after him. "He's going for reinforcements. More Security. Drag you out of here."

Garcia turned to look at the door. "Think so?"

"I know Ikans. That's what Adder would do."

"Huh." Garcia turned back and refilled her bowl. "Lily, lock the door." Merrell didn't move from her place at the communication board. Garcia didn't appear to notice. Velocity held her bowl out to be refilled as well and Garcia obligingly poured the mijui, adding, as if Velocity had spoken, "Never mind how many people die in the panic, we send out an evacuation order, where do you think they evacuate *to*? Dead of exposure, dead from plasma, just as dead."

"Maybe you should have thought about that before signing up to be Hayek-Lopaka's dog."

Merrell jerked her head up to glare in outrage, but Garcia just laughed. "As if I had anything to say about that."

"I'm giving up my ship to fix your, your—" Velocity hunted for the right phrase.

"My error," Garcia provided obligingly.

"My crew is dying to save you. Brontë Ikeda is. Wolf's brother rerouted a lifepod. Put it on a collision course with one of the frigates."

"Of course he did. Calypso. Just what I would have done. And you, am I right?"

"Everything isn't our genetic code," Velocity said irritably.

"Ha." Garcia stretched her legs out along the bench. "Why else am I still running after Combine approval, with everything I know?"

Velocity said what the Pirian genetic engineers had told her, when she had been feeling grim about being a Calypso: "Genes are the matrix. The basic programming. What we build on that is our own decision."

Garcia snorted. "My bony ass."

Velocity wasn't sure she believed the Pirians herself. "I left the Combine. You haven't been following their orders for years."

"And look what it got us. Plasma down our necks."

Merrell wheeled from the com board. "That's not you! That's the Combines. And they would have done it no matter what you did."

"It's the Atlas Society," Velocity said. "Not the Combines."

Merrell snorted. "Big difference."

"It is a big difference, though. What made the Republic work for so long—"

"The Republic works?" Garcia said, and laughed immoderately.

"What made it work," Velocity said doggedly, "as well as it has for as long as it has, is the Combines keeping each other in check. It's why the Republic used to have a law, way back, regulating how many Houses could make alliances. It used to be only two Houses could combine. Then they changed the law to three, but only if one agreed to accept non-voting status on the Combine Board."

"Like who holds voting seats even matters."

"It matters. But you're right. Behind-the-seat influence matters more. That's what makes the Atlas Society dangerous. They're abrogating Combine integrity."

"Abrogating Combine integrity," Garcia mimicked. "Tell me again how you aren't Combine to the bone."

"Atlas Society decides to create the Calypsos, and to seed them through the Combines. Then they decide that Calypso males are too dangerous. So they decide to kill off all these males."

"Sell off," Garcia corrected, and waved a hand. "Sell to mining platforms. Same thing, you're right."

"Then your Combine, Hayek-Lopaka, sends you out here to build a reserve of Calypsos. Maybe it was actually the Atlas Society in Hayek House that did it," Velocity said, thinking it through. "That's a House decision. At the most, a Combine decision. Then the Atlas Society, which is to say Isra Ikeda Lopaka, starts a takeover of Hayek-Lopaka. And someone, probably someone in the Society who is trying to stop her, finds out about Durbin. And they authorize a compliance raid."

"The Atlas Society built the Calypsos," Merrill objected. "Why would they wipe them out?"

"They're not wiping them out. That ship, the *Reynard*, it left the station, what, an hour ago?" Velocity asked. *Fifty-one minutes ago*, Uri told her. "Holds packed with Calypsos. Not to mention those already seeded through the Combine board seats. Probably zygotes in their freezers, too."

"The frigates are from Taveri-Bowers Combine," Merrell mentioned.

"Taveri-Bowers was part of the alliance Isra Ikeda Lopaka was forming. It's why she wants me back. She put a Calypso in the Primary Board Seat of Ikeda House, with at least one Calypso lined up as his potential heir. She wants the same for Taveri House." Velocity shifted on the bench. "That might be another reason someone is trying to stop her. Those Calypsos put in positions of power."

"Calypsos they have on their leash," Garcia said. "Not Calypsos in power."

"They wanted Calypsos they control," Velocity agreed. "What they got is Calypsos like you. And Brontë."

"And you," Garcia said, pointing her bottle at Velocity.

"And me," Velocity agreed. "Me. You. Wolf. Half this planet, apparently."

"Only about fifteen percent, so far."

"What percentage of Security, though?" Merrell said. "What percentage of Parliament?"

"Which is why the frigates," Velocity agreed. "But who sent the frigates? Not Taveri-Bowers, or Hayek-Lopaka, either. This isn't one Combine acting against another. This is someone in the Atlas Society, taking action against someone else in the Society. This is two people making decisions for all the Combines. It subverts the system. It's a new system. A dangerous one."

Garcia squinted, clearly thinking this over. "You're saying I'm not the insurgency. They are."

"I'm saying they're carrying out a coup while no one's watching. And it might be too late to stop them. It might be," she said, the idea occurring to her as she spoke, "that the only population capable of stopping them is this one. Right here. On Durbin."

The ensuing silence was so complete Velocity could hear the footsteps clattering down a staircase, somewhere in some distant part of the building. Then Merrell said, half under her breath, "Hence the frigates."

"Hence the frigates," Velocity agreed, and held her bowl out for Garcia to fill it up one more time.

Chapter 42

Off Planet Durbin, in the Deep

You should put on your skinsuit," Uri said.

Tai snorted. "Right, like that will help." But he dragged it from the locker and put it on, even sealing the throat, a detail he didn't usually bother with. He left the hood down for now. "Have they spotted us yet?"

"They have us on their boards. No alarm triggered yet."

"What about the *Prince*?"

"Also on their boards, as is the pod. I predict alarms will trigger in less than nine universal seconds."

His throat dry, Tai pulled himself down into the command saddle and fastened the restraints. "Will you be able to take control of their weapons array before then? Your other you, I mean."

"Unable to predict. Their proximity alarms have triggered. Firing engines." Before Tai could acknowledge, the force of the thrust slammed him down into the saddle.

ಠ ௲ ಖ

"Fire engines," Brontë said.

"Firing engines," Evans said. The push shoved them hard into their saddles; Brontë set her teeth. She could feel her heart kicking in her chest like an animal trying to escape. On the board before her, red circles marked the position of the frigates; a blue chip showed their own position. Off to their starboard was the yellow marker for the *Susan Calvin*; to their port, Lifepod C. The projected paths for each curved to intercept the projected paths of the frigates. Seven minutes to impact. An impossible stretch of time.

For the first time, Brontë understood what a bad idea this was—dying, *actually dying*, on the chance that they might get past the defense perimeter of three combat-class frigates. The *very small chance*. She shut her eyes, her teeth still set. What choice, though, really? Let the planet be destroyed without trying to stop it? Run away and leave the Captain to die? Not to mention Wolf. She could see no way that she could go on if she hadn't tried to stop that.

"Frigates have fired plasma cannons." Evans sounded calm and unworried. "Running projections. Chance of impact on our ship: Thirty-eight percent. Chance of impact on the *Susan Calvin*: Forty-one percent. Chance of impact on Lifepod C: Eleven percent."

Should have all taken lifepods, Brontë thought, her eyes shut. Uri spoke through the feed: "Recommend *Prince* and *Calvin* fire turbo, five seconds each."

"Fire turbo." Brontë was distantly surprised to hear that she sounded as calm as Evans.

"Firing turbo, five seconds," Evans said. The pressure on Brontë's chest increased sharply; she fought to breathe, spots blooming behind her eyes. "Plasma has missed. Frigates have fired a second round."

Brontë opened her eyes; her vision was blurry. *Pressure warping my eyeballs*, she thought hazily. *Still six minutes out. We're going to fail. Fail and die anyway*. Adrenaline surged hot in her blood. Despite this, she found herself calm. Everything she had worried over, all her life, fell away as she soared toward death. Even whether they would succeed at destroying the frigates seemed a matter of complete disinterest. They would succeed or they wouldn't. The Combines would destroy the planet or they wouldn't. All that was important, but it was important to some other world, one which she would never see. Uri spoke: "*Prince of Peace*, recommend you fire forward thrusters, full impulse, fifteen seconds."

"Fire forward thrusters," Brontë said.

"Firing forward thrusters. Second round has missed. Frigates have fired a third round."

"Station has fired," Uri said. He meant his counterpart had fired, the copy he had left on the station. "*Prince of Peace*, recommend you fire turbo, five seconds."

"Fire turbo," Brontë said.

"Firing turbo," Evans said. "This exhausts our excess fuel."

"Acknowledged." Brontë managed to focus her eyes. No excess fuel meant no way to alter their course. No way to get out of the way of the next load of plasma cannon fired at them. And they were still four minutes from impact.

ᘓ ᚈ ᘝ

I *don't understand*, Gecko said. *This tactic will fail.*

We don't know that yet.

For this tactic to succeed, all units must succeed. Probability of that outcome is less than three percent.

So you're saying there's a chance, Uri said. It was an old joke, and not a very funny one in these circumstances. Gecko sparked confusion. Uri relented. *What chance do we have if we do nothing?*

Gecko calculated, and said, *Essentially the same chance.*

Exactly.

I do not understand.

And he never would, Uri thought sadly. When the station was destroyed, along with the human population centers on the planet, Gecko would be left without servers or banks. He could no more survive without those things than humans could survive without their bodies. Uri had split himself before leaving Pirian space, leaving a copy behind with Taniwha on the *Sungai*. So he would, in a sense, survive. Gecko would die with the planet.

Is it like solitaire? Gecko asked.

What? Uri said, startled.

That game humans are always playing. Mom says it's something they do while they wait to die. Is that what this is?

Delight and grief filled Uri, bubbling up like oxygen in an Exchange tank. He wondered if this was what human parents felt like. If the Captain had felt this way about him. *Yes*, he said. *Very much like that. Now help me calculate our next shot.*

Chapter 43

Tauranga City, Republic Settlement Planet Durbin

To Velocity's utter lack of surprise, Wolf showed up with a quarter-squad of Security: six Durbin Security, all armed with Lopaka long rifles and charged sticks. But when he ordered them to escort Garcia to the stormcraft outside, they hesitated. "Are you telling us to arrest Madame Drury?" one asked, more confused than anything.

"I'm saying put her in that craft and get her out of the city," Wolf ordered. "Now move."

"Stand down," Garcia said, waving them back—though in fact none of them had moved. "No one is going anywhere."

Uri spoke: *The frigates are firing on our ships.*

The wine was almost gone. Velocity finished what was in her bowl. Up by the boards, Merrell said, "Frigates have fired."

Everyone turned toward her, and Merrell obligingly shifted her screen to the main wallboard. Multicolored triangles marked the positions of ships: green for their ships, yellow for the frigates. Curving arrow showed the trajectories for each ship. Pulsing orange vectors showed the plasma loads headed for the green triangles. Wolf moved closer to the board, the muscles in his back and face tense. "That's a miss," he said. "It's going to miss."

Velocity wondered which load he meant—the one aimed at the lifepod, or the one aimed at the *Prince of Peace*. Through the uplink, Uri said, *Next round fired*. Up on the board, new orange vectors began crawling toward their targets. "Second round fired," Merrell said.

Firing my first round on the frigates, Uri said. *Projected trajectory shows a miss. Recalculating. Firing second round.* Velocity shut her eyes, but the orange pulse of the plasma loads had printed itself on her retinas. "It's a miss," Wolf said, not very loudly.

Projected trajectory of my second round: a miss. Recalculating.

"Third rounds fired," Merrell said.

Firing third round, Uri said. He sounded remote, machine-like. Velocity opened her eyes just in time to see a splash of scarlet on the screen, a circle that bloomed and grew. She sat up, her breath caught in her throat.

"The lifepod has been hit," Merrell said, and a second circle bloomed bright red. "The *Susan Calvin* has been hit." Velocity's mouth was numb; so was the pit of her stomach. Her fists had clenched tight on nothing. Monkey reflex: hold on hard when you're falling. Up by the board, Wolf was pale except for dark red patches on his cheeks and ears. "The *Prince of Peace*," Merrell said. "Missed."

Another scarlet bloom. Velocity twitched, and Uri said, *My third round has hit Frigate A. Firing fourth round.* His last round, Velocity thought numbly. Even if Brontë…it would leave the third frigate undamaged. They had failed.

Wolf wheeled from the board. "Get Drury to the stormcraft. *Now*."

The Durbin Security officers looked at Garcia, still slouched at the worktable. She shook her head. "I'm not going anywhere. Take Lily, if you like."

"I'm staying," Merrell said, not turning from her board.

Wolf glared at the Durbin Security. One of them shrugged, spreading her hands, and Wolf wheeled back to the board, where the circles of scarlet that were the burning ships widened and widened. *Fourth round has missed*, Uri said. Velocity reached for her empty bowl, and then pushed it away. *Advise you remove yourself from the city forthwith.*

*Do you have the **Susan Calvin** on visual?* Velocity subvocced. Is there any chance…. She didn't bother finishing. No chance. And what if there were? They didn't have a rescue ship. Not one that could get there in time. Or maybe…*What about the **Ruka**? Where is she?*

Hold, Uri said. *We have unidentified ships.*

"What?" Velocity said out loud.

"Where did those come from?" Merrell said. Wolf put his hand on the board, fingers outspread, covering the bright blue triangles rushing toward the station. "Those weren't—Madame Drury, we have sixteen ships, less than twenty thousand kilometers from the station, type unknown—anji!"

Garcia sat up. "What is it?"

"They're firing—all of them! Mami! Sixteen, I don't, torpedoes, I think!"

"At the station?" Garcia was on her feet.

"No! At the frigates! Second round fired! The frigates are returning fire!"

"Who are they?" Wolf asked. It was a question aimed at no one; and no one answered, except Uri, speaking through Velocity's uplink: *Pirians. Those are Pirian ships.*

Chapter 44

**Commercial Space Station Webster-1,
Planet Durbin, in the Deep**

Velocity leaned her shoulder against the frame of the observation window, gazing dispiritedly down at the concourse. The metal of the frame was cold through her skinsuit; the air was cold around her. Down below, the concourse wasn't the dim empty place it had been when they had first come aboard Webster Station. Now, brightly lit, it buzzed with people—Pirians, mostly, but also local Security, Durbin administrators, and medics. No wounded left in what had been the triage area: the last of those had finally been given beds in the hastily constructed annex to the infirmary. Uri had examined every wounded brought onto the station, and Velocity had visited anyone likely, which included those who were badly burned. None were Tai.

Very few of the wounded were burned. If you were that close to a plasma burst, mostly you didn't survive. This was especially true on Combine ships, where skinsuits were not standard issue. Only those who had bought one on their own tag, and who happened to be wearing it, had had any chance of survival at all. That wasn't very many. Each of the frigates had a crew complement in the range of three thousand; the Pirians had picked up and brought in just over two hundred survivors. None of them Tai.

Mendoza, Tactical First on the Pirian squad that had come

to their rescue, said not to lose hope. They hadn't yet found the wreckage of the *Susan Calvin*. Tai might still be found alive. Not impossible, Velocity agreed, but with every minute that ticked past, less likely. The life pod Ruçar had commandeered had not been found either. But no one expected it to be, given it had taken a direct plasma burst. Well, Adder. Adder might be expecting that. Or at least hoping for it.

Yao Garcia entered the conference room through its big double doors, trailing her usual crowd of Security, aides, and petitioners. These included three different Parliamentary cabinet members: the Ministers of State, Transport, and Defense. Absent, notably, was the Minister of Trade, Imre Theriot.

Garcia dealt with her entourage briskly, sending them off in all directions. She was down to the Ministers and Wolf when Mendoza Sungai and Nur Che came in together. Velocity took the seat at the end of the table farthest from the Ministers. She was working hard not to resent these cabinet members. It was clear that parliamentary work was a hobby here on Durbin, and not one that they had ever given much attention to. The Minister of Transport, though barely in her thirties, was the most competent, and the only one who seemed willing to listen and learn from what she heard. All of them acted like Garcia was in charge. Garcia acted that way too, of course. Given that she was meant to be a clerk to a low-level Minister, Velocity wondered why all of them accepted her leadership so easily.

Garcia had been holding these briefs twice a "day" through the ten watches since the battle. (Why keep a planetary cycle on a space station?) Technically, Velocity knew, she herself had no right to attend the briefings. She wasn't in command of anything anymore. But Mendoza had brought her to the first one and she kept coming, and so far no one had objected. She supposed at a stretch she might be said to represent Free Trade interests. Or the Combines.

Garcia knocked her knuckles on the table to say they were starting. Mendoza and Nur stopped talking and sat down. Garcia brought the agenda up on the wallboard and considered it, her lower lip pushed out. "Mendoza," she said. "How's medical?"

"Two hundred seventeen survivors so far," Mendoza said. "Thirty-two of those are in critical condition. We'd like to transfer them to infirmaries on the *Kirikiti* and the *Anna Kauho*." She paused. "Those are Scorpions with full medical bays."

"And we'd get these thirty-two Combine citizens back afterwards," Garcia said. Mendoza did the Pirian sideways nod. Garcia studied her, eyes narrowed. "What does that mean?"

Velocity laughed. It was almost the first sound she'd made in hours, the first laugh since the battle: the noise was ragged. Everyone looked at her. She shrugged. "Just wondering why I never thought to ask that."

"It means," Mendoza said, "that if they wish to come to Durbin, we will see they get to Durbin."

Garcia grunted. "No, in other words."

"They are not slaves."

"They *are* prisoners."

"Our prisoners. Prisoners taken by Siji, and healed by Siji medics."

Garcia grunted again. "What about the *Reynard*? Any luck there?"

"We have visual confirmation from one of our itachi that it emerged from the jump point at Liberty-236," Mendoza said. This was no surprise, since Liberty-236 was the only exit for the antipodal jump point in Durbin's system. "The ship did not make dock there. It proceeded directly to Liberty's primary jump point which, as you know, is a hub. Destinations from there include Oz, Kyoto, and Jefferson. The last is their probable destination, but we lack reliable itachi in that system."

Jefferson was the usual route into the Drift. Its system had mining platforms and a single commercial station, orbiting the moon of a gas giant. Most ships didn't stop there, but went straight on through to the Drift.

"I assume you have people watching at Oz and Kyoto," Garcia said.

"We do. No sign of the ship at either of those." Mendoza paused. "Have you compiled the list of the contract workers shipped out on the *Reynard*? We would like to add that to the briefs we are sending to our itachi."

"Still working on that," Garcia said. Uri's investigations had shown that Imre Theriot had authorized the collection and export of the Calypsos from the child farms via the *Reynard*; that her orders had come from Pierre Hayek Ito, who held a seat on the Hayek House Board; and that Imre's records were fuzzy on who, exactly, had been shipped. Garcia had Durbin Security running their own investigation; but these Security officers were having to work from what individual clerks remembered, and by interrogating second parties—those who had been responsible for work assignments, for instance, who would now be missing workers. "We should have a complete list by tomorrow noon. I can give you a partial list now."

"That will be helpful," Mendoza said.

Garcia was studying her. "I want my citizens returned," she said. "None of this 'if they wish it' in this case. You find them, you send them home."

"If they wish to come to Durbin," Mendoza repeated, "we will see they get to Durbin." Garcia tapped her forefinger on the table, scowling, and Mendoza added: "They are not prisoners. And slavery is not recognized in Pirian space or on Pirian ships."

Garcia kept staring at her. Then, abruptly, she turned her attention to the head of Station Security. "Captain Che. Ordnance?"

Nur opened the port set into table and put a spreadsheet up on the wallboard to replace the agenda. "Eleven plasma cannons are back online. Siji have provided sufficient rounds for us to fire all eleven of them five times each. The torpedo system tests out as functional, but given that we have no torpedoes, they're useless at the present time." Nur paused. "Siji will bring us more plasma rounds as well as torpedoes when they return. They have the materials to rebuild our railguns. Also they can provide updated plasma rifles. I have sent the cost-estimate to your dropbox."

"To Garcia's dropbox?" the Minister of Defense said sharply.

"Pardon," Nur said. "To everyone's, I meant."

Garcia switched her attention back to Mendoza. "When do your Siji plan to leave us?"

"We're sending the ships with the wounded back to Pirian space on mainwatch first," Mendoza said. "The rest of the squad will remain until the fleet sends replacements."

This was new information. Velocity watched Garcia become entirely expressionless, which was the way she reacted when she was surprised. Or angry. Or amused. "Replacements," she said.

"A defense perimeter for Durbin," Mendoza explained. "Sixteen Scorpions and two courier ships, rotated every five hundred watches."

"You're going to occupy my planet."

Mendoza widened her eyes, miming shock. "You would have us leave this system undefended?"

The Minister of State spoke at almost the same moment: "*Your* planet?"

Garcia shot him an impatient look. "Can we focus on the point? An occupation by the Pirian Navy is not acceptable."

"The fleet has invested a significant sum in preventing the destruction of this system," Mendoza said. "A second, and possibly larger, flight of Combine vessels may well arrive while we are gone, and before you have any useful defensive capabilities. What then?"

"Invested," Garcia said. Mendoza stared at her. Garcia stared right back. "What return do you expect on this investment?"

The Minister of State leaned forward. "This is a sovereign

planet in the Republic of Worlds. We will not sell our loyalty for a few torpedoes."

Mendoza nodded. "Tell me, if your Combines have decided you and your planet are to be eradicated, like an infested Exchange, will you accept that decision? And call it loyalty?"

Garcia tapped her forefinger again. "Let's put this question to the side for the moment. I'd like an answer to the initial question. What will your fleet expect in return for the protection you will provide?" She gave the word 'protection' a delicate emphasis.

"We would expect any of our people now in contract labor on your planet, or who arrive there later, to be returned. We expect free trade between our fleet and your planet. We hope for the right of free movement between your planet and our fleet. We hope that you will allow our scientists access to your planet and society."

"Free trade," said the Minister of Transportation. "Scientists." Velocity smiled a dispassionate, reflexive smile. Those were the exact points that had caught her attention as well. The Minister of Transportation was learning fast.

Captain, Uri said through her uplink. *We have located the **Susan Calvin**.*

౧ ☖ ౺

Without her ship, Velocity had nothing—no transportation, no berth. No purpose. She was back where she had been at sixteen, loose in the universe with nothing but a data tag in her pocket and no idea where she would lay her head. Rida, now on the *Prince of Peace* along with Brontë, had suggested they just appropriate that ship. Prize of war, he said. This was a term used by pirates in the Drift, meaning to keep enemy ships defeated in combat. Everything was legal in the Drift. "Right," Velocity had said drily, "except we didn't defeat the *Prince of Peace*. She was fighting on our side."

Rida snorted. "You're saying Combines aren't our enemy?"

"We can't steal a ship whose Captain died trying to save us."

Rida grimaced but didn't argue further. The *Prince of Peace* was supposed to be hunting survivors, but Velocity knew their search had been more specific: Uri had plotted probable vectors for the *Susan Calvin*, post-impact with the plasma bolt, and they had searched those vectors exclusively.

Now they had found it. Velocity took the service ladders from the conference room out to her berth, a box of a room in the temporary workers quad. The clerk who assigned her the room told her that quadrant hadn't been opened in nearly fifty years. Hadn't been cleaned since then either, as far as Velocity could tell. It did have a hatch she could shut, though, and a working wallboard. When she arrived, Uri already had a link to the *Prince of Peace* established, and a capture from the ship up on the board: the black of space, with ice-sharp chips of stars. "Where's the ship?" Velocity asked, sealing the hatch behind her.

Uri put up a second capture, smaller and in the upper corner of the board, showing the com of the *Prince of Peace*, with Brontë, Corvo, and Evans in the saddles. Velocity wondered where Rida was. Evans tapped at something on his board and said: "The *Susan Calvin* is three kilometers off our port, and closing."

The image on the feed was zoomed in, once, twice, and again: the *Susan Calvin* appeared, tiny even at that magnification, its ovoid shape lucid in the pure light from Durbin's star. Its running lights and portholes were dark and its aft end gone entirely, torn away by plasma bolts. Burning plasma had marked its remaining skin with rippled scars. Velocity bit on her lip. "Rida and Jusuf are taking the *Ruka* over," Uri told her. "Its fuel reserves are sufficient."

The runabout had been almost to Durbin when Rida changed course to go meet the *Prince of Peace*—an expensive proposition in terms of fuel use, since they'd had to reverse their vector, which meant killing their velocity entirely, and then building back to speed. But they almost certainly had enough fuel left for this mission. "Where do they plan to dock?" Velocity muttered. The runabout bay had been aft, in the section destroyed by plasma.

"The hold," Uri said. "What remains of the hold. It should just fit." Velocity shook her head, doubting this—most of the hold was also gone—but given the time-lag, there was no point in objecting. Also, second-guessing those in the field was never wise.

"*Ruka* has launched," Brontë said. "Adding transmission from the *Ruka* to feed."

"Switching *Prince of Peace* to audio only," Uri said. On the wallboard, Rida's feed appeared. His voice, raw and tight, spoke over it: "I don't know if you can see this," he said. The feed showed flashes of the hold, of the scorched bulkheads. A branch drifted past, fragile with frozen leaves—part of a fig tree, from the Exchange. "Damage to the ship is extensive. I can…ah, cabins and hold are open to space. Uri is not responding to our hails."

"The other Uri, he means," Uri said. "My cloned self." Velocity grunted, dismay hot in her belly at the sight of the wrecked ship. No one had survived that. It was impossible. "The *Ruka* has fired thrusters," Uri said. "Slowing their momentum. Closing with the *Susan Calvin*…predicted vector acceptable."

On the board, the tiny chip that was the runabout drifted closer to the broken shell of the *Calvin*. Rida spoke again: "We're, I think we're going to…just fit. Oops. Hull check."

"They're in," Uri said.

"Activating mooring lock," Rida said, meaning the magnetic field which would lock them to the metal deck of the hold. "Lock fixed. Still nothing from Uri. We're going to board."

Velocity muttered. On the feed from the *Prince of Peace*, Brontë spoke: "Scan the ship."

Evans replied, "I'm picking up faint heat signals, forward upper quadrant."

"The com," Velocity said, at the same moment that Brontë said, "That's the com. Rida, head for the com. He might be there."

"Very faint," Evans warned. "Nowhere near a life sign. Sixteen degrees."

Brontë's voice was steady: "Head for the com."

"Heading for com," Rida said. Rida's capture, showing the exterior of the *Susan Calvin*, flickered and went black. A moment later a badly illuminated capture replaced it—the feed from Jusuf's skinsuit, according to the note on the board. It showed the interior of the hold, illuminated by his hood light. He ghosted up through a gap in the bulkhead, into the berth deck corridor. Plasma had burned through here, too, blistering the paint off bulkheads and the deck covering off the decks. Hatchways, designed to withstand pressure, had mostly held, but their surfaces, including their windows, were scorched grey-white. Rida drifted past him and caught a cleat to kill his momentum. It broke loose from the overhead, sending him tumbling. Jusuf caught him and held him until he was stable. "Structural integrity damaged," Rida said, his voice tense. "I'm going to try opening this hatchway."

Velocity bit her lip, biting down an objection. If there was atmosphere on the other side—if Tai was yet alive, and in that atmosphere—but how else to get to him? If there was even any point to reaching him. Sixteen degrees was far less than half of normal body temperature. A cooling corpse. Not a survivor.

On the ship, the hatchway grated halfway open and then froze. "No atmosphere," Rida said. "Going through. I see light in the com. That's…it kept power at least."

"Is the hatch sealed up there?" Brontë asked.

"It is sealed," Rida said. He was climbing the ladder to the com hatchway. The inset window there frosted over from the inside. He banged on the door with his gloved fist, a dull muffled thump. "No atmosphere here either."

"We have to go in," Jusuf said. "I'm getting a reading of fifteen point eight degrees from…the object inside." Object. Because he didn't want to say *body*.

"Overriding the seal on the hatch," Rida said, punching in code—the override code, Velocity knew. The hatch shifted, sliding open in stuttering increments. Light spilled out, pale, sharp, unmitigated by atmosphere. Rida gasped, and then dove into the com; Jusuf followed. Not until he reached the interior did his feed show what had made Rida catch his breath. Half the com was gone, just gone—open to space. Rida hovered by a body in a skinsuit—its hood was sealed, Velocity noted, and shook her head at her own idiotic hope. The body was pinned to the command saddle by full restraints, including the head frame. Rida touched the fogged-over helmet with his own. "Tai? Wake up! Tai!"

Jusuf nudged him aside and plugged his field doctor into the skinsuit's belt. It hummed and brought up a display. Uri zoomed in on this without being told: Straight lines, all the way across. Negative pulse, negative respiration, negative brain activity. Temperature: fifteen point seven.

"He's dead." Rida's voice was strangled. "Is he dead?"

"Let's get him back to the ship," Jusuf said, hitting the latch that opened the restraints. "Come now, hurry."

"Why? What's the point? He's dead!"

"He's not dead until he's warm and dead," Jusuf said, and yanked Tai from the saddle. "Go get the engines hot. *Move.*"

Chapter 45

**Aboard the *Prince of Peace*,
Inbound to Commercial Station Webster-1, in the Deep**

Rida hovered outside the courier ship's infirmary. Jusuf was muttering imprecations in Pirian as he hunted through the very basic banks of the medic, finding plenty for diseases of the leisure class—headaches, hangovers, heartburn—and very little for traumatic injury. A courier ship wasn't intended for combat.

With Brontë's help, Jusuf stripped Tai from the skinsuit and sealed him into a full-body treatment pod. He spoke to Corvo, still up in com, in Pirian; she replied the same way. The pod began warming Tai slowly. It also delivered repeated jolts to his heart, compelling it to beat and pump blood. Stripped of the skinsuit, Tai's body was greyish, his long bones and flat lean muscles slack. The scar under his ribs, the one Rida knew like the inside of his own mouth, was pale as dust. His feet and hands were ice-white. Dusky bruises showed on his shoulders and across his ribs—marks left by the restraints as the *Susan Calvin* was hit.

Jusuf intubated Tai deftly and programmed the pod to ventilate him with warm, highly oxygenated air. Rida folded his arms around himself, squeezing hard to keep from howling. Jusuf drove a giant needle into Tai's arm. "Fluid, push," he ordered the pod. "Warmed to twenty degrees."

"Do you think you can bring him back?" Brontë asked.

Jusuf didn't reply; he didn't even seem to hear her. He was watching the screen beside the pod. Rida rubbed at his hair, clenched a fistful of it, and made himself stay quiet, though he wanted to wail. "Corvo?" Jusuf demanded.

"They're on their way," Corvo said. "Eleven minutes. Ready him for transport."

"What?" Rida demanded. "Who's on the way? Transport to where?"

"Find the PPU," Jusuf ordered, and when Brontë gaped at him, snapped, "Portable Power Unit. We have to move him to the *Kirikiti*. Find the unit. It'll be in one of these lockers, probably."

"Locker 113. Up and to your right," Uri said through the feed. Brontë yanked open the locker and hauled out a PPU still in its factory seal. She began breaking the seals, fumbling in her haste.

"Is that…." Rida hesitated. "Which dagan are you?"

"The one from the *Susan Calvin*," Uri said. "I'm downloading myself into this ship. I have sustained some damage."

Rida felt a rush of relief, as if Uri's survival changed anything. "Do you know what happened to Tai? Can you access that data?"

"We were hit by plasma from Frigate A. Our structural integrity was damaged. We lost environmental support. I was not able to rectify this situation. Tai was able to seal his hood, but the temperature drop was precipitous. Also, he only had air for ten hours."

Rida nodded, feeling sick. Over by the pod, Jusuf had the PPU connect to the pod. He and Brontë shifted Tai onto a porter, and sent it gliding through the hatchway—Rida moved aside to give them room. Jusuf spoke to Corvo in Pirian; she replied. They headed along the corridor, toward the umbilical. Shivering with grief and terror, Rida followed.

Chapter 46

Commercial Space Station Webster-1, Planet Durbin, in the Deep

olf sat down at the bistro table across from her. "You missed the briefing."

"I plan to miss the rest of them, too." Velocity waved at Ahn and pointed to Wolf. A scattering of teashops and eateries had opened up here on the station over the last fifty watches, but Ahn was the only one who could make drinkable coffee.

"I don't want anything," Wolf said, when Ahn reached their table.

"Give him white tea," Velocity said. Ahn nodded and punched the order into her dock. Then she went back to scrubbing tables. "Did Garcia send you?" Velocity asked.

"She's wondering why you're sacking briefings."

Ahn's niece brought the tea. Velocity tapped the payment panel, adding a twenty percent gratuity. This was all still on the Pirians' tag. She didn't know how long that would last. What would they want with her, now that she didn't have a ship? It wasn't like she had a skill set, outside of command. Maybe she could at least get them to take her crew. Corvo was bringing the *Prince of Peace* into dock in—Velocity checked her uplink—forty-six minutes. Velocity intended to meet her at the umbilical. If she couldn't get a commitment, at least she could get a feel for what the Pirians might intend.

"Why are you missing briefings?" Wolf persisted.

"Why would I attend? Do you need someone to applaud?" Wolf frowned, and she added, "I've got nothing to contribute. You don't need me there."

"If that were true, would Garcia send me out looking for you?"

"I'm not interested in being Garcia's tool."

Wolf poured tea and looked out over the barren concourse. A clerk on her way somewhere. A Durbin Security officer talking to a Pirian off one of the Scorpions. It was mainwatch third, and most people who had work were at that work. "How's your crewman?" Wolf asked. "Still in a coma?"

"He is." Velocity forced herself to drink coffee. She had no appetite lately, but she could usually get coffee down. The medics on the *Kirikiti* said the coma was to be expected. They said Tai would almost certainly wake on his own. They said they wouldn't know until he did wake how much damage, if any, had happened to his brain. Rida, on the Pirian ship with him, was sending her posts every few hours, mostly just saying the same thing: no change.

"Pirian medics are the best in the universe," Wolf said. Velocity didn't bother with a reply. "Listen. Come talk to Garcia." Velocity looked over at him, and he spread his hands. "Do you have something more important to do?"

"Something more interesting to do," Velocity said, lifting the coffee.

You should go, Uri said through her link. *More information is always better.*

Velocity was not fooled. Uri was worried she was sliding into a depression. He thought she needed more human contact—even contact with Garcia, apparently. Depression! Why would she be depressed? Just because her entire world had been blown apart. Not like it was the first time.

On the other hand, it was true she had nothing to do until the *Prince of Peace* made dock. She swallowed the rest of her coffee and got to her feet. "Fine. Let's go." Wolf, who had clearly been marshalling additional arguments, looked surprised. But he got up and led the way.

Garcia wasn't in the conference room, or out on the letter decks in her big admin suite either. Instead, she was just down the concourse from Ahn's, in a noodle shop at a booth near the door, where anyone could find her. If this latter was her aim, it had succeeded: all the tables in the shop were crowded with waiting petitioners, and a queue had formed for thirty meters down the concourse. Wolf ushered Velocity past those waiting in this line, straight into the shop, where he halted by the tag stand and caught Garcia's eye. She nodded and leaned forward to say something to the kid sitting in the booth with her. This was the contract labor child who had come in with the Pirians, Jack Ngata. Jack said something back, and slid from the booth. On his way from the shop, he spoke to Wolf: "Need to see you about supplies."

Wolf nodded. "Topwatch first?"

"That works." Jack went out, and Garcia waved at Wolf, who fetched Velocity over.

"Anything else you need?" he asked Garcia.

"No. Go get some sleep. That's an order."

He grinned at her, the bare shadow of a grin that Velocity knew well from the past two years with Adder. "You can't give me orders," he said, and left the shop, stopping to talk to various people along the way.

"Are you planning to offer me a job?" Velocity asked, settling into the booth.

"I'm offering you coffee," Garcia said. "Noodles, too, if you'll eat."

"I just had coffee. And I'm not hungry."

"Would you take a job, if I offered one?"

"I might. I'm on empty. If the Pirians cut me off, I won't have funds to buy air."

"You're heir to the Primary Board Seat on a top Combine. I wouldn't call that empty."

"You still think they want me back?" Velocity gestured upwards, in the general direction of the temporary infirmaries, still stuffed with wounded survivors of the battle. "Or do they maybe want me back so they can cut my throat?"

"You have a claim to that seat. Which could be useful, later on."

"Veil of respectability kind of thing," Velocity said, imitating Jack's dialect.

"That kind of thing," Garcia agreed. "But that's long term. Right now it's your connections to the Pirians that interest me."

This was not what Velocity had expected. She sat back, her eyebrows lifting. Garcia nodded, registering the surprise, and added, "They'll come for us again. The Pirians are right about that. I don't see that we have any choice but to accept this defense squadron they have offered to provide."

"Offered."

"Exactly. We can't fight the Combines. We certainly can't fight the Pirians. They're here. We have to accept that. What I don't accept is them refusing to return our people. Stealing Calypsos. Taking over the planet."

"Taking over the planet being your job," Velocity said drily.

Garcia ate a radish. "Which is where you come in. I need a liaison. Someone who understands Pirians, and can explain them to me. And someone who understands Combines, and can explain us to the Pirians."

Velocity thought this over. "I don't understand Pirians all that well."

"Better than anyone else I've got."

"You've got Huna Sulavee. She's an actual Pirian."

"Who knows nothing about Combines. Are you trying to talk yourself out of this job?"

"I might be," Velocity admitted. "What's in it for me?"

"You need a job. Also, you're a Calypso. What better place for you?"

"Than here? A planet on a Combine kill-list? Almost anywhere, I would think." Velocity drummed her fingers on the table. "The Pirians will give me a berth. It's how they operate."

Garcia pointed the blunt tip of the knife at her. "That sort of knowledge. That's why I need you. I'll pay you. I can pay well. I've got a planetary budget more or less open to me. I'll pay your crew too."

This reminded Velocity of Tai, who she had managed not to think of for at least two minutes. She had enjoyed bargaining; now she just felt tired. She looked away, out over the concourse. "Can't have a crew without a ship," she muttered.

Garcia wound noodles on her fork. "Maybe we can get you a ship." Velocity looked back, surprised, and Garcia shrugged. "I've got a few ships in dock that need captains. You'd be under my command, obviously. Well. The Minister of Defense. His command."

"But you've got his leash."

"Durbin has a Parliamentary system of government, Miss Tallis. I just work with that system." Velocity snorted, and Garcia added, "Are you interested?"

"What's your goal? How do you see this ending?"

"So long as the Combines exist, they'll come for us. The ending is non-negotiable."

"Right. But are you taking down the Combines to put yourself in their place? Or do you have something else in mind?"

"Now that part," Garcia said, "that is negotiable."

Uri spoke through Velocity's uplink again: The **Prince of Peace** *is docked.*

"I'm wanted elsewhere," Velocity said, rising from the booth. "Let me get back to you."

"As you like," Garcia said, and waved the next petitioner forward.

Chapter 47

Aboard the *Kirikiti*, en route to Pirian Space

When Tai opened his eyes, the first thing he saw was Rida, curled up asleep in a knot on the infirmary bunk next to his. Alarm flashed weakly through him—was Rida injured? He tried to sit up, but restraints held him in place. He collapsed once more into sleep. When he woke again, a few hours or few watches later, Rida stood by the bunk, reading something on its board; his eyes widened and he looked down into Tai's face. "You're awake."

"Ridashi." His voice was a raw whisper. He tried to reach for Rida, and his hand wouldn't move. The restraints.

Rida took his hand. "We had to buckle you in. You kept trying to get up." Despite his smile, worried lines showed around his eyes. "Do you know where you are?"

"What?" Tai glanced around. Medical gear, e-pods, lockers stuffed with more gear. He had vague memories of waking earlier. Pirians saying his name. Someone coaxing him to breathe deeply. Pain in his throat. "An infirmary. A Pirian infirmary." He coughed, which hurt, and said, "How did we get on a Pirian ship? I was..." He shut up, memory seeping back. "I was dead?"

"Technically no," Rida said, laughing, or making a noise like laughter, gripping Tai's hand more tightly. "Close enough to scare my skin off, though."

Rida was explaining what had happened, and Tai was trying to focus well enough to follow it, when a Pirian medic loomed up on them, beaming. "Here we are!"

"They've been saying you would wake up sometime this watch," Rida explained, helping the medic unseal the restraints on his upper body. "Something in your brainwaves."

"Let's raise this." The Pirian did something that turned the bunk—no, it was a pod—turned the pod chair-shaped. "Are you thirsty?"

Tai realized that was why his throat hurt. He reached for the bowl the medic was offering, but she threaded it deftly through his hands and tucked the sip tube into his mouth. He drank: some sort of sweet liquid. Tart. Thin. Three swallows and he released the tube, exhausted. "Excellent!" the medic said, patting him on the shoulder. "Ali will be along in a moment. Rest now."

"Ali is Medic Mainwatch First," Rida explained. "You're the most interesting patient they've seen in years, I think."

"Where's the Captain?"

"The Captain stayed on Durbin. This is a courier ship, the *Kirikiti*. It's taking us back to Pirian space." Tai tried to get up, alarmed; Rida held him in the pod. "Don't, my love. The Captain's all right. She's fine."

"Why did she stay on…" Tai trailed into silence, remembering more. "The *Susan Calvin*. I destroyed it. Oh, shit buckets."

"The Combine frigates destroyed it. And Mendoza says if you and the others hadn't distracted the frigates, they would have lost many more Scorpions in their attack. So you're a hero. Lie still."

Tai shut his eyes. He realized he recognized this unsteady feeling. "They've got me medicated."

"A bit. Mostly they're using nerve blocks."

He considered whether he wanted to ask, and asked anyway: "Why do I need nerve blocks?"

Rida's grip tightened on his hand. "There was some cold damage. But don't worry. They say you'll be good as new."

Tai opened his eyes. He saw what he had been refusing to see—his lower legs were gone. Just gone. After his knees, nothing. When he reached out for the space where they should have been, Rida intercepted the gesture, taking his hand again. "They can fix you," he said. "They promised me. They'll make it like nothing happened. That's why we're going to Pirian space. Tai? They promise. You'll be fine."

Tai pulled his hand away, seeing why the medic had refused to let him hold the bowl himself: parts of his fingers were gone too. Nubs wrapped in med-skin. He made a sound of dismay, and Rida captured his hand and gripped it fiercely. "They can fix it," he insisted.

"What happened?" Tai asked, his voice sounding weak and airless. "Fix it how?"

"They say they can do it," Rida said. "You're going to be part ceramic and part metal and the rest cloned. They say they do it all the time." He bent his head to kiss the back of Tai's hand, and Tai saw his eyes were shimmering with tears.

"Hey," Tai said, alarmed. "Hey now, love. Dear heart. Don't cry."

"I love your hands," Rida said, his voice muffled. "They're so beautiful."

"Ridashi. I'm going to be fine. Didn't they promise?"

Kneeling by the bed, Rida rubbed his face against Tai's forearm. "I've been so scared. They kept saying you'd wake up. That you'd be fine. That they could fix it. But you looked…" He set his teeth, the tears spilling bright. Tai started to cup Rida's face, only when he reached out, he caught sight of his monstrous claw of a hand again, and froze. Rida caught his hand and kissed it again, fiercely. "You're going to be *fine*," he said. "It's going to be *fine*."

Tai lay back in the pod. His muscles felt light and strengthless. "What about the frigates? Did we stop the frigates?"

"We did." Rida brushed tears from his face and drew a deep

breath. "The Siji are establishing a perimeter, a blockade, to stop any other Combine attack ships. That's why the Captain stayed behind. One of the reasons. Jusuf and Corvo stayed, too. We're going to go back, once you're well."

Go back. He remembered, like a flash of terror, the plasma bolt hitting the *Susan Calvin*. He shut his eyes. "Go back to what? The ship is gone."

"The Captain says she'll handle that." Rida didn't sound entirely certain about this claim. "She says not to worry."

"One of the reasons."

"What?"

"You said one of the reasons the Captain stayed behind. What are the other reasons? Is the *Susan Calvin* one of those reasons?"

"The Siji say the *Calvin* is scrap," Rida said unsteadily. "They're salvaging it for parts. The Captain is working with Durbin Parliament. With Garcia, really. On the counterattack."

"The what?" Tai lifted his head, squinting. "Counterattacking who? Not the Combines? Counterattacking the *Combines*?"

"That's the plan." Rida shook his head. "A hostile takeover. By Durbin Parliament. Well, by Garcia."

"Garcia." Tai shut his eyes, exhaustion rising like heat through his body.

"And the Siji. Mendoza thinks it can work," Rida added. Tai started to ask who Mendoza was, but he was too tired. "Anyway," Rida went on, sounding distant, as if he were moving to some other room, "anyway, Captain says don't worry. She'll handle that part. You just get better."

"Right," Tai said, as he fell into sleep. "No worry. What could go wrong?"

As he slid downward, he felt Rida kiss the palm of his hand. "Everything is going to be fine, my love. I promise, I promise."

Chapter 48

Davaille Island, Planet of Durbin, in the Deep

Brontë pulled off her boots and her stockings and veered down to walk on the wet sand near the surf. When she was a child, back in Ikeda House, she and her cousins had spent two months a year on Gagarin, a resort planet near the Core. The sand on the beaches at Gagarin had been white as bone, so fine it squeaked underfoot. This sand was large-grained and a deep olive green, almost black in places. She padded along the edge of the water, the wind roaring past her ears. On the high bench of land above her, she caught glimpses of barracks, long and low, with long windows in every room. Built from some local bamboo-like plant, big as pine trees, they weathered golden in the sun.

Calypso children were everywhere on the islands. She could see at least thirty of them scattered along this beach, some of them net-fishing, but most wandering idly. This island, the biggest and rockiest, held about half of the farm's three thousand-plus Calypsos. Those who were old enough to work mostly lived on two islands to the east, which had originally been elaborate gardens and now grew rice and sugar beets; or they worked the fishing fleet that ventured far out to sea, returning once or twice a month. Here on this island, the younger children ran wild.

Brontë and her cousins had run free on Gagarin too; but it would be hard to find lives further apart than their life on those beaches and the life of these kids here. Every Ikeda House child had trailed a constellation of nannies, tutors, coaches, housemaids, physicians, and Security teams. These kids had teachers, and "big sisters" or "big brothers" who oversaw each barrack. There was a single infirmary to serve all the islands, and one kitchen for every ten barracks. A lone central laundry handled clothing for everyone, which was possible, apparently, because the children wore almost nothing. Shorts and a sunhat woven of straw seemed the usual costume; the youngest children skipped the shorts.

Brontë walked down to the place where the big river came roaring over a rocky cliff to crash into the sea, admiring the skill set of whoever had rebuilt this island. You could still see the evidence of its former life as a resort—the remains of an immense dock, for instance, and the elaborately archaic stone pagoda halfway down the cliff, where guests could get a close view of the waterfall. But now this was just what Drury claimed it was: a working farm, run by the children living on it. Calypso children.

Brontë heard a shrill whistle and turned to see Adder trotting down the beach, her expression rigid with temper. Sighing, Brontë went to meet her. "Didn't I say to stay right there?" Adder demanded.

"You're not my mommy," Brontë said, going past her.

Adder wheeled to stride beside her. "No. I'm your Security. How do you think I can keep you alive if you ignore my advice?"

"I'm not dead," Brontë said, spreading her arms to show how unharmed she was. Adder drew a breath to launch a rebuttal and Brontë added, before she could speak, "How did the meeting go?"

"Not as well as it would have if you had sat in."

"I don't want to stay here. Why would I help you find a way to keep me here?"

"Good news, the Captain agrees with you. She thinks Pirian space will be safer."

"It will be," Brontë said, though "safer" was not why she wanted to return to the *Sungai*. She and Uri had been talking.

*Return to the **Sungai**,* the AI said. *Study for and pass the ratings to become a Tactical Third. Join Siji.* In his opinion, if she worked hard, she would be able to get that done within six months. Siji would not waste someone with her connections. *Think of what a Calypso with training in Pirian tactics could do,* Uri said, *once she held the Primary Seat of the most powerful Combine in the Republic.* A lot more than she could do stranded on some backwater planet in the Deep. Even if the Combines didn't get past the Pirian defense perimeter and kill them all.

Down the beach, two children burst out from a clump of other children. One swung a clam rake; the other flung herself past the rake to knock the first child down. They rolled in the surf, all the children shrieking like seahawks around them. One shoved the other down under the surf and held her there. Beside Brontë, Adder tensed. The one underwater surged up, belted her opponent in the face, and took off running. Bleeding from the nose, the bigger child shouted something after her, and then squatted down to wash her face in the sea. Adder muttered. Brontë shrugged. "Raise kids without parents, what do you expect?"

Adder shot her a sidelong look. Brontë recalled too late that the Ikan16s hadn't had parents, not any more than any of the bonded labor sets created in the Houses. "You had house parents, though," she objected. "Coaches."

"Uh-huh," Adder said blandly. Her own biological mother—Sabra—had been occupied with raising Brontë. Sabra had spent far more time with Brontë than Isra ever had. Speaking of kids raised without parents.

Brontë started on toward the stairs, shifting her route so that they would miss the knot of Calypso children, still milling about and shouting, though their racket seemed more delighted than angry. This was the first place Brontë had ever been where everyone's reactions made perfect sense to her. "Are you staying here with Wolf?" she asked Adder.

"He wants me to."

"Will you?"

Adder scowled. "Of course I won't. I took an oath."

"What if I release you from the oath?"

"That's not up to you."

"Why not?" They reached the stairs up to the bench, and Brontë halted, facing Adder directly. "What if I cancel your bond? I can do that."

Adder flushed. "If you think I only protect you because of some bond to your Combine," she said, and shut her lips hard.

"All right, all right." Brontë started up the stairs. Though she would have willingly released Adder, she had to admit she was glad to be refused. Even though she knew Adder would give her constant trouble over the Tactics thing. "I'm still going to cancel your bond, though."

Adder made a rude noise. "Whatever helps you sleep."

Reaching the top of the stairs, Brontë stopped to get her breath. She'd been downplanet less than fifteen watches, and the gravity was still rough on her. Adder stood beside her, breathing easily, scanning for assassins while she waited for Brontë to recover. Beyond the barracks, Brontë could see groups of children learning Shtai. Another group had gathered on the wide plaza between the barracks, and were doing some sort of work on desk ports— as on Pirian ships, almost no one here had a personal dock. Two small children were running along the peak of a barrack roof, their balance perfect and fearless. Off to her left, other children were weeding the immense vegetable garden behind the kitchens. Or at least Brontë assumed they were meant to be weeding. Right now they were throwing dirt clods at one another.

"Captain's in the Big House," Adder said, nodding down the coast to the elaborate five story resort house that was left over from the island's days of glory. "She sent Dilgry out to kick up the runabout. Ready to leave in an hour, she said. That was half an hour ago."

Brontë headed that way. The Captain had come down for the final meetings between Garcia and the Pirians, the last set of negotiations to delineate who would owe what and when in their tenuous alliance. From what Brontë had seen, before she stopped attending meetings entirely, the Captain's main role had been to stress to Garcia what a terrible idea double-dealing Pirians would be. That, and making it clear to Garcia that giving the Captain a ship to command didn't mean that Garcia owned her.

The ship was a courier ship, the *Hachi*, one of the eleven Combine-held ships that had been in-system when the frigates attacked. Durbin Parliament (at Garcia's behest) had seized these ships and was using them as the basis of their own navy—privateers was the name they were using, pirates being such a chancy term. The Captain had forced Garcia to agree to the *private* aspect of the word: Garcia (or rather Durbin Parliament) might hold the ship, but the Captain would command it, and its crew. She would take jobs from Garcia and from the Durbin Parliament as a priority, but she would also be free to refuse these jobs, and to take others at her discretion. Also, she would have a free hand in signing on crew.

Garcia had fought all this—of course she had—but given that the Captain had the power to walk away and go work for the Pirians, Brontë suspected it had been a pro forma fight. Also, Garcia had been preoccupied by her negotiations with the Pirians. Among other things, Garcia had wanted both Brontë and Adder to stay on Durbin. For a while, she had made that one of the conditions of her agreeing to the alliance. Brontë knew why—if she couldn't control the Captain, then she wanted some other Combine Heir in her pocket—but she hadn't worried. Even if the Pirians had agreed to such a thing (impossible), the Captain would never leave her here.

Adder, still watching the swarms of children as if one of them might whip out a plasma cannon, caught up to her. The Big House was close enough now that Brontë could see the Captain standing on the steps talking to Wolf. "We're going to keep looking for Ian," Brontë said. "We'll find him."

"Uri says the probability of him being still alive is only forty percent," Adder said.

"We'll find him," Brontë repeated. Ian was not dead. They would find him. And the other two Ikan16s, Maggie and Nora, who were still at the Core, acting as Security for Theo—when Siji sent her to kill Theo, she would get them back, too.

"There you are," the Captain said as they drew near. "Time to go. Quinn's already taken our baggage to the shuttle. Sure you won't go with us?" she added to Wolf. "We'll need a good Security team, with the jobs we'll be running. You stay here, you'll end up teaching kindergarten."

Wolf grinned. He and the Captain were best friends these days. "I'm going to teach Combat Security," he said. "Quinn's my first cadet."

The Captain snorted. "She'll be good at it, if you can keep her from stealing your bullets. Come on, then," she said to Brontë and Adder, and set out toward the shuttle port, which was a flat sandy field about a kilometer from the barracks. There were in-line vehicles stowed in the shed by the Big House, but the Captain ignored these, striding off along the shell road. Adder stayed behind to speak briefly to Wolf; Brontë went with the Captain, though keeping the pace she set soon had Brontë wheezing. The Captain noticed and slowed down. "Planets," she said.

"What jobs?" Brontë asked.

"Mm?"

Brontë gulped for air. "You said the jobs you'd be running. What jobs? I thought you were just going to run transport. Cargo. That sort of thing."

"Oh, we'll be doing that too." The Captain gripped Brontë's shoulder briefly, more of a thump than an embrace. "Don't worry, we'll get you to the *Sungai* first. I have to go there anyway. Tai and

Rida are there."

"What jobs will you be running that you'll need Security for?" Brontë demanded.

"Uri integrated. Did I tell you that?"

Brontë frowned. "What, with his self that was on the *Prince of Peace*? I thought he already did that."

"With his self that was on the *Arago*." When Brontë looked blank, the Captain added, "The Combine frigate that had command. It also had banks and banks of data. Among other details, Uri from the *Arago* learned who authorized the funding for the raid. Guess who it was."

"We know who it was," Brontë said, still frowning. "It was the Atlas Society. Or whoever, your cousin, working through the Atlas Society."

"That's how it looked. But Uri followed data trails, and guess who they lead to."

"My mother." Brontë glanced at the Captain, wondering why she was grinning. Surely she didn't think Isra trying to kill them all was funny?

"Not your mother," the Captain said. "Your uncle."

"What? Do you mean…you don't mean David?"

"David Ikeda Ito," the Captain said, with satisfaction. Brontë stopped walking for a moment, and obligingly the Captain stopped with her. They had drawn near the landing field. The shuttle was lit: hot air wavered near its exhaust. In the shade beneath its belly, Quinn was loading bundles into the cargo bin.

"David wouldn't…" Brontë bit her lip. Of course he would act without her mother's knowledge. Of course he would. He'd done it during the coup; he'd do it now. "Do you think he thought I was on the planet?" she said.

"I don't. Though I don't think that would have stopped him."

"*David* wanted the Calypsos eradicated," Brontë said, saying it out loud to hear if it made sense. "*David* set all this up."

The Captain gave her another thump on the shoulder. "We don't know if he was really acting alone," she said. "That's one of the jobs I'll be doing. Finding that out."

"How will you do that, without...." Brontë looked up at her. "You're going to the Core?"

Out on the field, Quinn shouted, waving at them. "You need to hurry!" she shouted. "Dilgry says you gonna miss your window!"

"Are you going to the *Core?*" Brontë demanded.

The Captain grinned again. "You heard her," she said, starting toward the shuttle again. "Let's not miss our window."

Acknowledgments

This book would have been a very different object without everything I learned from my son, Hershel Burgh, and his father, Mark Burgh. I'd like to thank both of them, as well as Athena Andreadis, who continues to show me new ways to think about science fiction. I'd also like to thank my colleagues at the University of Arkansas-Fort Smith, especially my chair, Cammie Sublette, and my dean, Paul Hankins, both of whom encouraged me to apply for the sabbatical during which this book was completed. And finally, I'd like to thank my mother, who took me to libraries, bought me books, and was the first one to tell me I would certainly be a writer.

About the Author

Raised in New Orleans, Kelly Jennings now lives in the Boston Mountains, where she writes science fiction when she is not catering to cats. Her short fiction has appeared in many venues, including *The Magazine of Fantasy & Science Fiction*, *The Other Half of The Sky* and *Retellings of the Inland Seas*. Her short story "History of the Invasion Told in Five Dogs" appeared in *The Year's Best Science Fiction: 35th Annual Collection* (2018). She has published two novels, *Broken Slate* (2011) and *Fault Lines* (2018); and she co-edited the anthology *Menial: Skilled Labor in SF* (2012). She is a member of the Science Fiction Writers of America. Find her on Twitter @delagar